Advance Praise

A Tangle of Fates

"Leslie Ann Moore's *A Tangle of Fates* is an exciting start to a new, lushly written and deeply imagined fantasy trilogy."

— Steven Barnes
Author of *Lion's Blood*

"Rich in world-building and lush in its storytelling."

—Gary Phillips
Editor of *Black Pulp*

"Moore kicks off this series with a hot blend of future weapons tech, Zorro, and strong female leads. Add in a touch of the mystical...and sit back and enjoy!"

— Sherwood Smith
Nebula Award nominee, author of *Inda* and *A Stranger to Command*

"Leslie Ann Moore's *A Tangle of Fates* presents us with a lushly realized, scientifically plausible universe as marvelous and full of adventure as any high fantasy. While its mix of priestly characters, archaeology, and questions about the cycles of human history are reminiscent of both the Indiana Jones franchise and Walter M. Miller Jr.'s great novel *A Canticle for Leibowitz*, Moore's Tangle is also something unique and new. Highly recommended."

— Howard Hendrix
Author of *Spears of God* and *The Labyrinth Key*

"*A Tangle of Fates* mixes planetary romance with a fairy-tale subtext, and serves it up with an intriguing background of reimagined technology and religion. The result is delicious!"

— Emma Bull
Author of *War for the Oaks*

To Candy,

A Tangle of Fates

LESLIE ANN MOORE

Best Wishes!

Leslie Ann Moore
4/15

MHP

LOS ANGELES SANTA BARBARA

A TANGLE OF FATES

A Muse Harbor Publishing Book

PUBLISHING HISTORY

Muse Harbor Publishing paperback edition published August 2014

Published by Muse Harbor Publishing, LLC

Los Angeles, California

Santa Barbara, California

All rights reserved, including the right to reproduce this book in whole or in part. For information, contact Muse Harbor Publishing.

Copyright © 2014 by Leslie Ann Moore

Interior Design by Typeflow

ISBN 978-1-61264-158-4

Visit Muse Harbor Publishing at

www.museharbor.com

To my husband, Aaron Mason.
You are my One and Only.

acknowledgments

First of all, I want to thank fortune for placing Eileen Workman and me in the green room together at the first West Coast Writer's Conference in Los Angeles. Eileen, if not for your willingness to listen, this book may not have come to fruition.

Thank you, Dave Workman, for all the tough love you gave me during the long, grueling process of shaping this story into something that I couldn't be more proud of.

Thanks to my fellow writer friends at ScHoFan (the Sci-Fi/Horror/Fantasy Critique Group of the Greater Los Angeles Writers Society). You all provided me with the critiques and encouragement at the very beginning that I really needed.

Thank you, Mom and Sylvia, for your unfailing support over the years.

Lastly, thank you Aaron Mason, my soul mate, for being my rock.

un mapa

western realm

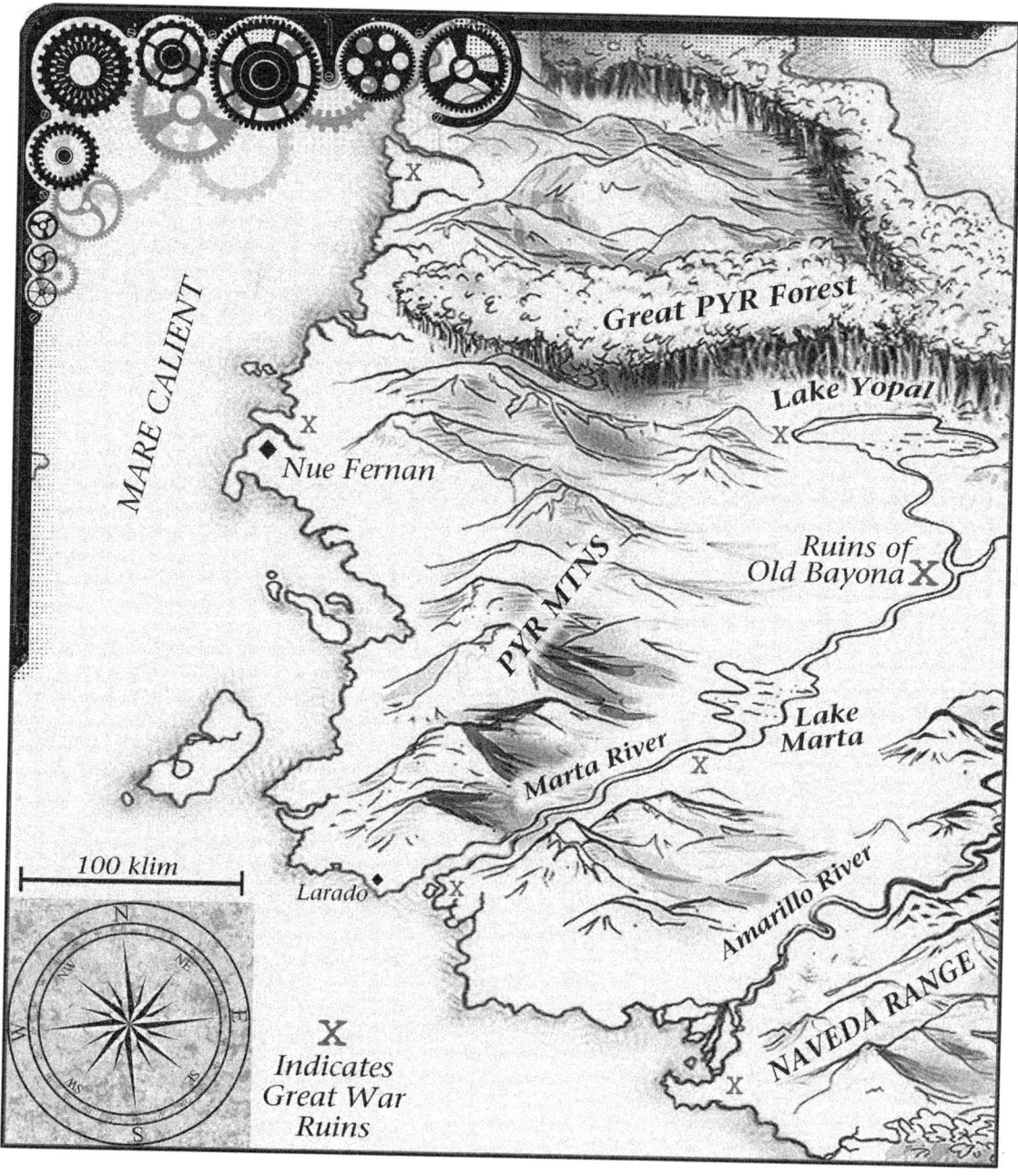

de nuetierra

eastern realm

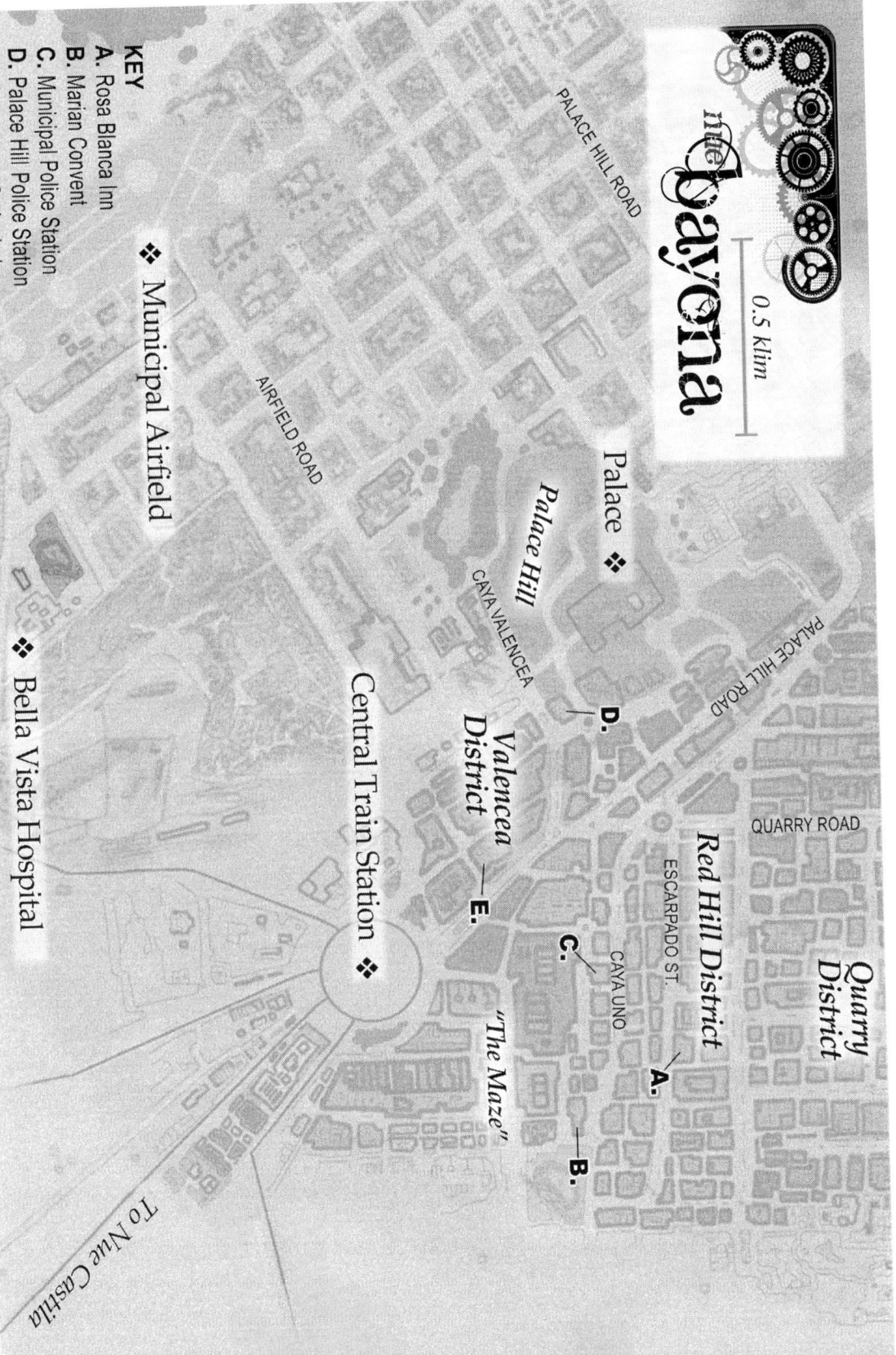

1

1

pursuit

"Maria's holy tits!"

Monseñor Gabril Ledesme, ever mindful of the proprieties of his sacred office as a priest of the Holy Church, nevertheless uttered the impious obscenity as a hot needle of pain spiked his temple. "Will you demon spawn ever leave me in peace?" He slapped at his silver-frosted hairline, then glared at the small, winged attacker crushed against his palm. He felt the venom-induced headache begin as a slow pounding behind his eyeballs. "Damned *skeeto*."

The myriad screeches, grunts, clicks, and whistles of a forest alive with hidden fauna surrounded him. Vegetation cloaked the tumbled ruins of the ancient city with a variegated mantle of green and brown against which daubs of brilliant floral colors — red, purple, blue, and orange — stood out like jewels in a nest of velvet. Overhead, yellow-breasted *doloras* rode the thermals in pairs and triads on black sickle-shaped wings, weaving lazy circular patterns through the cloudless violet sky.

Nothing of Ledesme's outward appearance marked his priestly station. Lean and as well-muscled as a man twenty years his junior, only the rake of fine lines around his eyes and the scatter of argent strands through sable hair betrayed his maturity. Dressed as he was for heat and hard trekking in tough, lightweight khakis and heavy brown boots, any observer would think him simply another wildcat salvager, scouring the bones of the dead city for useable tech; and in truth that assumption would be mostly correct.

Dragging his wide-brimmed leather hat from his aching head, Ledesme dropped to his haunches in the lee of a half-fallen section of glassite wall to rest and aerate his sweat-damp hair with his fingers. The translucent blocks at his back, shielded from hard sunlight by a forest canopy grown lush on spring rains, sent a frisson of pleasure through his overheated body as he leaned against them.

The *kittle kittle* cries of wild *turquia* calling to each other in the surrounding undergrowth mingled with the soft peeps of forest *ranas*, clinging with suckered feet to the pebbly green trunks of a cluster of *boca* trees. The delicate scent of *corella* flowers delighted his nose and the sough of the wind in the leaves overhead reminded him of the distant murmur of the sea. A pod of wild sky jellies, named for their resemblance to a marine creature of Old Earth, floated above the trees, their gas-filled bodies almost invisible against the firmament. The animals were too distant to pose a threat as they probed the canopy for small prey with their stinger-tipped tentacles. After a score of years spent in scientific exploration and salvage for the Church, Ledesme knew every sight, sound, and smell of this place as intimately as he knew his own skin.

Relaxed, he massaged his forehead and watched with delighted interest a rare sight: the boca tree closest to him, less than ten paces away, shuddered and rose out of the damp soil on roots like a pale clump of thick, squirming serpents. It then began a slow glide, made more amazing by the ponderous beauty of its movement, away from its watcher. A second later, its half-dozen herd mates uprooted themselves and followed in the wake of their leader. Ledesme suspected the creatures—not trees at all, but gentle beasts of flesh and blood evolved to an uncanny resemblance—were making their stately way toward a nearby creek where they could dangle their tentacles in the sluggish water to drink.

Wonder at the grace of Her works and gratitude for the granted privilege of witness filled Ledesme with joy. "Madre, You are truly great," he whispered.

When the bocas had disappeared among the sheltering trees, the priest sighed and lifted his gaze to squint at the patches of visible sky overhead. The others would wake soon from their mid-afternoon siestas and the absence of their leader would provoke irritated consternation, if not outright alarm. He stood to stretch the kinks from his back, then settled his hat down over the spiked locks of his hair. It was time to return to camp.

Turning in a half-circle, Ledesme sought the familiar gleam of metal through the trees. A pair of slim towers, once the lofty domain of the ancient city's elite rulers—or so the Church had always speculated—would serve him as a landmark from which to navigate his way back to camp. The crack of a fracturing tree limb froze the priest in mid-step. For an agonized run of seconds he held his breath as around him the forest's living chorus faltered, then fell silent.

Daring a glance over his shoulder, Ledesme felt shocked near to panic at the unexpected sight that met his keen green eyes. Near five meters tall, screened by a stand of young *sawtooth* trees, and rendered almost invisible by a camouflaging mottle of brown and gray spots, crouched a saber-tusked horror.

Mierda! What's a *kymera* doing here?

An apex predator of the deep woods, no kymera had ever been encountered within the precincts of war-shattered Veyho Bayona by any previous expedition, Church-sanctioned or otherwise.

Until now.

Like the blast from a steam locomotive, a chuff out of wide nostrils sent a shower of serrated golden leaves pinwheeling through the air high above Ledesme's head as the beast exhaled in preparation to charge.

Through a flushed haze of adrenalin, the priest seized upon a terrifyingly small chance for escape and took off at a dead run toward a vine-enshrouded mound of concrete slabs several meters away.

The kymera rocketed from its concealment in scorching pursuit, emitting a roar that seemed to shake the very roots of the trees.

Fit though he was, Ledesme knew he did not possess the speed to outrun the monster. Propelled along on six powerful legs, each ending in a paw armed with black claws half as long as a man's forearm, the kymera would scatter his gory remnants over the leaf litter long before he reached any refuge. He needed to stall the creature, and he needed to do it now.

Ledesme ripped his sidearm from its holster below his shoulder, twisting as he ran, and squeezed off three shots in rapid succession at the kymera's long snout. The glimpse he caught in the split second it took him to point his pistol would have loosened the bowels of a less intrepid man. One or two more strides and the monster would be upon him.

Diosa mia, it's too fast ...

A shriek like tearing metal rent the air. Ledesme risked another glance and saw the kymera prancing in a crazed circle, shaking its narrow head, the mane of quills sprouting like javelins clacking together with a fearsome racket. Streams of greenish-black blood oozed from a trio of puncture wounds below its left eye.

Pushing his body to the limit, Ledesme swerved to avoid a collision with the bole of an *ebon* tree and nearly lost his footing on a loose block of pavement. Slim branches like scourges cut stinging gashes across his cheeks. His lungs heaved and burned.

The kymera, once again barreling after him, plowed through the undergrowth with uncanny agility. A slap of displaced air hit the nape of the priest's neck at the same instant he felt a sharp pain slice across his shoulder blades. He flung himself to the side while firing another shot. The mound of broken slabs loomed a pace or two away, beckoning with shadowy crevices that promised salvation.

Blessed Madre, thank you.

Ledesme dove beneath an overhang into a dank cavelet and shoved forward until he could go no further. Squirming onto his side, he lay wedged in a casket-narrow space facing the entrance to what might turn out to be a tomb, rather than a refuge.

The kymera slid to a halt, its claws flinging up a hail of crumbled concrete and fallen leaves. Bugling in thwarted rage, the creature thrust a forefoot into the crevice to try to hook its prey and pry him free. Ledesme fired his last two rounds into the questing paw. The twin reports within the low, tight confines spiked pain through his ears and left them ringing. The kymera withdrew its injured foot, only to reach in with another of its five undamaged paws.

Ledesme flinched as four wickedly honed talons gouged a quartet of grooves into the dirt a finger span from his ankle, and then withdrew. The beast screeched and dropped its head to glare at him from one gold-shot, viridescent eye. Saliva dripped in mucinous ropes from the roots of sepia tusks curling on either side of its mandible. Then, as suddenly as it had appeared, the hideous face was gone. After a few moments the monseñor heard the beast moving away through the undergrowth, growling. Then all sounds of movement ceased.

Too wise to fall for this admittedly wily trick, Ledesme remained frozen in place, every one of his senses stretched to exquisite tautness. His headache, forgotten in the midst of frenzied flight, returned to hammer the inside of his cranium in time to his heartbeat.

He counted to one hundred, then counted again.

At four hundred, he snatched up a fist-sized chunk of concrete and rolled it through the bright-lit opening.

With force enough to crack stone the kymera hurled itself at the crevice, startling a curse from the priest despite his suspicion of its lurking presence. As the monster's head eclipsed the entrance, plunging the cavelet into darkness, Ledesme heard rather than saw its hideous muzzle thrusting toward him. The creature's breath enveloped him in a rancid fog.

Once, twice, three times the beleaguered man felt serrated jaws snap closed with jackhammer speed a handspan from his sweating face.

Exhausted, he was alerted to the seriousness of his wounds by a warm trickle of blood. Ledesme closed his eyes and prayed.

Oh, Blessed Madre Maria, deliver me from danger. Let the might of Your love, and that of Your Son, the Holy Yesu, protect me, in this, my time of need.

The kymera screeched and pulled its head from the fissure. Ledesme shoved backward, hissing with pain as his lacerated shoulders scraped against shards of concrete. He reached behind himself, and instead of unyielding soil and rock, his questing hands found an opening. Desperate, he clawed away the debris to enlarge the hole wide enough to wiggle through.

The beast plunged its rapacious snout into the crevice and bit at empty air where a mere second ago, its intended prey had huddled, helpless. That same prey now slithered down a narrow passage, the cold feel of metal beneath his hands and knees. Near-absolute darkness precluded speed as Ledesme felt his way forward, the turbulent roar of his own blood deafening in his ears. From the scant information gleaned from his fingertips, he guessed he'd stumbled into a ventilation shaft or service passage.

The frustrated shrieks of the kymera gradually grew faint and eventually stopped. Ledesme paused long enough to unclip a battered brass hand torch from his belt. Thankful he'd thought to replace the fuel cell early that morning, he thumbed the switch. The light of the thin white beam revealed a corroded metal tunnel…and something else that filled him with consternation. Less than two paces beyond where he crouched, the floor of the tunnel ended in a square black hole.

With exaggerated care, Ledesme inched forward and then pointed the torch down the hole. Caught in its illumination, approximately three meters down, a pile of broken metal furniture lay on a floor carpeted in a plush gray layer of dust.

The fall may not have killed me, but getting impaled on some rusty old chair leg might've. At least I've got a way back up into this shaft if I need it.

Torch wedged tight between his teeth, Ledesme rolled onto his stomach, gripped the beveled edge of the hole, and dropped feet first into the darkness. Pain, sharp as a white-hot splatter of molten lead, forced a groan past the torch barrel in his mouth as his wounded shoulder took the full weight of his body.

Can't drop straight down onto that mess. Gotta swing past it.

Tears of suffering spilling from his eyes, Ledesme kicked out with both legs, swinging pendulum-like through a long arc that he prayed would throw him clear of the lethal pile of metal below. He mentally recited a quick prayer and released his grip.

A second of sheer panic as he plunged through open space, and then he hit the floor with bruising force, unable to maintain balance. The torch flew from his mouth as he sprawled in the thick dust, throwing up a swirling cloud that clogged his nose and throat.

Ledesme staggered to his feet, violent sneezes and coughs doubling him over for several agonized moments. As he struggled to catch his breath, wiping tears and snot off his face with his sleeve, he bent to retrieve the fallen hand torch. Raising it to eye level, he swept the beam around to reveal a corridor stretching before and behind, featureless except for unmarked metal doors set at regular intervals. All were closed. The twisted furniture looked as if it had been deliberately piled below the opening to the shaft above.

Like someone needed a way to escape.

With no way to determine otherwise, one direction appeared as good as the other. Ledesme fished a kerchief from his back pocket to fashion a makeshift dust mask, then started walking.

Going off on my own was stupid. Mierda I know better! Arnau will send Francisco and Calderone to look for me and they might very well run into that blasted kymera. They'll have ee-rifles but still....

Gabril Ledesme had lived his entire adult life in service to the Madre and Her Church, much of the time spent prowling subterranean warrens like the one he now found himself traversing. The darkness and silence of these dead places held no fears for him; in truth, though his body ached and his wounds burned, at the same time he felt invigorated. The heady wine of curiosity coursed through his veins, damping the worst of his hurts. At his core he was an explorer, excited by the unknown.

Cool air, stale but breathable, reassured him, as did the undisturbed layer of dust underfoot.

I must be the first living man to walk this corridor in more than four centuries.

The sweep of Ledesme's light revealed matte metal walls scarred by burn marks from ancient energy weapons fire. All the light rods in the ceiling had been smashed. The dust carpeting the floor concealed the scattered glass, making each step a crunchy hazard. He swung his torch beam along the wall until the soft gleam of something not metal caught his eye.

Ledesme paused before a door. He noticed a small glassite tile inset above a recessed slot near the door's edge. He pressed his palm into the slot and pushed, but the door refused to budge. He tried the next three doors in turn with the same result. Sighing in frustration, he resumed walking.

Veyho Bayona, the largest city on colonial Nuetierra at the time of its destruction, had covered hundreds of square *klims*. Beneath its gleaming towers of metal and electrochromic glassite blocks, vast plazas, and parks filled with artwork and monuments of natural stone, ran many klims of corridors and tunnels, connecting underground chambers both small and vast; a seemingly endless complex that rivaled the size of the surface city. Ledesme walked within a tiny circle of light, step after step until he lost count, ignoring the corridors that branched off the one he traversed, determined to follow this main passage to its end.

So far, he'd seen no signage or writing of any kind. This anonymous passageway could be beneath a government building, hospital, or in the basement of an office complex. The only sure clue was the damage; like most of the city, this location had not escaped the cataclysm of the Great War.

The corridor ended in a heavy metal door, blackened and sagging open on twisted hinges. A whisper of breeze caressed his cheek, fresh and redolent of the forest. He stepped over the threshold into a large chamber. As the carbon filament bulb in his torch began to flicker, he switched it off.

Natural light, filtered through a screen of tangled vegetation, leaked through a broad fracture in the vaulted ceiling above, illuminating a jumble of debris piled around the jagged rim of a crater torn into the floor. Clearly this room had suffered a direct missile strike.

To the gritty crunch of glass and plastic beneath his boots, Ledesme moved farther into the room until he stood at the edge of the hole, contemplating the destruction surrounding him. Shattered concrete, broken metal rebar, pulverized glass, partly melted cables snaking like blackened vines through the rubble, and….

Bones.

Femurs, ribcages, hands and feet like bundles of brown sticks, phalanges, jawbones, teeth scattered like macabre dice…and skulls, some still intact, others broken.

Ledesme made the sign of the Holy Family on his breast and muttered a brief prayer for the dead. Though this discovery saddened him, it did not shock. He and his teams had come across remains before. The city had died in fire, and quickly. There wouldn't have been time for such a large population to evacuate. Most perished where they'd lived or worked, and the survivors had been too few and too traumatized to bury the countless corpses.

As he scanned the pile and pondered his next move, something on the wall opposite the door caught his attention. Beneath the layer of soot clinging to the concrete, Ledesme discerned an image that stirred vague recognition. He picked his way closer, avoiding the bones, until he stood close enough to puzzle out a symbol and words from the background grime. Excitement set his heart racing.

The logo he knew from histories studied during long hours in the Church's archives. Twin black lightning bolts contained within an equilateral triangle. The words, written in the language he himself spoke, passed down with only minimal changes from his Old Earth colonial forebears, read:

BAYONA DISTRICT ONE CENTRAL COMMAND
FIRST MECHANIZED FLEET

Sweet Madre Maria, this is it!

Ledesme laughed aloud. "Madre, You know I'd never presume to question Your methods, but did you have to send a kymera to show me the way?"

2
discoveries in the dark

By a miracle of the Madre, a few of the computer stations had escaped destruction. Sucking in a sharp breath at the pull of blood-crusted *algodon* fabric on his wounds, Ledesme righted an overturned chair and swept a thick pelt of dust from the seat. He positioned the chair at an undamaged workstation and perched on its edge to examine the console before him. A shard of light from above highlighted the ancient keyboard.

Familiarity with pre–Great War–era computers, gained through archival studies and practical experience using the Church's pair of working machines — only two other functioning machines existed on all of Nuetierra — guided the priest's perusal.

With gentle exhalations he cleared the console of dust; then, with hands poised, he paused to reflect.

Refugees from a dying world beset by famine and endless warfare, the men and women of the first colony ships to leave Old Earth for the vast unknown of interstellar space had entered their metabolic stasis pods with the knowledge that they and their children would be the first humans to walk beneath an alien sun. On the world they named Nuetierra — New Earth in the old tongue spoken by their great-great-grandparents—the colonists bent to the task of building a new society on a planet poor in mineral resources.

For nearly six centuries the autonomous city-states of Nuetierra's only inhabited continent prospered in a loose, peaceful confederation, but the lesson of conservation learned by ancestors from a depleted homeworld gradually faded. Resources grew increasingly scarce and competition more fierce, until the descendants of the people who'd fled a depleted planet savaged by warfare found themselves engulfed in the same nightmare.

A high-pitched squeak and the crisp rustle of vegetation overhead startled Ledesme from his musings. He looked up in time to see a black-and-white-striped *mono* scurry up a ladder of vines to perch on the jagged lip of the roof cleft. Hairless tail lashing, the tiny primate bared needle-slim fangs and unleashed a barrage of invective before leaping out of sight. Ledesme sighed, relieved. The fact that a mono chose to den here meant there weren't any large predators also in residence. He turned his attention back to the console.

Reverence lightened his touch as he set calloused fingers to the computer's dark, glassy surface. A red square abruptly winked to life beneath his left index finger. In shocked reflex, Ledesme pulled his hands away. An instant later the entire console lit up in a block grid of yellow, red, green, white, and orange.

"Madre preserve!" he cried, as a ghost materialized before his astounded gaze.

The phantasm hovered above the console, a semitransparent rendering of a woman no more than two handspans tall. She glowed, yet cast no shadow. Silver blond hair fell in a ragged plait across the shoulder of her black uniform jumpsuit. A smear of blood streaked her pale cheek.

Though her lips moved, Ledesme heard no sound. He watched, transfixed, as the desperation infused into her every gesture rendered words unnecessary.

The figure flickered and died. An instant later the console went dark. Ledesme gripped the arms of his chair, trembling. Though he'd never before witnessed such an image composed only of light, he knew what to name it. A remnant of power lingering within its ancient core had, by his touch, awakened the machine to a fleeting life that lasted long enough to show him a few seconds of a holographic distress call.

His compassion for her suffering and for all who died here so long ago triggered an ache in his chest. Ledesme resigned himself to the fact that the woman's identity and her final words would forever remain lost.

As a young seminarian, Gabril Ledesme had spent hours poring over histories of the pre–Great War period as well as original source material brought back by Church teams for its vast archives. What he personally discovered and retrieved over the long years of his career could fill its own catalogue, and in fact did. Now the priest stood on the verge of what might be his most important discovery, in a place that could yield an artifact the Church had been seeking for the better part of three decades.

As leader of this, his fourth expedition to the ruins of Veyho Bayona, largest of the pre-war city-states, Ledesme's mission was unlike any of his previous efforts. Data crystals, fuel cells, electrochromic glassite tiles, and rare, intact light rods that could be re-electrified added to the Church's wealth, and his team would not neglect to search for those artifacts; however, Ledesme had been tasked with a single, prime objective by the Archbishop himself.

We need technical specs, diagrams, an operations manual, anything you can find, Gabe. Bring back whatever you can carry and destroy the rest. I don't need to tell you what a disaster it would be if we're beaten to this.

Less than a month ago, Lugo Zerate, small-time salvager and cousin on his mother's side, had come to Ledesme's cramped office in Nue Bayona Cathedral with startling news. Grizzle-haired and rawboned, Zerate had skirted the edge of destitution for years, always chasing that one big strike. Phlegmatic by nature, the broad grin on his windburned face made him seem like a stranger. Ledesme had never seen his cousin so excited. "I think I've found what you've been looking for all these years, Gabe," Zerate said, as he dropped onto the only spare chair in the room, opposite Ledesme's cluttered desk.

"You're sure?" Ledesme prodded.

"Oh, it's a mech command post all right." Zerate's face had the look of a man tallying anticipated winnings. "Said so, in big letters right on the wall. I went in, though I didn't explore very far."

"You can find the entrance again?"

"Not exactly the front door, but a way in nonetheless, at the edge of a huge plaza. There's a round turret with a big hole blasted out of the side. It may have been a skylight or the top of a ventilation shaft. We'll have to lower ourselves on ropes."

"I'll need to take this to the Archbishop first, but I think he'll approve." In truth, Ledesme had always had standing permission from his superior for any expedition he wanted to mount.

"You'll vouch for me as guide." Zerate leaned forward, fixing his cousin with steel-rivet eyes.

"Of course. You're the only one who can find the place again."

It had taken two weeks to assemble a team and another week of travel by steam trike, first along dirt farm roads potholed and pooled by spring squalls, then across burgeoning scrubland criss-crossed by game trails, and finally, through the hardwood forests to the outskirts of the ruined city.

Emerging from reverie, the urgency of his situation once again uppermost in his mind, Ledesme looked at the broken dome overhead. *This must be how Lugo got in*, he thought. *Without a rope, I can't get out that way. I'll have to go back the way I came and hope the kymera has given up.*

Torch once more in hand, his kerchief covering the lower half of his face, Ledesme retreated from the chamber back into the corridor, moving with slow, deliberate steps to stir up as little of the ancient dust as possible. The thought that much of it had once been living human flesh gave him momentary pause.

When he reached the pile of broken furniture, he hesitated. The need to explore burned in his blood like a drug, pulling him away and sending him walking past the mound, up the passageway.

Blank door after blank door materialized and then vanished into the darkness behind him. After he'd passed twenty of the dull metal panels, Ledesme's torchlight bounced off a wall of rubble that blocked any further progress. Whatever lay beyond this cave-in would remain undisturbed, at least by him. As he turned to retrace his steps something caught his eye. He shined his light into an alcove half-choked with fallen debris that blocked a door. In the light of his torch beam Ledesme noticed a strip of black between the edge and the frame.

The temptation was too much to resist. The gap might be wide enough for him to pass through if he could clear away enough rubble. But without pick or spade, and weakened from his injury, he realized the task was beyond him.

I can look though.

Balanced on a flat slab of fallen concrete, Ledesme pressed as close as he could to the gap and aimed his torch into the chamber beyond. What he saw both thrilled and horrified him in equal measure.

Strewn across the floor amid a scattering of blackened and distorted human remains, drifts of plastic sheets, and other detritus were dozens of black, hexagonal-shaped data crystals.

Even as he felt sorrow for the dead, a heady rush of excitement quickened Ledesme's heart and breath. What he and his team had come here to find might very well be in this room. He stepped away from the door and shined his light on his left wrist. The glass face of his watch had shattered. Dismayed, he hastened back to the overhead shaft. The need to escape began to nip at him with undeniable urgency.

Surely the others have noticed by now that I'm missing and are looking for me.

By the time he completed the perilous ascent of the furniture mound and had hauled himself into the air shaft, Ledesme felt muzzy with pain and blood loss. Sprawled on the cold metal, he floated in a haze of disjointed thoughts until the fog lifted and he remembered the urgency of his predicament. On hands and knees, he retraced his path toward the crevice through which he'd entered.

When the glimmer of daylight ahead limned the walls of the shaft, Ledesme stopped to stow his torch and listen. Only the sound of his own breath, as soft and slow as he could make it, reached his ears. With no accurate sense of how much time he'd spent below within the derelict command center, he couldn't be sure if the kymera still lurked by the cavelet, waiting for him to emerge.

Trepidation held him back, but only for a few heartbeats. He crept forward out of the shaft into the cavelet, pausing once again to listen.

The hum of insects and the far-off call of a *risa* bird, which sounded like a woman's laugh, were all that he heard. Abandoning caution, he wriggled on his belly from the crevice and stood.

The kymera pounced with the speed of a whirlwind. Ledesme cried out as a single claw pierced the heavy khaki of his pant leg and jerked him off his feet. He landed on his back in the hard dirt with force enough to expel the breath from his lungs and choke off his cry of pain. Helpless as a gaffed *bacalao* fish, he lay staring up at his death.

"Blessed Madre, I consign my soul to Your care," he whispered as he sketched with a trembling hand the sign of the Holy Family on his breast.

With its hard-won prey pinned beneath one paw, the kymera seemed in no particular hurry to finish the hunt. Rumbling deep within its throat like a contented *gahto*, its whip-slim tail described languid arcs across its haunches. A black, blade-shaped tongue darted out to sample the salt of Ledesme's skin, rasping an abrasion across his cheek like an iron file.

"Come on, you effing piece of mierda. Get on with it and to the Adversary with you," he growled.

The kymera raised its snout, trumpeted in raw, bestial satisfaction, and opened its jaws to strike.

A horizontal bolt of blue-white light sliced through the trees, catching the monster at the base of its tubular neck and leaving a smoking black hole in the thick, mottled hide. Its victory cry spiraled to a shriek of agony as a second bolt scored a groove across its spine. The stink of charred flesh and the sharp tang of ozone filled the air. Hissing, the kymera turned to confront its unseen attacker, but a third blast caught it between the eyes, sending it crashing to the ground in a tangle of thrashing limbs.

Ledesme scrambled backward, curses flying from his lips, in time to avoid disembowelment by the kymera's flailing claws. Breath ragged with fear and relief, he crouched behind a moss-covered block of concrete and waited until all movement ceased, then he emerged from his hiding place to approach the carcass. With the kerchief still tied around his neck, Ledesme covered his mouth and nose against the reek of scat and urine voided by the animal during its death throes. He prodded the body with his boot, noting the exposed genitalia identifying this individual as female.

He relaxed for a moment, staring at the animal until he recalled a vital fact about kymeras and their habits.

They always hunted in pairs.

"Gabe! Gabe, are you all right?" Two men emerged from the forest shadows, beckoning with arms raised and waving.

"Diosa mia, Gabe…I thought the accursed creature had you for sure." Moonlight-silver hair a stark contrast against his chocolate skin, Benito Arnau, fellow priest and Ledesme's second in command, stood breathless and sweating beside Lazaro Francisco, leader of the expedition's security detail.

Ledesme pointed to the matte-black barrel of the ee-rifle Francisco held with the confidence of long familiarity. "I hope there's some juice left in that."

The big blond man squinted at the energy meter strip on the gun's barrel, frowned, then shifted the heavy weapon in well-muscled arms. "Maybe one more shot. These things eat cells like a fat kid eats cake." Once a fuel cell was depleted it became useless. The technology to recharge them had yet to be redeveloped.

Ledesme offered a grim look to each man in turn. "We need to get out of here now. You can be sure this beast's mate has already got our scent."

"Monseñor, you're bleeding pretty badly," Francisco said. "Did the creature…"

Ledesme cut him off. "No time to think about that. Let's go."

The three men took off at a run back toward their camp.

3
bayona district one

"You shouldn't have gone out alone, Gabe. You know better," scolded Padre Felip Osorio, the expedition's medic.

Two hours had passed since Ledesme had nearly met his death in the jaws of the kymera. Night had fallen, ushering its own distinctive chorus of nocturnal performers onto the stage of ruins surrounding the expedition's camp.

As the monseñor lay prone and shirtless on his pallet, his rangy, ginger-haired colleague fussed over the delicate task of closing the laceration in the skin and muscle over his left scapula. "Damn it, the skin keeps puckering." Osorio paused to readjust the position of the lantern illuminating his work area. Gore slicked his deft fingers like wine-dark ink.

"Yesu preserve, Felip, I don't need any of your lectures right now. I'm in too much pain." Despite the topical anesthetic tincture applied to the wound beforehand, Ledesme still felt each bite of the steel needle Osorio wielded with formally trained precision.

He ground his teeth and, for a distraction, pondered the mystery of the kymera. "We've been at this for over twenty years, and this is the first time ever that we've encountered a kymera," he said.

"They're deep forest dwellers, Gabe," Osorio replied. "The city is considerably more overgrown than when we first started salvaging here, you know. It's not so strange that eventually some might move in."

"I suppose you're right...Ah, mierda, Felip!"

Osorio sounded contrite. "Sorry. Nearly done...there."

"Praise the Madre."

"Let's get you cleaned up," Osorio said.

After enduring gentle strokes with a warm, water-soaked cloth, Ledesme rose to sit cross-legged. Osorio bound his handiwork in clean, soft bandages. "I'll crush a *morfo* tablet in some tea for the pain," the priest-medic said. "Stay put. Relax while I wash up."

Ledesme nodded. His head felt weighted with stones. He closed his eyes.

"Maceas has dinner ready, if you're feeling up to eating something." Arnau's soft drawl stirred Ledesme from his exhausted doze. He lifted his head to see his oldest friend squatting beside him, the lines carved by time and exposure into the ebon skin of his ascetic face deepened by worry. "Madre, Gabe. You look terrible."

Ledesme chuckled. "Thanks. After a good meal and a pain-free night's sleep, I'll look a lot better." Biting back a groan, he reached for his pack.

"Here, let me help you." Arnau dragged the heavy canvas pack to his friend's side and rummaged for a few seconds before drawing out a clean shirt.

With Arnau's assistance, Ledesme dressed and allowed his colleague to help him gain his feet. The three priests then joined the others around the campfire—Lazaro Francisco and his three-man security detail; the two camp servants; and the expedition's guide, Lugo Zerate. Maceas, the cook, had prepared a stew of jerked *puerco* and vegetables for the evening meal.

The burning sap of *pinya* and bloodbark infused the air with sweet incense and instilled within Ledesme a small measure of the peace he always felt when kneeling before the High Altar in Nue Bayona Cathedral. Little by little, the trauma of the day seeped from his body and psyche, like receding mist.

"You're lucky to be alive, Monseñor," Lazaro Francisco, ex-policeman turned gun-for-hire, commented from his seat across the fire pit. Save for his fellow priests, no other member of the team enjoyed Ledesme's absolute trust. Built from a working relationship that spanned the better part of twenty years, his confidence rested on Francisco's impeccable skills and unswerving devotion to the Church. "A second or two later and, well…" The former *poli* drew a finger across his throat.

"What possessed you to go out alone?" Arnau asked.

It was a reasonable question; nevertheless Ledesme felt a flash of annoyance, followed by the painful realization that his anger came from a place of shame. He had put the lives of his team in danger by his foolish act.

"I felt restless and wanted to walk awhile," he replied. "Why? I don't know. I've been through here before and have never encountered anything bigger than a *pantera*, and they only hunt at night. I had my pistol…I thought I was safe enough. I know that's *not* much of an excuse. I'm sorry."

His sidearm probably still lay in the small cave where he'd taken refuge from the kymera. He deeply regretted its loss and had already decided to go back to look for it after the expedition had completed its mission.

Francisco pointed his fork at one of his fellow guards, a broad-shouldered, bald man seated on his right. "Good thing Calderone heard your shots."

"Never could sleep during the day," Calderone's voice lisped through a mouth distorted by some past calamity that had left his face a scarred ruin. Though he'd worked as hired security for Ledesme twice before, never had the man offered up the tale of his wounding, and the monseñor had never asked. Calderone in fact spoke very little.

"And thank the Madre for Francisco's ee-rifle," Osorio added. "Bullets alone wouldn't have stopped that monster."

Francisco rose to help himself to another ladle of stew from the bubbling pot on the camp stove. "We'd all better hope we don't run into another one, or that we find a cache of cells soon. Otherwise it's our slug shooters or nothing."

"I didn't see any cells," Ledesme said, "but I was only down there a short time. The complex is big and there may be storerooms that escaped looting. I saw no evidence that any other salvage teams have ever found the place."

"I think you're right, Cousin," Zerate agreed. "The place looked completely undisturbed to me as well."

"I did find a records room. The door was open, but partly blocked by debris. I looked through a gap and saw computer crystals all over the floor." He looked at each of his fellow priests in turn. "This could be the single most important find in decades, brothers. A trove of material to keep the Church research archivists busy for years."

"And once it's secure we'll have prevented any of this from falling into the wrong hands," Arnau said.

"The Church should have claimed exclusive salvage rights to Veyho Bayona years ago." Osorio glared at no one in particular, the look on his face that of a man vexed anew by an old grievance. "Then we wouldn't have to worry about staying ahead of the city teams, not to mention all the damned privateers."

"Nue Bayona is not, and never has been, a theocracy, Felip," Ledesme pointed out, "though I know you sometimes wish otherwise. The Church has no legal authority to hold for itself the sole right to search for and possess lost knowledge."

"I've never argued for a theocracy, Gabril," Osorio retorted, "though, considering what the city has had to endure over the last six years... Again, you misinterpret my intentions."

Ledesme shook his head. "I don't think so."

"All I'm saying is…"

"I know your arguments very well and my rebuttals haven't changed."

"Enough, you two." Arnau threw up his arms, his tone equal parts joviality and annoyance. "I've heard this debate too many times in the past. Not tonight, for Yesu's sweet sake!"

"You're right." Aware of Osorio's still-smoldering ire, Ledesme offered his fellow priest an olive branch and a tired smile. "I do respect your views, Felip, even though it sometimes doesn't seem that way."

The tense muscles around Osorio's mouth relaxed. "We are both brothers in the Madre's service. That's all that matters."

The other men had busied themselves with their meals, feigning indifference to the heated exchange. Now that the storm had passed, they visibly relaxed. Bandy-legged Maceas and the other servant, Ignacio, a young lay brother with tragically large ears, began clearing away the dishes. Osorio stood and went to the camp stove, to return a few moments later gripping a blue-enameled metal cup. He reached into the breast pocket of his shirt and withdrew a small packet, then offered both cup and packet to Ledesme.

With a nod of thanks Ledesme tipped the contents of the packet into the hot liquid and set it beside his foot to cool; the morfo needed a minute or two to dissolve and he didn't fancy a burnt tongue to go along with the rest of his aches. "Tomorrow you'll lead us to the hole in the roof, Cousin," he said to Zerate. "How much farther up this road, do you think?"

The small, wiry man scratched a chin covered in a week's growth of black stubble. "Maybe a half hour. We'll have to travel the last bit on foot. Too much undergrowth to drive trikes through."

Ledesme shifted in his chair, trying to get comfortable, and allowed his mind to wander, but the pain of his wound proved too insistent. Admitting defeat and feeling a need to rest, he retrieved his drug-laced tea and drained it in three gulps, grateful that Osorio had thought to sweeten it. Even so, he grimaced at the underlying bitterness of the morfo.

He rose from his seat and placed the empty cup into Ignacio's outstretched hand. "Don't let me sleep past sunrise," he said to Osorio. "We've got a lot of work to do tomorrow. A peaceful night to you all."

"Mariche and Casetas will take first watch," Francisco said.

After removing his boots and whispering his nightly devotions, Ledesme lay on his pallet, floating on gentle waves of narcotic bliss that carried him away into troubled dreams. He found himself lost in a lightless, endless maze of twisting corridors, and always close, the sound of claws clicking and scrabbling in pursuit.

WHEN LEDESME AWOKE, the few stars visible through the forest canopy were fading with the dawn. He sat up to find the others already moving about like shadows in the cool dimness. The smell of frying bacon and *café* wakened his appetite.

"You tossed and turned all night, Gabe." Arnau emerged from the dark, his white hair wet and slicked back from his forehead. "Bad dreams?"

"I asked Felip to not let me sleep late," Ledesme grumbled as he threw back his blanket and reached for his boots.

"You said you didn't want to sleep past sunrise. It's still dark."

"I can see that." Ledesme threw an exasperated look at his friend, not caring if it was visible or not. "And yes, my dreams were not especially sweet."

Arnau didn't pry. Instead he asked, "How's your shoulder feeling?"

Ledesme did a quick mental assessment. "Still hurts, but I can manage. Though I'm not looking forward to climbing any ropes." He dare not dull his senses with more morfo until after they finished for the day.

The team assembled around the fire pit to eat a quick breakfast of bacon, hard rolls, dried fruit, and café, then broke camp with brisk efficiency. Maceas and Ignacio had the trikes loaded and fired up before

Ledesme finished his daily cigarette, his one and only vice and a habit since late teen-hood.

Powered by small, coal-oil-fired boilers affixed to the rear of open-framed steel chassis, the trikes were the all-terrain transport of choice for any well-funded salvage team. One machine could carry two riders in tandem while pulling a fully loaded supply wagon. Freelance teams with no backing and most wildcatters had to rely on *eelats*, the three-toed indigenous ungulate long ago domesticated by the Earth colonists to replace their virally decimated horse stocks.

Francisco and Zerate took the lead, riding double. Ledesme and Arnau followed, then Osorio and Calderone. Maceas and Ignacio, sharing a machine, towed the larger supply wagon. Casetas and Mariche brought up the rear, pulling the smaller wagon.

As the sun crested the horizon, the diurnal forest stirred into full-throated life. The wind rushing across Ledesme's face began to warm. Fat tires helped stabilize the trikes as they rolled along the uneven pavement of the ancient road, for which the monseñor was grateful. Less jarring meant less pain.

After a quarter hour of travel, Zerate signaled for the trikes to pull over to the verge. The expedition halted and everyone dismounted to cluster around him.

"Here's where we go in." The guide pointed to a narrow path leading into the trees. Once paved, now the walkway was broken and overgrown, impassable to their trikes. "Shouldn't take more than twenty minutes from here."

Ledesme glanced down the path and gave his orders. "Casetas, you'll stay here with Maceas and Ignacio." The guard acknowledged with a nod. "Everyone else, let's divide the equipment and get going."

With a full pack on his back, Ledesme followed Zerate into the forest, gritting his teeth at each painful step. The demands of his mission took precedence, no matter the ultimate cost to his damaged flesh.

Fifteen minutes of tramping passed. Before Ledesme could spot the clearing ahead, Zerate declared, "This is it."

The team emerged from the trees onto a vast plaza pocked with impact craters and studded with small mountains of debris. The expanse had undergone a softening of its fractured topography as the forest made inevitable inroads over the centuries. Here and there, clumps of vegetation formed green islands between the mounds, while solitary trees stretched leafy crowns skyward from the bottoms of the shallower craters.

"Fissure's this way." Zerate pointed and headed off to his left, leading the others to a concrete turret jutting from the ground and partially split asunder, as he'd described. A mass of flowering sugar creepers cloaked the structure, rendering it invisible to anyone unaware of its presence. Tiny, winged *abehas* buzzed among fragrant trumpet-shaped yellow blossoms.

Ledesme gingerly shed his pack, retrieved a hand torch from a side compartment, and dropped to his belly in front of the opening. Shoving a tangle of greenery aside, he shined the light downward. "Yes. I was definitely here." He climbed back to his feet, wincing, and looked at the others. "Once we're below we'll split into teams. Francisco, Calderone, you're with me. I'll need you to shift the debris away from the records-room door. Benito, you're with Mariche. Felip, you're with Zerate."

No additional words needed to be said. Each man knew his business. Osorio removed a coil of rope from his pack and secured it around the base of a nearby *bloodbark* tree. Francisco added an additional length, and a harness from Mariche's pack completed their rappelling rig. Within minutes, the team stood inside the ruined Bayona District One Central Command.

"Have a care where you step." Ledesme swept his torch in an arc across the treacherous footing. "There are human remains here." He paused, then said, "You know what we're looking for. We'll all meet back here in four hours." Within the beams of their torches, the team synchronized their timepieces.

Ledesme surveyed the faces of each man, secure in his confidence. "Good hunting, everyone."

4
trust betrayed

It took Francisco and Calderone the better part of an hour of sweaty labor to clear enough debris away from the door before they could slide it open. Ledesme entered first, flushed with anticipation. Before the other two could follow, he held up his hand. Obedient to his command, they lingered on the threshold.

The extent of the trove revealed itself to him with every sweep of his torch beam. Between the space of each heartbeat and snatched breath, his excitement grew. He looked back at the others. "Come in."

"Don't step on anything," Francisco cautioned. Calderone grunted.

The prime objective of the mission remained the guarded secret of Ledesme and his two Church colleagues. Not even Zerate knew its true purpose, although he thought he did. For the rest of the team, even the trusted Francisco, this expedition was no different than any other—take in salvage anything useful to the Church.

Francisco turned in place, whistling, his light slicing arcs through the gloom. "You were not exaggerating, Monseñor." He bent over and peered at one of the corpses.

"Let's get to work," Ledesme said.

Dead computers; data crystals winking amid drifts of dust; brushed-steel folders containing plastic sheets imprinted with schematics and dense strings of numbers; a long, thin black box that rattled when shaken; sundry small plastic and metal objects— the three men filled their packs to bulging capacity, then left the remainder among the dead, and the dead to their rest.

For three more hours they navigated the stygian corridors, leaving notations in chalk on doors to rooms that contained salvage too big to carry but worth returning for at a later date. Much of the complex was inaccessible, cut off by debris piles from collapsed ceilings. They discovered few skeletons; the dearth of remains stood as proof that most of the people escaped before the missiles began falling. How many had survived the destruction could not be known.

After rejoining the others back in the primary control room, Ledesme confirmed that, between the three teams, the entirety of the complex that could be accessed from their present location had been effectively explored. Besides the salvage from the secondary control room, their haul included an artifact of surpassing rarity: in a small room lined with metal storage lockers, Osorio had discovered a protective suit constructed of some unknown material, complete with helmet.

Though several hours of daylight remained, Ledesme decided nothing more could be gained by further exploration. If there were sections of the complex still navigable beyond the rubble-choked passages they'd encountered, finding an alternative way in could take days. He'd leave that task for a future expedition.

Climbing back out through the fissure took a good deal more effort than rappelling in had taken. To lessen the likelihood of another salvage team stumbling upon the opening, Ledesme ordered the three hirelings to pile slabs of broken concrete over the fissure and shove the tangle of vines back in place, rendering the turret effectively invisible.

Casetas and the camp servants, Maceas and young Ignacio, had not been idle while the rest of the team had been away. Ledesme and the others emerged from the forest to find a fire pit ringed with camp chairs and the plucked and gutted carcass of a turquia hanging by its scaly feet from a rope tied to a sapling.

"Casetas bagged it 'bout two hours ago," Maceas told Ledesme. The flightless birds were crafty and their mottled plumage made them tough to spot amid the undergrowth, but a lucky shot had provided the team with a much-appreciated break from canned and dried supplies.

After shedding their packs, Francisco and Mariche sought their bedrolls for a nap, as did both of Ledesme's fellow priests. Zerate broke out a deck of cards and lured Casetas and the two servants into a game of *corzones*. Calderone sat near Ledesme with his back against a tree, gazing into the shadows beneath the boughs, a rifle across his lap and a lit cigarette dangling from his lips.

The past hours had taxed the monseñor's diminished stamina to its limit. He felt feverish and his wound throbbed with each heartbeat. Though he desperately needed rest, Ledesme could not siesta like the others. While the men took their leisure, awaiting sundown and the evening meal, he sorted through the data crystals and file folders taken from the auxiliary control room.

Surely there's something in all this? The mech command center would have technical specs. There'd be pilot logs, communications logs...Maybe if we're very lucky, some of these crystals contain uncorrupted sound or vid files, or even...

"This could be it, Gabe."

Ledesme looked up into the eyes of his oldest friend. "I thought you were asleep."

Arnau squatted on lean haunches beside the monseñor and picked up a crystal the length of his thumb. As he turned it in his fingers, its black surfaces gleamed iridescent, like oil on water. "The Church has been looking for schematics of the Annihilator since before you and I entered the seminary," he said. "The fact that nothing has been found yet must be the grace of the Madre at work. Once we get all this back to the city…"

"The real work begins," Ledesme finished. "Let's pray our machine can read these."

"If it can't," Arnau said, "the Archbishop may have to go to the Sedanos."

Ledesme's reply was swift and sharp. "No. That's not even a consideration. I don't care if they do have the only other working computer in all of Nue Bayona. The mere possibility that information on the most destructive machine this world has ever known might fall into Gregorio Sedano's hands...it doesn't bear consideration."

Arnau held up a hand. "Easy, Brother. It was only a suggestion. There's always Doctor Alba, I suppose."

"That would mean trekking across the desert for days."

"If that's what is necessary, Gabe, I'll take the material to him myself." Arnau rose and gazed down at his friend. In the failing light of the gathering dusk, his eyes appeared like dark holes against the duskiness of his face. "This feels like the biggest find of our careers."

Ledesme heard the satisfaction in his colleague's velvet voice. "It does, doesn't it?"

On the other side of camp, the card game broke up amid much crowing from Zerate and good-natured curses from the other players. "I'll put all that into the wagon," Arnau offered, pointing to the trove. "You look as if you don't feel much like moving at the moment."

Ledesme gathered up the disks and folders, sweeping the lot into a canvas bag. "I don't. Thanks." He passed the bag to Arnau and lay down on his pallet, hoping to get a little rest before Maceas called them to eat.

He awoke to the rhythmic clang of a spoon against a pan, surprised that he had fallen asleep without benefit of drugs. Dragging his aching body off his bedroll and over to the fire pit left him woozy.

"...never in my life seen anything like how those bodies were damaged," Calderone was saying as Ledesme fell into a camp chair.

Francisco grimaced into the steaming cup cradled in his large hands. "Can't imagine what it must've felt like." It looked as if the bones were...

melted or fused together. What kind of gun does that?" He took a cautious sip and added, "I hope for their sakes it was quick."

Arnau, the team expert in pre-war tech, spoke up. "From what we know about the types and power of energy weapons of the era, certainly not an ordinary ee-rifle or cannon. No, something else entirely was at work."

" Why weren't any of the data crystals damaged?" Ledesme mused. "They were scattered all around the remains, some even beneath the pile, and yet…." The implications both terrified and excited him. It suggested that the colonials possessed a type of weapon unknown to Church researchers, something that could destroy human flesh without damaging the surroundings. Perhaps the very artifact he'd come here to find had been equipped with this mysterious, destructive force.

"If you ask me, that kind of tech should stay lost, even from the Church. It's too dangerous," Francisco said, his chiseled face pensive. "Maybe it's wrong for us to use any tech from the pre-war days."

Casitas snorted. "You don't seem to have any problem with that ee-rifle of yours."

The ex-poli gave his colleague a look like sharpened steel. "I said maybe. I'm questioning, is all."

Ledesme regarded Francisco with fresh, astonished perspective. "I had no idea you felt that way."

Francisco shrugged. "I don't want my kids to wake one day to a world going up in flames."

Ledesme had no sound response to such a simple, yet harrowing, statement.

Neither did Osorio or Arnau. Francisco's oblique indictment had silenced both his fellow priests and cast a pall over the group.

For the first time in his long career, Ledesme felt doubt prick his conscience like a thorn.

Maceas' turquia stew gave off a savory aroma that should have made Ledesme's mouth water, but instead it only roiled his stomach to the brink of rebellion. Osorio noticed and quickly mixed him a concoction of morfo and sweet tea, which he drank while the others ate. He excused himself to seek his bed before the rest had finished.

That night he dreamt of fire.

"Gabe. Gabe, wake up."

Ledesme groaned, wanting to ignore the insistent whisper in his ear, but the voice sounded urgent. He opened sleep-crusted eyes to Arnau's face, peering down at him with grim intensity. "What is it?" he rasped.

"You need to come see this."

Ledesme felt a shiver of alarm course through him. "Help me up," he murmured.

"Madre's grace, Gabe. You're burning up." Arnau slipped an arm beneath his shoulders, bringing Ledesme to his feet, hot, dizzy, and with a murderous headache.

"What's happened, Beni?" he asked.

Arnau remained silent. Instead he slowly led Ledesme across the camp to where the rest of the team had gathered in a circle around the trikes.

At first, Ledesme didn't understand what he was seeing. The fever made concentration difficult, but then the full scope of the disaster swam into focus.

"Blessed Madre," he whispered.

All the trike tires had been slashed.

Wait. There's one missing…and a wagon's gone as well.

Francisco stepped forward, looking both furious and embarrassed. "Monseñor, Casetas is hurt. He's got a cracked skull. And Calderone is gone."

5

machinations

Surrounded by the plush velvet and wood-paneled luxury of her palace office, Lourdessa Hernaan, Dama Alcalde of Nue Bayona, gazed at her reflection in the old mirror and frowned. Turning to three-quarter profile, she lifted her chin to tauten the gentle sag of skin on her neck.

That's better.

She studied her face, admiring the well-formed nose and brows tweezed to perfect arches. No matter that a fine spray of lines now radiated from the corners of her eyes. She reached up to tuck a mahogany strand of hair back into her otherwise neat chignon. Where only a moment ago generous lips had grown tight with irritation, a smile now displayed a flash of even white teeth.

You are still quite the beauty, my dear.

A three-note chime broke the silence. Her smile vanished. She turned from the mirror to see her private secretary, Mari, prim in a starched white blouse and long gray skirt, standing in the open doorway. "Señor Nunyez has arrived, Dama."

Lourdessa sighed then returned to the red velvet and gilt chair behind her desk. Once seated, she smoothed the spill of ivory lace at her throat. "Show him in."

A stooped man in black sidled past Mari, glided across the room to Lourdessa's desk, then inclined his head. "Dama," he said in a rasping voice.

Lourdessa's lip curled as she remembered the day she'd promoted Saviero Nunyez to his current post. He'd been among the most difficult of the former Alcalde's ministers to persuade; in fact she'd had his arrest warrant drawn up and ready in case he'd refused her offer.

The former Chief of Palace Security smelled like an old trunk that had recently been opened after years in storage. A fine powder of red clay speckled his threadbare frock coat and trousers. The mottled skin of his face and balding head reminded Lourdessa of a spoiling corpse. Her dislike of this man bordered on loathing, but she'd never allowed that to interfere with their working relationship. As Minister of Intelligence, he and his network of Special Police operatives provided the Alcalde with her most powerful tool—information.

Nunyez regarded Lourdessa down the length of his patrician nose. His black eyes glittered with cold satisfaction; for what, Lourdessa didn't wish to contemplate.

"Oh, do sit down, for Maria's sake." She hated when he hovered, like a carrion bird atop a carcass. The Minister inclined his head again and, flipping the tails of his coat out of the way, he folded his lanky frame onto the mate of the chair Lourdessa occupied.

"You look like a gahto that's just eaten a sand mite," Lourdessa said. She picked up a fountain pen and rolled it between her fingers.

"I have good reason, Dama. One of my operatives has discovered a resistance safe house in The Maze. I'll have a team there to clean out the rebels within the hour. After a few days in detention, perhaps one of them will value his miserable hide more than solidarity with the suffering masses and give up Faustin's location."

Lourdessa sniffed her distain. "You and your Specials have been looking for Faustin for over a year now. You're not even sure what he looks like."

"No one has seen his face. The rebels we've captured and questioned tell us he always wears a mask." Nunyez's air of smugness had evaporated. "Despite our best efforts, all we know about his physical appearance is that he's tall and slim."

"I don't know why you bother. So far, what have he and his pathetic band of misfits managed to do? A few small explosions, nothing more. He's his own worst enemy." Lourdessa rapped the desktop with a clenched fist. "My stepdaughter is the real danger to my administration."

"Dama, the airfield bombing was hardly small," Nunyez replied. "There were significant casualties. Faustin has never struck so high profile a target until now. He's growing bolder. Pardon my own boldness, but Faustin and his cells seem more of a threat, especially now that he's targeting centers of governmental power. And have you forgotten the Castilians? They're due here in two weeks. This concern with your stepdaughter's influence over the people is, well, perhaps misplaced."

A mix of fury and concern surged through Lourdessa's body. "The rabble loves Deanna because she is Eduard's child. She's a symbol to them. A word from her and the lower classes might rise against me." The Alcalde leaned forward in her chair and stabbed a manicured finger at Nunyez. "My son and I didn't risk everything, only to have it all undone by my dear husband's skinny brat."

Lourdessa rose from her chair to stalk the room, the heels of her shoes beating a staccato complement to her racing thoughts. She imagined she could feel Nunyez's serpentine eyes boring into the back of her skull. "I don't care what you or my brother think," she said. "Gregorio hides in that dreary pile he calls a house and believes he knows what's really going on out here in the world. He doesn't!" She spun to face Nunyez. "My brother is a fool. The time has come to act."

The tip of Nunyez's tongue flicked across his lips. Lourdessa shuddered.

"You should listen to your brother, Dama," he said. "The girl is no real threat. The resistance, however, is growing stronger and the Castilians are poised to take serious action against us if we don't renegotiate our gas and coal contracts in good faith. Worry about that, not Deanna."

Though irked by the undeniable fact that her brother and Nunyez had a point, Lourdessa refused to bend. "Make no mistake, Señor. I've given the so-called resistance all the consideration it merits, and as for the upstart Castilians," she picked an imaginary thread off her sleeve, "they will get exactly what they deserve. Now. I've made up my mind. You'd do well not to fight me on this." She left the implied threat unspoken.

A tiny muscle by Nunyez's eye twitched. "What, then, do you have in mind, Dama?"

"The girl takes her auto out for a drive in the country every Mercoles. She always has an escort, a man named Valdis." Lourdessa perched on a corner of her desk and faced her intelligence chief. "Next week she will find a different man waiting to escort her. Choose a man who will get the job done and bring me proof afterward."

"How will you explain her...disappearance?"

"I will make an official announcement next Hueves, on the steps of Nue Bayona Cathedral," the Alcalde said. "Deanna has decided to join the cloistered Sisters of the Blessed Maria, so that she may dedicate her life to contemplation and service to the Madre and Her Son, the Holy Yesu."

"The girl has never been very devout, Dama. She only attended worship services because her mother requested it. I'm not sure the people will believe this sudden conversion, and there's the matter of the Marian Sisters themselves. When Deanna fails to present herself at the convent, then what?"

Lourdessa dug her fingers into the varnished edge of the desk. "Even those dreary, sanctimonious hags will keep quiet for enough *reáles*." She glared at Nunyez. "Get this done. Now if you don't mind, I have more important business to attend to."

He unfolded himself from his chair, inclined his head, and departed. Lourdessa took a deep breath to slow her racing heart. She slid from her perch and crossed the room to stand once more before the antique mirror. The heavy cast-silver frame had been in her family for four generations, undamaged, though the glass had been replaced several times. Her mother always maintained that the silver had come all the way from Old Earth, but Lourdessa believed that to be no more than a family legend.

Though dark eyes met their twins within the glass, the hated image of her stepdaughter taunted Lourdessa's inner vision.

Once Deanna's out of the way, the people will no longer have any reminders of the past. It will help them accept things as they are now.

"Admiring yourself in that old mirror again, Mother?"

Lourdessa tore her gaze from the mirror to face her son. "Allie. I didn't hear you come in."

"Clearly. And I've asked you to stop calling me 'Allie.' I'm twenty-seven years old, Mother. 'Allie' is a child's name."

Lourdessa sighed. "You may be grown up, but you'll always be my beautiful boy." She kissed his cheek and ran a hand through bronze-chased chestnut curls. He snorted and pulled away, making a show of rejecting her caresses, but Lourdessa saw secret pleasure in his hazel eyes.

Alehan, her only child, had inherited his father Ricardo's high cheekbones, slim build, and fair skin. Whenever she looked at him, an intense longing for her first love—dead from throat cancer ten years past—tore at her heart. "Your dressmaker's here. I told her to come in." He waved toward a shimmering cloud of indigo damasked silk hovering by the door. The cloud glided forward on severe, low-heeled black shoes and spoke.

"Good afternoon, Dama. I think you'll be pleased with how the dress has turned out." Round and plump as a ripe melon, the small woman freed her bespectacled face from the obscuring folds of silk filling her arms. "Shall we see how it fits?"

"Son, whatever brings you here, can it wait until after I'm finished?" Lourdessa ran a fold of the sumptuous fabric through her fingers, admiring the costly, glassite crystals sewn into the grain. When exposed to an electric current, the crystals would twinkle like tiny stars in the midnight sky.

A triumphant smile lit Alehan's face. "You'll want to see this now."

Lourdessa gripped his shoulders, feeling hard muscle sliding beneath the fine blue algodon of his shirt. "Did you…?" she whispered.

"Yes." With a flourish he extended his hand. A small black hexagonal crystal rested on his palm. "Our agent delivered this, along with a cache of others, two days ago."

"Diosa mia," Lourdessa murmured, then to the dressmaker, "Señora Luz, I'll only be a few minutes."

"Of course, Dama." The dressmaker turned and scurried toward a triple-paneled bloodwood screen that closed off a corner of the room, cascades of indigo silk trailing in her wake.

Taking Alehan's hand, Lourdessa led him to the large open window behind her desk. The red velvet curtains hanging to the floor in heavy, plush folds stirred in the lukewarm late afternoon breeze.

"The Archbishop will be howling mad when he finds out we have this," Alehan said.

"Let him howl. The crystal is readable, then?" Lourdessa hardly dared to breathe.

Alehan nodded. "Olivas was able to retrieve most of the data. Now you need to convince Eduard to build it."

Lourdessa looked into her son's eyes and saw her own exultation mirrored there. "Oh, he'll agree. He knows what I'll do to his children if he doesn't."

Alehan frowned and rubbed his jaw. "Why use Eduard at all? Can't Olivas build this wondrous machine of yours? He is your chief engineer, after all."

Lourdessa stared at him for a moment, then dismissed his sarcasm with a shake of her head. "It's true that Raul Olivas is a clever man, but

Eduard is the most brilliant engineer in Nue Bayona. If anyone can resurrect the Annihilator, he can."

"I still have my doubts. We're talking about tech that's over four hundred years old. Where will we find all the materials?"

Lourdessa smiled. "My husband is very resourceful; and besides, he'll have ample incentive."

Mother and son stood in easy silence, gazing out at the city below. In the near distance beyond the high sandstone walls that enclosed the palace grounds, the stately homes of the elite Palace Hill district nestled like jewel boxes within the vibrant greens of well-watered private parks. Further below, the lush landscape gave way to smaller gardens surrounding the neat brick and wood townhouses of the middle-class Valencea district, home to Bayona University.

Fanning north and east from the base of the uplands like the drab skirts of a kitchen drudge, the working-class districts of Red Hill, Quarry, and Rio Gran blended into the frayed hem of the city, the slums known as The Maze. Beyond that, lost in a brown haze of coal soot that hung like a dirty veil over the valley, lay the factories and farmlands that kept the city alive and functioning.

Lourdessa recalled the last time she'd spoken to Eduard, nearly four months ago. Since staging the coup that had deposed her husband, she'd made the trip to Central Holding beneath the Justice Ministry twice yearly to check personally on his well-being. A special guard detail assigned to the former Lord Alcalde saw to his every comfort, within reason. Even after six years, Lourdessa could not bring herself to have him discreetly murdered. Eduard Hernaan was still her husband after all, and she was not a monster.

The little porcelain clock on her desk broke the stillness with a run of bright notes. As the fifth chime shivered away to silence, the shriek of a steam whistle signaled the arrival of the weekly airship from Nue Fernan—one of the last old-style sky jelly flotation ships in service—at the municipal landing field south of the palace. Lourdessa looked at Alehan. "I must have the Annihilator," she said.

"Why is it so important, other than as a symbol of power? You already control the government and the elite families are afraid of you. What do you really want it for?" Conspiratorial interest gleamed in Alehan's eyes as he returned his mother's gaze.

Not yet ready to divulge her plans, Lourdessa replied, "To help me become more than I am now. When the time is right, you'll know everything."

Alehan's unblemished forehead creased. For a moment Lourdessa thought he might demand an explanation. Instead he leaned in to kiss her cheek. "Very mysterious of you, Mother. I admit I'm intrigued, but now I must go. Lilliana's birthday party is tonight and I have things to do beforehand."

Lourdessa trailed her son toward the door. "Little Lilli...all grown up. How my ugly cousin produced such a beautiful child defies explanation." To Alehan's retreating back, she added, "Make sure she received the necklace I sent."

Alehan replied with an uplifted hand as he departed.

"Señora Luz, I'm ready now," Lourdessa called.

A moment later, she stood before a full-length mirror while Señora Luz's quick fingers secured new seam allowances in her gown's bodice, using dressmaker's pins. Meanwhile, Lourdessa's mind occupied itself with a more pressing matter. She had a letter to compose.

People of Nue Bayona, I come before you to announce that my beloved stepdaughter Deanna, after much soul-searching and prayer, has decided to take holy orders...

"You have my delivery?"

Guided by the red glow of a burning cigarette, Alehan approached the smaller shadow that had detached itself from the deeper mantle of darkness cloaking the façade of an abandoned warehouse.

"You have my money?" The wiry little supplier held out his hand. Moonlight bounced cool reflections off multiple silver rings.

Alehan struggled to conceal his contempt. "Three thousand reàles as agreed, but you get nothing until I inspect the product."

The small man grinned with lupine slyness. "Fair enough. It's very pure. The best, my source tells me. Procured from the special garden of one of their most important medicine women. Guaranteed to have your clients begging for more." He sucked on his cigarette and discarded the stub with a flick of slim fingers. Pale smoke trickled from his nostrils to wreathe his dark head. He unslung a leather pack from his shoulder, picked apart the ties, then pulled out a fist-sized square parcel. The waxed paper wrapper crunched in his grip as he passed the package to the Alcalde's son.

"It'd better be as good as you say for this price." Alehan slit open the paper with a small pocket blade, releasing a rich burst of scent like wet earth and wood smoke. He peeled back the paper to reveal a block of dried, compressed leaves, blackened from fermentation. With the tip of his knife, he worked loose a single leaf, then placed it on his tongue. A heartbeat later, eyelids fluttering, he sucked in a sharp breath and then let out a long, soft sigh, as the sweet familiar heat surged along his nerves.

"Diosa mia...this is good...," he whispered. In a stronger voice he said, "All right. I'll need at least three bricks a month. Can you handle that?"

The supplier nodded. "I can." He fished two more packages from the depths of his pack, but held fast to both, waiting.

Alehan reached into the inner breast pocket of his duster and removed a wallet fat with bills. He resisted the urge to drop the money on the gravel at the little mongrel's feet and instead placed it into the man's hand. The supplier relinquished his merchandise.

"Excellent. Now leave," Alehan commanded. "There could be squatters lurking about. I can't risk being seen with you, not even by squatter scum."

"I won't insult you, Señor Estes, by insisting you stay while I count my money." A hint of steel edged the little man's bland tone. "It will be a pleasure doing business with you, Señor. See you next month."

He spun to a squeak of gravel beneath hobnailed boot soles and melted away into the shadows.

"*Perro*," Alehan muttered.

6
an unacceptable proposal

For want of intelligent conversation, Deanna Hernaan found herself isolated in a corner of the crowded ballroom, bored near to tears. Announced upon arrival by a liveried doorman ten minutes past, she had yet to receive any further acknowledgment of her presence. Her stomach growled in protest at having been fed nothing since midday, and the flute of sparkling wine in her hand, snagged off a silver tray carried by a passing white-coated waiter, had lost its initial appeal.

Three sets of floor-to-ceiling double doors stood open to cooling night breezes. Ornate brass sconces, each cradling an electric bulb, studded the walls. A magnificent cast silver chandelier, ablaze with priceless, salvaged light-emitting orbs, flooded the room with a soft white glow. From atop a small dais, a chamber orchestra struck up a lively merengue to entice guests onto the parquet dance floor. Even if she had wanted to dance, Deanna had no one to partner her, for which she felt no particular sorrow.

Though she tried to ignore it, the vapid babble emanating from the quartet of young women clustered in earnest worship around an impeccably dressed young man kept intruding on her self-imposed solitude. She wanted desperately to escape their insipidness and heavy perfume but the group had her hemmed in. None paid her any heed. Deanna knew each one well, having grown up with all of them, but she counted none as friends.

"Have you seen Lilliana's gown? It's the most beautiful thing ever," Nadea Derezo gushed, her plump cheeks flushed with wine and excitement. "All that gorgeous beadwork!" She clapped her hands, causing the fist-sized, juvenile sky jelly attached to her wrist by a silken tether to flutter and spin. Jewels glued to the creature's skin spattered colored reflections across her face and neck.

Nadea's family had made its money from the breeding and sale of domesticated, nonpoisonous sky jellies for the Nue Bayona Air Service. With the replacement of jellies by faster, modern steam-powered ships, the Derezo family's fortunes were in serious decline, which explained why Nadea was dressed tonight in a dove-gray silk gown from last season.

"Ooh, I did! I'm so jealous." Tatyana Pinyas, youngest daughter of Estrella Pinyas, principal soprano of the Nue Bayona Opera, chimed in with a toss of her auburn ringlets.

"Juan, *dulzor*, don't be angry with me for telling you this, but there's a rumor going around that your sister is secretly engaged to Jorge Leon." Francisca Lorca, blade-slim in fashionable, shoulder-baring teal, shook her head in feigned sympathy.

Juan Guteriz, scion of Nue Bayona's most important banking family and older brother of Lilliana, whose birthday they had gathered to celebrate, raised one elegantly arched blond eyebrow. "The butcher's brat? That's ridiculous and I'll thank you not to repeat it. I don't care how rich his father is. Jorge Leon is a disgusting puerco who's unfit to clean the dirt off my sister's riding boots."

Francisca's acerbic snigger set Deanna's teeth on edge. Jorge Leon was a gentle, shy boy, the only son of the city's biggest purveyor of fine meats. Deanna knew him from her mechanical engineering courses at Bayona University. He had a quick mind and sly sense of humor, but his rotund figure made him an easy target for the vicious barbs of Juan and his friends. Francisca, in particular, had no right to such disdain. As the granddaughter of a man who'd escaped poverty by turning a single garbage cart into a citywide refuse-hauling business, she was only two generations removed from The Maze.

"I hear your father was furious over how many reàles your mother spent on this party, Juan." Heiress to a railroad fortune, Josefina Torez, looking like a bakery confection in a cream-colored gown of frothed lace and pink bows, tapped the young man's forearm. "I say it was money well spent," she added with a coquettish flutter of false eyelashes.

"It is my sister's twenty-first birthday, after all. She's officially an adult now."

Josefina's pursed lips looked like a painted doll's mouth. "My twenty-first birthday party will be equally as grand. Mama will see to it."

Juan glanced over the heads of his admirers toward the center of the room where a tiered silver fountain, rising as tall as his own height, dispensed sparkling wine to thirsty revelers. "I think I'm ready for another drink," he announced. "Coming, ladies?"

The five of them disappeared into the swirl of the crowd, releasing Deanna from her confinement. Sighing with relief, she smoothed an invisible wrinkle on the bodice of her forest-green silk party dress; then, with a copper pin, she resecured an errant strand of brunette hair that fell in thick waves below her shoulders. The dress had once belonged to her mother and lacked the full skirts so much in fashion for formal wear these days. Deanna loved the older styles precisely for their simplicity. She glanced over her shoulder at the pearlescent round face of the grandfather clock sharing her corner. Eight o'clock. One more hour and she could excuse herself without offense to her hosts, return home to change clothes, then head to the Book and Quill in time to meet Zander.

Though Deanna counted herself among Nue Bayona's elite by virtue of her family name, the eldest daughter of the deposed Lord Alcalde Eduard Hernaan felt no affinity for others of her station. Serious-minded since childhood, she had made few attempts to fit in with the hedonistic cohort of people her age, eschewing the endless rounds of parties for engineering studies and charitable pursuits. She had few friends among her peers, but one was Lilliana. Wine glass abandoned on the floor behind the clock, Deanna plunged into the crowd in search of the night's honoree, avoiding attempts by well-meaning dowagers to draw her into conversation. She neither desired nor needed their pity.

Since her father's overthrow and imprisonment at the hands of her stepmother six years earlier, Deanna and her mentally ill younger sister Ceilia had found themselves in very strange circumstances—not exactly shunned by the people they'd known their entire lives, but not especially welcomed either. She could ignore the pity when directed at her, but when the object was Ceilia, it infuriated. Even worse was Lourdessa's deliberate withdrawal of her younger stepdaughter from society. She claimed reasons of protection, but Deanna knew the true reason—embarrassment.

Though herself apolitical, Deanna understood politics for the blood sport it was. Those members of her father's administration who fought at his side against the coup were now in prison or exiled. The rest had thrown in their lot with the winners to save their skins and fortunes. Deanna's mere presence in the Alcalde's palace and at the occasional social gathering served as an awkward reminder to all who had betrayed her father.

Lilliana's parents, Anjel and Sofia Guteriz, presided over the festivities from a pair of rose-silk-damask-covered chairs near the wine fountain. Anjel Guteriz's left leg was weighted down by a plaster cast. Two weeks earlier, he'd been caught in the explosion that had destroyed the passenger waiting area at the airfield.

During the perilous days after the coup, Guteriz had maintained strict neutrality, publicly declaring his business was finance no matter who ran the government. Despite his stance—and because he'd always been kind to her—Deanna bore no grudge against him.

As Deanna approached, he broke off conversation with his wife and beckoned her with a warm smile. "Deanna, how lovely to see you. We're so glad you could come, aren't we, dear?" Guteriz glanced at Sofia, whose tight expression conveyed the opposite opinion. "Please excuse me for not getting up."

"Of course, Señor. I understand. I'm so glad you escaped with only a broken leg."

The portly banker shifted his bulk, grimacing. "Praise Maria and Yesu's mercy, I was lucky. If my flight hadn't been late, I would've been inside the terminal when the bomb went off."

Sofia Guteriz, Lourdessa's red-haired cousin on the distaff side, snapped open a painted silk fan and regarded Deanna as though she were an annoyance in need of removal. "I can't help but wonder if you are secretly pleased to see this so-called resistance movement against my cousin's government getting bolder, Deanna."

Guteriz scowled and huffed past his magnificent gray brush of a mustache. "Nonsense, my dear. Why would you say such a thing?"

Her caramel eyes narrowing, Deanna drew a slow breath before responding. "Only a monster would be happy to see innocent people hurt, Señora. I don't support terrorism, and I'm shocked you'd believe that I could."

Sofia flapped the fan in front of her face, perspiration carving runnels through her heavy makeup. "My husband was nearly killed by those animals. The rabble supports them and refuses to cooperate with the police to catch them...the same rabble, I might add, that you spend so much time defending, Deanna. One of these days your sympathies are going to get you into trouble."

Guteriz's furred jowls quivered. Voice laden with an undertone of warning, he said, "Enough, Sofia. Deanna is our guest and Lilli's friend." He shifted his gaze to Deanna. "You just missed Lilli. I believe she's out on the terrace getting some air."

With a twist of her thin, rouged mouth, Sofia added, "My daughter is simply overwhelmed with friends and admirers, Deanna. You might find it hard to get her attention."

Addressing Lilliana's father as if the chair beside him stood vacant, Deanna replied, "Thank you, Señor. I'll try the terrace."

As she turned her back on the pair and steered toward the double doors piercing the east wall, Deanna fantasized about ripping the glittering necklace of bezel-set diamonds from Sofia Guteriz's freckle-splashed décolletage and shoving it up her pinched little nose.

It wasn't the horrid woman's personal dislike of her, or her implied threats that annoyed Deanna. Her contempt for those of the elite—people like Sofia Guteriz—stemmed from their near total lack of empathy for the common citizens of Nue Bayona.

The terrace proved to be only a little less crowded than the ballroom, but the fresh evening air dissipated most of the heat generated by the crush of bodies. Ornate brass oil lamps provided gentle illumination, and potted *jenjibre* perfumed the air. Deanna sighed with relief as the sweat prickling her brow began to dry.

She stood just beyond the threshold and scanned the crowd. A high-pitched, familiar laugh drew her gaze to a knot of people near a set of broad, shallow steps that led off the terrace and into a formal garden.

Perched on a stone railing, Lilliana held court like a blond pixie contemplating mischief. A group of laughing, fawning young men and stiletto-eyed girls gathered in a semicircle before her. She had hitched the skirt of her dusky rose gown up around her knees to expose pale pink silk stockings. Her pretty mouth curved upward in a manic grin. Spotting Deanna, she extended her arms like a signalman, then jumped from the railing and, with a flourish of taffeta, rushed to embrace her friend.

"Deanna, I'm so glad you came," she cried. "I wasn't sure you would."

"You're my friend, Lilli. I'd never miss your big day." Smiling, Deanna brushed a spun gold lock from the other girl's forehead.

"Oskar was saying how we should all take off our clothes and jump in the fish pond." Lilliana's aquamarine eyes flashed in wicked merriment.

"Wouldn't that thrill your parents," Deanna replied, laughing.

"I'm officially an adult now. I can do what I want."

"Oh, how I remember that feeling."

Lilliana's mood sobered. "I know things haven't been easy for you these last few years," she said, catching Deanna's fingers in a grip surprising for its strength, "but at least your stepmother can't tell you what to do anymore."

"She never could."

A minor stir among the clusters of people congregating by the doors caused both friends to turn their heads. Melting aside, the crowd called out greetings as Alehan Estes and his entourage of swaggering young bravos swept onto the terrace. Deanna bit back a curse. She had hoped to avoid her stepbrother and the inevitable tangle of unpleasant and conflicting emotions an encounter with him always engendered.

As children she and Alehan had counted themselves friends, but even then Deanna disapproved of his insufferable arrogance and the way he wielded the power of his beauty to get what he wanted. Though she could not fix the precise day on which her stepbrother decided that mere friendship could no longer satisfy him, his attitude had subtly shifted soon after her eighteenth birthday, four years ago. Since then Deanna had found herself locked in an ever-escalating struggle against his advances.

Lilliana's hands slipped from hers, the other girl drawn, inexorably as a *polilla* bug to a lamp, into Alehan's beauty-spun snare of charm.

"There she is, the birthday princess." Alehan lifted Lilliana by the waist and whirled her in an arc of flying skirts. Setting her on her feet, he pressed his lips to hers in a kiss that ended just shy of impropriety. "I've been waiting years to do that," he said.

Drunk on wine, high spirits, and the thrill of being the center of attention, Lilliana dissolved into a fit of giggles.

Deanna considered slipping away and letting the press of people conceal her escape, but the protective instinct that compelled her to watch over Ceilia extended to Lilliana as well. She remained rooted in place.

One of his friends spotted her first. "Alehan. Deanna's here."

With Lilliana still in his arms, Alehan turned to pin her with eyes that gleamed like polished onyx in the soft light of the oil lamps. He drifted away from Lilliana, leaving her blinking in confusion, until he stood—pale and heartrendingly gorgeous—at arm's length before Deanna.

"I was hoping you'd be here," he said, a faint rasp burring his voice. His black evening coat accentuated the pallor of cheeks dusted with a day's growth of stubble. Dilated pupils and the faint aroma of *sueño* leaf on his breath confirmed Deanna's suspicion.

"You're high...again," she replied.

He laughed. "Would you like a taste? It's premium product." Alehan counted many of Nue Bayona's young blue bloods as clients, though he had trouble meeting the demand. His taste for his own stock often left him short.

"You know my answer," Deanna said. "When will you get it through your thick head that I'm not like your friends?"

Sneering laughter from Alehan's companions drew his lacerating stare. Like cowed puppies they ducked their heads, their shoulders slumped in submission. Turning his gaze back to Deanna, Alehan edged a step closer until a mere handspan separated them. Wise to the tactic, Deanna stood her ground, refusing to succumb to the spell woven from awe and intimidation he so skillfully used against every person he encountered. The insidious effects of the drug in his bloodstream lent his eyes the illusion of sincerity. "It's because you aren't like them that thrills me, Deanna. You make me feel like no one else does. I don't, I can't ..."

The words left unspoken hung like hungry ghosts between them. Alehan raised a hand and traced the line of her jaw with a forefinger.

"Alehan, stop," Deanna whispered. "Don't say anything you know will only make things worse."

He flinched as if slapped and his eyes narrowed to gold and black slits. A stain of color crept across his high cheekbones. "Do you want me to beg? Is that it?"

The noise of the crowd fell away until it seemed as if a bubble of silence sealed them in their own private space.

A surge of anger coursed through Deanna's body. Never before had Alehan played his cruel game with such intensity. If his plan was to entrap her before all of Nue Bayonan society, she vowed he would not succeed.

"Don't be ridiculous," she snapped, then in stunned disbelief, gasped, "Yesu! What are you doing?"

Alehan had fallen to his knees upon the fired terra cotta tiles of the terrace. Too late Deanna realized her mistake. Her stepbrother's intentions were deadly serious.

Berating herself inwardly for not following her original impulse to leave, she now found herself hemmed in by Alehan's friends. There could be no escape. She must play through this terrible scene to its bitter end.

"Deanna, this is what you've brought me to." The naked pain in Alehan's voice raked Deanna's heart.

"Stop, Alehan," she said. "Stop now."

He raised slim hands clasped in supplication like a man before his deity. "I'm begging...on my knees. Me. The son of the Dama Alcalde." He dropped his hands to swipe at his face, then groaned, "Ah diosa mia...I love you. I've loved you for so long now, I've forgotten what it feels like to *not* love you."

"You don't mean any of this." Even as Deanna denied his words, she knew with sick certainty that at this moment Alehan believed he meant every one. She also knew he possessed a drug addict's boundless capacity for self-delusion.

He seized her fingers in a grip made unbreakable by passion. "Deanna, right here and now, I'm asking you to be my wife."

All sound and movement on the terrace ceased, save for the soft strains of a rhumba floating through the open ballroom doors.

Surrounded by a crush of onlookers, Deanna felt like a long-eared *conayho* caught in a snare. Into the well of stillness and anticipation, she spoke.

"Alehan, we were friends once. I've always thought of you as my brother. Tell me, when have I ever given you the slightest hint that I felt anything for you other than...sisterly regard?" The true measure of her feelings she dared not express, not while her stepbrother's emotions remained in such a drug-heightened state.

Alehan staggered to his feet, his hold on her hands never slackening. "That kind of affection can easily become love, Deanna. Give me a chance to show you. Once we are husband and wife..."

Struggling to break free of his grasp, Deanna cried, "Alehan, no! That is never going to happen. I can't marry you." Shocked whispers rippled through the crowd at her back.

The chiseled planes of Alehan's face settled into frigid stillness. His hands fell to his sides, releasing Deanna's fingers to the hot-needle rush of returning sensation.

In a voice devoid of inflection, he asked, "What are you saying?"

"Haven't I made myself clear?" she replied. "I don't love you."

A tiny muscle fluttered like a trapped insect beneath the skin of Alehan's temple. "Deanna, think very, very carefully before you reject my offer. Consider what marriage to me will mean. Status. Wealth. Power. You will be a Sedano." He raked her with a look like hurled acid and added, "What are you now?"

"What am I now?" she repeated on a rising note of anger.

"I'll tell you. The daughter of a traitor." Quick as a pouncing *felion*, Alehan grabbed Deanna's shoulders with enough force to bruise. "The only reason society still tolerates you is because of me and my mother."

"You're hurting me." Deanna dug blunted fingernails into the solid muscle of his forearms. "Let go!"

He shook her hard enough to rattle teeth, turning her brittle anger to cold fear. "My mother would have been well within her rights to throw you and your idiot sister out on the street the day she had your traitor of a father arrested but she didn't. Why? Because I asked her not to. So, you see," Alehan shouted, "You owe me!"

"I don't owe you anything," Deanna responded in crisp, chill tones, "especially not gratitude. My father was no traitor. Now, let me go or so help me, I'll break that pretty nose of yours." She planted her palms flat against Alehan's chest and shoved. He had no choice but to release his grip or risk stumbling. Backing away, she rubbed her aching flesh.

Alehan stood with hunched shoulders, his mouth twisted in an ugly sneer. Breath ragged, he said, "It's him, isn't it? That street scum you sneak around with. Zander Montoiya." He spat out the name like a piece of offal. "Oh, I know all about how the two of you eff like a pair of filthy perros. By Yesu, he'll pay."

"Shut up," Deanna whispered, shaking.

Alehan threw back his head and let loose a wild bark of laughter. "Your dirty secret is out, dear sister. Everyone knows what kind of woman you really are. One who takes a street *raton* to her bed. Not so sweet and innocent after all."

"Puerco!" Before she could stop to think of the consequences, Deanna swung at Alehan's face. His cheek and her palm connected with a sharp crack, snapping his head to the side. The agitated crowd cried out in alarm and anger.

Alehan's posse engulfed him within the protective shield of their black-clad bodies. From their midst, Deanna heard his icy warning. "You bitch. You'll regret that…you'll regret everything."

Deanna stumbled backward into a pair of arms that pulled her into a sheltering embrace. Blinded by tears, she allowed Lilliana to lead her from the center of the chattering, staring crowd back into the house.

"C'mon, Dee. Let's go hide in my father's library," Lilliana whispered.

Head resting on her friend's shoulder, Deanna squeezed her eyes shut. The sounds of the party faded behind them. Not until she heard the library door close and felt Lilliana gently push her down on a couch did she open her eyes.

The smell of old leather and *limón* oil polish acted as a balm that soothed Deanna's frayed nerves. "Maria damn him," she murmured, wishing she could erase the scourge of Alehan's vicious outburst from her mind. Lilliana pulled a small square of fine algodon from her bodice and pressed it into her hand. With a grateful sigh Deanna accepted, and dabbed at her streaming eyes. "My makeup must be ruined," she added, chuckling.

"It's a little smeared," Lilliana replied.

Deanna stroked her friend's slender arm. "I'm so sorry, Lilli. I let things get out of hand. I should have left as soon as I saw Alehan."

"It wasn't your fault, Dee. He was high on sueño."

Deanna slumped back into the *vaca* hide couch and gazed in pensive silence at the heroic mural decorating the library ceiling. She wondered if the Old Earth colonials had really looked so muscular and fearless as they took their first steps on Nuetierran soil. Lilliana leaned against her, a comforting presence.

The distant strains of dance music licked at the edge of Deanna's consciousness. A large brass clock holding pride of place on a sandstone mantle chimed the hour. "I'd better go," she said.

Lilliana stirred as if awakened from a doze. "No. Please, stay. There'll be cake soon."

With a shake of her head, Deanna stood. "It's better if I don't."

"I'll take you out through the kitchen, then." Lilliana rose, smoothed her skirts, and slipped her arm through Deanna's. Together they made their way through quiet back corridors and entered the steamy bustle of the manor kitchen. The servants cast curious, sideways glances as Lilliana guided Deanna through the controlled chaos to the scullery and then out a small back door leading to a gravel-paved yard. She paused and turned to face her friend.

"Dee...Alehan had no right to humiliate you like that in front of everyone," she said. "It's none of his business who you spend time with. I promise I won't speak to him again until he apologizes."

Deanna smiled and stroked the younger girl's cheek. "Lilli...you are very sweet, but Alehan is your cousin and he is never going to apologize to me."

"Distant cousin," Lilliana insisted. "You are my dear friend."

Bright, swift Nayna—the smaller of Nuetierra's two moons—sailed high overhead, flooding the yard with quicksilver light. Larger, slower Luna, named after the lone moon of Old Earth, would not rise for another two hours.

From the open doorway came a clatter of kitchen tools, punctuated by the shouted orders of the manor chef. Deanna finally said, "I'd better go."

The two girls wrapped their arms around each other in a tender embrace. "Happy birthday, Lilli," Deanna whispered in her friend's ear, turned, and headed up the path toward the front of the house, where valets waited to fetch autos from the lot across the road from the manor.

Though Deanna had a car of her own, tonight she had chosen to travel the short distance from the palace to the Guteriz estate by the power of her own muscles. Hidden in the dark beneath an ancient *roble* tree, well back from the bright electric light that bathed the sweep of sandstone brick driveway fronting the main house, Deanna's bicycle leaned against gnarled bark, waiting.

Slim skirt gathered in a crinkling bunch above her knees, Deanna pedaled toward the twin iron gates thrown open in welcome to only those with permission to enter. The breeze of her passage flowed over her bare arms like chilly water, pricking her to regret for not bringing a shawl. Though the cold air caused her to shiver, Deanna trembled more from the emotional aftermath of tonight's harrowing encounter. How Alehan would exact payment for her rejection remained to be seen, but Deanna had no doubt that she would suffer a heavy price.

Drawing in deep breaths of air scented with night-blooming *jazmin* and tamping down her fear with sheer force of will, Deanna put on a burst of speed to drive all thoughts of Alehan from her mind. By the time she rolled up to the north gate of the palace and hailed the guard to let her pass, the breeze's cool caresses felt welcome and her only thoughts were of Zander.

7
dangerous resolve

On a gust of cool air, Deanna pushed through the vermillion door of the Book and Quill into welcoming warmth and noise. She paused on the threshold to unbutton her canvas coat and swing the satchel from her shoulder. She scanned the crowd, searching for a familiar shock of black hair.

This tavern did not have the same reputation for rowdiness as others in the university district, but tonight, the crush seemed livelier than usual. A mix of gas lamps and candlelight bathed the room in a mellow glow. The smells of hot grease, beer, and *tabac* smoke hung thick in the air. Black-robed professors in pairs or small groups occupied leather-upholstered booths, sipping wine from long-stemmed glasses. A trio of young women occupying a small stage dashed off the sprightly chords of a popular drinking song on guitar and recorders, while a clutch of tipsy boys, clad in the loose maroon gowns of freshmen, sat with arms entwined by the sandstone hearth, singing in a multiple of discordant keys.

Several voices called out to Deanna in greeting. She acknowledged them with a wave and a smile. The Book and Quill had been her tavern of choice for the last two years, ever since she had entered the university as an engineering student. She knew most of the regulars by name.

A hand shot up above the sea of bobbing heads. Deanna pushed her way through the densely packed bodies pressed against the roble wood bar, pulled a wobbly chair up to a corner table and sat. "*Hola, Zan.*"

"Hey, *dulzor.*" The whip-slim young man slouched in the chair opposite leaned over and pecked her cheek. "Did you bring them?" He stared at her leather satchel with hungry blue eyes.

Deanna nodded and fished around the bottom of the bag until her fingers found their quarry. She withdrew a smaller pouch and placed it in the center of the scarred wood tabletop. "Three mini fuel cells, as promised. Two are about half-charged, and one's down about a third. Still, they should fetch you a good price."

Since the coup, possession of pre–Great War tech without a license was illegal, insuring that the elite controlled the felion's share. Deanna kept Zander supplied with small tech items she pilfered from forgotten storerooms beneath the palace, mostly fuel cells salvaged by licensed teams from the ruins of Veyho Bayona and other smaller, dead cities. The increasing scarcity of cells in recent years had driven prices to such heights as to put them beyond reach for the common citizen, even those who could afford the licensing fee. Zander sold these partially charged cells on the black market, but not without some risk. Undercover police operatives posed a constant threat.

Despite the danger, at least a third of Nue Bayona's commerce transpired beyond the bounds of official sanction. For many people, including Zander, it provided the only way to make a living. He had been her friend since childhood, and for as long as Deanna had known him he had been on his own, relying on his wits to survive. The clothes on his back, a rucksack stuffed with toiletries, a silver ear hoop, and a gold ring—his most valuable possession and the only link he had with his dead mother—made up the sum total of his personal wealth. The tidy amount of reàles made by selling the mini cells would keep him in a rented room for a month.

Deanna pushed the pouch across the table and watched it disappear into an inside pocket of Zander's shabby brown coat. "Have you eaten yet?" she asked.

He replied with a wan smile and a shake of his head. "I used my last reàles a couple of days ago to buy shoes."

"Yesu, Zan. Two days?" Deanna touched his hand. "Why didn't you come to my place?"

He shrugged. "I figured I'd find something on my own, but the pickings weren't very good."

The thought of him scrounging through trash tips for food pricked Deanna with a special kind of pain. Zander had been her first love; she'd given her virginity to him when they'd both turned sixteen. Now, six years later, sexual passion had transformed into the tender affection felt for a dearest friend.

Who hadn't eaten in two days. She scanned the room and spotted a waitress. Raising her arm, she shouted, "Service, please!"

A curvaceous young redhead shouldered her way past standing patrons to the table. Tablet in hand, stylus poised, she acknowledged Deanna with a nod. "What can I get for you, Dee?" For Zander she spared only a glance.

"Hey, Kata. What's the daily special?" Deanna inquired.

Kata tapped her cheek with the blunt end of her stylus. "Umm, I think it's *patok* soup."

"Two bowls of patok soup please, and I'll have a glass of *manzaniya* juice," Deanna said.

"Beer for me." Zander grinned and tweaked her cheek. "Fruit juice is for babies." Deanna rolled her eyes. Kata scribbled the order onto her pad and disappeared into the crowd.

"She doesn't like me at all," Zander said. "I wish I knew why." On planted elbows he leaned forward and fixed Deanna with a worried gaze. "What's up with you, Dee? You don't look happy."

Hiding her emotions from him had always proven futile. "Something happened at Lilliana's party tonight and it's got me a little rattled."

Alehan's vitriol still burned like a fresh wound. She took a steadying breath; then in terse detail she recounted the entire ugly encounter to Zander's swelling fury.

"Effing bastard," he whispered through clenched teeth. "I'll kill him if he hurts you."

Deanna laced her fingers through his. "Don't talk like that." Part of the sting of Alehan's diatribe came from the fact that it contained some truth. In the absence of any other man worthy of her love, she still allowed Zander to stay with her at her palace apartment several times a month; though now more often than not all they did was sleep.

"Estes thinks he can snap his fingers and you'll jump into his arms and marry him?" Zander shook his head. "Effing bastard."

Deanna untangled her fingers from Zander's fierce grip. "I didn't come here tonight to talk about Alehan, but I'm afraid what I want to say will make you just as mad."

Zander's simmering anger morphed into wariness. "Diosa mia, what now?"

"I know you and Sonia have gotten close lately and it has me worried."

"Dulzor..." He chucked her under the chin. "Sonia's gorgeous and she likes me. A lot."

Deanna laid her hand on his forearm, ashamed at the momentary twinge of jealousy heating her cheeks. Pitching her voice so only Zander could hear, she said, "Rumor is she's part of the resistance." Talking about the resistance in public could get a person hauled off to detention. Though she enjoyed a certain amount of immunity, she was acutely aware of Zander's vulnerability. "Do I have to remind you of what could happen?"

He shrugged.

Deanna wanted to scream. "Please..." Her voice caught and she looked down at her hands. After a heartbeat of silence, she murmured, "Please stay away from her. I don't want anything to happen to you."

Zander opened his mouth to reply but Kata reappeared, a laden tray in her arms. She set steaming bowls of soup before them, along with a basket of heavy brown bread, spoons, and a couple of mugs. "Enjoy." She turned and headed back to the kitchen.

Zander attacked the food like a famished *coyote*. Deanna ate her own soup in sorrowful silence, remembering him as the boy she had met for the first time while playing in Valencea Park with her sister.

Little more than a bundle of sticks clothed in an oversize shirt and pants, and crowned with a mop of black hair falling in tendrils across his lean face, he'd approached with a hesitant smile, offering to climb a nearby *cirilo* tree to pick fruit for her and Ceilia. Deanna offered to pick fruit for him instead, recognizing how much more of a struggle life was for this boy than for her. Before she could perform her small act of kindness, her nanny drove the boy off with verbal abuse and flung pebbles. For the first time Deanna felt the sting of injustice, like a needle, digging into her conscience. The next day she slipped her nanny's leash and rode her bicycle back to the park to search for the skinny boy with the black hair. She found him sitting beneath the cirilo tree, waiting for her. They had been best friends ever since.

Zander finished his soup and wiped the last drops from the bowl with a hunk of bread, which he stuffed into his mouth. He leaned back in his chair, chewing.

"Order another bowl if you want," Deanna said in response to his raised eyebrows. He flashed her a grateful smile.

Deanna laid down her spoon. "I'm asking you again. Please stay away from Sonia and her gang. I wouldn't be surprised if they had something to do with the airfield bombing."

"You don't know that," Zander said. "And so what if they did?"

Deanna curbed the urge to thump him on the top of his head. "Innocent people got hurt. Doesn't that bother you?"

His eyes narrowed. "Of course it does."

"Zan, they're going to get caught, most likely sooner rather than later. The resistance is no good. It can't succeed. My stepmother and her cronies are too powerful."

Zander regarded her for a quiet moment, pensive. "The power they have over us is only what we let them take," he said in a low voice. "It's time the people took back what's theirs." Resolve infused his face with a new maturity.

The change intrigued and worried Deanna. "I've never heard you talk this way before."

"I've been asleep. I'm awake now." He curled his hands around her closed fists. "You could join us. People would listen to you. The Hernaan name still means something."

Fear thrummed along Deanna's nerves. "So you're admitting you're resistance?"

Zander caressed her fingers. "I'm not admitting anything."

His answer neatly sidestepped his sworn oath to never lie to her. She shook her head. "Even if I wanted to join, Lourdessa threatened to hurt Ceilia if I ever step out of line. I can't let that happen, any more than I can let you get thrown into detention."

"I'm not afraid," Zander replied. "Faustin says only cowards refuse to stand up and fight for what they know is right."

Deanna sucked in her breath. "So, it's not only Sonia you've been hanging around with." Her insides turned cold. "Faustin is a terrorist. He's not a revolutionary, despite all his rhetoric about freeing the suffering masses. You're going to get yourself killed."

"Better to die fighting like a man than live as a perro." Zander's eyes flashed like the sharp edge of a blade. Deanna squeezed his hand. For a heartbeat she feared he would pull away. He didn't, and she dared to hope.

"You know I love you," she said. "We've been best friends practically our whole lives. Faustin is dangerous, dulzor. He hurts innocent people while claiming to fight for their freedom. Don't throw your life away for a man who cares only about getting what he wants, no matter the cost."

The muscles of Zander's jaw worked. At last, he spoke. "I love you, too. Always have, but for the first time in my life I know what I have to do."

A single tear leaked from the corner of Deanna's eye. "Zander, I…"

Across the room a woman screamed.

8
a call to witness

Deanna spun to see a pack of black-cloaked men pushing their way into the room. Horrified, she watched a slim black truncheon swing in a vicious arc to connect with the back of a maroon-clad student's head. The boy screamed and crumpled to the floor, clutching his skull in bloodied fingers.

People scrambled in all directions. Some of them cried out in fear; others shouted incoherently. A tow-headed girl staggered past Deanna and Zander, dragging a young man by the elbow. His eyes rolled like a drunk's in a pallid face sheeted with blood.

Still gripping Zander's fingers, Deanna surged to her feet and yanked him, but he refused to budge. "Come on," she cried and pointed toward the rear of the common room. "We can get out through the back."

Zander gently pried free of her grasp. "You go. I'm staying."

"What? No…you can't." Deanna's heart thudded so hard against her breastbone she feared it would tear itself free. "Zander, it's the Special Police."

"I know." In the flickering gaslight, his eyes gleamed with a strange feverish intensity.

The sharp report of a slug pistol tore through the room. The ceiling exploded above the bar; bits of plaster, wood, and hot lead rained down on the people below. All pandemonium ceased as if a switch had been thrown to douse the chamber into electrified silence.

"Everyone, stay where you are." The crowd shrank away from a man holding a .38 Trueno in one gloved hand. A curl of blue smoke wafted from the gun's polished black barrel. The poli's face, round and pink like a mustachioed melon, surveyed the cringing assembly. The three gold stripes of an inspector decorated the stiff collar of his cloak.

Deanna pulled together scattered memories to join the face to a name.

Inspector Hugo D'Lucio. She knew him by sight as well as reputation. A man with a known taste for violence, like as not he would shoot first and sort out the particulars later.

His gaze trained on the crowd, D'Lucio slipped the pistol back into the holster at his hip. As his hand lifted the fabric of his cloak, Deanna caught a glimpse of the neural stunning baton clipped to his belt. Unlike the blue-uniformed City Police, the Specials were licensed to carry energy weapons. No doubt D'Lucio and his men would employ their batons with alacrity before this night was over.

"Pay attention, all of you." D'Lucio spoke into the well of silence his pistol shot had produced. "We've got good intelligence that says some of Faustin's terrorists are in this bar, right now."

Deanna blinked in confusion. The Book and Quill catered to professors, students, and university workers. In the two years she had patronized it she had never once heard so much as a rumor about any resistance cell using the bar as a meeting place. Why a raid tonight?

D'Lucio scanned the crowd. His keen gaze lighted on Deanna's face, lingered for a heartbeat, and moved on. She wondered if he had recognized her in the uncertain light. She glanced at Zander, who stared at the inspector with unflinching directness as if daring the poli to notice him.

"You know who you are," D'Lucio added in tones of sharp menace. "Give yourselves up now, and no one else will get hurt."

Deanna counted eight uniformed officers besides their commander. They all clutched wicked looking truncheons in their black-gloved fists. She shuddered, dimly remembering the wet sound of leather-wrapped wood smashing down on a man's head, which she'd heard years before when her stepmother's troops seized the city.

"I will count to ten. If you don't come forward, everyone in this room goes to detention."

Whispers flowed through the throng like the sough of wind in high grass. A girl sobbed near the bar; her male companion quickly stifled her. Zander muttered something too low for Deanna to hear.

"One," D'Lucio said.

"Please, Señor. There's no resistance here. Just folk havin' a nice evening." Portly Luis Olvera, the Book and Quill's owner, pushed his way forward to stand, hands clasped in appeal, before the inspector. "I don't let those troublemakers in my place. This is a nice, respectable establishment."

D'Lucio's lip twitched beneath his waxed, gray mustache. "Two."

Zander rose to his feet. "It's no use, Luis. Since when do the polis ever listen to a common man?" he said.

Deanna turned toward him, mouth agape. "Shut up. What are you doing?" she whispered.

Cold black eyes fixed on defiant blue ones. "Three."

"Are we going to let these puercos treat us like this?" Zander shouted. He looked around the room and Deanna saw people shifting from foot to foot, heads nodding.

"Four."

I can't stand here and do nothing, she thought. "Inspector D'Lucio…"

All eyes in the room turned to her. Her inner voice begged her to keep silent, but she ignored it. "I eat and drink here all the time. Would I come to a place where resistance members were welcomed?"

The officers arrayed behind their leader looked like a pack of hounds awaiting the order to attack. D'Lucio pushed his cloak aside to rest a hand on the butt of his neural baton.

Deanna drew in a deep, ragged breath and forged ahead. "These people are my friends. I will vouch for them."

"You don't have to do this," Zander whispered.

Deanna ignored him. The smell of fear and the threat of violence hung too thick in the air for her stop now. "There's no reason for anyone else to get hurt. If you're worried about not carrying out your orders, I'll speak to my stepmother."

"Leave now, Miss Deanna, while you still have the chance," D'Lucio replied. His lip curled in ill-concealed contempt. "Once the round-up starts I can't be responsible for your safety. Five!"

"Inspector, please." Deanna started to move forward, but strong hands gripped her shoulders from behind, pulling her back. She spun into Zander's embrace, her face pressed into the rough weave of his shirt.

"Get out of here, Dee," he whispered in her ear. "The puercos won't stop you. Remember…I love you."

A memory flashed unbidden to Deanna's mind of a night several months ago, when last she'd invited Zander into her bed. He'd whispered words of love to her. With a sudden flash of insight she realized he'd dared to speak the truth then, just as now. She pushed away from him, searching his face for any trace of fear, but found none.

"Six," the inspector intoned.

Zander bent to place a kiss, light as a *spinner's* web, on her lips. "Don't be afraid for me," he said with a crooked smile. "I can take care of myself."

"Not in here you can't." Deanna tried to focus, but Zander's face had become a blur of light and shadow. "Damn it, I won't leave you."

"Diosa mia, Dee…For once, quit being so stubborn." Deanna felt Zander slip something into the pocket of her trousers. "Just go," he added, the soft tone drawing the sting from the command.

Deanna shook her head. "Eff this," she muttered, knuckling her eyes clear of tears. Drawing herself straight like a martyr facing death, she called out, "Inspector D'Lucio…I'm not leaving." Zander gasped as she slid from his arms to push forward through the crowd. People jostled from her, clearing a path to the front of the common room. Hands reached out to pat her back, arms, and shoulders as she passed.

D'Lucio stood in rigid stillness. His men had formed a semicircle at his back, a bulwark against the now-restless crowd. "Miss Deanna, what you are doing is incredibly foolhardy," he said as she stopped within striking distance of his neural baton. Its activated tip shimmered with the blue, electrical charge that would knock her into twitching unconsciousness with a single touch.

"That may be, Inspector, but I still refuse to abandon my friends. Whatever violence you are planning, know this." With a sweep of her hand, Deanna encompassed the whole of the crowd. "I am their witness."

"Madre Maria bless Eduard and Deanna Hernaan!" a female voice shouted from somewhere near the bar.

"Get her out of here," D'Lucio snarled. The Specials pounced.

The room erupted in chaos.

Strong hands seized her arms and legs and hoisted Deanna off her feet. Like a sack of flour, she was flung in humiliating fashion over the shoulder of a Special, her nose bumping his backside with each stride.

"Put me down!" she screamed, pummeling the backs of his knees with her fists. "Zander!" She twisted from side to side in an effort to locate Zander, but the veil of hair falling across her face obscured her vision.

"Stop that wiggling miss, or else," the Special commanded. He backed up the implied threat with a slap to her thighs.

"How dare you," Deanna shrieked, growing lightheaded with fury and the rush of blood to her head. In perverse reaction she redoubled her efforts to escape. Just as she thought she might break free, the Special whipped her off his shoulder and set her on her feet beside the back door. Pure, impulsive rage drove Deanna's hand in a tight arc toward his face, but the man thwarted her blow with a quick elbow block.

"Please Miss Deanna, stop this nonsense," the poli growled. Before Deanna could counter-swing, he hauled open the heavy wood door to admit an onrush of blue-uniformed City Police from the alley behind the bar. Shoved into the arms of another poli, Deanna was hauled, stumbling, away from the melée.

The staccato blast of pistol shots, punctuated by screams, spilled from the open doorway.

"Miss Deanna, you shouldn't be here." The gray-haired City Police sergeant who held her hand glared in stern rebuke at Deanna from beneath the brim of his helmet. "This is a resistance watering hole. What would the Alcalde say?"

Deanna pulled her hand from his grasp. "There's been a terrible mistake, Sergeant. The resistance never comes here." She felt the tickle of fresh tears on her cheeks as she gazed back in cold fear at the rear door of the bar.

The man's scowl softened to a kindly smile. "There, there, Miss. No need to cry. I'm sure you don't know about such things. I'll give you a ride back to the palace, shall I?"

"That's not necessary, Sergeant. I have my bicycle. I can get home on my own, thank you."

"I'm sorry Miss, but that won't do. It's not safe."

The poli's crossed arms and set face told Deanna that further objection was useless. She'd lost her chance to sneak back into the besieged bar to rescue Zander and render any help she could. "Forgive me, Zan," she whispered.

Turning her back on the noise, she saw a pair of police wagons parked in the center of the alley, their rear doors flung open in menacing readiness. That there were two told Deanna the polis had come tonight expecting to arrest many people. The thought of Zander in custody, coupled with her total inability to stop the travesty pierced her to her core. Her stomach lurched. She pressed her hand to her mouth. "I...I'm not feeling well, Sergeant," she mumbled. Ignoring the poli's solicitous questions, she staggered out of sight around the nearest wagon, went to her knees in the gravel, and vomited.

Weak-kneed and sweating, she pulled her coat closed and regained her feet. A stray breeze lifted a tendril of dark hair and blew it across her face. She thought about Zander's kiss and the clarity in his eyes.

Remember...I love you.

Why hadn't she seen the truth of his feelings before now?

She reached into the back pocket of her pants for a handkerchief to wipe her mouth. Tangled in the cloth she discovered Zander's ring. The sight of it warmed her heart. Knowing he faced arrest he'd entrusted his most prized possession to his best friend, for safekeeping.

She knew the perfect place to hide it—on the gold chain around her neck next to the locket her father had given her for her twelfth birthday. She slipped the metal band onto her right thumb, thankful for the snug fit. She would secure the ring on her chain once she'd reached home.

I swear...until the time I put this back on your finger, dulzor, it won't leave my neck.

The poli's polite cough signaled his impatience to be away. "Are you all right, Miss?" he called.

Deanna emerged from behind the wagon, dabbing her lips on the handkerchief. "My bicycle's parked out front, Sergeant. I'll go get it."

Before she could make good on her escape, the poli locked a gentle, but firm hand on her arm. "Leave it, Miss. I'll send someone back for it tomorrow." A subtle note in his tone warned her against any further attempts at deception. "Car's this way."

The commotion spilling from the bar had faded to an ominous silence. Dispirited, Deanna offered no resistance as the sergeant led her from the alley to one of several squad cars parked at the curb. He held the door for her while she climbed into the back.

Beneath the strong light of the twin moons, the car sped northwest along winding Caya Colina, the main road that led back to Palace

Hill. The sergeant made no effort to converse, for which Deanna was grateful.

Tomorrow she would go to her stepmother, humble as a penitent before the altar of the Blessed Maria, and beg if she had to. She could not let Zander rot in prison. The possibility he might not have survived the raid did not bear consideration.

Until that night Deanna had not thought much about the resistance. She took it as immutable fact that Lourdessa and her regime held all the advantage. Even if the eldest daughter of the beloved, deposed Lord Alcalde Eduard Hernaan dared to raise her voice against the repression, nothing would change.

Another auto rolled past the squad car, heading in the opposite direction. Through her half-opened window Deanna heard the telltale hiss of escaping steam from a faulty boiler valve. She breathed in the cool wind blowing against her face, and shivered with the ache of old and fresh sorrows.

The people know I'm not my father. Why would they ever follow me? Tonight proved how useless I am to them. Zander is wrong. Lourdessa and her allies hold this city too tightly in their grip. There's nothing I can do.

Oh, Father. I miss you so much....

AWAKENED AND SHIVERING in cold aftermath from amorphous nightmares, Deanna sat by her bedroom window, gazing out at the city.

Red Hill, Rio Gran, Quarry, and The Maze slumbered in near total darkness. Three years ago, in order to save an unwarranted expense to the city's coffers, Lourdessa had decreed that two-thirds of the public street lamps in Nue Bayona's working-class districts be extinguished at midnight. Only Palace Hill and Valencea, home to Nue Bayona's elite class, remained illuminated with expensive electric lights.

As fear faded with the aid of deep, slow breaths, Deanna sifted through what she knew about the Book and Quill, searching for clues. Tonight's raid defied explanation, unless...

Could it have had something to do with Alehan's threat, sworn in cold rage before his peers at Lilliana's birthday celebration? The question punched to the fore of her consciousness with the force of a clenched fist. Her stepbrother knew she frequented the Book and Quill. He also knew she occasionally met Zander there.

An all too plausible answer to the mystery took shape in Deanna's mind. A small bribe—either to a hungry student or one of the tavern's kitchen staff—could have purchased Alehan notification of Zander's location. And so much the better if Deanna was present to witness his arrest. A single call to the police, and Alehan's jealous vow would be brought to its full and violent fruition.

Sick with regret, Deanna returned to bed where she lay in rigid anguish. Zander had always been tough and full of bravado, even as a boy, but she doubted he could withstand what the Specials would do to him.

For what little remained of the night, she tossed and turned to the din of guilty thoughts that robbed her of any rest.

9
at bella pacifica hospital

The morning after the raid, Deanna—as she had sworn to do—brushed aside her stepmother's protesting secretary and entered the gilt-wood and wine-velvet inner sanctum of Lourdessa's office. She came to plead for leniency; for her temerity she received a tongue-lashing, meted out in naked contempt while the sweating, red-faced Chief of the Nue Bayona City Police looked on.

"How dare you interrupt me for this." Lourdessa's tone cut deep as a butcher's knife. "The boy is obviously a rebel. Otherwise he wouldn't have been arrested. I always knew he was no good." The Chief, joined to the Sedano family by marriage to Lourdessa's younger sister, opened his mouth to speak, but a sharp look from the Alcalde quelled him. She added, "I will not ask Chief Deltoro to release him."

"But he's innocent."

"Oh, I doubt that very much. This may come as a surprise, but I do care about you, Deanna. Your choice of...friends...is troubling. You are too kind and trusting. This boy is nothing but street scum looking to use a naïve elite girl for his own purposes. He's a perfect recruit for

Faustin's terrorist organization. You are much better off with him out of your life."

"Why my father married such a hateful woman as you, I'll never understand."

Lourdessa's eyes and voice grew chilly. "Take care, dulzor. Remember who you're speaking to."

"How could I possibly forget?"

"Get out…now." The three words carried an unassailable ring of authority.

Realizing the futility and risk of further confrontation, and determined to deny Lourdessa the sight of her tears, Deanna chose retreat. Only after she'd put several corridors and an expanse of sandstone-paved courtyard between her and her stepmother's office did she allow the brutal pressure of restrained anger to vent. In the privacy of the garage reserved for the autos of the mayoral family, Deanna let out an enraged scream and pounded the steel bonnet of an unresisting roadster with clenched fists.

Fury spilled from her like molten steel from a crucible, leaving her drained and uncertain. Rubbing her bruised hands together, she acknowledged that tantrums had no effect. She needed a walk among the bowers of her late mother's favorite garden to clear her head.

Along gravel paths winding through fragrant beds of jazmin, *rosa*, and *lavanda*, Deanna wandered. The perfumed quiet soothed her mind to a state of near stillness in which she could simply be. For a time she lingered on a marble bench, watching a flock of dun-breasted brown *gorrions* pecking in the grass, until a glance at her wristwatch warned her she'd stayed longer than intended. Ceilia would be done with her therapy session in less than an hour.

Twice weekly a palace driver chauffeured Ceilia to and from Bella Pacifica Hospital. There, she spent her mornings in therapy to knit up the raveled threads of her sanity, so cruelly ripped apart on that terrible night of their father's defeat. Witnessing his struggles as turncoat members of his own police force dragged him away, and then being forced to live with the woman who had destroyed their world—all that had heaped too much trauma on a young girl already burdened with exquisite emotional sensitivity.

Over time Deanna had noticed only slight improvement in her sister's condition; still she lived in hope and continued to pay for Ceilia's treatments from the none-too-generous allowance Lourdessa provided her.

Today Deanna had decided to make the twenty-minute drive to the hospital herself to fetch Ceilia. If she left right away she could arrive in time for them to share lunch. When she rose from the bench, the gorrions took flight to settle in cheeping rows on the limbs of a *jacaran* tree a few paces away. Though reluctant to leave the garden, Deanna didn't want to keep her sister waiting. She bid the little birds good day and returned to the garage.

Her personal auto, a two-seater Tormenta, had been a rusted derelict when she'd rescued it from the wreckers. Rebuilt and restored to brass-fitted and leather-upholstered perfection, it now stood parked inside her private workshop, a brisk five-minute walk from the garden. None of the autos in the mayoral garage could match her Tormenta for speed, but a minor repair she'd yet to finish had put it out of commission. The roadster she'd lately abused would have to serve as a mundane substitute.

She pulled a handkerchief from the side pocket of her menswear trousers to tie back her hair and filched a pair of goggles from the glove box of Lourdessa's private sedan to complete her preparations. After firing up the boiler, she slid behind the wheel to wait. Five minutes later she steered the car out through the double doors and onto the driveway that led to the main gates.

The sentries at the gatehouse waved stiffly as she rolled past and turned left onto Caya Palacio. The wide avenue coursed along the entire southeast-facing front wall of the palace complex before turning south to wend past the high-gated estates of Palace Hill. At the bottom the road narrowed to become Caya Colina.

The roadster was no Tormenta, but it handled well. The pleasures of driving beneath the clear skies of a warm spring day soothed her frayed nerves, and as the tidy brick townhouses and shops of Valencea flowed past, she began to feel almost serene.

A whitewashed signal shack stood on the weedy verge where the main rail line leading from Nue Bayona Central Station crossed Caya Colina. As Deanna approached the tracks, the signalman on duty stepped out, unfurled a small red flag, and began waving it overhead. Deanna recognized him as Sanchez, the same man who had stood guard at this crossing for more than two decades, earning a wage that — despite his long years of service — barely kept his family out of poverty. Sanchez lowered the iron barrier arm and waited while Deanna's car slowed to a stop. The vibration of the oncoming train rattled the roadster's floorboards.

Though his slate-gray uniform was clean, the mended rips at the signalman's threadbare elbows and knees spoke of long, hard use. He acknowledged her with a tug on the brim of his cap and a broad, gap-toothed smile. She returned the greeting with a wave, uncertain if he recognized her behind the wheel of the unfamiliar auto. "Señor Sanchez," she called out, but the steady blast of the train's whistle drowned out her voice.

The locomotive rolled through the crossing at a pace just shy of a sprinting man, belching a thick column of white steam from its stack that shredded to tatters in the wind of its passing. The squealing interface between wheel and rail birthed sparks like stars that flared and died in the bright sunlight. A string of cars clattered along in the engine's wake: a windowless boxcar for cargo and baggage; a plush, fully enclosed first-class coach for the elite, followed by a pair of comfortable but more modest coaches for middle-class travelers; bringing up the rear, three open carriages that were little more than boxcars fitted with wood benches. A third-class fare bought a spot inside the car, on a bench, if one arrived early enough. Latecomers stood in the aisles or traveled rough on the roof.

The first- and second-class coaches were only half filled. The three third-class cars overflowed with riders, baggage, and small livestock.

The contrast could not have been starker.

As the train passed, Deanna's fragile serenity evaporated, supplanted by sorrow, frustrated anger, and a measure of guilt. For though she had had no direct role in creating the system, still she bore some responsibility for its maintenance by not rejecting the privileges it bestowed upon her.

Three small boys waved to her from their perches on the rear platform of the last car. One cradled a toddler on his lap. Deanna waved back. When the train cleared the crossing, Sanchez raised the barrier to allow two vans, Deanna's auto, and a hay wagon pulled by a pair of draft vacas to resume their travel.

On impulse she dug in her pocket for the small leather purse she always carried and plucked out a twenty-reále note. Shifting into gear, she let the roadster roll forward until she reached Sanchez. Braking, she lifted her goggles to reveal herself and proffered the bill. "For your children's school books, Señor."

"Madre bless you, Miss Deanna. Thank you." Sanchez pressed the paper to his lips and slipped it into his waistcoat pocket. As Deanna drove away, in her rearview mirror she saw him dab at his eyes with a handkerchief.

Bella Pacifica Hospital occupied a sandstone mansion set amid bucolic parkland a half klim southwest of the airfield. The estate once belonged to a family of wealthy algodon farmers named Alvares. The last Alvares died without heirs over fifty years ago and had willed the estate to the city for use as a private sanatorium. Since then those members of the elite class in need of medical care came to the hospital for its up-to-date therapies.

Deanna steered the roadster through ornate iron gates onto a narrow drive hemmed by massive old sawtooth trees. She followed the slim ribbon of road through the grove and across a stone bridge beneath which flowed a placid stream, then up a gentle rise to where the main hospital grounds began. After leaving the roadster with the auto park attendant, Deanna headed on foot toward the main entrance.

The fine weather had drawn many patients outdoors to take the sun on the vast stretch of the hospital's manicured front lawn. The nurses' and orderlies' white uniforms seemed especially dazzling against the deep teal of the grass. Deanna blinked in the glare, wishing she'd brought along a pair of tinted glasses. Making her way up the gravel path leading to a broad stone porch, she nodded at the words of greeting called out by the staff. Though she might not know all of them by name, she recognized most of their faces.

A particular face caught her eye this day, stopping her in mid-stride. "Captain Varges," she whispered, shocked.

She stepped onto the springy grass to approach the veteran Air Service captain who'd once been her father's private airship pilot. He lay on a wheeled cot beside a gushing stone fountain, swaddled in bandages, a soft gray blanket draped over what remained of his lower body. In dawning horror, Deanna realized Varges no longer possessed his legs.

"Hola, Miss Deanna." The nurse in attendance rose from her stool, smiling. "Have you come to see the Captain today? He's napping now, but I can wake him."

Deanna shook her head, fighting back tears. "I had no idea he was here. What happened?"

"Oh, Miss, something terrible…terrible." The nurse pulled the blanket a little higher over the sleeping man's torso, her broad, kind face flushed with emotion. "The Captain's ship got blown up when those awful terrorists attacked the airfield. He's a hero, you know. I heard tell he went into the burning gondola to rescue two passengers… dragged them right out. That's how he got burned. His legs were so cooked the doctors had to amputate. He might lose his left hand as well. The docs don't know yet."

"He must be in dreadful pain." Deanna recalled a snippet of childhood memory. She stood on the bridge of an old-style airship, wild with excitement, gazing out the gondola's front windshield. Captain Varges gripped her shoulders with comforting strength as she held the wheel and her father looked on, smiling.

"He's heavily medicated. Might be a bit groggy, but I'm sure he'd love to talk." The nurse bent to place her lips against the Captain's ear.

Reluctant to have Varges drawn from his refuge of sleep, Deanna said. "Please don't…"

Her words went unheeded.

"Captain Varges, you have yourself a visitor." The nurse paused, scrutinizing her charge's face for any sign of response. A heartbeat later, she beckoned a second time. "Captain, do wake up. There's someone here to see you."

Varges' eyes fluttered open, rheumy and unfocused. He uttered a soft moan. "Is it time to go back in already?" he whispered.

The nurse adjusted her starched white cap as she straightened. "Not yet Captain, but look—Miss Deanna came over to say hola."

"Miss Deanna…" Varges rolled his head to face her. "What a lovely surprise."

Deanna had to strain to hear his threadbare voice above the merry splash of the fountain. "I can't stay long, Captain. I'm here for my sister, but when I saw you I had to come speak to you."

"Nurse Portiyo, will you…" Varges scratched at the pillows beneath his head.

With Deanna's help the nurse soon had the injured man propped up on a mound of cushions that supported his back and shoulders. "There, now you two can talk properly." She gave the blanket a final smoothing and pushed her stool toward Deanna, indicating with a nod that she should sit.

Deanna kept her gaze fixed on the captain's wan and weathered face, afraid that if she allowed herself to look any lower, she would weep.

"I'd barely gotten the ship settled. Most of the passengers had disembarked…that's when the explosions hit…boom, boom." He drew in a laborious breath and exhaled through his teeth before continuing.

"The landing cradle was on fire, the ropes and harness were about to catch, but I knew I had some time. A sky jelly's gas bladder is harder to ignite than one might think. There's the skin that has to burn through first, and that's pretty tough. Even so, I had to move fast."

Varges winced in pain, the strong sunlight draining his sunken cheeks of all color.

"If it's too much, I can go so you can rest, Captain."

"No, no. Please stay. It's been quite a long time since you and I have had a chance to talk. So much tragedy has happened…to a lot of good people."

Deanna picked up on the double meaning underlying the captain's words. As one of the few Air Service officers to remain loyal to her father, Varges had paid a heavy price for his steadfastness in the aftermath of the coup. A once proud master of his own ship, the thirty-year veteran had found himself denied assignment to one of the sleek, new steam-driven ships and reduced to an assistant pilot's chair, subordinated to captains with half his age and experience.

"You were saying?" Deanna prompted the injured man.

"Yes…yes. I had to move fast. I pushed through the cockpit door into the passenger compartment, yelling for everyone to get out. The jelly was reacting to the fire by this time. The lines and harness were burning and the poor beast's skin was smoking. I only had a matter of a minute or two before the gas ignited. And there was an elderly man still in his seat, unable to get his safety belt undone. Smoke was thick in the cabin, making it very hard to breathe, and the old man was choking and crying for help. I tried to calm him down while I undid his belt. The buckle gave way, but he was overcome by the smoke and fainted. I had to throw him over my shoulder and carry him out. Fortunately he weighed almost nothing.

"The jelly was really thrashing and groaning, knocking the gondola from side to side. I stumbled on the threshold and nearly pitched the old man headfirst to the ground, but praise Holy Yesu I managed to hang on to him. The entire landing cradle was one big inferno. There was no way down except through the flames. So I went. As soon as I stepped out, the whole thing gave way. The last thing I remember is falling…and the smell of burning flesh. When I woke up I found myself here."

Awed and heartbroken in equal measure, Deanna laid her hand on his shoulder. "Captain…I don't know what to say."

"You don't have to say anything, child. You being here is comfort enough. You're my one and only visitor."

Deanna remembered Varges had lost his wife several years ago, but he had two grown sons with children of their own. "Captain, your family hasn't come to see you?"

"No." The single word, uttered with no elaboration and in such quiet despair, tore through Deanna's resolve. She brushed away tears while Varges patted her arm with his good hand. "Don't cry, my dear. I'll be fine…"

"You were always kind to me, Captain. My father thought highly of you. I've never had a chance to say how sorry I am about what my stepmother did to you. If I could change things…"

"What's done is done, child. Worry about yourself and your sister, not me. I understand." Varges yawned and his head fell back against the pillows.

"The Captain is tired, Miss Deanna. Time to let him rest." Nurse Portiyo bustled forward to adjust Varges's cushions. "Thank you for coming over," she added in a low voice. "He's a proud man and will never let on how lonely he is, but I see it in his eyes." The small woman's lips twisted in a fierce frown. "If only his children would come visit. It would mean so much to him, but I suppose…well, let me stop before I say too much."

"Do you know why his sons don't come?"

Portiyo's round cheeks flushed crimson as she plucked at her starched white collar. "I…well…"

Deanna raised her hand in reassurance. "You don't need to say anything more. I think I can guess."

The nurse regarded Deanna with a mixture of relief and sympathy. "Yes, I believe you can." As Deanna stood to leave, she added, "Don't lose hope, Miss. I haven't."

Deanna smiled. "As long as my father is alive, I won't. Please tell Captain Varges I'll come see him again next week." From the corner of her eye she saw the nurse trace the sign of the Blessed Maria on the breast of her apron.

THE HOSPITAL FOYER, cloaked in cool shadows and suffused with calm efficiency, stood empty. Deanna bypassed the front desk as the bespectacled woman whose duty it was to check in visitors waved her on. With the ease of familiarity, Deanna navigated the hallways and staircases leading to the fourth floor of the east wing. Here, in the section dedicated to the study and healing of mental illness, Ceilia had spent the morning in private therapy.

The dayroom, where patients not sick enough to require restraint were allowed to interact, occupied a smaller chamber off the former grand ballroom. A row of tall windows in the east wall flooded the space with natural light. The ornate fixtures and faded frescoes adorning the ceiling whispered of an opulent past. Deanna had always suspected this room had served as a small recital space.

A handful of men and women occupied comfortable chairs scattered around the room, some dozing in the warm sunshine, while the rest engaged in board games or conversation. Deanna spotted Ceilia sitting alone at a small table, the highlights in her long, auburn hair kindled to flame in the sunlight. Dressed in a lace-collared white blouse and mauve algodon skirt more suited to a girl half of her nineteen years, she was bent over a sheet of paper with a slim pencil pinched between thumb and forefinger, drawing.

Not wishing to break her concentration, Deanna slipped into the chair opposite her sister. Ceilia acknowledged her arrival with a curt nod and kept working, leaving Deanna to watch in intrigued silence as an image took shape on the page. From her upside-down vantage, she could not at first understand what she was seeing, but after a minute of intense scrutiny, the tangle of lines resolved into a startling composition.

"Cece, dulzor, is this a picture of an airship on fire?"

"Yes. Someone blew it up."

Deanna always tried to shield Ceilia from news that might frighten her. Annoyed that somehow her sister had learned of the incident, she forced her voice to remain calm. "Who told you about what happened at the airfield? Was it one of the other patients?"

Ceilia paused with pencil poised above the detailed drawing. "No," she replied, then resumed her work.

"Then, how do you know?"

"A boy told me. He's my friend."

"A boy here at the hospital?" Deanna regarded her sister with a mixture of curiosity and faint unease.

"I already told you it wasn't another patient," Ceilia said.

"You've never mentioned this friend of yours." Deanna reached out to caress Ceilia's arm. A dusting of cinnamon freckles stood out on her pale, soft skin. "What's his name?"

"I can't say. It's a secret."

Ceilia lived a sheltered life, supervised by her older sister and a nanny. Though a grown woman, her mind still lived in childhood's innocence. She'd never once spoken of a desire for male companionship, even of a strictly platonic nature, which made her revelation all the more puzzling. Deanna wondered if this mysterious boy could be make-believe.

Ten years of loving care and close observation had taught Deanna patience and when not to push. Still, it worried her that Ceilia would keep a secret, even one spun of pure fantasy. "Is this your friend?" She pointed to a figure Ceilia had drawn with considerable skill, a young boy or man dressed in black who stood at a distance from the burning airship, his hand raised as if shielding his face from the heat.

Ceilia froze. For a moment Deanna looked into her eyes and saw only windows, behind which lay a dark void. Before she could react, her sister's childish sweetness had returned; but for some inexplicable reason Deanna felt like she'd gazed, however briefly, into the cold, dead eyes of a stranger.

Her breath caught in her throat.

"Why are you staring, Deanna? Is something wrong?" Ceilia cocked her head, sending an auburn lock coiling across her throat.

"Uh, no, but…"

Ceilia put the pencil down and folded the drawing into quarters. "It's time to go home now. Diosa mia, how this effing place bores me."

Deanna frowned, uncertain she'd heard her sister's last muttered sentence correctly. Ceilia never cursed; at least not to her knowledge. "What did you say?"

"It's time to go. I'm hungry. Aren't you?"

"Yes, but I have to talk to Doctor Lovos first." Deanna rose from her seat.

"He's only going to tell you what you want to hear, you know."

Taken aback and at a loss for a response, Deanna took a moment to untie her tongue. "Wait for me here, Cece. I won't be long."

Ceilia slipped the folded drawing into a pocket on the side of her skirt. "All right, but please hurry. I don't want to miss lunch. It's *tortas*, my favorite."

"I'll hurry, I promise." As she turned to leave she glanced back at Ceilia, who stared out the window, chin in hand, seemingly lost in daydreams. Deanna sighed, wondering if she'd fallen prey to her own morose and overactive imagination.

10
the last quiet day

"Doctor Lovos, it's been five years now. I haven't noticed any real improvement in my sister's condition. In fact, only today something very strange happened, like nothing I've ever seen before."

Doctor Salvedor Lovos, Chief of Mental Therapies at Bella Pacifica, leaned forward to rest his elbows on his leather desk blotter. The coarse gray hedges of his eyebrows dipped to meet at the bridge of his patrician nose. "Can you describe what you saw?"

Deanna pondered before answering. "I was talking to my sister. And suddenly, her eyes go blank for a second, and then it's as if someone who looks exactly like Ceilia but is not her, is sitting across from me. Even the quality of her voice changed. It was…odd."

The doctor stroked his chin, nodding. "I've witnessed the same phenomenon," he said, "but only twice before. I don't know what it means yet, but I'm certain it's part of your sister's illness. That's why it's so important not to withdraw her from therapy. I feel I'm very close to a breakthrough."

Deanna glanced around Lovos's office. The expensive carpets, hand-painted wallpaper, and plush silk damask curtains all served as pointed reminders of how much of her limited income she had given over to him. Never before had it rankled her quite so much. "Doctor Lovos, you know my situation. I have to pay for this out of the allowance my stepmother gives me. She's never been generous and, frankly, your fees are quite steep. I feel like…"

Aware of the ire in her voice, Deanna paused to take a deep breath and rethink what she was about to say next. An accusation of fraud would be both unjust and untrue. Doctor Lovos had never been anything but kind and professional; still, perhaps the time had come for them to both admit that Ceilia's condition could not be reversed.

Lovos looked hurt and sympathetic in equal measure. "If it's a matter of my fees, then I'm willing to work with you, Deanna."

"I'm sorry, Doctor." Quashing a stab of guilt, Deanna voiced her honest opinion. "I'm not sure my sister can be cured, and maybe she's better off. She doesn't seem unhappy, and as long as I'm around she'll be protected. I'd rather spend the money I'm paying you to keep her comfortable."

Lovos sat back in his chair, a tiny muscle in his jaw twitching; whether from anger or consternation Deanna couldn't tell. Finally he said, "I don't agree, but Ceilia is your sister and you have the final word. What choice do I have but to acquiesce? But before you go I want to show you something." He reached into a lower drawer and withdrew a stack of papers. He passed them to Deanna, who spread the sheets out on the desk before her.

"What am I looking at?"

"These are some of the drawings you sister has made during our sessions these past five years." Lovos indicated the pictures with a sweep of his hand. "They're arranged in order from early to most recent. I've only saved the most interesting ones."

Deanna had always known about Ceilia's artistic talent, but never before had she seen a comprehensive collection of her sister's drawings. "I never realized how good she is," she said as she perused each image in turn.

"What's important to note is how her style changed about three and a half years ago," Lovos commented, "and how it corresponds to the appearance of this figure." He pointed to the image of a boy, repeated in each successive drawing. The backgrounds varied—a garden, a city street, Ceilia's bedroom—but the figure was the same as the one she had witnessed her sister create in the dayroom not ten minutes past. A boy wearing dark clothes, his expression blank, standing to the side of the image and never at the center; an observer with unknown motives.

"Today, my sister drew a picture of a burning airship." Deanna riffled through the sheaf of papers a second time. "She said a boy told her about the attack, a friend. She wouldn't tell me his name." Deanna looked up to meet Lovos' grave stare. "Ceilia has no male friends that I know of. In fact she has no real friends at all. Why would she start drawing pictures of a boy who doesn't exist?" "I don't know. But given more time I'm confident I can find out."

Deanna scrutinized the collection of images awhile longer, then arrived at a decision. "Thank you for showing these to me, though I wish you'd shared them sooner. Perhaps I've been too hasty." She swept the drawings into a neat pile and passed them back to Lovos. "All right, Doctor. You've convinced me. I won't withdraw Ceilia from therapy."

Lovos nodded. "You've made the right decision. And I meant what I said about my fee. I'm willing to work with you on that."

"Thank you. Any little bit helps."

As she left the doctor's office, the mystery of Ceilia's condition gnawed at Deanna. Had she made the right decision? Was it so disturbing for her sister to have an imaginary friend? If it helped Ceilia to cope, then where was the harm? Deanna wasn't certain.

She would give Lovos another six months. If during that time he failed to make progress in lifting the mental block that had frozen Ceilia's mind in unnatural adolescence, Deanna would accept reality and withdraw her from therapy, no matter the doctor's admonishments.

Ceilia met her in the doorway of the dayroom. Deanna smiled and reached for her sister's hand. "Ready for lunch?"

Ceilia smiled in return and entwined her fingers with Deanna's. "Oh yes. I'm really, really hungry."

"Perhaps while we're eating you can tell me about your friend. The boy you like to draw." Deanna studied her sister's face, searching for any clue that would help her to understand, but Ceilia's expression revealed nothing.

"Did I tell you they're serving tortas today? Hurry, Deanna, before there's none left for us." Ceilia tugged at Deanna's hand.

Deanna sighed and allowed her sister to lead her away.

THE DRIVE BACK to the palace passed in companionable silence. Throughout lunch, Deanna could glean no useful information about her sister's mysterious friend. All Ceilia would admit was that he was real and that he "helped her with things." What kinds of things she would not say. In frustration, Deanna had given up trying to question her sister any further. After returning the borrowed roadster to the garage, Deanna offered to accompany Ceilia back to the suite of rooms they shared in the residential wing, before retreating to the refuge of her workshop, but the younger girl demurred.

"I'd like to come watch you work today," Ceilia said.

Surprised and yet pleased, Deanna replied, "Really? All right then. Let's go."

Deanna's shop occupied a corrugated tin-roofed shed in the northeast corner of the palace grounds. Years ago the structure had served as a stable for the mayoral family's personal riding eelats. When Deanna first stumbled upon it, as a child out roaming with her sister, it had held nothing but dust, cobwebs, and the faint odor of manure.

As a grown woman—engineer-trained and in need of a workspace—Deanna had remembered the shed with the hard-packed clay floor and gravel yard. A new concrete floor, some racks for tools, a workbench, and an overhead pulley for lifting heavy loads completed the renovation.

Deanna's prized Tormenta convertible stood in the center of the shop, the case hatch at the rear opened to reveal the boiler and pistons within. Ceilia pulled up a wooden stool while Deanna fetched her box of hand tools from the workbench.

She held up a small cylinder for Ceilia to inspect. "You see this?" It looked like a fat white ceramic caterpillar with a tapered metal tail. "It's a sparking cone. When I turn the key, this little cone will provide the spark to light the coal oil I poured in here." She removed a screw cap from a funnel-shaped opening at the base of the boiler. "The coal oil will flash-heat the water in the boiler and give me the necessary pressure within two minutes."

"I don't know why you like machines so much," Ceilia said. "They always seem so dirty. I like pretty, clean things." She twirled a lock of auburn hair around a forefinger, her pale rose lips pursed.

"Machines are amazing, dulzor. They make people's lives easier." Deanna eased the sparking cone into a socket atop the coal-oil tank and, as carefully as a master jeweler setting a diamond, she crimped it in place with a pair of needle-nosed pliers. Too much pressure and she could damage the invaluable part. She had paid fifty reàles to the man who had made it for her, a sum that would keep his family fed for a week.

For a time the two sisters did not speak; the younger watched the older minister to her mechanical charge as lovingly as any mother would to her child.

"Papa says terrible machines that made everything burn destroyed the old world."

Deanna paused to stare at her sister, but Ceilia's gaze remained focused inward. "Yes...that's true," she replied, "but the machines we have now help us. Those other machines are gone." In a bid to change the subject, Deanna added, "Today's the day Lourdessa lets me drive out past the city limits. Would you like to come?" She closed the engine case and wiped her oil-coated fingers on a rag.

"Oh, no. Not today," Ceilia said. "The dolls are having a tea party, you see, and I'm the hostess." She stood, smoothed a wrinkle from her skirt, and drifted toward the open shop doors. Deanna watched her retreating figure, pondering the odd episode at the hospital and the questions it raised.

Alone again, her thoughts gradually turned to Zander.

She wondered what the Special Police would do to him when they found the fuel cells hidden in his coat pocket. Those cells alone were enough to earn a street raton like Zander a beating and a detention cell. Under such duress, Deanna wouldn't blame Zander for telling the police the truth. Even if they forced him to talk, she had nothing to fear from them.

Lourdessa was another matter.

Her stepmother had no qualms about resorting to house arrest—or worse, forcing her to take holy orders—to quell her perceived rebelliousness. The Sisters of the Blessed Maria had long specialized in taming the disobedient and recalcitrant daughters of Nue Bayona's elite.

A polite cough from the doorway interrupted Deanna's reverie. A tall, muscular man strode into the shop wearing a beige canvas driving coat, brown gloves, and a leather cap.

"Hola, Miss. I'm here to drive you today."

Since the age of eighteen, Deanna had enjoyed the freedom to drive herself anywhere within the city. That privilege didn't extend to journeys outside Nue Bayona's limits. Deanna suspected Lourdessa feared that one day she'd pack up Ceilia and drive away, never to return.

Whenever she wanted to take her auto any further than Bella Pacifica Hospital, her stepmother forced her to accept a chaperone.

"Where's Valdis?" Deanna asked, and then added, "Sorry. That sounded rude."

"He's sick, Miss. I'm Gomaz." The man's blue eyes betrayed nothing of his thoughts. Deanna felt a twinge of unease. She shook it off, gesturing to the car.

"Help me push this outside," she said as she climbed in to release the brake. Gomaz walked to the rear where Deanna joined him. They set their hands to the boot and pushed the machine out into the warm afternoon sunshine.

"Let me get my cap and driving glasses," she said. As Deanna turned to reenter the shop, a gust of wind lifted the edge of Gomaz's coat away from his body, revealing the chromed glint of an ee-pistol on his belt. Deanna's heart skipped a beat.

Of course he carries a gun, she thought. *He works for my stepmother. He'll no doubt report back to her everything I say. Well, as usual, she'll be disappointed.*

Deanna slipped into her driving coat and stuffed her thick dark hair beneath a soft leather cap. She snatched a pair of brass and leather goggles from a peg on the wall and strode to where Gomaz waited by the car. Her eyebrows shot up at the sight of the man's frown.

"The boiler hasn't been fired up yet, Miss. We're going to have to wait around until the pressure builds. Why didn't you...?"

"Do you know much about engines?" Deanna interrupted, grinning.

"For one this size it takes a good ten minutes for the pressure to build up enough to drive the pistons."

"Watch this." She reached into the open carriage and turned the key.

Gomaz fixed his eyes on the pressure gauge embedded in the polished roble-wood dashboard. The slender brass needle swung upward almost immediately. Deanna counted the seconds under her breath as it climbed past a row of tiny red numbers into the black.

"Eighty-six seconds!" she whooped, throwing her arms into the air in triumph. For the first time since introducing himself, Gomaz smiled.

"How is it you have a car that can start this quickly?"

"I designed a new boiler system. Get in. I'll explain it as we go."

"You are a very clever young lady." Gomaz looked at her and smiled.

"Thanks. The main problem is getting enough coal oil," Deanna replied. The volatile liquid distilled from coal served as the main fuel source for Nue Bayona's poorer citizens. The city's only distillery kept up with demand, but little surplus remained for things like newfangled flash boilers for autos.

For the next half hour Deanna gazed at the countryside rolling by. The gravel-paved road arrowed through fields of spring wheat ruffled into waves by the wind, past orchards of manzaniya trees sporting crowns of white flowers, and alongside pastures carpeted in plush teal grass. The open carriage allowed her to feel the wind on her face and to drink in the myriad aromas. Off in the distance a pod of wild sky jellies floated like clouds in the violet sky, their reflections chasing them across the shirred waters of Playa Reservoir, the city's main water source. The animals were too far away to worry about, so she did not alert Gomaz, but seeing them jogged and clarified her childhood memory of that day aboard Captain Vargas' ship.

The Lord Alcalde's entire family had boarded their private airship in high spirits, bound for the lakeside resort of Anjelas. Her father had not yet replaced the old-style craft with a steam-powered machine, so the encounter was Deanna's first chance to see a sky jelly up close. Staring in wonder at the huge beast wrapped in its padded harness of ropes, she imagined it returning her gaze with its flat black eyes. She tried to guess at its thoughts, or if in fact it harbored any thoughts at all. Every time the beast farted jets of malodorous gases from its rear vents, she and Ceilia dissolved in gales of laughter. That had been the last time she, her sister, and both her parents had been together and happy. Soon after returning home, Deanna's mother had fallen ill.

"Are you all right, Miss?" Gomaz said. Deanna turned to face him, wondering if the concern in his voice was real or feigned. His driving goggles hid his eyes, denying her even that uncertain source for clues. He was Lourdessa's spy after all, and so the safe bet rested on insincerity.

"Why do you ask?" The engine made no sound as the steam from the boiler drove the pistons. With the rush of the wind filling her ears, she had to strain to hear Gomaz' answer.

"You seemed very sad just now."

Deanna looked away. "I was thinking about when I was little and my mother was still alive." She instantly regretted allowing that confession to slip. She did not want such a personal memory shared with her stepmother.

Gomaz drove on in silence, his gaze fixed on the road. Deanna checked her wristwatch and cast a surreptitious glance at the Special Poli's profile. The uneasiness that had plagued her since leaving home smoldered, approaching a flashpoint. Two minutes past the spot where he should have turned the car around for the return trip to the city, Gomaz continued on with no sign of stopping.

After several more minutes had passed, Deanna finally said, "It's time for you to take me back."

"I can't."

For one confusing instant she refused to trust her ears. "What did you say?"

Gomaz reached toward her, stopping short of physical contact. "Don't be afraid, Deanna. I promise no harm will come to you. We're almost there."

His assurances only heightened her suspicion. She shrank against the door, closing her fingers over the handle. "Tell me right now what's going on."

"Please, stay calm. I'll explain everything once we get to where we're going."

A stand of trees appeared in the near distance, resolving on closer approach into a windbreak. Gomaz turned onto a packed-dirt driveway that led to the front yard of an old farmhouse. Roof shingles, like flaking scales—along with a sagging porch and empty window frames—spoke of its long-ago abandonment. Gomaz brought the car to a stop and applied the brake.

For a few moments Deanna remained frozen, too nerve-struck by the total isolation of the place to move. There was nowhere to run. No other farmhouses stood nearby; beyond the screen of sawtooth trees she saw only empty fields beneath open skies.

She pushed her goggles up onto her forehead, still gripping the door handle, and turned to face the poli. "Why'd we stop here?"

Gomaz removed his own goggles, revealing eyes like blue ice set deep in his rugged face. "Your stepmother has ordered your death."

11
a sudden turn

"I knew you were Special Police the minute I saw you." Deanna felt as if she stood on a precipice with a rapidly crumbling edge. At any moment it might give way and pitch her headlong into a lightless abyss. "I hope Lourdessa's paying you well for this," she said, then drove her elbow into his jaw. Flinging the car door open, she tumbled out and bolted for the road.

Like a pouncing felion, Gomaz seized her from behind before she'd gone half a dozen steps. He lifted her, struggling, into granite-hard arms. His breath hot against her cheek, he growled, "Deanna, listen to me please."

She sunk her teeth into the back of his gloved hand. He hissed in pain and, for a split second, his grip loosened. With wild strength born of terror and a desperate imperative to survive, Deanna tore free. Overbalanced, she stumbled forward and nearly fell to her knees, but her natural agility saved her.

Her perception of time grew distorted, granting her a preternatural visualization of each moment as it happened. Hands outstretched and grasping, Gomaz lunged toward her. She twisted under his reach and dove for the ee-pistol on his hip. Caught by surprise, the poli reacted too late to prevent his own disarming.

With no thought for the consequences, Deanna turned the weapon on him and pressed the trigger node. He slammed into her, driving her down onto the hard-packed dirt. The weight of his body crushed the air from her lungs. She writhed beneath him like a trapped serpent, trying to raise the gun so she could fire, but he had both her arms securely pinned.

"Drop it," the poli commanded, his viselike fingers tightening on Deanna's wrist until the pain forced her to release the pistol. "Now you're going to listen to me."

"Why should I?" she wheezed.

Frowning, Gomaz pushed up into a crouch, relieving the pressure on her chest while maintaining his hold on her arms. "I'm not who you think I am." His voice sounded kind, soothing even, which only amplified Deanna's fear.

Incredulous, she spat, "You're my stepmother's assassin. You said so yourself."

"I said no such thing. I'm not here to take your life, Deanna. I'm here to save it."

The absurdity of that assertion forced a cynical laugh from her throat. "I don't believe you. Why are you torturing me? Just do it."

In one smooth motion, Gomaz rose to his feet and pulled her up with him. He thrust the ee-pistol into her hand and backed away several steps. "I'm at your mercy now," he said. "You can shoot me, or you can listen to what I have to say."

Deanna pointed the gun at his chest, stunned to speechless confusion by this sudden turn. Overhead, the mournful cry of a dolora bird drifted on the light breeze. The smell of dust, machine oil, and wildflowers filled her nostrils. The ee-pistol grew heavy in her grip, as if gravity and the weight of her own uncertainty conspired to spoil her aim. Gomaz held himself in poised, watchful stillness, his hands hung relaxed by his sides. His face wore the serene look of a man at peace with his fate.

To press the trigger now would be an act of murder. Deanna lowered the gun. "I'm listening."

"I'm a Special, that's true, but I'm also a member of a clandestine group working to restore the rule of law in Nue Bayona. Our goal is to overthrow Lourdessa Hernaan and return your father to office. Saviero Nunyez is our leader."

Gomaz took a step toward her. "Stay where you are," Deanna ordered, raising the pistol to once more take aim at his chest. "You expect me to believe Saviero Nunyez is a resistance leader? He turned on my father and sided with Lourdessa. He's her Minister of Intelligence, for Yesu's sake."

"I know how it sounds, but it's true," Gomaz said. "Nunyez, Raul Olivas, and a handful of others…"

"Raul Olivas is part of this too?" Deanna felt light-headed from so much revelation.

"And the Archbishop of Nue Bayona, as well as a few other elites in your stepmother's administration. They formed the core group several months after the coup."

"Then who the hell is Faustin?"

"A useful diversion. Nunyez allows him free rein in order to provide cover for us."

"But…that's monstrous!" Deanna exclaimed. "Faustin and his gang have hurt innocent people. Men and women have gone to detention on just the suspicion they might be part of the resistance. My best friend…"

The memory of her last moments with Zander at the Book and Quill tore her heart. "How can you let that go on?"

Gomaz remained unflinching before her furious gaze. "We keep our eyes on the greater good, Deanna. Toppling your stepmother's illegitimate regime and restoration of the rightful, elected Alcalde."

"No matter the cost?"

A tiny muscle in the poli's jaw quivered. Deanna sensed she'd touched a sore point. "When there is a grand cause to be won," he said, "sometimes, there are unavoidable casualties. None of us are happy about that, but it's a painful reality." He paused and added, "We've all accepted our culpability, none more than Nunyez."

His candor surprised her. "If Nunyez and his group had truly believed in the rule of law," she asked, "then why did they support my stepmother?"

"Good people make mistakes, Deanna. They all realized they'd been misled with false evidence fabricated by Lourdessa against your father." Gomaz pointed to the ee-pistol. "Do you mind lowering that? I really don't relish getting shot by my own weapon. I have a family to get home to tonight."

If he felt any anxiety over the delicacy of his situation, he gave no outward sign. He remained the picture of calm, nonthreatening professionalism. Deanna felt something in her shift. Her mistrust began to cede incrementally toward hope. She let the gun drop. When Gomaz stepped forward this time, the reflexive urge to flee did not overwhelm her. She stood firm and met his eyes without fear.

The poli made no move to repossess his gun. "When your stepmother ordered your death, Nunyez devised a plan to get you to safety," he said. "I was sent to drive you out of the city, but instead of killing you I was to bring you here." He waved a hand at the abandoned farmhouse.

"For what?" Deanna asked.

Gomaz started walking toward the ramshackle structure. After a split second of hesitation Deanna followed, still holding the ee-pistol in a firm grip. Gomaz paused at the foot of the porch. "Another resistance agent is on his way," he said. "He's to take you from here to a safe house, where you'll remain until we can make arrangements to get you to Nue Castila."

The only other sizable city on the continent, Nue Castila lay almost five hundred klims to the east, a five-hour journey by steam-powered airship.

"Come inside," Gomaz said.

Deanna eyed the three decayed risers, fearful they would collapse under her weight, but Gomaz navigated them without mishap. He must have interpreted her hesitation as continued suspicion, for when he reached the open doorway he said with gentle patience, "You still have my blaster, Deanna. Stay out of my reach, if that makes you feel more comfortable."

He disappeared inside. Deanna climbed the steps and entered the front parlor, wrinkling her nose at the musty smell of mold and raton urine. Paper faded to murky brown by age still clung to some sections of the wall, and dangled in ragged strips from others. Spinners' webs, black with dust, festooned the rafters. Shattered glass lay in blade-like shards beneath the window frames. Two doorways opened off the main room, neither one fitted with panels. Both rooms beyond were empty.

Gomaz stood in the middle of the parlor, sweeping a patch of the worn plank floor clean of dust and glass with an old broom. He looked up as the aged wood squeaked beneath Deanna's steps. "I left some supplies out here a couple of days ago." He laid down the broom and walked to a corner, pried up a loose floorboard, and lifted out a canteen, a folded blanket, and a small cloth bag. "I hope you like *pacana* nuts," he said.

Looking around the room, Deanna tried to see past the decay and imagine what life must have been like for those who'd once called this place home. "How long am I going to be here?" she asked.

"Not more than three hours at most." Gomaz shook out the blanket and settled it on the boards. "This'll make your wait more comfortable."

Deanna glanced at the ee-pistol still in her hand, gleaming softly in the dim light. Contrition igniting her cheeks, she offered the weapon back to him. "I'm sorry I tried to shoot you," she murmured.

Gomaz accepted the gun and re-holstered it. "No need to apologize." With a smile that reminded Deanna of her father's, he added, "I was never in any danger. The safety latch was engaged the entire time."

Contrition morphed to mortification. "I've never fired an ee-pistol before, but still I should have known it'd have a safety," she said. "Thank the Madre I didn't think of that." She pulled her driving cap from her damp hair. "So, what happens now?"

"You'll wait for my colleague. His name's Diego. When he arrives, he'll say he's here to sell you an eelat. That's how you'll know it's him. We're far enough outside the city limits that I doubt there'll be any traffic, and this house has been abandoned for years; but even so we can't be too cautious."

"I'd feel safer if I had a gun." Deanna looked at the ee-pistol.

"How well can you shoot?"

The question sparked memories of the times spent with her father at the palace firing range. "Well enough," she said. "My father taught me."

"I can't give this to you," Gomaz said, tapping the ee-pistol's grip. "It's police issue, but I do have an old slug revolver you can have. It's my personal gun." He reached into his coat, drew forth the weapon, and held it out to her, butt first. The pistol, a .45 Poltro with its sleek black barrel and gold chasing, had the look of a cherished family heirloom. The initials "RG," inlaid in gold, graced the polished ebon wood grip. Seeing it caused Deanna's heart to skip a beat.

Gomaz had been armed the entire time. He could have drawn and shot her at will. The fact that he hadn't done so snuffed out the last vestiges of her mistrust.

Deanna's hand hovered over the weapon. "This looks valuable. If there's any chance for me to return it to you, I will. I promise."

"I know," Gomaz replied.

Deanna took the gun and checked to see that it was fully loaded. She weighed it in her hand and sighted down the barrel. "Nice balance," she said, tucking it into the waistband of her trousers. "Thank you."

Gomaz had gone to stand by the window. After a moment's hesitation, Deanna joined him. One particular question nagged her. "Nunyez, Olivas, the Archbishop…the true resistance has a lot of powerful members. Why hasn't it made a serious move yet against my stepmother?"

"We may have resources, but the Sedanos have more. Gregorio Sedano runs an extensive network of mercenaries and agents—the

Black Corps—whose sole duty is to protect his family's interests. His spies are everywhere. Your stepmother is rumored to have a list containing the names of all immediate family members of her closest advisors. If anything happens to her, Sedano assassins will slaughter everyone on it. It's been an effective deterrent...until now."

"What's changed?" Deanna asked.

Gomaz reached into his inside pocket and withdrew a cigarette and a box of matches. He lit the cigarette, took a drag, and exhaled a stream of pungent smoke. The sun had dipped below the trees, casting long violet shadows into the yard fronting the house. "It's late," he said. "I have to get back to the city."

A little irked that he'd ignored her question, Deanna trailed Gomaz from the house to the car. "I'm not surprised Lourdessa has a kill list," she said. "What I don't understand is why she wants me dead. I'm no threat to her."

Gomaz paused, his hand on the driver's side door handle. "She believes otherwise."

Deanna smiled with bitter amusement. "Lourdessa's delusional. I couldn't lead an eelat to water, let alone a people's uprising."

"Why do you say that?" Gomaz said.

Struck by his quiet intensity, Deanna searched his face. The sincerity in his eyes broke through her instinctive defenses. Disarmed, she spilled her heart's most secret shame. "Is it such a mystery? What Lourdessa did to my father made me a coward. Leadership requires courage and conviction. I don't have either."

"You were a child when the coup happened." Gomaz laid a hand on her shoulder. This time, his touch elicited no fear. "A child isn't expected to be brave."

Deanna looked at her boots, coated with the red dust of the yard. "I'm not a child anymore. I can't use that excuse."

Gomaz shook his head. "Why you think you're not brave is the real mystery. The girl who caught me off guard and got my gun away...she was no coward. I have the bruise to prove it." He ran a cautious finger over his jawline.

Unable to provide other than her own heartfelt conviction, Deanna remained silent. Gomaz leaned against the car, smoking, his face grown pensive. His eyes seemed to look inward at something that worried him. After a few moments he straightened and looked at her, all trace of worry gone.

"What if I told you the resistance has need of you?" he said.

Deanna stared at him for a moment in wary silence. "I'd say I can't do much in my present circumstances," she replied.

"You're wrong. There's a very important job for you, if you're willing to join us."

"Even if I were, how can I do anything from Nue Castila? I don't know anyone. I have no money. How am I supposed to live?" To land in an unknown city, bereft of resources, wearing only the clothes on her back, held little appeal.

"You won't be abandoned, Deanna." Gomaz seemed surprised at her concern. "Your father has allies there. They'll shelter you until our plans have come to fruition."

"What plans? What job? You're not telling me anything."

"You haven't answered my question yet."

Exasperated at Gomaz's evasiveness, Deanna turned her back on him to gaze at the panorama of empty countryside beyond the windbreak.

"Forgive me, Deanna," Gomaz said softly. "For your own protection, I can't divulge certain information unless you agree to join us."

His apologetic explanation drew her back out of herself. She sighed and faced him once more. "I can see you want me to say yes, but I can't, at least not yet. Too much has happened. I need time to think. I'm sorry."

He gave her a long, measuring look. "Don't be. I asked a difficult question and you gave me an honest answer." He climbed behind the wheel and turned the key.

With the poli's imminent departure came a disturbing thought. "How will you convince Lourdessa I'm dead?" she asked.

Gomaz chewed the ends of his mustache, frowning. "I'm to bring back your heart."

Until that moment Lourdessa's murderous plan had seemed like one of political expediency, but Gomaz's reply made it horribly personal. Deanna felt queasy with disgust. "I had no idea she hated me so much."

"A puerco's heart would be a good substitute. It's the right size." He buckled the chinstrap of his cap. "I know a butcher in Red Hill. I helped him with a problem once, so he'll be only too happy to reciprocate." Gomaz caught Deanna's gaze. They stared at one another for a few moments. Finally the poli spoke. "Never doubt your own courage, Deanna. The resistance needs you."

Unswerving dedication infused Gomaz's lived-in face with quiet zeal. Deanna sensed a complex soul hidden behind his enforcer's façade, which made her want to know more about him. "What's your first name, Gomaz?"

"Roberto."

"Roberto, will you do me an important favor?"

"Of course."

"Please check on my sister Ceilia if you can. She'll have no one but her nanny to look after her now. She's a child in a woman's body. She won't understand why I'm not there for her."

"If I can, I will."

"There's someone else I need you to take a message to. His name's Zander Montoiya. He lives in Red Hill. He rents a room when he has money. Other times he stays with friends." The memory of Lourdessa's callous dismissal of Zander's plight stung Deanna to fresh anger. "He may still be in detention…I don't know."

"I'll find him. Don't worry," Gomaz said. "What would you like me to tell him?"

You only know the real value of a thing once it is no longer yours. Never before had the truth of that old saying cut so close. Heart-sore, Deanna replied, "Tell him I finally understand now."

"I will." Gomaz pulled his driving goggles over his eyes and released the brake. "Remember. Stay hidden until Diego arrives."

"Will I see you again?"

"That depends on circumstances. I sincerely hope so." Deanna needed no further elaboration. Hers was not the only life at risk.

"Goodbye and good luck, Deanna," Gomaz said.

"Good luck to you too, Roberto." She stepped away from the car, and watched Gomaz drive out to the road, turn left, and disappear.

Now I'm completely alone, she thought.

The day's events prior to this fateful drive seemed so distant now, like half-remembered scenes from a dream. Her life as she'd known it had been irrevocably derailed. What path it would take next had yet to be determined.

Drawing forth the chain that held both her locket and Zander's ring from its hiding place beneath her blouse, she pressed the metal to her lips and cried.

DEANNA ROUSED FROM a fitful doze, opening her eyes to darkness. She sat up and groped for the slug pistol. Angry with herself for falling asleep, her pique soon turned to apprehension. It was past sundown, and Diego had yet to arrive.

Her left arm had gone numb from the weight of her body. Shaking the tingling out of her fingers, she rose from the blanket and went to the window, careful to stay out of the square of moonlight pooled on the floor.

A soft breeze wafted the pungent scent of sawtooth sap through the empty frame. Outside, the yard lay half-cloaked, still in the black shadow of the house. What if Gomaz's compatriot had already come and called for her, received no answer, and then departed?

That makes no sense. Surely I'd hear him. And even if I didn't, he'd come looking for me.

Dismissing the unlikely scenario allowed an even more frightening possibility to take root. Darkness and isolation provided fertile mental soil, especially when watered by anxiety.

He should have been here hours ago. What if this Diego isn't coming at all? Could this be an elaborate hoax?

Deanna returned to the blanket and sat with the pistol across her lap, her mind spinning a pair of grim explanations.

Diego was not coming because he'd been captured…or worse.

Gomaz's entire story was a lie, and there was no Diego.

Either option meant perhaps Lourdessa already knew about her current hiding place, and would send another of her operatives to finish the job.

Madre, is this a trap? What am I going to do?

If sunrise found her still breathing, she determined she would not wait to test her luck any further. She had a gun, some water, and a little food. The resort town of Anjelas, sprawling on the shore of the lake from which it took its name, lay about one hundred thirty klims to the southeast, a three-day journey on foot. Many of Nue Bayona's elite families maintained holiday houses there, including the Hernaans, though she'd not visited her parents' relatively modest cabin for years. If she could reach it she'd have a temporary refuge from which to plan her ultimate escape. Avoiding the main road to travel cross-country would add at least a day or maybe two to the trip, but she had no choice. Once Lourdessa's agents realized she'd slipped their net, they'd have all the roads covered.

Deanna spent the remainder of the night in a tense vigil. At the first blush of sunrise she rose on sore, stiffened legs and secured the blanket into a bundle with her belt. Canteen slung over her shoulder and pistol in her waistband, she peeked around the doorframe, scanning the yard for any sign of movement.

Confident no assassin lay in wait, she slipped out the door and made her way up the drive to the road. A light ground mist curled silver tendrils around her ankles. The air smelled damp and earthy. With a quick glance from side to side, Deanna darted across the road into the weeds and started walking.

12
a dangerous problem, solved

A sea of screaming, chanting fans packed the wooden bleachers of the municipal bullfighting arena. Sweating beneath the glare of Nueva Sol, those citizens too poor to afford seats in the shaded stands stood in the dirt clearing at the base of the bleachers, voicing their excitement with as much enthusiasm as their betters. Two meters below Lourdessa's private guarded box and on the far side of the sandy arena, the reed-slender young matador and the vaca bull—its hide burnished to an obsidian gloss by the light of the sun—danced their ancient pas de deux, hurtling to an inevitable bloody climax.

Lourdessa occupied the middle of a row of three plush green upholstered chairs at the front of the box, sipping from a glass of white wine. A pair of binoculars languished unused in her lap. Alehan perched on the edge of the chair next to her, his gaze riveted on the spectacle below. Saviero Nunyez stood near the rear of the box, sipping brandy from a cut-crystal tumbler. A white-coated attendant hovered, decanter in hand, ready to pour refills.

"I don't see why a meeting with the Castilians is necessary, Mother," Alehan said. Just mobilize our defense forces, send them to teach those perros their place, and be done." Without taking his eyes off the action, he snatched the binoculars from Lourdessa's lap and raised them to his face.

"Yesu, Alehan…It's not that simple. You really have no idea how certain things work, do you?" Lourdessa retorted. "I can't just mobilize the defense forces. That would take…"

Before she could finish, Alehan sprang to his feet, shouting, "Bravo! Did you see that? What a pass." He cupped a hand to his mouth and howled.

"Alehan, please." Lourdessa snapped. "Must you…"

"Mendosa's a true artist," Alehan continued, oblivious. "It won't be long now before he makes the kill."

Irritated by her son's lack of subtlety and mercurial attention span, Lourdessa drained her wine glass and reached up to slap the back of Alehan's head.

"Damn it, Mother, what was that for?" he exclaimed, turning to glare at her. The binoculars dangled, forgotten, from his hand.

"Now that I have your undivided attention…" Lourdessa paused to settle her temper and said, "Even if we could mount a quick military strike, it's always the wisest course to try diplomacy first."

"I must side with your mother on this," Nunyez said. He finished his drink and held his glass out to the attendant, who nodded and poured a second dram. "We should avoid hostilities if at all possible." Fresh drink in hand, Nunyez ensconced himself in the chair behind Alehan.

Before Alehan or his mother could respond, the crowd bellowed as one, a deep primal roar that made conversation impossible.

"The original mining and gas extraction contracts between our two cities were negotiated over two hundred years ago," Nunyez continued when the noise died, "back when Nue Castila was little more than a collection of miners' shacks and squatters' hovels. Hardly a recipe for fair dealing."

Alehan flung a withering glance at the older man. "The first Alehan Sedano—my ancestor and namesake—discovered those coal and gas deposits. He built the first pipeline and dug the first seam. His own

brother and grandson died so Nue Bayona could have what it needed to grow. Now, that upstart commoner Stefan thinks he's entitled to a cut of what's rightfully ours."

"Ectorio Stefan was duly elected. He's a populist doing the people's bidding."

Alehan threw up his hands in exaggerated bewilderment. "Will someone explain to me how the eff that happened? I thought we owned Nue Castila."

Nunyez regarded him with hooded eyes. "The Castilians were desperate for a change. Because Stefan came from the mines himself, he was able to overcome the Sedano political machine. His nullification of all the existing coal and natural gas contracts makes sense when viewed in that light. I know you don't like to think about this, but the Castilian miners have also given lives to your family business over the years. They only want fair compensation for their labor."

"There's fair and there's foolishness." Lourdessa reclaimed her binoculars from Alehan and lifted them to her eyes, training them on the drama in the arena below. "I am no fool, Señor," she added.

His handsome lips curling in a snarl, Alehan said, "Whose side are you on, old man? You talk like those perros in the resistance."

Nunyez remained motionless except for his hands, which twitched in his lap like large white spiders. "And you bark like an overexcited puppy," he rasped.

Alehan spat an obscenity as he leaned over the back of his chair to menace the older man with a cocked fist.

"Alehan." Lourdessa's voice cracked, whip sharp. She lowered her glasses to glare at her son. "Stop this at once."

Curbed by his mother's command, Alehan froze. He doused Nunyez with a final look as bitter as spilled venom and then turned his attention back to the action.

As the fight neared its finish, a hush settled over the crowd. It held its collective breath in simmering anticipation of the kill. The bull, weakened from blood loss and exhaustion, stood a few paces from its executioner, pawing the sand. The matador stepped forward and the beast swept the air with horns like twin scythes, trumpeting its helpless wrath through foam-flecked nostrils. The matador's long slim blade flashed in the sunlight.

"Do it...do it...kill him," Alehan murmured. For one disturbing instant, Lourdessa couldn't decide if his words were meant for the man or the animal.

With a final flourish of his cape and a shout of exultation, the man closed in on the bull. It charged forward nobly and without fear, as if welcoming death. As the matador buried his sword in the heavy muscles at the base of the bull's skull, the beast crashed to its knees in a spray of blood and fell onto its side, quivering.

Alehan's guttural cry of delight mingled with the howls of the fans crowding the arena. From an enclosure at ground level opposite the mayoral box, a brass band struck up a lively tune.

To make himself heard over the tumult Nunyez was obliged to shout. "I only wish to remind you both of what you are dealing with. If you fail to understand the mindset of your adversary, you will inevitably make mistakes. Perhaps disastrous ones. Dama, the people of Nue Castila threw off the Sedano yolk when they elected Stefan. Your brother Gregorio no longer controls the political levers. The Castilian envoy is coming here to negotiate new contracts with you. He has no intention of leaving with any deal that is not in the Castilians' favor. He also is no fool, this Jon Santo."

Like a man attempting to flag down a hansom, Alehan leaned with precarious abandon over the railing of the box, shouting, "Mendosa! Over here...give it to me."

Lourdessa checked the urge to seize her son's waistband and haul him back. "Be careful, Allie," she called out.

The young matador appeared below the railing. The dozens of tiny mirrors sewn onto his costume sparkled in the sunlight. In his hands he cradled the severed ear of his slain adversary. Lourdessa watched him strain to place it in Alehan's outstretched hand, his azure eyes riveted on her son's face. When their fingers touched, Alehan whispered something and the matador's high cheekbones flushed. He bowed and backed away. A moment later Alehan tumbled backward, to safety. Thrusting his fist high, he crowed with triumph.

"Do you have to yell so? It's not as if that's your first trophy," Lourdessa snapped.

Alehan brandished the ear with childish glee, heedless of the blood leaking down his wrist. "No, but it is Mendosa's first kill. And he has sworn to dedicate this and all future kills to me." With an exaggerated sigh, he flopped down onto his chair, his erstwhile exhilaration softened into wistfulness.

Lourdessa pondered the scene between her son and the handsome matador. The unexpected intimacy of their interaction raised an emotion in her she couldn't quite make sense of, but before she had a chance to question him a sharp rap on the box door forestalled her. She turned to see the attendant admitting her personal bodyguard, Higerra. Touching the brim of his cap, he leaned close and whispered, "Dama, there's a Special here to see you. He says it's urgent."

"Thank you." She glanced at Nunyez, whose only reaction was a raised eyebrow. Ignoring Alehan's curious look, she stood. In a quiet voice she said, "Wait here."

A tall, well-built man clad in a dusty car coat stood in the foyer. He clutched a leather driving cap in his hands, his knuckles looking like drawer knobs. A canvas satchel hung from one shoulder. With a flick of her fingers she signaled for him to approach.

"Dama Alcalde," he said.

"Show me," Lourdessa demanded.

The man's mouth compressed, forming a hard line. He reached into the satchel and withdrew a small parcel wrapped in brown butcher's paper. "It was quick," he said in a clipped voice. He held the bundle in his hand, making no move to give it up.

"Show me," Lourdessa repeated through tight lips.

He proffered the package and folded his arms behind him after she took it, his eyes never leaving Lourdessa's face. He radiated a faint air of distaste.

Impudent perro, she thought as she pulled on the strings binding the package, releasing the paper to reveal its contents. Inside rested a rust-brown lump. Blood clots still clung to what had once been living tissue. Lourdessa prodded the cold mass with a forefinger.

Now that she held the evidence of her stepdaughter's death in her hands, the Alcalde wondered why all emotion deserted her. Where triumph should blaze in fervent glory, numbness settled instead, cold and bleak like winter fog. Perhaps her lack of feeling came from the fact that she had felt nothing for the living girl. Why should things change for the dead one?

Lourdessa glanced at the assassin. "What's your name?"

"Gomaz, Dama."

"Well done, Gomaz. Give me the bag." She folded the paper back over the heart and concealed it within the canvas. "Nunyez will see to it you get paid. You may go now."

The Special's jaw worked, but he remained silent. With a stiff bow he turned and strode to the staircase, disappearing downward amid the heavy thump of boot heels on wooden risers.

Lourdessa reentered the box, dropping the satchel into Nunyez's waiting arms before reclaiming her seat. Alehan sat on the edge of his chair, tapping his foot to the strains of a popular song rendered in sprightly two-four time by the house band. "What was that all about?" he inquired.

"Nothing you need concern yourself with, dulzor."

Alehan's pale brow knit above his fine nose. Seeking to deflect his attention onto less perilous subjects, Lourdessa patted his forearm and pointed to the wine-dark stain marring his otherwise spotless cuff. "You've ruined your shirt. Blood is impossible to remove once it's dried."

Alehan shrugged. "I've got plenty of shirts. What does it matter if I ruin this one?" He twirled the severed bull's ear between his fingers.

The brass ensemble belted and wheezed through another tune, then fell silent. The roar of the crowd waned to the low murmur of a lazy river. The day's sport had come to an end; the citizenry now flowed through the arena exits in cheerful disarray, clutching half-eaten bags of salty roasted pacana nuts, spun candy floss remnants, and empty beer cups.

Higerra announced that the Alcalde's car stood ready for her departure whenever she wished to leave.

"Come back to the palace with us, Minister. We need to discuss a few things," Lourdessa said.

Nunyez already stood by the half-opened door, the satchel wedged beneath his arm. "Of course, Dama, but there is the matter of my bicycle. I do not wish to leave it here."

"Send one of your men back for it later. Why you insist on pedaling around the city on that old machine when you have access to a car and driver whenever you want is beyond me."

"I enjoy the exercise."

Bracketed by Alehan and Nunyez, Lourdessa swept from the box into the foyer where knots of well-dressed people—fellow elite patrons leaving their own private boxes—milled about or drifted toward the stairs. She ignored the soft words of greeting offered by a few of the more intrepid people among the gathering. Higerra fell into step to lead the way and the crowd fell back to allow the mayoral party to pass.

Lourdessa's sleek black limousine waited at the curb. Cabriyo, the driver, waited until everyone was settled before joining the swirl of pedestrians, bicycles, and private autos wending its collective way along the arena access road.

Silent since leaving the mayoral box, Alehan sat on the banquette beside his mother, staring out the car window. Faint trembles coursed through his muscles, perceptible only because their bodies touched at shoulder and thigh. Lourdessa tapped his knee and he jerked like a perro startled from sleep, turning dilated eyes on his mother.

Lourdessa felt annoyance and alarm in equal measure. "Are you feeling well, dulzor?" She reached out to touch his misted forehead.

He dodged her hand with an irritated snort. "Yes. Why are you asking me that? Do I look sick?"

Lourdessa sighed. "I'm your mother." Rather than press the issue and risk a tantrum, she asked, "How are preparations for our special project coming along?"

Alehan's waxing bad humor dissipated in a flash. "So far, everything is on schedule. Olivas has recovered most of the data from the Veyho Bayona data crystals. We've got schematics and most of the operations manual to work with. All the equipment'll be in place in another week."

"Excellent." Lourdessa allowed herself a tiny smile of satisfaction. "It would've been an effing disaster if we'd allowed Archbishop De La Roha to get his hands on this. No telling what that bleeding heart would've done with it."

"This machine, Dama," Nunyez said. He sat across from Lourdessa, Higerra stone-faced beside him and the satchel tucked between his feet. "Are you sure it can be re-created? And if so, will it function? So much about pre-war technology remains beyond our skills and understanding."

"Mother is letting Eduard out of prison to direct the project," Alehan said. "If anyone can resurrect the Annihilator, it's him."

"How will Doctor Olivas feel about that?" Nunyez said.

"Raul Olivas may be Chief Engineer of Nue Bayona," Lourdessa replied, "but my husband is the best engineer in the city. Besides, Olivas serves at my pleasure. He'll do what he's told."

Nunyez regarded her with a flat expression. "Once this machine is operational, then what?"

"Nue Bayona needs unfettered access to all the coal and natural gas this continent has. Fuel cells supply only a fraction of the energy the city needs. We're finding fewer and fewer every year. Eventually, there'll be no more to find." Lourdessa paused, the implications

striking her anew. "No," she continued. "We can't allow Nue Castila to cut us off. Until Stefan came into power, we had nothing to fear, but now..."

The minister pursed his lips while stroking his chin with a bony forefinger. "You'll have the perfect stick with which to bring him to heel."

The remainder of the trip back to the palace passed in silence. Alehan fidgeted the entire way, bouncing his knees and passing his grisly trophy from hand to hand. Before the car had rolled to a stop in the courtyard fronting the residential wing of the palace, he'd reached past Higerra to fling open the door and clamber out onto the pavers. I've got some things to do before dinner," he mumbled.

"I've told the kitchen to serve promptly at seven. Your favorite. *Ovehas* medallions in red wine sauce." Lourdessa said.

Alehan merely grunted. With long, swift strides he headed off toward his private quarters.

Lourdessa dismissed Cabriyo and Higerra. Only after the two men had driven off in the limo did she acknowledge the satchel dangling from Nunyez's hand. "I trust you know what's in there."

He stared at the bag for several moments, a raised eyebrow the only clue to his thoughts. At last, he looked up at Lourdessa. "It saddens me, this. Strange, I know, to think a man in my profession could feel regret over a necessary occurrence; but well...there it is." Though he sounded sincere, Lourdessa doubted the truthfulness of his admission.

A wave of disgust washed over her like dirty water. Nunyez held out the bag as if expecting her to take it; she turned away instead and whispered, "Get rid of it."

"Dama?"

Knowing full well his puzzled response was nothing more than pretense, Lourdessa rounded on him in narrow-eyed fury. "You heard me."

Nunyez shuffled back a pace, nodded, and slung the satchel over his arm. "Then I will see you in the morning."

Filled with all the equanimity of a trampled serpent, Lourdessa returned to her office. Now that the deed was accomplished she found herself strangely disquieted; if she allowed it, she could almost feel a tiny particle of regret.

No! Never that. There's far too much at stake for foolish sentimentality, she thought as she stared out her office window at the city below, burnished to a sheen of gold and copper by the setting sun. *Greg will be angry, but he'll get over it. I'll go to the mansion first thing in the morning and tell him in person. Then I must deal with the Marians. The dreary biddies will have to be bribed, of course.*

Lourdessa moved to her desk. From the drawer where she'd hidden it nearly a week ago, she withdrew the false announcement of Deanna's conversion she'd crafted for the newspapers, written on official mayoral letterhead.

Scanning the words, she nodded in satisfaction. She folded the heavy paper into thirds and affixed her seal in gold wax.

This will go out tonight, special dispatch.

13
prisoner #253-1950

In a roble-wood-paneled study made uncomfortably warm by sealed windows and a gas fire, Lourdessa lounged in a heavy, high-backed chair. She sipped strong café from a porcelain cup and regarded her brother over the rim. Imprisoned in a steam-driven wheelchair of his own design by the muscle-wasting disease he'd contracted in his youth, the head of the Sedano family looked like a wizened little mono enthroned on a frame of gilded metal tubes, velvet upholstery, and clockwork gears. On rubber wheels, Gregorio glided across the hand-knotted ovehas wool carpet toward his sister, fury like a storm cloud darkening his brow. "I warned you, Dessa. I warned you not to do this."

"I had no choice, Greg. The girl is...*was*, too popular. Eventually, the resistance would have drawn her in and used her against us."

"Deanna Hernaan was no threat to us. Your obsession with her had more to do with your jealousy than anything else. The girl was too young and pretty. You just couldn't stand having a rival."

"You really believe I'm that petty? That I'd order a girl killed because I was jealous of her?" Lourdessa slammed down the delicate cup and whipped a handkerchief from the pocket of her green linen trousers to dab away the fine sheen of sweat on her forehead. "Diosa mia, my son was in love with her. He even proposed marriage. She turned him down."

"For which I'm sure you are grateful." Gregorio's thin jowls quivered. "Dear sister, you've only ever cared about getting your way, no matter what you have to do. This time you've gone too far."

Though only two years her senior, Gregorio had taken on more of a paternal role in Lourdessa's life since the death of their father Lucien, including the meting out of chastisement. Stung to brittle annoyance by his indictment, Lourdessa resisted the urge to hurl the café cup at her brother's head. "The deed is done." Defiance sharpened her tone. "The resistance has been robbed of their symbol. And in time the people will forget about her."

"The true resistance doesn't need a symbol," Gregorio said. "You are seriously underestimating its danger. You believe it to be no more than a street rebellion, but you're wrong. The real rebels lurk among your own inner circle."

"No one in my government would dare betray me. They all have families to protect." With a dismissive wave Lourdessa added, "I don't want to talk about this anymore. I have something far more important to tell you. Raul Olivas has decoded the Veyho Bayona crystals. The Annihilator project can go forward."

Gregorio's spindly fingers tightened on the plush arms of his chair. "So. Not only do you ignore my warning against harming Eduard's daughter, you now intend to spend a huge amount of my money on resurrecting an ancient machine that no one knows for sure will even work."

"It's our money, Greg." Lourdessa responded, her voice clipped with resentment. "I own an equal share in Sedano Industries, which you seem to have forgotten. I can spend my income on whatever I please."

"Why do you want this machine so badly?"

Lourdessa shook her head, incredulous. "You have to ask me that? We've lost control of Nue Castila!"

"Assuming Olivas can construct a working prototype, then what? The Castilians have a standing defense force. Threatening them will only strengthen their resolve." With a soft whir of gears, Gregorio maneuvered his chair closer to the ornate iron hearth anchoring the south wall of his study. The flames sparked blue reflections from the surface of his wire-rimmed spectacles as he stared into their fluttering depths. "Times have changed." He turned the chair to face his sister. "I backed your takeover because you convinced me Eduard was about to seize control of our mining interests. I've since learned that perhaps I should not have trusted you. A war with the Castilians will be very bad for our business."

"And Stefan seizing our mines and gas pipelines isn't?"

"Stefan is a reasonable man. His claims have merit. When his envoys arrive you'll negotiate with them in good faith."

Lourdessa raked her brother with a look that could scald flesh. "Since when did you become such an effing socialist?"

"I'm trying to avert an unnecessary war." Gregorio's voice swelled as high as his weakened chest muscles allowed. "If you'd bothered to pay attention to your history lessons in school, you'd understand." A paroxysm of harsh coughs wracked his thin frame. He subsided into the cushions and covered his mouth with a hand. Lourdessa watched, unmoved. After several agonizing seconds, Gregorio regained his breath. "Tell me you'll do as I say," he whispered.

Lourdessa lifted her chin. Her full lips twisted. "Oh, I'll negotiate with the Castilians. And the Annihilator will serve as my leverage."

"No. I forbid you to go forward with this."

Lourdessa rose to her feet and turned her back on her brother. "Too late. It's already begun." She walked to the door. As her hand touched the knob, Gregorio growled his final warning.

"Damn it, Dessa…if this all blows up in your face don't come running to me, because I will not protect you."

A JINGLE OF keys and the whispered turns of well-oiled locks alerted Doctor Eduard Hernaan, Prisoner #253-195B, to the arrival of a visitor.

The erstwhile Lord Alcalde of Nue Bayona looked up in mild surprise from his diary to see a guard usher his wife into his cell.

"Hola, dulzor," Lourdessa said with cloying sweetness.

Eduard closed the cover on the day's musings and removed his wire-framed spectacles. He placed book and pen in the top drawer of his little writing desk and stood to face her. "Dessa. To what do I owe this unexpected pleasure?" He knew his tone and the real meaning of his words would not be lost on her.

"Can't a woman visit her husband without a reason?" Lourdessa stepped across the threshold and said to the guard at her shoulder, "Wait outside." She motioned for the man to close the heavy steel door behind him.

"It hasn't been six months yet," Eduard said. He ran a hand through his silver hair. "Forgive me if I seem surprised." Lourdessa's biannual visits had been a constant until now. That she was here two months early raised droves of alarming questions.

"I could do with a drink," Lourdessa said.

"Of course." Eduard moved to a sideboard where a crystal decanter and four tiny glasses stood on a brass tray. He poured each of them a finger of *jerez*—last year's birthday gift from his daughters—noting how little of the amber liquid remained. From the corner of his eye he watched Lourdessa wander the confines of the cell, knowing full well her casual glances hid a search for contraband books or papers.

"I see the new cot arrived," she said.

"Yes, thank you. It's much more comfortable than the old one." He handed her a glass. "I could use another fuel-cell lamp. The one I have is small, and if I light too many oil lamps, the air gets smoky."

I'll see what I can do."

"How are the girls?"

"They are well...for now."

Eduard pulled the wooden chair from beneath his writing desk and sat, leaving the more comfortable leather armchair—the only piece of furniture from their apartments in the palace she had allowed him to keep—for his wife. He sipped his drink, watching her as she watched him.

Six years had passed since Lourdessa's betrayal; and though the rage and pain of that treachery still lay coiled deep in his soul, it no longer burned white-hot. Like the ache of an old injury it was always there; never forgotten, but manageable. Lourdessa saw to it that his jailers kept him comfortable. They fulfilled most of his requests and allowed his daughters to visit on holidays and his birthday.

He had dreamed of escape often enough over the years; in fact he knew the exact layout of the ventilation shaft grid and which ducts would take him to freedom. He stayed only to protect his children. Deanna and Ceilia served as guarantors of his good behavior.

Lourdessa had dressed in emerald green, a color she knew he found particularly attractive against her complexion. The fitted blouse and slim trousers showed off her still-youthful figure to perfection. A pair of greenstone studs, a gift from him on their second wedding anniversary, glinted in her ears. He felt the familiar stirrings of desire heat his body.

Madre Maria, will I never be free of her spell? Even after all she's taken from me...I could forgive her, if she asked.

Eduard took another sip from his brandy and broke the tense silence. "Tell me why you're really here, Dessa."

She drained her glass and set it aside. "You always were an impatient man, dulzor. I never liked that...except in the bedroom." A tiny smile curled her lips and then vanished. "What would you say if I told you I'm willing to release you?"

Eduard frowned. "I'd say you were lying."

Lourdessa leaned forward in her chair, breasts straining against the fabric of her blouse. "I'm not."

"There's a price, of course." Eduard's eyes remained fixed on her face. He tried not to think of the last time his hands had caressed her breasts.

"I need your engineering skills in service to the city."

"What do you mean?"

"Two weeks ago a Church salvage team discovered a cache of data crystals in the ruins of Veyho Bayona." Lourdessa gripped the arms of her chair. "The covert agent I placed in their midst was able to confiscate the entire lot. I turned the trove over to Raul Olivas for analysis."

Eduard couldn't help but marvel at his wife's staggering audacity. The fact that she could rob the Church with impunity only served as further proof of how tight her grip on the city's power structure had become. "I can imagine the Archbishop's reaction to that," he said.

Lourdessa raised a single, impeccable eyebrow. "The Archbishop knows who stocks his pantry. If he's dared to whine I've heard nothing of it."

"Has Olivas made any headway?"

"Yes. He and his research group spent the last three days working. Most were too corrupted, but not all. He may not be you, but the man does have some skills. He finally managed to get our computer to read a few of them. And Eduard, my darling, you'll never guess what he found."

"I'm in no mood for guessing games," Eduard grumbled. "Just tell me."

"Schematics and an operations manual for an AX238 assault mech." Lourdessa sat back, a look of triumph on her face.

The Annihilator. Eduard stared at her, astonished. Every citizen of Nue Bayona learned the history of the Great War in school, the war that ended the technologically advanced society established on Nuetierra by the original colonists from Old Earth. The two factions had unleashed arsenals of weaponry upon each other that had shattered their cities and devastated most of the continent. The AX238 Annihilator was the most fearsome of these weapons.

"I need you to resurrect it," Lourdessa said.

When he finally found his voice, Eduard realized he had to speak with care, lest he scream. "You want me to build an Annihilator."

Lourdessa's café eyes gleamed with predatory intent. "That's right."

"What possible need could you have for that kind of power?" A cold knot of dread coalesced in the pit of Eduard's stomach.

"You should know the answer. Faustin's insurgency has been terrorizing the city for nearly a year, or don't you read the newspapers I send you?"

There would be no insurgency if you hadn't betrayed me. "That can't be the only reason," Eduard shot back.

"You're right, there's another," Lourdessa replied. "That peasant Ectorio Stefan is sending two of his lackeys to renegotiate the terms of the coal and gas contracts between our two cities. If I don't give in to his demands, he's threatening to cut Nue Bayona off completely."

Eduard shook his head in sardonic amusement. "The people of Nue Castila have finally gotten rid of that puppet Narcisso Cruze and you can't stand it."

"Cruze provided stability. He was the best man for Alcalde."

"Cruze was a dictator. Your—or should I say, your brother's—creature, right down to his corrupt bones. The Castilians are tired of austerity. They only want a fair share of the profits for their labor. This is all about the Sedano's excessive wealth."

Lourdessa's counterattack was swift. "I never heard a word of protest from you about my family's money before. You were perfectly willing to spend it on things you wanted."

"Like better sanitation and more access to electricity for the common people," Eduard parried, fighting to rein in his mounting fury. "That's why they elected me. It's why they support Faustin's rebels. What have you done for the citizens, Dessa?"

Lourdessa stood, the full force of her implacable will burning in her gaze. "I need you to build that machine. You are the only one who has the skill."

Eduard abandoned his own chair to meet her will with his. "You don't need the Annihilator." Disgust roughened his voice. "You just want a way to intimidate Nue Castila and protect the Sedano monopoly." He took a step toward Lourdessa, his hands clenched. "What if I refuse to help you?"

"You won't, dulzor, because I know how much you love your children." Lourdessa's voice was low and cold as winter fog.

Eduard turned his back on his wife to hide the tears welling in his eyes. There it is, the true face behind the beautiful mask. Why did I not see the danger until after it had struck me down? He gazed at a little framed photograph of Deanna, Ceilia, and their mother—his beloved Louisa—hanging on the whitewashed wall above the sideboard. His daughters had been quite young at the time when he'd taken the picture. He'd used his own equipment, in the small palace garden that had been Louisa's favorite spot. The laughing faces of his lost family tore at his heart.

Resigned to the futility of resistance, he took a deep breath.

"When do I start?"

14
to the edge and back

Zander lay curled on his side in darkness, shivering. Cold, unyielding concrete brutalized cheek, shoulder, hipbone, and knee. The dark pressed in, alive with furtive rustlings, the plink-plink of dripping water and the rhythmic hum of distant machinery.

The first time the hooded men in black came for him, they beat him with truncheons. As the blows descended on his writhing body, Zander's torturers answered his cries for mercy with laughter. He couldn't decide which hurt worse—the blows or the scorn.

When next they came, they dragged him from his cell to a small room with rust-brown splatters on the walls and ceiling. They strapped him to a board and tied a cloth bag over his head. As he struggled against leather restraints, water sluiced over his nose and mouth in a steady stream, choking him.

They took him to the threshold of death and yanked him back. While he fought for each precious breath, a guttural voice screamed questions in his ear that he could not answer. His tearful denials only seemed to enrage his tormentors. Water flooded his mouth once again, cutting off his pleas. This time it did not stop. Zander's consciousness fled in terror.

With his returning awareness had come the realization that he still lived. Surprise, quickly followed by despair, made a jumble of his thoughts. Dripping wet and stripped to his underpants, he could do nothing but lie in searing misery on the merciless concrete.

His stomach had long since ceased to gurgle with hunger. Thirst had become his greatest tormentor. That…and the pain.

A metallic rattle echoed in his ears. With a harsh groan the door to his cell swung open. Zander squeezed his eyes shut against the sudden glare pouring in from the corridor.

"No, please Madre Maria…no more," he begged in a cracked whisper.

Rough hands hauled him to his feet. He fought to stave off the darkness that threatened to snuff out his consciousness. "Shut up, perro," a voice snarled in his ear. Two guards, one on either side, dragged him stumbling into the corridor. He blinked, bleary eyed, and struggled to walk on legs robbed of all strength.

"Just kill me now," he whispered.

The guards remained silent. Their fingers clamped on his shoulders with such force it felt like his bones would crack.

At the end of the corridor a flight of stairs led down to a loading bay. A large black police van waited, its rear doors hanging open. Zander's guards marched him up to where a third man waited. Together all three lifted and sent him sprawling atop several other bodies on the floor of the van. The doors shut with a hollow crash, closing him in darkness once more.

One of the bodies stirred beneath him. A muffled voice cried, "Get off me…" Zander rolled away, coming to rest on the slick metal floor as the van lurched into motion. He tried to lever himself up but his head slammed into something hard. An explosion of sparks erupted behind his eyes as pain blasted his skull.

"Ah, mierda!" He flopped back to the floor, straining to see in the dimness. After a few heartbeats he realized he had rolled underneath a bench along one side of the van. Struggling against the motion of the vehicle, he pulled himself onto the unyielding wood where he sagged, panting from pain and exertion.

His eyelids drooped shut for what seemed only a moment; then the rear doors flew open. Before he could react, two guards seized him by his arms and legs and threw him out over the tailgate like a trussed carcass. His head hit the pavement with a sickening crack.

The last thing he remembered before the darkness closed in again was the sound of a woman's scream.

"Zan...Zander...Time to wake up."

Dee, is that you?

"C'mon, Zander. You're scaring me. Please...wake up!"

Zander opened his eyes to golden light and moving shadows. The light drove pain like a steel spike through his forehead. He groaned and raised his hand to block the tormenting glow.

"Get the lamp out of his face, idiot. Can't you see it's hurting him?"

A female voice, but whose?

Recognition came in a rush.

"Sonnie," he whispered, or tried to. His lips felt as thick as patok tubers. The iron taste of blood filled his mouth. He reached out and felt the comforting warmth of her fingers clasping his.

"You're safe now, dulzor." Sonia's long dark hair fell around her shoulders and breasts as she leaned over him. Her sorrowful gaze filled his vision. "How do you feel?"

Dizzy with relief, he pondered the question and finally answered, "Like mierda." His injured mouth slurred the words but Sonia must have understood, for she gave him a little smile.

"Ask him if he remembers anything from the last three days," a man said. Zander thought he recognized the voice, but he couldn't be sure. The speaker remained hidden behind Sonia.

"It's alright, Zan, you don't have to say anything right now." Sonia ran a gentle hand through his hair. "We know you were in detention. They hurt you bad, but there's nothing that won't heal. You'll be as handsome as ever in no time. You can stay here for as long as you need to."

"No he can't." The unseen man's voice thrummed with hostility.

"Shut up, Tony." The name conjured a vague image of a sharp-faced blond. Sonia glared over her shoulder. "I say he can. Zander is our friend."

"Your friend, you mean."

"I can go." Zander attempted to sit up, but Sonia gently pushed him back down. Just that small effort awakened every agony that had lain dormant within his flesh. He stifled a sob behind gritted teeth.

"I've got some morfo." Sonia said.

Zander knew how much the potent painkillers cost on the underground market. He shied away from contemplating what Sonia must have had to trade for them.

"No, thanks. As long as I don't move much...I'll be all right." He tried to smile, but it felt more like a grimace. Sonia disappeared from view and returned a few moments later holding a small vial. She drew the stopper and shook a single white tablet onto her palm.

"Chew this, you twit. And no arguments." Before he could object Sonia pushed the tablet between his lips. "Now you can actually sleep, which is what you need," she said in a soft voice.

Zander let the pill dissolve on his tongue. The drug trickled into his bloodstream, gradually transforming his agony into bliss.

"I have to get word to Deanna. She needs to know I've been released," he said, but his lips had gone numb, so he couldn't be sure if Sonia heard.

"Go to sleep, lover." Sonia kissed him.

Zander closed his eyes.

15
battle for survival

Deanna shoved a sweat-slicked lock of hair from her eyes and renewed her assault on the *canteen plant*. Lack of a knife forced her to chop at the bulbous, waxy base with a sharp-edged rock. As she worked she listened to her father's voice, speaking to her from memory.

Remember this ugly plant, Dee. If you ever find yourself in the Wilds with no water, the canteen will save your life. First, cut through the base, then take a long stick and stir the pulp. Then, you drink.

Deanna grimaced. "Easier said than done, Papa," she muttered. "You assumed I'd have a knife or a hatchet."

Her father had taught her many lessons during their trips into the untamed country beyond the city limits. The one about this plant could prove the most valuable. Yet despite the many she'd chopped down, each contained barely a sip or two of sour juice, hardly enough to satisfy.

A brisk wind off the prairie tempered the late-afternoon heat. Deanna stopped to catch her breath and give her sore hands a much-needed rest. She gazed across a ruffled sea of umber, waist-high grass broken by scrub-topped, rocky outcrops and drought-tolerant *choa* trees that stood solitary or in small groves. A mountain range formed a distant wall to the north—the high Pyrs, the jagged backbone of the continent. Many klims to the south lay the vast, desiccated wastes of the Siyera Desert.

The landscape held a harsh beauty that moved her in spite of the fear lurking beneath the surface of her thoughts. She mentally ticked off the number of days that had passed since she'd fled the abandoned farmhouse.

Three. No…four.

On the morning of the first day Deanna had avoided the main road to follow a secondary dirt trail about fifty meters parallel to it. She kept the paved road always to her right, alert for the approach of any traffic, but none appeared. As that day wore on, the road and track began to diverge, with the road continuing east toward Nue Castila while the dirt track curved south. Deanna stuck to the trail, thankful she didn't have to forge her own path through the high grass.

Shortly before sundown the track ended at the door of a tumbledown shack. At one time, it might have served as a storage shed for salvagers or ranchers. The roof had fallen in, but the standing walls afforded modest shelter. A quick circumnavigation of the shack revealed no other trails. She'd had no choice but to continue southeast across unbroken terrain. Worry robbed her of any sleep that first night.

Dawn of her second day in flight had found her exhausted and regretting her decision to make a run for Anjelas. What originally seemed like a reasonable conclusion in hindsight had begun to appear both hasty and ill conceived. If Gomaz had truly been tasked to kill her he would have done so. He had no need to spin an elaborate hoax for her benefit. Some logical explanation must have existed for Diego's failure to appear. Had she stayed put and waited instead of panicking and running, it seemed likely that either Diego or Gomaz would have eventually come for her. She'd allowed fear to overrule logic; as a consequence she now found herself lost deep in the bush, precious days having passed and with no end to her suffering in sight.

The close, harsh screech of an unfamiliar bird refocused Deanna's mind back on the present. In the near distance a small pod of wild sky jellies floated by on warm air currents. Their supple, ropelike tentacles skimmed the ground, trolling for prey. Flushed from hiding, a herd of dun-striped *gazelas* sprang into bounding flight. The slender, lance-like horns of the males stabbed skyward with each leap. The jelly pod put on a burst of speed to close with the fleeing herd. Deanna watched in queasy fascination as they snared several of the gazelas and lifted them, bleating with terror, to their deaths. Twice during the last two days, foraging jelly pods had forced her to seek cover. Sky jellies would as happily dine on human flesh as they would on gazela, wild eelat, or vaca.

Every bit as harrowing, an earlier encounter with a felion lying in ambush had cost her two precious bullets and nearly her life. Cursing her ill fortune, Deanna had scrambled to sanctuary on a high choa tree branch while the russet-and-brown-spotted beast circled below, bellowing and rattling its mane of needle-sharp quills in frustration. Lucky for her that particular animal proved too old and debilitated to climb. After a few lackluster attempts to reach her by rearing on its hind legs to grope with an outstretched paw, it gave up. With a last hiss and gnash of yellowed fangs, the felion vanished amid the camouflaging grasses.

The memory left her trembling, but immediate need demanded that she master her anxiety and return to the business at hand.

After a few more chops at the canteen plant, the stem gave way. Snatching up her prize, Deanna retreated to the shade of a choa tree. She settled amid knees of thick, spreading roots to rest her back against its smooth silvery trunk.

She reached into her coat pocket and pulled out a stick. She stirred the purple pulp to release the juice. With a frown she downed the sour liquid in one gulp, then pillowed her head on folded arms and closed her eyes.

I'm so hungry and thirsty, she thought, *and I'm not sure how far off-course I am.* Without proper equipment she couldn't wrest enough nourishment from the harsh terrain, nor navigate with any certainty. Still she had no choice but to press on. To give up now would mean death, and victory for Lourdessa. Somehow she would find the strength to reach Anjelas.

Dull aches coursed through her back and thighs. With a sigh, she shifted in an attempt to find a more comfortable position against the tree trunk. *I only have a few bullets, no knife...I'm so tired, I don't know how much farther I can walk...I'd love a tall, cold glass of water or manzaniya juice or maybe a beer, yes, a cold beer...*

A loud crack overhead propelled Deanna out of her daydream and onto her feet. The thick canopy of the choa thrashed above her as if caught in a winter gale. It showered her with small red leaves. A rope-like object as thick as her wrist whipped past her head, followed by several smaller ropes. Each ended in a slim black spike. The stench of rotten meat permeated the air.

Crying out, Deanna darted from beneath the tree. Looking up, she saw a sky jelly pod had surrounded her erstwhile shelter. The animals were busily dismembering it in a quest to reach their prey. Deanna sprinted into the grass, putting distance between her and the pod before stopping to look back. She counted nine of the beasts, led by a large male sporting a bright red dorsal ridge.

What sky jellies lacked in intelligence they made up for in persistence. Once a pod fixated on their prey they would pursue it for hours; unless another, easier choice presented itself. Deanna knew she could outrun the pod in the short term, but exhaustion precluded a swift escape, and the creatures moved quickly when they sensed an imminent kill.

She scanned the horizon for a new place to shelter. A large, rocky outcrop loomed in the middle distance. If she could reach it in time she might have a chance.

Fear banished fatigue from her limbs as she took off running, but the thick prairie grass tangled around her legs, slowing her flight. The jellies had no such encumbrance. Propelling themselves through the clear air with strong jets of gas from their rear vents, they gained on her.

Deanna felt the low frequency clicks and moans of the jellies rumble through her as they called out to each other. Her lungs burned and her strength began to flag. One long tentacle whipped past her head, then another. She stumbled and, before she could recover, a thick, gray rope snaked around her torso and legs.

Deanna screamed as her feet were yanked from beneath her.

Pain seared through her thigh and stopped her breath. Her leg lost all feeling as the venom invaded her body. A strange prickling tingled in her hands, chest, and face.

Several more tentacles wrapped themselves around her, forming a living net in which she hung suspended, several meters off the ground. Though her legs and feet were immobilized, she still had use of her hands, but for how long, she had no clue.

She withdrew Gomaz's gun from her waistband, where it had, by some miracle, remained wedged. Her fingers felt pierced by a thousand hot needles. Gritting her teeth against the pain and surging dizziness, she aimed at the jelly's small head, cocked the hammer, and squeezed the trigger.

The first shot missed. The second tore a hole in the animal's gas bladder. It shuddered; for an instant the net of tentacles loosened around her. Deanna felt her grip on the gun grow weaker. Darkness frayed the edges of her vision. A strange, pungent taste filled her mouth. She fired a third time, too groggy to know if the shot had found its mark. She managed to squeeze off one last bullet before the pistol slipped from her nerveless fingers.

She hung upside down, unmoving, in the deadly embrace of the jelly's tentacles. Her thoughts gyrated in a venom-induced haze. The pain had vanished; in fact she felt nothing at all, not even fear. She'd become a being of pure thought, divorced from any physical concerns. All she needed to do now was close her eyes and wait for the darkness to spirit her away. Even as the tentacles relaxed and sent her spinning into the void, she felt only a calm anticipation. When the dark reached out to swallow her, she was ready.

Migeyl Diego tugged his eelat mare to a stop and whipped a spyglass from his saddlebag, training it on the distant jelly pod. What he saw horrified him. He drew his slug rifle from its saddle holster and took aim, but better sense stayed his hand. He was too far out of range. He had to get closer.

He drummed his heels into the eelat's piebald flanks. The beast snorted and shied, her neck streaked with sweat. Even from this distance, her terror of the jellies had driven her close to bolting. Desperate, the man lashed her shoulders with the ends of his reins. She nearly unseated him as she sprang forward, but galloped only a few meters before swerving into a bucking, plunging circle. With every bit of strength he possessed he wrestled her at last to a shivering standstill.

A pistol shot echoed across the waving grasses, followed a second later by another. The man again raised his spyglass in time to witness the girl fire twice more. Helpless, he could do nothing but watch as together, jelly and girl plunged to the ground.

Diego barked an obscenity and slammed his spyglass closed.

If only I'd arrived sooner, he thought.

Though she may have survived the fall, nothing he knew of could help her survive the sting of a full-grown, wild sky jelly.

The frantic pod circled its fallen leader, uttering sharp clicks of distress. The man knew he had to retrieve the girl's body, but that wouldn't be possible until all the jellies had departed. With a heavy heart he retreated a few meters back to a small outcrop, where he dismounted and settled down to wait.

16
the power of the curaro

Beneath the sheltering canopy of a small stand of choa trees, three riders lounged in the tough grass beside their mounts, guarding the carcass of a freshly killed vaca calf. Sunset was less than two hours away. Once the day's heat waned, they would return with their kill to the scrub-shagged outcrop where their companions camped in a cave at its base. After two weeks in the bush scouring ruins and subsisting on *capra* jerky, flatbread, and dried fruit, roasted vaca would be a welcome change.

The three had been friends since childhood. Ghost Dog and New Moon, twin siblings, and River, New Moon's husband, had no need for the crutch of small talk; the empathy they shared allowed companionable silence as meaningful as spoken words.

Brother and sister shared other traits as well. The same glossy black hair crowned both their heads, though Ghost Dog's fell below his shoulders, while New Moon kept hers shorn close above her ears. Cinnamon-hued skin, high cheekbones, fine noses—his marred by a small knob on the bridge from a childhood accident—and eyes the color of amber defined their beauty in both masculine and feminine form.

Though Ghost Dog had arrived into the world two minutes ahead of his sister, he had never claimed the privilege of being firstborn that was his by right. As children they'd shared everything, forging an unbreakable bond into adulthood. To him, New Moon was, and always would be, his equal.

Ghost Dog yawned and rubbed his stubble-roughened chin. Tired from a long day in the saddle and drowsy from the heat, he stood to retrieve his canteen from his saddlebag and splashed a handful of water on his face. Grim, his gray eelat gelding, grumbled and butted its earless head against his shoulder. Ghost Dog poured a little water into his palm and let the beast suck it down; he then took a single, tepid sip from the canteen and closed it.

He glanced at his sister and brother-in-law, curled in sleep together between a pair of knobby roots. From the start they'd made an unlikely couple. River's spun-copper hair, pale skin, and green eyes—so different from the norms that defined their people—had deflected most girls' favors away from him. New Moon could have had her pick of the clan's comeliest men for her mate, but she saw beneath the superficial and fell in love with the substance. Two months hence they would celebrate their first year as husband and wife.

The grasslands rippled beyond the oasis of shade provided by the choas. As Ghost Dog watched he thought of his own betrothed, left behind in camp with a stomach ailment. Next spring would see them married.

A small pod of sky jellies hove into view. Ghost Dog frowned. Something about the way the animals were moving pricked his hunter's sense to full alert. Perplexed, he squinted at the pod through sun glare and the distortion of heat shimmer, trying to sort out the puzzle. Over the crunch of dry grass and the noise of the eelat's bits jingling as they chewed, he heard New Moon's sleepy voice at his shoulder. "What are you looking at?"

Ghost Dog pointed at the pod. "Those jellies. I think they've caught something."

A flash, followed by a faint pop echoed across the swaying prairie. The jellies jetted closer. Brother and sister looked at each other, eyes widening with concern.

A second flash from among the clump of tentacles hanging beneath the red-crested head of the dominant male, followed by another pop, left no doubt in either sibling's mind. New Moon's cheeks paled beneath her russet complexion. "I'll wake River," she said.

Rubbing the sleep from his eyes, River stepped up beside Ghost Dog. "Moon says there's someone in trouble..." He stared at the circling jellies. "Ancestors preserve! You don't think they've caught a person, do you?"

"Both Moon and I heard gunshots," Ghost Dog said.

New Moon looked first at her husband, then her brother. The knuckles of her hands whitened against the dark leather of her breeches. "We can't just stand here. We have to try to help!" she cried.

As she took a step forward, Ghost Dog laid a hand in gentle restraint on his sister's arm. "Moon, stop. You know it's too dangerous."

"*Sunaiya*, your brother is right." River slipped his arm around his wife's waist and pulled her close. "There's nothing we can do."

As the three young hunters watched, the big red-crest shuddered. What looked like a human body fell from its tentacles. A heartbeat later the jelly also plummeted from the sky, trailing tatters of ruptured gas bladder like streamers on the tail of a kite. The creature hit the ground and a thin cloud of dust geysered upward to dissipate in the hot breeze. The remaining pod members spun in a confused circle above their fallen leader, dragging their tentacles over the rapidly deflating body.

"Did you see that?" New Moon pushed away from River, as if ready to race out to the fallen jelly, no matter the danger. "Maybe whoever that is, he's still alive."

"Even if that were so, we can't risk riding out there while the rest of the pod is hanging around," warned Ghost Dog.

"If there's the slightest chance that person survived, we can't ride away without checking," New Moon insisted in a quiet voice.

Ghost Dog gazed at his twin, acquiescence mellowing his amber eyes. "Come darkness the pod will move on." Jellies, he knew, were primarily visual hunters. They almost never attacked at night, not even in bright moonlight. "We'll look then. If the Ancestors will it, we'll find our brother or sister still alive."

At nightfall the pod departed. The three young hunters waited until the creatures' clicks and squeals had faded away before riding out to the carcass. Overhead the spring constellations glimmered like spilled diamonds on black silk, their glory unchallenged by the moons. Nayna wouldn't rise for an hour, her sister Luna for yet another two.

With only dim starlight to see by, the trio had to rely on hand torches and the superior night vision of their mounts to navigate the uneven terrain. Ghost Dog rode in the lead, the bright white beam of his torch trained on the ground ahead of Grim's forefeet. The dead jelly rose from the grass like a small hill, a darker shadow against the black of night. The closer the three hunters approached, the balkier their eelats grew. Eventually no amount of persuasion could force them nearer, no matter that the creature lay silent and still.

Ghost Dog dismounted and handed his reins to River. Drawing his pistol, he aimed his torch at the massive body and advanced with cautious steps. The carcass exuded a powerful odor comprised of equal parts rotting meat and fermented vegetation. He battled his rising gorge between quick shallow breaths.

Alert for any movement, Ghost Dog prodded a tentacle with the toe of his boot. When that elicited no response he drew his hunting blade and buried it to the hilt in the rubbery flesh. Still nothing. He called out, "Clear!" to the others.

New Moon and River dismounted, leaving the nervous eelats ground-tied several paces from the corpse.

"I'll cut some pieces from the gas bladder," River said. When properly tanned, jellyskin made the best waterproof garments. "If you find someone alive, yell."

Ghost Dog tugged the sleeve of his sister's brown gazela-suede jacket. "Let's look near the head first."

The siblings paced alongside the carcass, scanning the ground by the light of Ghost Dog's torch. A soft sound, like the whimper of a baby, drifted from the darkness ahead.

"Did you hear that?" New Moon whispered.

The two paused to listen. Another sound, more of a moan this time, raised the hairs on the nape of Ghost Dog's neck. He trained his beam on the knot of tentacles sprouting from the jelly's head. "It's coming from over there."

The siblings ran toward the jumbled mass. Ghost Dog swept the light over the pile of dull gray appendages. Something white and brown lay entangled in their midst. Without hesitation he waded into the snarl to discover a figure caught in the net of dead jelly flesh. He staggered back as if struck.

"What's wrong?" New Moon fetched up against her brother, steadying him. "Is he alive?"

Wordlessly, Ghost Dog pointed.

"Blessed Ancestors," New Moon murmured. "It's an *alta*. City-dweller, by the look of the clothes."

"What's one of the tall folk doing alone all the way out here?" Ghost Dog bent over the prone figure, his torch revealing a profile of fine angles amidst a snarl of mahogany hair.

New Moon drew in a sharp breath. "It's a girl...ai, look at her skin."

"Let's get her free," Ghost Dog said. Together they pulled at the young woman's shoulders and legs until they removed her from the creature's cold embrace.

"Mierda," New Moon whispered. "Is she alive?"

The alta's face, neck, and hands gleamed stark white in the moonlight. An irregular dark stain marred the torn fabric of her pant leg. Ghost Dog placed his cheek against the victim's colorless lips. A wisp of exhalation stirred the fine hairs on his skin.

"Barely," he said, "but there may still be time for the antidote."

"I'll get River." New Moon disappeared into the darkness. Ghost Dog sat back on his haunches to stare at the alta's face, his mind filled with questions.

How did a city girl end up out here, dying from a sky jelly sting? She looks so young. Who is she, and where are her companions?

Tall folk from the cities never ventured this far into the Wilds unless they came seeking fresh slaves for the mines, and they never traveled alone. This young woman's presence presented a dangerous mystery. Ghost Dog ran a hand through his hair, compassion warring with well-founded fear. After an interval of tense contemplation, compassion won out, at least for the moment.

Whoever you are, alta girl, despite what you are...I won't let you die.

A spasm rippled the girl's muscles and a faint moan escaped her bloodless lips. Ghost Dog laid a hand on her forehead; clammy, chilled flesh told of the ruthless advance of the poison.

"You don't have much time left," he whispered.

Rapid footfalls signaled the return of New Moon, with River following at her heels. River muttered a curse and bent over the unconscious girl. With a heavy sigh he shook his head. "Her skin is already white. It's too late."

"No, it's not," Ghost Dog insisted. "Remember when Looks Past got stung last year? Her skin had already changed, but she survived after I made the antidote."

Both River and New Moon squatted beside Ghost Dog and the unconscious alta girl. In the reflected glow of the torch beam, Ghost Dog saw the incredulous look on his brother-in-law's face. "Curing Looks Past nearly killed you, Brother. Transmuting jelly toxin is too dangerous. Why risk your life for an alta? She and her kind wouldn't do the same for us."

Without hesitation Ghost Dog answered. "I'm a *curaro*. I took an oath. I can't stand by and watch another human being die, even if she is alta."

"You took an oath to heal our people," River replied.

"She's a human being, Brother. Like us."

River shook his head. "But she's not like us, Dog."

Ghost Dog saw fear for him on the faces of his sister and brother-in-law. His heart ached. He knew how much they loved him, and how grief would tear them apart if he perished, but he had no choice. River opened his mouth to press the argument, but New Moon held up her hand. "Peace, sunaiya. Dog has to do this." She caressed her brother's cheek. "Give me your torch. I'll get your canteen."

"Dog, will you make it back to camp?" River asked.

"We'll have to ride fast."

New Moon returned, dangling Ghost Dog's canteen by its leather strap. She passed the torch to him but kept the bottle. River gripped his shoulder. "I'm sorry, Dog, but I have to say it one last time. You don't have to do this. No one will think you've broken your oath."

Ghost Dog pulled his long knife from the sheath at his waist and swept the beam of his torch over the mound of tentacles. Stooping over an appendage the thickness of his own arm, he sliced through the rubbery flesh just above the black thorn-like claw at its tip. He then passed the torch back to his sister.

While New Moon held the torch steady, Ghost Dog filleted the poison sac from the remainder of the tissue with a few deft passes of his knife. He touched the alta girl's leg. "Lift her up."

River knelt, slipped the girl's limp arm around his neck, and hoisted her torso into his arms, bracing her against his chest. She whimpered as he steadied her lolling head with his hand. He looked up in tense expectation at Ghost Dog.

Putting the slimy globe of tissue to his lips, Ghost Dog bit deep, fighting the urge to gag. A thick rush of bitter liquid filled his mouth.

The tingling sensation in his lips and tongue started within moments. As he swished the milky fluid over his palate, the tingling grew more intense until his entire mouth and face felt as if the flesh burned from within. Sweat beaded his forehead and the ground rippled in a slow roll beneath his feet.

Just a little longer. Not quite there yet.

Pain exploded downward from his face and into his neck. It raced like a whirlwind of fire through his arms, chest, back, and legs. He squeezed his tearing eyes shut to focus with desperate intensity against the unbearable need to spit out the toxic liquid. His stomach twisted and heaved.

No! It's not ready...

He felt himself slipping sideways, but strong arms caught and held him upright.

Just when his brain screamed that he had reached the limit of endurance, the pain retreated. What had once been bitter poison now filled his mouth with a taste as sweet as corella flower nectar.

It's done.

He opened his eyes and reached for the girl. River pushed her forward into his arms. He allowed her head to tilt back just enough so he could administer the antidote without it spilling down her chin. Pressing his lips to hers in a kiss as intimate as any lover's, he let the antidote flow from his mouth into hers. He then pinched her lips closed with his thumb and forefinger while massaging her throat with his free hand. The girl swallowed convulsively once, then again. For a heartbeat Ghost Dog saw the gleam of her eyes beneath half-open lids.

"Let me take her now," River whispered.

Ghost Dog nodded and relinquished his hold. New Moon pressed a canteen into his hand. He rinsed his mouth and took a long drink. "We need to go now," he mumbled through lips rendered numb by the poison.

"As tall as she is, we'll have to carry her trussed like a *cervena* carcass," New Moon said.

"Use Grim," Ghost Dog replied, breathing hard to stave off insensibility. "I...I'm better...off riding...double anyway." He tried to stand but the ground upended him.

River raised him up and steadied him with gentle hands. "Hold on to my shoulder, Brother."

Nayna had risen by the time they rode away from the downed sky jelly. The land rested quiet and still beneath the black mantle of night. New Moon led the way with Grim's reins tied to her saddle, and the unconscious alta girl bound hand to foot like a sack across the eelat.

Ghost Dog rode slumped in River's arms. He struggled against the rising tide of sickness engulfing his body, even though he knew he would eventually succumb. The singular ability of the curaro demanded a high price from those who chose to wield it. Both gift and curse, it enmeshed the curer and the cured in *iyahuya*, a lifelong unbreakable bond. How his life and this alta girl's would now intersect Ghost Dog could not begin to fathom, but whatever the future held they would see it through together.

May the Ancestors protect us both, he prayed.

HIDDEN IN TALL grass and darkness, Diego sighed. From a safe distance he watched as the bobbing lights of the hunting band's torches moved away. Showing himself now would likely get him shot before he could explain his mission, so strong was their mistrust of his kind.

Fate had once again torn his plans asunder and rearranged things in an entirely unexpected fashion. Though relieved that immediate disaster had been averted, he still lamented his failure to secure her safety. Even so, knowing their people as he did, he believed that if the girl's rescuers ultimately decided that she posed no threat they would do her no harm. Already they'd chosen compassion over indifference.

With this realization came a shift in perspective. He now saw the girl's rescue as a stroke of serendipity, rather than a setback. Once his colleagues heard his report he believed they too would agree, though their original plans would need revising. Finding the girl again might prove a challenge, but they could all take comfort in knowing her enemies would have a harder time than her allies.

From close by an eerie, high-pitched howl raised the hairs on Diego's neck. A second, then a third ululating cry joined the first. His eelat mare growled in warning. Recognizing the time had come for retreat, the man gathered his reins and swung into the saddle. Holding his slug rifle at the ready and with a hand torch to light his way, he set off toward a nearby stand of choa trees. He would camp there for the remainder of the night. At first light he would start the journey back to Nue Bayona.

17
the rosa blanca

When Zander woke, he still hurt, but at least the morfo had doused the flames of his pain to smoldering embers.

He found himself on a cot in a small room with floors and walls of whitewashed adobe. A wooden staircase in one corner led up to a closed door. A rough-hewn plank table and several battered chairs made up the room's only furnishings. Rows of shelves filled with boxes, bags, and colored ceramic jars lined the walls. A single oil lamp rested on the table, illuminating the room with dim yellow light.

Zander recognized the basement beneath the common room of the Rosa Blanca Inn. How he had arrived there he had no clue. He threw back the thin wool blanket covering his naked body and hissed in dismay at the large blotches of purple and red that discolored his torso, thighs, and calves.

Sitting upright on the edge of the cot, he gingerly explored the damage to his face, wincing with every probe. A few moments later, the door rattled and swung open with a squeak of sticky hinges.

"Good. You're awake." Sonia thumped down the stairs on bare feet, a bowl and spoon in one hand and a beer bottle in the other. Struck by inexplicable embarrassment, Zander dived back under the blanket.

"Oh, please." Sonia's tone matched the amusement in her dark eyes. "It's not like I've never seen that before." She placed the bowl and bottle on the table. "Hungry?"

Zander knew she referred to his nakedness and not the evidence of abuse marking him as a recent detainee. He should feel no shame, and yet....

"What happened to my clothes?" He used the blanket to fashion a scratchy kilt around his hips.

"You didn't have much on when we found you," Sonia replied.

Zander breathed a prayer of thanks that he'd given his mother's ring to Deanna for safekeeping. The rest of his meager possessions he'd carried in his pack. Now that the police had taken it, he had nothing.

"Don't worry. My aunt's already found some clothes for you. Come eat." Sonia helped him to his feet with a hand beneath his shoulder, and guided him toward the table.

Zander sat and sniffed the contents of the bowl. "Mmmm. Your aunt's vaca stew. I love this stuff." He picked up the spoon, then ate as fast as his swollen mouth would allow. Sonia took the chair opposite him, propped an elbow on the table, and rested her chin in her hand.

She looks like a little girl when she does that, he thought. *Not at all like a woman who'd put a bullet in the Alcalde's head if she got the chance.*

Guermoe Espinoza and his wife Beatrichia owned the Rosa Blanca. They'd raised their niece Sonia from the age of ten, after her parents had perished in a textile workshop fire. When the elected government of Eduard Hernaan had fallen to the coup, they'd offered aid and shelter to the nascent resistance. Sonia used the inn's basement storeroom as a meeting place for her faction.

"How did you find me?" Zander inquired through a mouthful of stew.

"The puercos dumped you in the alley behind the Marian House," Sonia said, "right in front of two nuns. One of them recognized you."

The Sisters of the Blessed Maria ran the only orphanage in Nue Bayona. Zander had spent most of his childhood within its austere red sandstone walls.

"The Marians help us out whenever they can," Sonia continued, "but harboring a member of the resistance within their compound...that's more risk than even they are willing to take."

Zander shook his head. "The Marians are sworn to offer sanctuary to anyone who asks," he said, "and besides, I'm not resistance. At least not yet."

"You didn't ask for sanctuary, Zan."

"How could I?" Zander slammed his spoon down. "I was unconscious, for Yesu's sake!" He pushed aside his half-eaten meal. The mix of emotions tugging at his psyche had killed his appetite. He felt hurt, betrayed, and angry all at once. "I can't believe the Sisters would turn their backs on me like that," he said quietly.

"They didn't, not really. It's just that they can't afford to have the puercos sniffing up their skirts right now. As soon as she realized it was you, Mother Elizabette got word to me. I sent Tony and Alberto to bring you here. That was three days ago."

"Diosa mia...I've been unconscious for three days?" Zander looked hard at Sonia, frowning. "Who took care of me? I mean...who...you know?" He couldn't make himself finish the sentence.

Sonia laughed. Flushed with indignation, Zander muttered, "What's so damned funny?"

"You." She pointed to the rumpled cot. "We've made love on that very bed. I've seen, touched, and tasted every part of your body, and now you're shy?" She wiped away the tears leaking from her eyes. "For your information, my aunt did all the nursing. So you needn't worry about your precious dignity."

"That's not what I was worried about." Zander knew the words were a lie, but for reasons he could not articulate, the thought of Sonia dealing with his battered, unconscious body profoundly disturbed him. Knowing Beatrichia's maternal hands had tended him came as an enormous relief.

Sonia's amused expression disappeared. "We heard about the raid on the Book and Quill," she said. "It made no sense. That place has never been a resistance hangout."

"You should've seen her, Sonnie. The polis gave Deanna a chance to leave before the trouble started, but she chose to stay and stand up for the people." Zander shivered with the remembered emotions—anger, fear, pride, and love—that accompanied the memory of that harrowing night. "I hope her stepmother didn't punish her for it."

Sensing unease in Sonia's attitude, Zander leaned forward, his gut twisting with alarm. "Did something happen to Deanna?"

Sonia bit her lower lip.

Zander reached across the table to grip her forearm. "Tell me, please. I have to know."

"I'm sorry, Zan. Deanna joined the Marian Sisters three days after you were arrested. The Alcalde announced it in the papers." She winced, plucking at his fingers. "You're hurting me."

With a whispered apology, he relaxed his grip. "That's...crazy," he said. "Dee has never been religious." His mind reeled in disbelief.

"It is strange," Sonia agreed. "No one can figure it out."

"If she is at the Marian House," Zander stared at the scarred wooden tabletop, his bruised knuckles between his teeth, "then she's not there of her own free will."

Sonia frowned. "You think the Alcalde's holding her hostage?"

"Maybe. Or...what if she's not there at all?" Zander looked up into Sonia's eyes. "What if her stepmother's done something else to her?"

"If you mean something...permanent, she wouldn't dare. Deanna's still her family."

"Family or not, Lourdessa Hernaan has always hated Dee...mierda!" A host of fearsome scenarios whirled through his mind, propelling Zander to his feet, swaying. "I have to find her."

Sonia stood and grabbed his wrist. "You're in no shape to go anywhere. You need more time to heal."

He tried to pull away, but Sonia held firm. She drew him close and wrapped her arms around him. "Zan," she whispered against his neck, "Wherever Deanna is, she's safe. She's a Hernaan. She's not like us. She'll always be safe."

For a long moment, Zander resisted Sonia's embrace, but he finally relaxed into its comforting warmth. His arms crept up to encircle her waist. "You know how I feel about her," he whispered.

"Don't say any more." Sonia pulled the blanket from around his waist and draped it across his shoulders. He allowed her to lead him back to the cot. He collapsed on the thin, lumpy mattress and she lay down beside him.

She covered them both with the blanket and placed a gentle kiss upon his sore mouth. Zander sighed. "I can't," he said.

"I know." Sonia combed her fingers through the tousled black mass of his hair. "I just want to hold you while you sleep."

He laid his head against her breasts. The faint smell of rosa blossoms clung to her skin. As he drifted into a deep sleep, he thought he heard weeping.

18
dreams and visions

In a thatched roof longhouse standing near a reed-fringed lake, a woman sat slumped in a chair cushioned with a pantera's pelt, held fast in the grip of a drug-induced vision.

She stands at the hub of a great wheel, a place she has visited many times before. Around her spins a complex whirl of colors and shapes— an infinity of possible futures, not yet set by choices made or not made. She begins her search by focusing upon a single point. Instantaneously, as if through a window, a series of grim images unfolds. She has made this search before. Though prepared, still she trembles at the scenes of destruction, misery, and death. She looks away to another point, and it too expands to reveal a slightly different, yet equally horrifying string of images. Again and again she seeks a path that leads to a different outcome, refusing to bow to despair. But no matter where she focuses her inner gaze, she finds only calamity for her people. Until....

A new path opens before her. The woman spies a shape, distorted at first, but as she sharpens her perception it resolves itself into the figure of a girl. She has seen this girl before, on other paths. She is not of the woman's people. Tall and lithe, her face is as white as chalk. Always she is running, but whatever pursues her has so far remained hidden.

The woman has not yet been able to scry far enough to discover how the girl's fate is entwined with that of her people. It is enough to know that it is.

She draws in her consciousness and wills herself to wake.

The woman roused to the sour aftertaste of the drug clinging to her dry lips. Already the effects of withdrawal roiled her stomach and head. She opened her eyes and called for her son. He came and pressed a cup into her hand. She drank the tangy liquid in one swallow, sighing as the antidote began to smooth the worst of the withdrawal.

"Did you see the girl again, Mother?" the boy asked.

"Yes, my love, I did." She tenderly stroked his face. "She's coming very soon."

"I hope she's nice and will want to stay," the boy replied.

The woman took her child in her arms and rested her cheek against his shiny black hair. "So do I," she said.

Deanna hurtles through *the sky on the back of a giant bird. The heat from the sun warms the top of her head. Her hair whips her face with a multitude of tiny, stinging lashes. The wind shrieks in her ears. She trembles with fear and exultation, sensing her life hangs in the balance, but she does not know why.*

Daring to look down past the mighty sweep of the bird's wings, she sees an unbroken landscape of sere brown grass, rippling in the wake of her mount's passage. A touch on her shoulder draws her attention to a russet-skinned boy. Long sable hair streams out from his head like silk ribbons. He sits at her back, regarding her with intelligent amber eyes.

"Hold on," the boy cries. "We're going down!" He wraps his arms around her waist.

The bird lurches sideways, pitching her and the boy headfirst into the empty air. Deanna opens her mouth to scream, but only a thin wail emerges. As the ground rushes to meet them, she clings with all her strength to the boy, as he clings to her. His embrace takes away all her fear. She senses he will keep her from dying if only she can hold on.

"I'll see you soon, alta," the boy says. Before they strike the ground, the sun winks out.

DEANNA AWOKE TO a relentless headache and a strange, sweet taste in her mouth. She opened her eyes to dancing shadows and light. A small, blurred face hovered close above hers.

"Ai, she's awake. Father!" The small face vanished; a larger one took its place.

"So she is." Deanna heard the deeper register of a grown man. She understood the words, but the inflections sounded odd.

"Where am I?" Her voice rasped like a rusty hinge.

"Do you remember what happened to you?"

"No," she whispered. She didn't remember anything beyond falling asleep beneath a choa tree — that, and a crazy dream about a giant bird and a dark-haired boy.

"You were stung by a sky jelly. It nearly had you for its dinner."

Deanna tried to push up onto her elbows, but the pain beating the inside of her skull like a mallet drove her back down, whimpering.

Who is this?

"Don't move," the man counseled in soothing tones. "You almost died. If my son hadn't intervened, your body would now lie beside the red crest you killed, and both of you'd be fertilizing the grasses."

"Thank...thank your son for me," Deanna murmured. She sensed the missing memories lurking at the edges of her mind, creeping ever closer.

"You can thank him yourself as soon as he recovers," the man replied. "Now...sleep. You need as much rest as you can get."

"My...name is...Deanna Louisa Hernaan and I...need...help." She wanted to stay awake to question her unknown benefactor, but she felt as if someone had attached stones to her eyelids.

"No more talk, Deanna Louisa Hernaan. There will be time for that later."

Yes. Later.

When Deanna woke again, her headache had subsided. Swaddled in blankets, she lay in cool dimness on what felt like a cushion of dried grass. She sat up to take stock of her surroundings and realized two uncomfortable truths — her clothes had disappeared and she was alone.

Deanna found herself in a small cave, sitting on a pallet against one wall. Rays of mote-dusted sunlight angled through the irregular entrance, illuminating a section of the wall opposite the doorway, and the pile of bundles stacked against it. Wisps of gray smoke curled up from a stone circle in the center of the floor.

So, it wasn't all a dream.

She gathered a blanket around her and tried to stand, but the sudden pain spiking her leg stopped her. She peered beneath the blanket at the neat bandage bound around her upper thigh and grimaced.

She tried again, mindful of her wound, and managed to gain her feet. She glanced around for her missing clothes, but a shadow passing across the cave mouth sent her back to huddle on her makeshift bed.

"Don't be afraid. You're safe." The shadow glided toward her and settled with feline grace beside the pallet. Deanna could now discern a face in the gloom.

"You're the boy from my dream," she whispered.

"I am called Ghost Dog. You look much improved. This is good."

He wore a sleeveless tunic of butter-yellow leather belted at the waist, brown leather leggings, and sturdy boots. His dark hair hung loose past his shoulders, except for a thin braid tucked behind each ear. He smiled and small, straight teeth flashed white in his russet face. Though he stood no taller than a twelve year-old boy, he possessed the well-muscled body of a man in his prime. Deanna felt a mix of anxiety and excitement as she realized who and what this young man must be. She pulled the blanket closer around her, wide-eyed with fascination. "Excuse me for staring," she said. "I've never seen a Tiqui before. That is what you are?"

Ghost Dog nodded. His smile broadened to a grin.

What few facts Deanna knew about the diminutive race she had gleaned from history books; the rest of her limited knowledge consisted of rumor and racist fables. Most Bayonans believed the Tiqui to be savages at best; and at worst, vermin to be exterminated.

"How many of you are there?" she asked.

"If you mean how many Tiqui exist on Nuetierra, I don't know exactly, but there are enough of us that we can survive as a people," Ghost Dog replied. "There are seven of us in this hunting band. My blood father Strong Hand leads us. We've been away from our village for over two weeks, scavenging in the ruins to the west."

The sunlight filtering in through the cave entrance flickered as another person entered.

"Dog, Father says to...oh...she's awake again."

The newcomer approached Deanna and crouched beside Ghost Dog. "This is my sister, New Moon," he said.

Even if Ghost Dog had not confirmed it, Deanna would have immediately noticed the resemblance. New Moon shared the same amber eyes and high cheekbones as her brother, but unlike him, she wore her straight sable hair cropped short. The curved yellow fang of a large predator hung suspended on twisted copper wire from each of her earlobes.

"How are you feeling?" New Moon asked.

Deanna thought for a few seconds before answering. "My thigh hurts…a lot. I'm tired and thirsty, but otherwise I feel well enough. Though I'd appreciate some painkillers, if you have any."

"We still have some *amapola* juice left. I'll get it." New Moon stood and crossed the cave where she bent to rummage among a pile of packs.

"A sky jelly's stinger, especially on a red crest like the one that nearly killed you, can be as long as a grown man's forearm." Ghost Dog indicated his own arm with a nod. "You're lucky it didn't sting you in your chest or belly. You would've bled to death before the poison killed you."

Deanna closed her eyes as the memories of the sky jelly pod flooded back. "I remember now. It grabbed me. I drew my pistol and fired. After that…things get a little fuzzy."

"We heard the shots," Ghost Dog said. "You blew a hole in the pod boss's gas bladder."

New Moon returned bearing a small glass vial. She held it out to Deanna, who accepted it with a quick, grateful smile. "We waited until the pod moved on to search the carcass. We weren't sure what we'd find," she added. "You were nearly dead from the venom. My brother made the antidote that saved your life. We've been camped here for the last two days, waiting for you both to recover."

"Both of us?" Deanna looked at Ghost Dog, confused. "Were you stung as well?"

"No, he wasn't. My brother is a special kind of healer," New Moon explained. "He takes the poisons of plants and animals and transforms them into antidotes."

"Our people call those of us who have this ability *curaros*," Ghost Dog added.

"It's a very rare gift," New Moon's face reflected the quiet pride in her voice, "only manifested in our men."

"The ability comes with a price," Ghost Dog continued. "The *curaro* falls ill after every healing. It's as if we deplete some vital essence in our own bodies during the process. Sometimes, the curaro dies, especially after a difficult healing."

"Thank you," Deanna said, fighting back grateful tears. "That you would take such a risk for a stranger…"

Ghost Dog laid a hand on her blanket-covered shoulder and squeezed. "I took an oath the day I became a curaro. I knew the risks when I decided to undergo the training."

Brother and sister shared a glance, then turned their matched golden gazes on Deanna.

"We were wondering…" New Moon began.

"How an alta girl, a city dweller, came to be out here," Ghost Dog added.

"Alone," New Moon finished. "If you're not ready to tell us now, we'll respect your decision, but…"

"We want to help you if we can," Ghost Dog said.

The grave expressions on the siblings' faces only served to underscore the subtext of their words.

They needed to know if their altruistic act might bring them trouble.

Deanna understood. "No one knows where I am." She paused and added, "I'm not here by choice."

"You don't have to talk about it now," Ghost Dog assured. "We promise we'll listen when you're ready."

"Don't make any promises to this alta, Son."

From the cave mouth, a new figure approached, man-shaped and backlit by the glow of the sun. Startled by the naked hostility of his tone, Deanna watched with trepidation as the man strode across the small space to stand at the twins' backs. He pinned her with a gaze like frost-glazed iron.

"This is our other father, Shadow." New Moon glanced up, then back at her brother.

Though New Moon had called Shadow "father," he looked no more than a dozen years her senior. His hair, the color of strong café rather than true black, brushed the neck of his forest-green tunic, sleeveless like Ghost Dog's. Two yellow dolora feathers threaded a lock he'd wound into a topknot.

Ghost Dog stood to face Shadow, his posture one of respect, yet his voice carried a hint of defiance. "Father, why do you say this?"

Anger, like a flame, kindled in Shadow's dark eyes. "She is alta, and not to be trusted."

19
a message of hope

"Faustin's called a meeting for tomorrow night," Sonia said. "And you're coming with me."

With the lunch rush past and the dinner service yet to begin, the quiet of late afternoon reigned over the common room of the Rosa Blanca. Zander and Sonia slouched side by side on stools at the kitchen end of the bar. A platter of Beatrichia's sandwiches—accompanied by mugs of strong, dark beer—rested within easy reach.

Zander scrutinized Sonia's patrician profile. "I've been asking you for months to let me in. Why now?"

"Because I think you're finally ready."

Her ambiguous response sparked suspicion. "Who knew all I had to do was survive detention to prove myself," Zander said in an even voice.

Sonia gave him a narrow-eyed look. "You really believe that?"
"Yeah. I do."

She turned away, silent. Zander took a drink and said, "I understand. You had to know for sure. I've been..." His voice trailed off as Guermoe bustled through the kitchen door, still wearing his driving cap and radiating an aura of urgency.

"Back so soon?" Sonia asked. She lifted an eyebrow and gazed at her uncle. "I thought you'd be running errands all afternoon."

"Yes, well I finished quicker than I'd expected." He turned a troubled gaze to Zander. "Son, there's a man been going 'round the neighborhood asking 'bout you."

Zander sat up as if prodded by a vaca goad. "Mierda…that can't be good."

"He came in yesterday around lunchtime, ordered a beer, and asked me if I knew you."

Cold sweat prickled Zander's brow and armpits. "Did he say what he wanted?"

"Take it easy, Son." Guermoe rested a thick-fingered hand on Zander's shoulder. "He doesn't know anything about you other than your name."

"What did this man look like, Uncle?" Sonia asked.

"Tall. Heavyset, but with muscle—not fat. Sandy brown hair and a mustache. Kinda ordinary, actually. No one you'd notice in a crowd." Guermoe pursed his lips and scratched his head. "I told him I didn't know anyone named Zander Montoiya, but I don't think he believed me."

"Why not?" Sonia asked.

"The way he looked at me…like he was annoyed, but at the same time like he understood why I'd lie. Before he left, he told me he had an important message that Zander needed to hear."

Zander took a deep breath. "If this man says he has a message for me, maybe I should let him find me."

Sonia laid her hand on Zander's forearm and squeezed. "What if he's Special Police?"

"The Specials already questioned me…" For a moment Zander couldn't speak. He felt the warm grip of Sonia's hand and the comforting presence of Guermoe's bulk beside him. "The puercos beat everything they could out of me, which was a whole load of nothing. I wouldn't have told them mierda anyway. But why send someone undercover to trap me now?"

"Maybe he's trying to trick you into leading him to the resistance," Sonia said in a soft voice.

Zander shook his head. "How could I?"

"If he comes back, what should I say?" Guermoe asked.

Zander stared at the scarred tabletop for a long, silent moment. "Tell him you know me after all. I want to hear the message, but I'll only talk to him at the Marian convent."

"Smart move," Sonia said. "If he is a poli, you'll be at the only place in the city where he can't arrest you."

Zander raised his mug to take another drink, but the look on Sonia's face, caught from the corner of his eye, stopped him. "What's wrong?"

She glanced away for a moment and then returned his gaze. The hard glint in her eyes softened with a fresh sheen of tears. "You think this man has a message from Deanna, don't you?"

The near imperceptible quaver in Sonia's voice felt like a razor drawn across his skin. "I don't know. But…yes, I'm hoping he does." Unwilling to lie, nevertheless Zander hated how his admission affected her.

"What if it is a trap?"

"Then…I don't know. But I have to go. Besides, Deanna might be a prisoner there, after all. If she is, I'll get her out…somehow."

"Damn it, Zander!" Sonia shook her head, her eyes never leaving his. She reached up to dash away the tears collecting in her lashes. "Why can't you just want to be with me?" Abandoning her stool, she strode across the deserted common room to the front door. Before Zander could call her back, she'd pushed through it and disappeared.

Zander approached the red sandstone walls of the Marian convent, his senses alert to any sound or movement. Over the imposing wooden gate of the main entrance, a single oil lamp burned, casting a pool of golden light on the threshold. Despite the day's heat, the air had grown chilly with the coming of night. Zander shivered and pulled his borrowed coat tighter. He wondered, not for the first time that night, if the man he was supposed to meet, the one who called himself Gomaz, would even show up. If he did, would Sonia's suspicion prove correct?

If Deanna was imprisoned within, then nothing else mattered but to get her free. He had to find out before Gomaz arrived.

The narrow street fronting the convent lay deserted. Hugging the wall, Zander advanced upon the gate and stepped into the guttering lamplight, the skin between his shoulder blades prickling. He pulled on a rope dangling through a hole near the top of the weathered portal. From somewhere beyond, a bell clanged.

To the sound of wood scraping against wood, a small square of darkness appeared within the central gate panel. Zander could just make out the wet gleam of a single eye peering out at him.

"Yes?" a soft voice inquired.

"Good evening, Sister. I'm here to see Deanna Hernaan. I'm a friend of hers." Zander held his breath.

The eye vanished. The metallic screech of a thrown deadbolt preceded the squeal of iron hinges. A door set within the bulk of the left gate panel swung open to reveal a small, stout woman dressed in the black gown and veil of a Marian nun, an oil lamp dangling from one hand. A silver circle within a teardrop—the *lagrima*, symbol of her divine patroness—hung on a sturdy chain about her neck. She squinted at him through thick-lensed spectacles.

"May I come in, Sister...?"

With a tiny squeak, the nun grabbed Zander's sleeve and dragged him across the threshold into a small courtyard garden. She slammed the door shut and slid the deadbolt home. Whirling on him, her spectacles flashing in the dim light of her lamp, she said, "I know you, Zander Montoiya."

Zander combed through childhood memories, searching for a name to match the fierce, round face. "I'm sorry, but I don't remember..."

"Sister Monica, you scoundrel. You used to steal candied manzaniyas and custard tarts from my pantry."

Soft, baritone laughter drifted from somewhere beyond the nun's light. A second later a well-built man clad in a long, black coat stepped out of the darkness.

Zander's heart sank. "You must be Roberto Gomaz," he said.

"And you most certainly are Zander Montoiya." Gomaz flashed an easy smile. "Smart choice, this place."

Sister Monica raked Zander with a look as sharp as razor wire. "What fresh trouble have you brought to this holy house now?"

"None, Sister. I swear." Zander took a step toward the nun, hands outstretched in supplication.

Sister Monica held aloft her lamp, illuminating Gomaz's face. "Señor, if this young miscreant is attempting to lure you into some sort of scheme…"

"I assure you that Montoiya here could not lure me into anything," Gomaz replied.

Though he'd lost the advantage, Zander determined not to abandon his set course. "Sister, is Deanna here? I need to talk to her." From the corner of his eye, he watched Gomaz for a reaction.

The nun regarded Zander with consternation. Her lips worked as if she wanted to speak, but dared not.

Gomaz intervened. "The good sister can't answer truthfully. Nor can she lie to you, Montoiya. Deanna isn't here. I know that for a fact."

Sister Monica looked both relieved and dismayed. "Mother Elizabette swore us all to secrecy." To Zander's amazement, she patted his arm and whispered, "I'm sorry."

Zander turned to Gomaz, still wary, yet yearning to know the truth. "Then you do have a message for me from Deanna."

"Would you care to come inside, Señor Gomaz?" Sister Monica asked. "You can speak to Zander in the chapel."

"We'll stay out here in the garden, thank you," Gomaz replied.

"Ring the bell when you're ready to leave, then." The nun shuffled away, taking the sole source of artificial illumination with her, plunging the garden into shadows and starlight.

"Are you...?" Zander strained to see the other man's face.

"Yes, but I'm not your enemy," Gomaz said, then added, "Hold on. I really need a cigarette." A tiny flame hissed to life in his hand, then winked out. The pungent aroma of tabac smoke filled Zander's nostrils. He could now see the poli's face revealed by the silvery light of Nayna, which had just crested the convent's tiled roof.

"Why should I trust you?" he asked.

"The fact that you aren't on your way to detention right now is as good a reason as any."

Cold sweat filmed Zander's brow. "Why would Deanna trust a Special to get a message to me?"

Gomaz raised his hand to his mouth. The glowing tip of the cigarette blazed and then subsided. "Things aren't always what they seem. Right now, all I can tell you is this. Deanna is safe."

Zander felt the knot in his gut begin to loosen. "What's the message?"

"She wants you to know that she finally understands."

Zander had loved Deanna from the first moment he'd seen her that long-ago day in Valencea Park. That love had remained constant, even in the face of her changed feelings for him. He had never let the hope die that one day, she'd give her whole heart to him again. "Where is she?" he asked, blinking back tears.

"I can't tell you that," Gomaz replied, his sympathetic tone softening the refusal.

Swelling frustration scraped at Zander's self-control, but he held fast to his temper. "You expect me to trust you, yet you won't tell me anything."

"It's for your own safety," Gomaz said, "and mine. If the Alcalde ever discovers that her orders weren't carried out, the consequences will be dire."

Zander now felt more confused than frustrated. "What are you talking about?"

Gomaz took another drag on his cigarette, his face a mask of darkness and argent light. "I've said too much already." Smoke curled, wraith-like, from his lips. Nocturnal insects among the fragrant *romara* and *sajaro* bushes whirred and clicked like a multitude of tiny machines.

Zander felt like the only thing left to do was bare his soul. "Deanna means everything to me. Please. I need to know where she is."

Gomaz let the spent cigarette drop from his hand to the ground, where he consigned it to extinction with his boot heel. He stared at Zander for several contemplative moments, sizing him up. At last he said, "Now I understand."

From high in the chapel tower, the convent bell rang the hour. Zander knew it summoned the entire community before the high altar to sing the Night Office. Soon a double score of women would be kneeling in orderly rows, their voices raised in sacred ecstasy.

"You've come too close to something that you can't be involved in," Gomaz continued, "but I'm not so jaded that I can't recognize true love when I see it. Deanna's no longer in Nue Bayona. Her life was in danger. Arrangements were made to get her out of the city. If you insist on knowing specifics, you'll only jeopardize her safety."

"The Alcalde ordered Deanna killed, didn't she?"

Gomaz lit another cigarette. "We weren't going to let that happen." *We...*

Zander immediately grasped the meaning of the plural pronoun. Gomaz might be a Special, but he was something else as well. It was to that other affiliation he referred.

Zander sensed the hidden presence of great forces at work, too rarified for the likes of him. And yet he had to try to understand, for the sake of the girl he loved. "Tell me that I'll see her again," he said.

"I sincerely hope you will."

To never again hold Deanna in his arms, or savor her unique scent, or hear her voice? That meant the condemnation of his soul to eternal misery. Zander refused to accept even the possibility. "Is there anything I can do for her?"

"Stay alive and hold fast to your love." Gomaz pinched out his cigarette and tucked the stub behind his ear. "I have to go. I'll leave first. Wait a few minutes before you follow me out."

Without bothering to ring the bell, Gomaz threw the deadbolt and opened the sally door wide enough to allow him to poke his head through. He stood unmoving for several seconds and then turned back to Zander. "Growing up an orphan must have been difficult."

Childhood memories resurfaced—clothes that never fit, knees forever bruised from kneeling on hard tile floors, cold showers in winter, the sting of a switch across his bare backside. Zander shrugged. "The nuns took care of me. Why?"

Gomaz looked back out into the street. "I have a son. It makes me sad to think of any boy growing up without his father. If you ever need to talk, get word to me through Mother Elizabette. She and I are friends."

"What? Wait, you know Mother Elizabette?" Zander reached out to seize Gomaz's sleeve, but the poli had already slipped through the gate.

"Remember. You'll never have to fear me," Gomaz said. An instant later he disappeared into the night.

20

the tiqui

"I don't know what alta means, but I can see by the way you look at me that it must be bad," Deanna struggled to meet Shadow's hostile stare without flinching. "I promise you that whatever bad thing you think I am, I'm not."

"Alta is our word for your people. The tall folk," New Moon said.

Shadow remained rooted in place, sculpted arms crossed, his expression unwavering. "You and my son are iyahuya...bonded in the way of his calling. He can't turn his back on you now."

"Thank you. I..."

Shadow cut her off. "But know this. I feel no such obligation. I don't trust you and if I find out you are trying to deceive us, I will not hesitate to do whatever is needed to stop you." With a final glance at the twins, Shadow stalked out of the cave.

Deanna exhaled and raked shaking fingers through her tangled hair.

"Shadow is my adoptive father and I respect him. But he speaks from anger and grief," Ghost Dog said, touching Deanna's shoulder. "Two years ago, an airship carrying an alta raiding party struck our village and kidnapped six of our people, including Shadow's brother, Rain."

Deanna shook her head, frowning. "I don't understand. Raiding parties from the city kidnapping your people? That can't be true. Who would do such a terrible thing, and why? It makes no sense."

The look of dismay that Ghost Dog and New Moon exchanged puzzled her. She wondered if she'd somehow given offense. "I'm sorry, did I say something wrong?"

"No," New Moon replied, tight-lipped. "We're just surprised that you'd have no knowledge of…"

Ghost Dog squeezed his sister's hand. "There'll be plenty of time to talk about that later," he said softly.

Deanna looked at each sibling's face in turn. She realized she'd unwittingly stumbled into sensitive territory. "I've lived my entire life in the Alcalde of Nue Bayona's palace, and I've never heard anything about raids," she said.

"Are you a servant of the Alcalde?" Ghost Dog asked.

Deanna laughed softly at the bitter irony of the question. "My life might be easier in some ways if that were so. No. I'm her stepdaughter."

Ghost Dog's eyebrows shot up in synchrony with his sister's.

Deanna retrieved the amapola juice, resting forgotten on her lap during the tense confrontation with Shadow. She uncorked the vial and took a hearty sip, then looked toward the pile of gear against the far wall of the cave. "May I please have my clothes back?" she said. "After I get dressed I'll tell you my entire story. Then, maybe you'll answer my questions."

New Moon tsked and shook her head. "I'm sorry for you, Deanna," she said. "Your own stepmother. Such a thing could never happen among our people. Family is sacred."

Deanna took another sip of the amapola. "Lourdessa uses fear to keep all the people of Nue Bayona in line, elites and commons alike. The resistance movement began only a few months after she stole power from my father. She hates me because the common people still love him. She believes I'll one day lead a coup against her."

"Would you? If she hadn't forced you to flee?" New Moon asked.

Deanna sighed. "I wish I could say yes, but that would be dishonest. Roberto Gomaz, the man who tried to help me, asked a similar question. The truth is, I don't think so. I'm an engineer, not a revolutionary. I spent my days going to university, looking after my sister, and tinkering with my auto."

New Moon's expressive face lit with excitement. "Then you know about machines. Our people could use your skills, Deanna. We find a great deal of ancient tech in the ruins, but so much of it is beyond our understanding."

"I don't have much experience with pre-war tech other than fuel cells, but I can try to help. It's the least I can do, after all you've done for me." Deanna corked the little vial of painkiller and set it aside. Feeling gratitude mixed with shame, she said, "I'm beginning to see that I don't know the truth about your people. I want to learn."

Ghost Dog started to speak, but the sound of voices outside the cave entrance drew his attention and brought both young Tiqui to their feet.

"Father and the others are back," New Moon announced.

"Now you'll meet the rest of our band," Ghost Dog said as he and his sister moved to greet the newcomers. After a moment's hesitation, Deanna stood, though she had to stoop to avoid scraping the top of her head against the jagged ceiling.

Shadow entered first, followed by an older man. Three others trailed after them.

"*Hausi*, Deanna. You are awake at last," the eldest said. "How are you feeling?"

Deanna recognized his voice as the one she'd heard when she first regained consciousness. Guessing the unfamiliar word was a greeting, she replied, "Hola, Señor. Much better, thank you."

Though he stood only as tall as her breastbone, the lines on the man's face and the silver threads woven through his short, dark hair and close-cropped beard spoke of his age and experience. He wore a laced brown-leather vest over a long-sleeved shirt of fine, lightweight unbleached algodon, buff leather breeches and brown boots. A set of felion claws, strung on a leather cord, decorated his neck. Deanna sensed he commanded the respect due a leader. She would show him respect as well.

"I'm called Strong Hand. I'm Ghost Dog and New Moon's blood father." He gestured to Shadow. "You've already met my co-spouse."

Deanna blinked, confused. Strong Hand laughed. "Tiqui chiefs, or *ithanis* in our ancestral tongue, are allowed more than one mate. Shadow and I are both married to the ithani of our village. I am *Natome Ehame*—First Husband. Shadow is *Nexa Ehame*—Second Husband. I know this is not the practice among the tall folk."

"No, Señor. It is not." Deanna now understood why Ghost Dog and his sister called Shadow "father."

Strong Hand named the others. "This is River, my daughter's husband." A young man with red hair and cool green eyes moved to stand beside New Moon. "Hausi," he said. Like the other men he wore a sleeveless tunic, breeches, and boots, but the dark brown hue of his leathers emphasized the comparative fairness of his skin. Struck by the contrast of his appearance, Deanna wondered if there were other Tiqui like him.

A girl not much younger than New Moon stood within the circle of Ghost Dog's arms. Her pretty, heart-shaped face remained unreadable. Her black hair fell to her slim, bare waist in a single plait threaded with blue and red ribbons. "Three Stars, my son's betrothed," Strong Hand said, as he waved the last member of the band forward.

The youngest of the group, a boy of no more than fourteen or fifteen years, gave Deanna a big smile. He seemed as eager as a puppy to move closer to her, but Strong Hand quelled the boy's enthusiasm with a firm grip on his narrow shoulder. "Red Stone, my nephew. This is his first salvage trip."

Deanna regarded the seven small people, feeling like the role of foreign emissary had been thrust upon her without her knowledge or consent. The mix of emotions she saw on their faces made her both nervous and hopeful.

"I apologize for not being here when you woke, Deanna," Strong Hand said, "but we wanted to do some hunting before sunset."

"May I sit, Señor? My leg…" Deanna's shoulders and neck had begun to cramp as well.

"Yes, of course," Strong Hand said. "I was growing weary of looking up at you anyway." He smiled and sat as she did. Shadow hunkered down beside his co-spouse, regarding her like a felion ready to pounce. The others formed a semicircle with her at its center.

"Ghost Dog was about to tell me about the Tiqui," Deanna said. "Most of the history books I've read were written after the Great War. They don't say much about you, other than to paint you as savages. The one book I did read from before the war claimed that the Tiqui were happy. Contented servants of the city dwellers…the people you call altas."

"History is always written by those in power, child." Strong Hand's air of gentle authority stirred up memories of Deanna's own father, causing a momentary pang of grief to catch at her heart.

"I have so many questions," she said.

"Which I'm happy to answer, in time. But first, you must tell me why a young alta woman is out here alone in the Wilds."

Deanna repeated her story.

After a few moments of silence, Shadow said, "How do we know you aren't lying?"

Strong Hand gave his co-spouse a sharp look. "What reason would she have to lie, Brother?"

"Perhaps she was sent out here as a spy. She gets us to trust her, we take her home, and then before we know what's happened she's betrayed us to her comrades and we find ourselves under attack." Shadow's eyes burned with such anger, Deanna trembled.

"No! That's not so," she cried. "I'm telling the truth, I swear."

"Father, listen to her." Ghost Dog laid a hand on Shadow's tense forearm. "I believe she's sincere."

"As do I, Brother," Strong Hand added. Shadow's lips compressed to a thin, hard line. His eyes still smoldered, but he said no more.

Strong Hand turned his gaze back to Deanna. "I promised to answer your questions. But first, I want to tell you some things that will help you understand us as a people."

"I'm listening," Deanna said.

"We Tiqui don't refer to the conflict that destroyed the original colonial civilization here on Nuetierra as 'The Great War,'" Strong Hand continued. "We call it 'The Liberation.' Our ancestors came to this planet from Old Earth, as yours did. But, unlike yours, ours had no choice." He paused, his gentle demeanor hardening to sternness. "The Tiqui were brought here as slaves."

Shocked into silence, Deanna could only stare in confusion at Strong Hand. His words had shattered everything she thought she knew about the colonization of Nuetierra.

"I can see this upsets you," Strong Hand said.

Trembling, Deanna looked away, trying to collect her scattered thoughts. "But our history books, our teachers, our parents..." she protested, "they all taught us that the original colonials—*including* the Tiqui—fled Old Earth to escape political persecution. To live life free from tyranny."

"All lies," Strong Hand countered. "And what else did your books and your teachers say about us?"

"Very little. Your people and mine lived together in the cities before the bombs destroyed everything. My ancestors were the technocrats and professionals. The Tiqui worked as servants and laborers—not as slaves. At least...that's what I've always believed."

Shadow snorted and shook his head. "Typical," he muttered. Deanna felt her cheeks flush. A feeling of profound shame crept over her. She could no longer look at Strong Hand or the others. She cast her gaze downward onto her still trembling hands.

"Go on," Strong Hand prompted.

"After the fighting stopped, the histories say the Tiqui refused to help rebuild civilization. They abandoned their fellow human beings and fled into the Wilds." Deanna's voice sounded weak and shaky to her own ears. It was as if the weight of the Tiqui's rejection of her official version of history bore down on her like a great stone. "Without the labor and support of your people, it took my ancestors twice as long to rebuild. No book—at least none I've ever read—explained why the Tiqui ran away."

"So the descendants of our masters have chosen to paint us as faithless traitors." Strong Hand sighed heavily. "The Great War cost the human race on this planet nearly everything, but one good came of it," he said. "My people gained their freedom. The Tiqui didn't abandon the tall folk. We escaped them."

The Tiqui elder's fingers gently brushed her wrist. Deanna looked up and where she expected to see disgust, she found only compassion. "It's no surprise that your books contain a warped version of the truth," Strong Hand continued. "Acknowledgment would mean taking responsibility for the great injustice perpetrated by your ancestors against our people. Our ancestors boarded the original colony ships as free folk, but they disembarked as slaves. How this happened is not entirely known to us, but our traditional stories hold some important clues."

"I'm ashamed to admit it, but even if every alta knew the truth I doubt it would make any difference," Deanna said. "My people don't care much about the world as it was before the war. In Nue Bayona, the elites are too preoccupied with safeguarding their privileges. It's caused tremendous resentment among the lower classes. Even now there's a resistance brewing."

"This is welcome news," Shadow said, a grim smile on his face. "If the alta are fighting amongst themselves, then perhaps they'll stop raiding our villages."

"Perhaps so," Strong Hand replied to a chorus of agreements from the others.

"Ghost Dog spoke earlier of a raid on your village by alta city dwellers," Deanna said. "I reacted without thinking. It came as such a shock to hear."

Ghost Dog glanced around at the faces of his family. "Ours is not the only village that has suffered, but we've been lucky. Only once have the alta attacked us."

"Young Tiqui are captured and sent to work the coal mines in the hills north of Nue Castila," River chimed in for the first time. "Only a few have managed to escape. The stories they bring back are harrowing."

Disgust over the profound state of ignorance she'd lived in for so long left a bitter taste in Deanna's mouth. Ripping away the blinders hurt. "My father was Lord Alcalde of Nue Bayona for many years before my stepmother overthrew him. He's a good, compassionate man. I refuse to believe he'd condone such atrocities." A sudden suspicion came over her. "When did these raids begin?"

"About six years ago," Strong Hand said.

The pieces to the ghastly puzzle fell instantly into place. Deanna knew with sick certainty where to lay blame for the entire ugly enterprise. "That's when my stepmother seized power. I'm so sorry for what your people have suffered," she said. "If only I'd known…"

Strong Hand interrupted. "You would have been powerless to stop it. One young woman alone can't hope to win against organized evil." He paused, stroking his beard with a forefinger "But a young woman with allies? That is a different tale."

21
joining the resistance

The tiny basement room beneath a Maze tavern named Lucie's sweltered with the heat of many bodies. Zander felt the prickle of sweat on his forehead and underarms. He looked at Sonia, who was fanning her face with her hand. "Do you always meet with Faustin down here?" He wiped his brow on his sleeve.

"No. The locations rotate every time. C'mon. I'll introduce you."

Zander followed Sonia down the rough plank stairs, unnerved by the combined energy of twenty pairs of staring eyes. The feeble light cast by the few candles burning in sconces on the walls made it difficult to discern faces, but he recognized two men as members of Sonia's cell—the blond, sharp-faced Antonio, who answered to Tony, and pudgy, balding Alberto. Both acknowledged him with terse nods. Most of the others wore expressions of guarded politeness.

"Comrades, this is Zander Montoiya." With gentle pressure at the small of his back, Sonia guided Zander to the center of the room. "Some of you already know he's been living at my uncle's place."

"Welcome, Zander. Faustin should be here soon." A man with a crooked nose and curling red hair caught up in a ponytail stepped forward. He wore a small pistol in a shoulder holster, and a knife with a distinctive brass hilt in the shape of a fist on his belt. He offered his hand. "I'm Ernesto. We've actually met. Or rather I've met you, though you probably don't remember."

"Ernesto was at the Rosa Blanca on the night the polis released you," Sonia said. "He supplied your morfo."

Zander shook Ernesto's callused hand. "I owe you my thanks."

"No worries." Ernesto smiled, revealing two chipped incisors. "Looks like you came through well enough."

"I did."

Ernesto turned his attention to a shaven-headed youth who'd come from behind to tap his shoulder. Sonia touched Zander's elbow and steered him into a corner. Catching her chin in his hand, he pecked her lips. "Thank you," he whispered.

Sonia's breath fluttered warm against his cheek. "It was time," she said.

Tony and Alberto emerged from the press to join them. "We wondered when you were going to bring him around," Tony said.

"She got tired of me nagging her." Zander offered his hand. With narrowed blue eyes and a heartbeat's hesitation, Tony seized Zander's fingers in a grip that felt more like a challenge than a greeting. Zander ground his teeth even as he smiled, then shook out the ache behind his back. In contrast, Alberto's soft, moist palm enveloped Zander's hand in a caress that made his stomach flutter with uneasiness.

From the far side of the room a tenor voice called, "Greetings, friends."

All conversation died. A tall figure swathed in black parted the crowd like a boat at flood tide to stand at the center of the chamber.

Zander stared in disbelief. "That's Faustin?" He had not realized he'd spoken aloud until Sonia elbowed him in the ribs.

Slender to the point of delicacy, the leader of the resistance bore no resemblance to the heroic figure of Zander's imaginings. Clad in a formal black evening coat, a white shirtwaist, and black pants and shoes, Faustin looked more like an elite dandy dressed for a formal ball. A black silk scarf wound in many layers concealed his hair. A mask of black leather, molded into the shape of a snarling pantera, hid most of his face. Only his lips and eyes remained uncovered.

"Sometimes he comes dressed in women's clothes," Sonia whispered.

"What...? Mierda." Zander shook his head.

"I hear that we have a new recruit with us tonight." Faustin's gaze fastened on Zander's face. His eyes glittered like peridot in the lamplight. Something in their depths sent a needle of ice through Zander's gut.

"This is Zander Montoiya, Sonia's friend," Ernesto said.

Faustin glided toward Zander with a dancer's grace and offered a hand sheathed in fine black kidskin. "Sonnie has told me so much about you. Any friend of hers is a friend of mine." Surprised at the strength of the resistance leader's grip, Zander reconsidered his first impression. Faustin's effeminate demeanor might be a deliberate deception designed to cause his enemies to underestimate him.

"Welcome, Zander." The warm overtones in Faustin's voice sounded inviting enough, but a wild light gleamed in his eyes. Zander was struck by the sudden feeling that he'd gazed into those same eyes before.

Faustin turned away to address the gathering. "Comrades, the time has come for another strike. The airfield attack was almost three weeks ago." Heads bobbed in eager agreement.

Zander remembered the date of the bombing with special clarity. Twenty-two years ago to the day, a disgraced young Marian Sister had died giving birth to him.

"The tyrant Hernaan refuses to take us seriously," Faustin continued, "so we must step up the pressure. We'll initiate two strikes in rapid succession. The Hall of Records and the Red Hill Police Station. The station on the twenty-third of Maio, and the Hall shortly after midnight on the twenty-fourth." Faustin turned and pointed to Sonia. "Your cell will carry out the station strike."

"But...isn't the Hall of Records full of civilians?" The words sprang from Zander's lips of their own volition. "And there are prisoners in the station," he added. "Not just polis."

The entire room went still. Zander suddenly felt like a cervena surrounded by a pack of wild perros intent on tearing him apart.

Faustin stared at Zander. For a long moment he said nothing; then he turned and addressed the room. "Our new comrade is correct." His affirmation seemed to dissipate some of the hostility. "Innocent people may get hurt," he added. "But this is war. War requires bloodshed. We can't let that shake our resolve. However," he turned back to Zander, "all precautions will be taken to ensure no civilians come to harm when the bombs detonate. Ernesto."

The red-haired man raised a hand.

"Your cell will destroy the Hall of Records."

"Right." Ernesto nodded once.

Faustin inclined his head. "You all know what to do. The puercos' fury will no doubt fuel an especially nasty retaliation. We'll need to lie low for longer than usual. I'll contact all cell leaders when I decide it's safe."

As gracefully as he'd descended, Faustin mounted the stairs leading to the basement door. Halfway up, he paused to face his followers. "Freedom never comes without a struggle. Keep the faith. We *will* win." With a pumped fist, he slipped through the door and disappeared. To Zander, it felt like a switch had been thrown and the room's main source of power had winked out.

Sonia elbowed him hard in the gut.

"Oww!" Zander rounded on her, glaring. "What the hell was that for?"

"Opening your mouth when you should've kept it shut, that's what," Sonia matched his frown with her own. "New recruits don't talk, they listen. And Maria's blessed tits, Zan...they sure as eff don't challenge Faustin's plans." Her scowl deepened. "I vouched for you, you know."

Zander kept his voice low. "Do all of you follow this *hombre* like a herd of vacas?"

"Shh...not here." Sonia looked at Tony and Alberto. "We'll meet at my uncle's place tomorrow night at seven." Seizing Zander's hand in a merciless grip, she dragged him from the tavern basement, out into the cool of the late spring night. Azure-tinted moonlight illuminated the alley behind the bar. Sonia headed for the street, her quick footsteps bouncing echoes off the walls.

Keeping pace a step behind her, Zander stared at Sonia's rigid back. "Is it so wrong for someone to point out that ordinary citizens aren't supposed to be targets?"

"Faustin is our leader. *Nobody* questions him." Sonia threw a furious look over her shoulder. "You're here to listen and follow orders. That's all."

Zander skipped ahead and blocked Sonia's path. She stopped, hands on her hips. "Why are you so angry?" he asked, clasping her forearms

"You embarrassed me." In the moonlight, her face looked ethereal and achingly beautiful, despite her anger. Or perhaps because of it; Zander wasn't sure. He longed to pull her close and kiss her until her fury melted away, but feared she would punch him.

"I'm sorry," he said. "I didn't mean to embarrass you. That's me, you know. Always wanting to be the center of attention."

Sonia shut her eyes and a growl escaped her lips. It sounded to Zander like a mix of frustration and amusement. An instant later her mouth curled up in a reluctant smile. "Madre Maria…damn you, Zander. Why can't I ever stay mad at you?"

"Because I'm so cute?" He smiled and danced away to avoid her half-hearted swing at his face. This time when she started walking again, he fell in beside her.

After a few moments of companionable silence, Zander's unsettled thoughts forced him to risk rekindling her anger. He still needed some answers. "I'm not against any of this, you know. I'm worried, that's all. It's why I'm questioning things."

"You heard Faustin. We'll take every precaution."

"How can you be sure?"

"Alberto's our demolition expert. He knows what he's doing. The blast will only damage the inside of the station. He'll set it away from the holding cells so no drunks or *putas* get hurt."

Surprised by his own ambivalence, Zander considered the fates of Red Hill's officers. "I can't believe I'm saying this, but what about the polis?"

Sonia snorted. "What about them?"

Zander slowed to a stop. "I'm wondering if there's a way to…not kill anyone, and still make our point."

Sonia looked at him as if he'd spouted gibberish. "Are you serious? Most of the polis in that station are Specials."

"I know, but some aren't. There's City Police in there too. They may bust heads, but they don't torture."

Sonia's lips twitched. The incredulity on her face slowly softened. "You're a good person, Zan." She stroked his cheek. "We'll create a diversion to draw as many of the polis as we can away from the blast. But you have to accept that some will get hurt. This is a war."

He had one final question. "How's Alberto going to get inside?"

"He works there. He's the janitor. See? We know what we're doing."

Sonia's answer laid the last of his misgivings to rest. "Seems like you do," he said. After a moment she clasped his hand and started walking once more. He matched her pace, savoring the warmth of her fingers in his.

Although satisfied that their mission would be accomplished with a minimum of bloodshed, Zander thought of yet another set of questions. "Faustin's a strange hombre. What's with the mask?"

"It's for his safety as well as ours," Sonia replied. "He hides in plain sight among the other elites. As long as we don't know his true identity, if any of us are captured we can't give him up."

"Convenient," Zander muttered. "Have you ever seen his face?"

"No." Sonia shrugged. "I don't think anyone has. Maybe Ernesto. He's Faustin's top lieutenant."

Zander turned over in his mind the memory of Faustin's peridot eyes. "He's nothing like what I imagined."

Sonia slowed. "What do you mean?"

Zander studied her profile as he spoke. "He's, well...you say he's a transvestite. I think he's more than that."

"You think he's a *mariposo*." Sonia laughed. "That's pretty obvious. What difference does it make who he sleeps with? He's a good leader."

Zander shrugged. "None, I guess."

The alley opened onto a side street lined with shabby tenements. Laughter, angry voices, and the wails of fussy babies drifted from open windows. Of the three public lampposts on the block only one gave off a feeble glow, leaving most of the area doused in darkness. As Zander and Sonia stepped out to the sidewalk, a man shambled past them, reeking of alcohol.

Only the city's most wretched souls dwelled within The Maze's twisting lanes and alleys, packed like canned fish into crumbling apartment blocks. Though streetwise and capable of defending himself in most situations, Zander would never have come to this section of town alone, or by choice. But he had to acknowledge the area's suitability for clandestine meetings. He linked his arm in Sonia's and pulled her close.

"Nervous?" Amusement colored her voice.

"Only an idiot wouldn't be," Zander replied. "How does Faustin come and go without getting mugged? He makes himself a big fat target dressed in those fancy clothes."

"Faustin takes care of the people around here, gives them food, clothes, coal oil...medicine for their sick kids."

"Oh?" Zander made no effort to hide the edge to his voice. "He sounds like a real hero." *Except he doesn't seem to mind if some of these same people end up dying for the cause.*

If Sonia noticed the hint of scorn, she gave no sign. "Don't worry. No one will bother you. You're one of us now."

The avenue known as Caya Uno separated the slums of The Maze from the less impoverished Red Hill district. The clock dominating the stone gable over the entrance to the police station struck eleven as Zander and Sonia hurried past. Zander caught a glimpse through the open door of a lone, blue-uniformed City officer sitting at the raised reception desk, head cradled in one hand.

Several more minutes of brisk walking brought them to the rear entrance of the Rosa Blanca Inn. Closing time would not come for another hour.

"Let's have a beer before we go to bed." Sonia led the way down a narrow corridor toward the common room.

Red-haired Beatrichia, round and soft with breasts like bed pillows, stood behind the bar, wiping the already gleaming ebon wood with a moist cloth. The half-dozen silver bangles adorning her wrists chimed as she moved. "I didn't expect to see you two again tonight," she said.

"We got done early. Quiet night?" Sonia settled on a barstool and Zander sat beside her. Except for the three of them, the common room stood empty.

"Oh, not so bad. We had a decent dinner crowd. Your uncle came down with one of his headaches, so he went to bed early. You kids want a drink?"

"Yes, please," Zander said.

Beatrichia laid down her rag and drew two foaming mugs from the tap. With an expert flick of her wrist, she sent them sliding down the bar to stop at Zander and Sonia's hands. "I'll be making the breakfast buns," she said. She gave them each a warm smile before disappearing into the kitchen.

They sipped their beers in silence, comfortable enough in each other's company not to need small talk. After a few minutes, Zander swiveled on his stool to face Sonia. "The police station strike...what do I do?"

"You'll be part of the diversion, along with Tony and me," Sonia replied.

"It'll have to be big. Otherwise, the polis might not take the bait."

"Don't worry. We've got it figured out." Sonia's expression, until now mellowed by drink, hardened with purpose. She pinned Zander's hand beneath hers. "Remember what Faustin said, Zan. This is war. People get hurt. Are you ready for that?"

He drained his mug. Pressing his lips to her ear, he whispered, "Let's go to bed. And I don't mean to sleep."

With a lascivious smile Sonia slid from her stool, looped her arm around his waist and pulled him toward the cellar stairs.

22
journey to reed valley

After an evening supper of roasted wild vaca tongue and a salad of *alazan* leaves, brown cup fungus and sweet *azur* berries, Deanna sat on a woven reed mat outside the cave mouth, nursing a steaming cup of blackthorn tea. The heat of the day had subsided into comfortable coolness. Neither of Nuetierra's moons had yet risen. From the velvet darkness beyond the spill of firelight, insects shrilled and clicked.

Strong Hand's words replayed themselves in her mind. *The Tiqui didn't abandon the tall folk. We escaped them.*

Shadow's seething resentment made sense. Historical injustice and the ongoing predation on the Tiqui gave his outrage an unassailable legitimacy. Deanna didn't believe in the ancient Earth proverb about inherited guilt, but she did feel some personal responsibility to help with the righting of old wrongs. How—or even if—she could, still remained to be seen.

She blew on the surface of her tea, took a sip, and made a face as she swallowed the first bitter mouthful.

"Drink it all." Like a wraith Ghost Dog materialized by her side, holding a teacup of his own. "I know it's not the best-tasting stuff, but it's a great restorative. The jelly toxin took a lot from both of us."

Deanna moved to make room for him on the mat. "It's not so bad. One could get used to it." She took another sip and shuddered. "Maybe."

Ghost Dog settled cross-legged beside her. "You don't have to sit out here alone."

"I know," Deanna replied. She gazed at the glittering infinity of stars above. "I needed time to think."

"I'll leave."

Before he could rise, Deanna snagged the hem of the young Tiqui's tunic. "Please stay."

He resettled. His warm, bare shoulder felt solid and comforting against her arm.

Deanna steeled herself and took a big gulp of tea. She swallowed and silently congratulated herself for not gagging. When she could speak again, she asked, "Is it against your customs to tell an alta how the curaro's ability works?"

"Even if it were, I'd still tell you. Once a curaro has healed someone, he's bonded—iyahuya—to that person on a spiritual and emotional level. We are like family now." Ghost Dog took a drink and set down his cup. "No one knows the exact science of it, but we believe it's linked to a unique quality found only in the blood of the curaro himself. In order to transform a poison, I must first take it into my mouth and hold it for a time. How long depends on the strength of the toxin."

"How do you know when the antidote is ready?"

"The taste of the poison changes. Most start out bitter or sour. A few are sweet, which makes them much more dangerous. Training and experience have taught me to recognize the precise moment when the transformation occurs."

Deanna shifted her injured leg into a more comfortable position, pondering the enormity of her good fortune. If she'd fled a half klim in the opposite direction, she'd be dead. "Thank you again for saving my life. It couldn't have been an easy decision."

"You're wrong," Ghost Dog replied without hesitation. "There was never a question in my mind. I took an oath."

An angry squeal drew Deanna's attention to the line of eelats tethered by the cave mouth. "How many days' ride to your village?" she asked.

Ghost Dog seemed unfazed by the animals' outburst. "From here… two. Maybe three, with the extra loads the pack eelats will have to carry."

Deanna laughed. "You mean me, don't you?"

The dark concealed the details of his expression, but she sensed Ghost Dog's smile in the lilt of his voice. "Our pack beasts are strong, but carrying you means the rest will have to assume your mount's load between them. Do you have eelats in the city?"

"Yes, but they're much bigger and used only for pleasure," Deanna replied. "My father and mother rode in the park near the palace every morning. After my mother died and Father remarried, he stopped."

"Why?" Ghost Dog asked.

Deanna tried to disguise the bitterness in her voice, but it leaked out anyway. "Because Lourdessa hates riding. She says eelats are dirty and make whoever rides them stink."

"Then I must smell awful."

Even in the dark, Deanna saw the flash of his teeth. "No, you don't, not exactly…" She bit her lip, wondering how far Tiqui rules of politeness bent toward honest answers. "Diosa mia, I haven't had a bath in days myself. I'm certain I'm the one who smells awful."

"Well…"

After a moment's charged silence, they burst into helpless laughter. To Deanna, the sensation of genuine merriment after so many days of darkness felt like salvation.

She wiped her streaming eyes and tried to think of a witty response, but the arrival of Ghost Dog's betrothed refocused her attention.

"I thought I'd come out and join the fun," Three Stars said. Ghost Dog held out his hand to steady his betrothed as she sat beside him. "What has you two laughing so hard?" she asked with a smile.

"Deanna and I are just admiring each other's aromas." Ghost Dog replied.

Three Stars leaned close and sniffed Ghost Dog's neck, then grimaced. "You could use a bath, my love. Deanna, why don't we drag him to that little water hole over by the choa trees and throw him in?"

"What?" Ghost Dog gasped in mock horror. "But...it's full of algae."

"I hear algae's very good for the skin," Deanna said, trying to sound serious but having no success.

"When we're married, I won't allow you into our bed smelling like you do now," Three Stars declared. "Do the alta bathe every day, Deanna?"

"Most of the people I know do," Deanna replied.

Ghost Dog stood and pulled his future wife close. "Foul-smelling or not, you still love me," he said.

"Ancestors help me, I do." Three Stars caressed his cheek. The firelight from the cave entrance silhouetted the two young Tiqui as they melded in a passionate embrace.

Sensing that the lovers desired some privacy, Deanna drained her teacup in three gulps. "I'll leave you two alone." She rose, limped past them to the entrance of the cave and turned to wish them a good night, but Ghost Dog had already led a giggling Three Stars away into the darkness.

For two days Strong Hand and Shadow led the band east toward a range of low, forested hills. Deanna's wide-backed mount, a bay with the ironic name of Slim, bore her with martyred sighs, plodding between

Ghost Dog's gelding Grim and New Moon's mare Swift Foot. The Tiqui passed the time by sharing stories and songs. Deanna found them eager to hear about life in Nue Bayona, and about her life in particular.

"This stepmother of yours...how was she able to overthrow your father?" Strong Hand asked. "Surely he had allies and soldiers to protect him?"

"Lourdessa put her plans into place over many months," Deanna replied. "The Chief of Nue Bayona City Police is her brother-in-law. She bribed half the city council, and those she couldn't turn through greed she had arrested and imprisoned alongside my father."

"So, your father still lives," Ghost Dog said.

"Lourdessa keeps him in a cell below the mayoral palace. He's been there for six years now. She lets me and my sister visit every couple of months."

"Why keep him alive?" Shadow said. "She should just kill him and be done with it."

"Maybe she still loves him in a warped sort of way. I don't truly know. I live in constant fear she'll change her mind." Deanna glared at the back of Shadow's head. "Despite what you think, my father is a good man. He had nothing to do with the raids on your people. They started after the coup. I'm certain my stepmother and her brother are behind them."

Shadow twisted in his saddle to face Deanna. "That doesn't matter, alta. They are all your family."

Deanna opened her mouth, an angry retort on her lips, but Strong Hand spoke before she could.

"Peace, Brother. Deanna is our guest."

Shadow turned his back, leaving Deanna shaking with frustration. He ignored her the remainder of the day and spoke only once to her that evening as they made camp. "Tomorrow, we will arrive home and then, alta, my wife will decide what to do with you."

For most of the night Deanna lay sleepless in her borrowed blanket, wondering if she should leave the band now to take her chances in the Wilds or stay and eventually face the judgment of the Tiqui ithani. If she harbored the same sentiments against the altas as her junior husband, Deanna wondered about her chances, even if Strong Hand spoke up for her.

She eventually fell into an exhausted slumber. When Ghost Dog woke her at sunrise, she arose with her mind still unsettled. After a cold breakfast of vaca jerky and bread, while the band went about the task of breaking camp, she sought out Strong Hand, hoping for reassurance. She found him with his nephew Red Stone, redistributing the loads between the pack eelats. "Señor, may I speak with you?"

"Of course." Strong Hand tightened a cinch and told Red Stone, "Go help River with the mounts." The boy gave Deanna a sunny smile before loping away. Strong Hand faced her, radiating warm expectancy. "What is it?"

"You've been nothing but kind to me, and Ghost Dog saved my life," she began, "but I don't think I can expect such a welcome from all your people. Your co-spouse showed me that." She looked down, feeling suddenly reticent.

"Go on," Strong Hand gently prompted.

"I'm worried your ithani will turn me away."

"That won't happen, Deanna. You are a fellow human being in need of our help. My wife is wise and merciful. She could no more turn you away than she could banish one of our own. You and my son are iyahuya. In time, you'll grow to understand what that means."

Strong Hand's words fell like a gentle, warm rain on Deanna's psyche, washing away her gnawing uncertainty and replacing it with fresh purpose. She would remain with the Tiqui, seek acceptance and immersion into their culture, and recuperate. And then….

She met the elder's gaze. "I don't know what my future holds, Señor, but I'm grateful to you for giving me time and a safe place in which to find out."

Strong Hand reached into one of the packs. "I have something that belongs to you," he said, handing her Roberto Gomaz's pistol.

"You found it," Deanna exclaimed. "I promised I'd return this to its owner, if possible. Now, there's a chance I can keep my promise." She tucked the pistol into her waistband. The return of the weapon spoke of Strong Hand's trust. "Thank you," she said.

"We're ready to go, Father," New Moon called from across the clearing.

Strong Hand smiled and gestured to their waiting mounts.

Midday found the band following a game trail winding through a thick stand of trees, the likes of which Deanna had never seen before. The sturdy trunks and branches were sheathed in a thick outer layer of the deepest scarlet, topped with bushy crowns of brilliant green leaves.

"They're called bloodbark," Ghost Dog explained. "If we're lucky, there'll be some ripe fruit today."

The group stopped so Red Stone could shinny up one of the larger specimens. He cut loose a cluster of bulbous orange fruit that hung near the top. The band ate their midday meal in the saddle, so as not to waste time, feasting on the fruit for dessert. Deanna peeled away the tough rinds to get at the soft red pulp, and quickly decided she had never tasted a fruit quite so delicious.

As the day wore on, the band moved deeper into hills clothed with towering stands of broad-leafed roble and needle-bearing pinya trees. Sunset found them at the base of a sheer rock face that rose many meters above the tree line. Strong Hand led the group to a fissure in the rock barely wide enough for the eelats to slip through. Slim pushed his way in, scraping Deanna's legs against the rough stone. The fissure opened into a narrow, twisting defile.

Less than three paces beyond the opening, near-total darkness reigned. Deanna clutched at her mount's reins, straining to see what lay ahead. She willed her heart to cease pounding.

"Don't worry, Deanna," Ghost Dog called out from behind her. "The eelats know this trail as well as their own arses." Grateful for his intuition, Deanna chuckled, feeling some of her anxiety evaporate.

An instant later a high-pitched wail sounded from somewhere ahead, followed by an answering call from Strong Hand. Deanna peered up into the gloom, wondering how many Tiqui sentries crouched hidden in the rocky crevices above. Though she couldn't see them, she imagined the heat of their gazes boring into the top of her skull. Her eelat snorted and jerked on its reins. Deanna forced her hands to relax, easing the pressure on the animal's mouth.

The eelats pressed on, sure-footed even in the darkness. Eventually the dark began to lift, giving way to a rosy glow. The group rounded a bend and emerged into the full light of the setting sun. They had reached the end of the defile. A hard-packed trail led from the base of the cliff, down a gentle slope, and onto the grassy floor of a small vale.

Near the center, sheltered among scattered trees, stood several dozen thatched-roof wooden houses, along with a few larger structures that looked like barns or storage buildings. A pair of windmills and a round, stone tower that Deanna guessed was a grain silo anchored the perimeters. Neat plots of cultivated land spread beyond the settlement like a patchwork quilt across the valley floor. A small, reed-fringed lake shimmered like a mirror beyond the far edge of the fields. The bucolic scene filled Deanna with something she had not felt in a very long time.

Peace.

"Welcome to Reed Valley," Ghost Dog said, smiling.

4

23
the best-laid plans

Beneath a low ceiling of bruised nimbostratus clouds, the city of Nue Bayona was shrugging off the somnolence of siesta. Steam-powered autos, commercial trucks, and vaca-drawn wagons trundled along rain-slicked streets, while office clerks in dark coats and shop girls beneath colorful umbrellas hurried back to work. Laborers swallowed the last of their midday sandwiches and café and returned to their tasks. Merchants were unlocking doors and raising awnings.

In the privacy of his well-appointed office at Nue Bayona Cathedral, His Eminence, Archbishop Javyer De La Roha, sat at his desk, struggling with his conscience as he had so many times in the days since the airfield bombing. He sighed and leaned back in his cushioned leather chair, ignoring the little aches in his once athletic frame—now gone soft from disuse—to ponder the moral dilemma at hand.

To allow Faustin's depredations to continue unchecked would result in the spilling of more innocent blood. And yet there was the greater good to consider. All just wars created martyrs. The responsibility of those to whom fell the prosecution of the war was to assure that the sacrifices of the innocent held meaning and purpose.

His personal copy of the Scriptures of the Madre lay open amid a clutter of papers on the desk before him. He had never yet failed to find solutions to any question or problem within its splendidly illuminated pages, but so far, a clear-cut answer had proven elusive.

For the third time that hour, De La Roha folded his thick, square hands in prayer to the Blessed Madre. A soft knock upon the door interrupted his devotions. "Come," he called.

"The Castilians have arrived," Saviero Nunyez announced. He entered the room, clutching a worn brown leather valise to his chest. He crossed to the cane-backed visitor's chair beside De La Roha's desk and sat. They needed no formalities; both men related to each other as comrades since forming their covert alliance against Lourdessa's illegitimate rule over five years ago.

The Archbishop closed the holy book and pushed it to one side. "Any chance Sedano can sway the Alcalde into abandoning her course?"

"None," Nunyez replied. "She is determined and will take no counsel, not even from her brother."

"Well, then. It's in the hands of the Madre and Her Son." De La Roha spun his chair to glance at the gilded, amethyst-studded lagrima hanging on the wall behind his desk. "All we can do now is stay our course." With a rustle of purple silk, he rose and went to a sideboard behind his desk, where he poured brandies for himself and Nunyez. "Any news of Eduard's daughter?" he asked.

"Our plans for her have gone slightly awry." Nunyez held out his hand to accept the snifter offered by the Archbishop. In response to De La Roha's dismayed exclamation, the Minister added, "The situation is under control, thank the Madre. She is safe for the moment, though not in an ideal location."

"What happened? Where is she?"

"Read for yourself." Nunyez opened his valise and passed an envelope to the Archbishop. "Our agent's report."

De La Roha perused the account in silence. He handed the paper back to Nunyez. "Madre preserve...A wild sky jelly attack," he murmured. "It's a miracle she survived. Does Gomaz know?"

"I informed him myself," Nunyez replied.

The men shared a moment of silence and the pleasure of fine brandy, each wrapped in his own thoughts.

Nunyez spoke first. "How is Gabril Ledesme?"

"Getting better each day," the Archbishop replied, resuming his seat. "He nearly died, which would have been a tragic loss. He still blames himself for the theft of the data crystals, even though I've assured him I don't hold him responsible. That culpability rests with me."

"You couldn't have known the Sedanos had an agent so close to him," Nunyez said. "This man Calderone had worked for Ledesme before. His cover was perfect."

De La Roha drained his glass, but the warmth of the brandy did little to soothe his raw conscience. "That still doesn't absolve me. I'm the head of the Church. I should have known."

"Nevertheless, we still remain one step ahead of Lourdessa," Nunyez assured him. "As long as she continues to be preoccupied with the Castilians and convinced that Faustin's street rebellion is the true domestic threat, she will never think to look elsewhere."

De La Roha frowned. "My failure to recognize Calderone isn't the only thing weighing on my mind. Faustin has crossed a line, Saviero. If he grows any more reckless..."

"Then, I'll rein him in." Nunyez swirled the golden liqueur in his snifter. "I don't want to do that, if at all possible. He provides us with too good a cover."

"I'm pleased you agree. I can't condone much more bloodshed." De La Roha settled into his chair, hands folded on the soft bulge of his belly fat. "So. What now?"

"We go forward with our plan. Lourdessa thinks she has the advantage, now that she's gotten the Annihilator schematic, but, in truth, we hold the ace. Not her."

"What do you mean?"

Nunyez once again reached into his valise and withdrew a thick sheet of folded paper. "Olivas retrieved a piece of data from one of the crystals when his minder wasn't looking. He did not give it to Lourdessa. Instead he brought it straight to me." He spread the sheet open atop the Archbishop's desk, smoothing it flat with his hand. "This is a copy of the original AX238 schematic, provided to me by Olivas. I thought you should see what Lourdessa intends to replicate."

Drafted in crisp black ink strokes, the diagram itself seemed infused with some of the deadly power of the ancient high-tech machine it depicted.

Six slim, jointed legs supported an armored elliptical body, from which sprouted an array of energy-powered weaponry too advanced for duplication. De La Roha felt a mild frisson of dread travel the length of his spine as he leaned forward to scrutinize the image. "I've seen diagrams of the Annihilator before, of course. But never this detailed. For some reason, seeing a fresh rendering like this…it makes it feel so much more immediate."

"Olivas believes this file was meant to be viewed as a three-dimensional interactive image," Nunyez explained, "but his computer is simply too old to read the crystal properly. The detail you see is a mere fraction of what the file actually contains."

The Archbishop sighed. "The Church's computers are not any better, I'm afraid." In an awed whisper, he read from the diagram's legend. *Forward optical sensor array. Satellite transmission receiving dish. Plasma cannon. Laser rifles…* Diosa mia. The tech level of this thing is so far beyond our modern capabilities to even understand, let alone replicate. Lourdessa is mad to think otherwise." He looked at Nunyez. "She truly believes Olivas can do this?"

"Not Olivas," Nunyez replied. "Lourdessa plans to coerce Eduard into designing her a contemporary facsimile and then supervise the construction of a working prototype." He tapped the schematic with a finger. "With conventional guns and grenade launchers augmented by salvaged ee-cannons, it will be as fearsome a machine for this age as its predecessor was for the last. Eduard will have no choice but to make it so. Though the task weighs most bitterly upon his conscience."

It took little effort for De La Roha to deduce what leverage the Alcalde would use on her husband to secure his cooperation. His heart ached for the man he still considered a friend. "You said Olivas brought you a piece of information that he's kept hidden from Lourdessa. Is this the ace you speak of?"

"Indeed, it is the very lynchpin of all our plans," Nunyez replied. "The Chief himself discovered a partially degraded vid file containing what seems to be location coordinates for an intact AX238, deactivated and buried somewhere in the Siyera Desert."

"Praise Maria and Yesu," De La Roha exclaimed, his entire body shot through with electric excitement. "The Church has long suspected at least one Annihilator survived the war. We've been searching for it for decades. No wonder the Sedanos have infiltrated their agents into our salvage teams." He stared in grim silence at Nunyez for a heartbeat, then added, "If Lourdessa and her brother had gotten their corrupt hands on that file…"

"Fortunately they did not." Nunyez tossed back the remainder of his brandy and placed the glass on De La Roha's desk. "What we need to do now is try to pinpoint a more precise location. We can't move forward otherwise. The Siyera is simply too vast to search at random. Gomaz is prepared to leave at a moment's notice, once we know where to look."

The Archbishop pointed to the brandy decanter, but the Minister shook his head. "I'll put my best researchers on it. But even the Church's archives aren't complete," De La Roha said. "A great deal of military knowledge was deliberately destroyed during the immediate post-war years. The most we can hope for is an approximate position."

"Then that will have to suffice."

To discover and gain control of an Annihilator for the purpose of safeguarding the world had long been the Church's most pressing secular mission. De La Roha fingered the chain of office hanging around his neck. The solid gold links felt heavier than usual.

Are we doing the right thing?

He wondered. Why, when the goal was nearly within reach, did he suddenly feel such a growing ambivalence? To awaken a machine that had the power to destroy entire cities...

Is this wise? Or simply rank hubris?

Aloud, he said, "I'm beginning to wonder if this plan is truly the right path, Saviero. What if we find we can't control this thing? Then what?"

Nunyez cocked a thin eyebrow. "Are you getting cold feet, Javyer?"

"I'm just questioning," De La Roha replied. "I have that right and the duty to do so. We're planning to retrieve and activate a pre–Great War Annihilator. We can't pretend there won't be repercussions."

"I understand your concerns. But what other choice do we have?" Nunyez refolded the schematic and tucked it back into his valise. "Once the Alcalde has built her squadron, she will be nearly invincible. Nue Castila will fall and all the rest of the smaller towns on the continent will surrender without a fight. The Sedanos will claim undisputed hegemony over all of inhabited Nuetierra. But as terrifying as their machines will be, one pre-war AX238 can stand against an entire fleet of steam-driven replicas. We can stop Lourdessa in her tracks."

De La Roha's uncertain gaze met Nunyez's dark eyes. "Pray to the Madre that it be so," he said.

WITH A PHALANX of black-cloaked Specials at their backs, Lourdessa and Alehan waited in the Arrivals lounge at Nue Bayona Municipal Airfield, watching through the floor-to-ceiling windows as the antiquated airship bearing the Castilian envoys drifted toward a landing.

Two hours earlier, a detachment of Specials had descended on the airfield. With determined efficiency they had cleared the entire terminal, leaving angry citizens with derailed travel plans to stand in grumbling knots outside the doors. Most of the workers had been ejected as well. Only a skeleton crew remained to service the inbound ship, and see to the Alcalde's needs.

Specials stood guard at both the entrance and exits, their gleaming black neural batons held at the ready. The sour tang of fresh paint lingered in the air. This part of the complex had been heavily damaged by the terrorist attack three weeks ago. Repair crews had only recently finished replastering the walls and ceiling.

The late afternoon sun burnished the jelly's translucent skin to glorious, gold-shot iridescence, but cold resolve rendered Lourdessa immune to the beauty of the moment.

"Shouldn't we be out on the tarmac?" Alehan asked.

"No. Let them come to us."

Mother and son continued to watch in silence as the complex operation unfolded.

The ground crew, comprising a dozen men in gray coveralls, fanned out within the shadow below the approaching ship. Their shouts, intermingled with the ultra-low frequency groans of the sky jelly, floated in through the open breezeway doors.

When compared to the modern, steam-driven vessels of the Nue Bayona Air Service, the Castilian ship seemed to Lourdessa a small, poor thing. The jelly's dorsal crest had faded from bright red to rust-brown, a sign of advancing age. It looked no more than twenty meters from rostrum to tail, less than a third the length of a commercial, steam-powered vessel. The tiny cabin, secured by metal clamps to rings in the leather harness encircling the jelly's gas-filled body, was constructed of wood, rather than riveted steel. Lourdessa doubted it held more than six people in total, passengers and crew together.

In contrast, the Sedano family's private airship could carry twenty guests and six crew members with ease.

Two of the ground crew rushed toward a tall wooden landing cradle, pushing a cart containing the dismembered carcass of a freshly slaughtered vaca. They wheeled the cart in place beside the cradle and secured it to the frame with heavy chains.

Smelling the blood of its reward, the jelly released a burst of malodorous gas and sank closer to the landing cradle. Eight helmeted crewman stood ready to grab the cables dangling from its harness. The tentacles sprouting from its head like a ropy beard thrashed against the tough netting that restrained them. Though smaller than its wild cousin, and de-venomed at hatching, a domesticated jelly still posed a significant danger to its handlers. One swipe of a tentacle could crush a man's skull as if it were made of paper.

With a final spurt of flatulence, the creature settled onto the cradle. The ground crew secured its harness to metal rings protruding from the cradle's sides. The passenger cabin now rested on the tarmac atop three sturdy landing struts.

Two crewmen wheeled a set of stairs to the cabin's doorsill. The door swung outward and a heavyset man dressed in a dark-blue frock coat, trousers, and black silk top hat hurried down the stairs. A taller, slimmer man in spring-weight bleached linen and a straw panama followed at his heels, carrying a leather valise. With quick strides they crossed the tarmac and entered the lounge.

"Dama Alcalde," the heavyset man said as he swept into the room. He halted before Lourdessa, doffed his hat and sketched a small, quick bow. "I'm Jon Santo. Alcalde Stefan sends his warmest greetings. May I present my aide," he nodded to the taller man, "Dominic Higar."

"Dama." Higar raised his panama off a lush thatch of blond curls.

Lourdessa rested a light hand on Alehan's shoulder. "This is my son, Alehan Estes. He serves as one of my most trusted advisors."

Outside on the tarmac, the ground crew had released the jelly's tentacles to allow it to feed. For a few moments, Lourdessa watched the creature as it lifted dripping gobbets of meat into its eager maw, then, with a tiny shudder, she turned away. "Señors Santo and Higar," she said, "my car is waiting outside to take us to the palace." She gestured toward the exit doors. "Shall we?"

24

unintended consequences

"Help...a man's just been hit by a car!" With one foot on the threshold and the other on the sidewalk, Zander paused in the doorway of the Red Hill precinct office, a look of horror on his face. He waved his arm toward the street with what he hoped was a convincing air of panic. "Hurry...he looks like he's gonna die!"

The desk sergeant and another officer had already rushed into the reception area, drawn by the shrill squeal of skidding tires. They pounded past Zander out to the sidewalk and ran down the block toward a car surrounded by a crush of people. Glancing around the room to assure himself that no civilians remained in the danger zone, Zander started walking toward the commotion.

Rising winds gusted and swirled around him. Above, clouds like piles of purple fleece darkened the sky. The air smelled of ozone. The skin on the back of his neck prickled in the electrified breeze. He calculated he had less than five minutes to get clear of the station.

The epicenter of the disturbance lay in front of a nearby public laundry. From all directions people were rushing to investigate, swelling the crowd that already blocked the flow of traffic. He slowed his pace, seeking a way around the chaos. He worried that if he attempted to push through the crowd he might end up getting stuck. Paused at the fringe, Zander glanced back at the station. A few polis had emerged and were standing in the dimming shadow of the clock tower, smoking cigarettes, and watching the action.

What's taking so long? he wondered.

His primal instinct to flee from imminent danger grew more difficult to ignore with each passing second, but Zander had sworn an oath to Sonia see this thing through. He took a deep breath and waded into the chattering crowd, pushing his way to the front.

He broke through in time to see the desk sergeant drop into a crouch beside the front tire of an expensive convertible sedan. A man wearing shabby dun coveralls lay sprawled beneath the sedan's front bumper. A blond woman dressed in a faded, floral-print dress knelt beside him, wailing. Another man, this one dressed in a fitted black chauffeur's uniform, wrung his hands and paced beside the sergeant. His long face looked as pale as moonshine beneath the crisp brim of his cap.

The second poli stood facing the crowd with outstretched arms. He brandished his baton and yelled at the crowd to stay back.

"Hey...that's my brother and sister!" Zander shouted. He tried to duck beneath the poli's upraised arms, but the officer threatened him with the baton. "Please," Zander insisted. He didn't have to feign the urgency in his voice and expression. "Let me through."

The officer glanced back at his superior, who nodded in consent. He grudgingly lowered his arm and allowed Zander to pass.

Tony lay on his back, arms and legs akimbo. His eyes were closed and his mouth hung open and slack. For one terrible moment Zander feared the ruse had gone horribly awry. He knelt on the blacktop beside a weeping Sonia. She'd tucked her dark hair beneath a blond wig and straw bonnet. "Is he...?" he whispered, as Sonia flung her arms around his neck. Zander saw her sly wink.

"Our poor brother," she moaned.

"I didn't see him, Officer, I swear," moaned the man in the chauffeur's uniform.

From the back seat of the sedan, a woman's voice called out, "Is he all right, Sergeant?"

Tony let out a loud groan and sat up, clutching at his head.

The sergeant rose to his feet, regarding Tony with narrowed eyes. "You hurt, hombre?" he asked. "D'you need a doctor?"

"Naw. I'm all right," Tony mumbled, still playing the role of dazed accident victim.

Zander pressed his lips to Sonia's ear. "We've got to get the eff out of here...now."

She nodded. He slipped his arms beneath Tony's shoulders, pulling him to his feet. Sonia stood as well, maneuvering herself between her accomplices and the two officers.

Zander glanced back at the station, then at Tony and Sonia. The look in their eyes told him they were all thinking the same thing.

Something's gone wrong.

Until now he'd kept his anxiety in check, but it was beginning to slip its leash. If Sonia had made contingency plans to deal with possible failure, she hadn't discussed them with him.

Some polis could smell fear in a man. Zander prayed this sergeant wasn't one of those.

"Everyone involved needs to give me their statements," the sergeant said. He pulled a notebook and pencil from his hip pocket.

His partner yelled again for the crowd to disperse.

As the chauffeur opened his mouth to speak, a mighty roar rent the air and reverberated off the façades of the buildings. The pavement heaved underfoot, sending Zander sprawling. A maelstrom of dust and flying debris engulfed him. Something hard slammed into his temple. For a few moments the world spun and darkness threatened to take him.

He fought off the swoon. Blinking grit from his eyes, he scrambled to his feet. The scene that confronted him wrung a shocked cry from his lips. The entire front wall of Red Hill Station lay demolished in the street. Bodies sprawled like broken, discarded dolls amidst the wreckage. An injured poli—the bloody and blackened tatters of his uniform flapping in the wind—staggered from the shattered interior. He swayed for a heartbeat and crumpled to the ground.

Zander drifted toward the ruins past people covered in plaster like powdered sugar. Some stood in dazed silence. Others sobbed, while still others lay bloody and unmoving on the rubble-strewn pavement. He bent down to help an elderly woman to her feet. Multiple, fine lacerations scored her cheeks and forehead. She pawed at his shoulders, her face a mask of fear. Zander could see her lips moving but her voice sounded muffled, as if his ears had been stuffed full of algodon wool.

He shook his head in confusion. She frowned and turned away. He moved on.

The paralyzing shock of the explosion had begun to wear off, and all around Zander, the crowd was disintegrating. He froze in his tracks, his arms wrapped around his body in a defensive hug as he was buffeted on all sides by running people. From out of the chaos, a hand seized his forearm and yanked him around.

It was Sonia.

Her wig and bonnet had disappeared. Fine white dust coated her clothes and the tangled locks of windblown hair whipping her face. She fixed Zander with eyes that held no fear. Grasping his hand, she turned and together, they let the stream of fleeing humanity pull them along in its wake. From somewhere behind, Zander could hear the muffled wail of approaching sirens.

By the time they reached The Maze side of Caya Uno, they were running. Sonia led the way off the main road onto a side street, then into a narrow, trash-strewn alley between twin rows of dilapidated tenements. Feeble light from the curtained windows overhead did little to banish the shadows. Shoulder to shoulder, they paused and leaned against a decayed brick retaining wall, breathing hard. A few moments later another figure entered the alley.

Revealed within the split second duration of a lightning flash, Tony limped toward them, his mouth stretched in a grimace of pain. He joined them against the wall. Pointing to his ankle, he said, "I think it's sprained." His voice sounded to Zander as if it came from the bottom of a well.

Zander rubbed his ears, trying to massage away the ringing caused by the blast. The effort set off a ferocious sting at his temple. Something hard was lodged beneath his skin. Ignoring the pain, he picked at the mysterious bleb until he'd worked it free and then held it up to his eyes.

It took a moment for his brain to register that the small, blood-smeared object in his grasp was a human tooth.

Like a jab to the solar plexus, the sight of it stopped his breath and shattered the last remnants of his emotional detachment. He pushed away from the wall and glared at Sonia. "It wasn't supposed to be that big." He flicked the tooth away, sick with horror. "You said Alberto knew what he was doing, that he'd make it so only a few polis got hurt."

"Alberto did exactly what he was supposed to do," Sonia replied. The shadows hid her expression, but her tone confirmed Zander's suspicion.

"Diosa mia...You lied to me." He couldn't decide which felt worse — his anger over being manipulated or his hurt from knowing that, despite everything, she still didn't trust him enough to tell him the truth.

"I'm sorry." Sonia's voice sounded sad, yet uncompromising.

Fresh guilt for the part he'd played in bringing about the carnage only added to Zander's fury. "Innocent people are dead, Sonnie."

"Keep your effing voice down," Tony hissed. "We did the job like we were supposed to, Montoiya. Stop being such a *gatito*."

"Better to be a gatito who cares about not hurting shop clerks and old ladies than a cold-blooded *pendayho* like you."

Zander sensed, rather than saw, the jab Tony aimed at his face. With reflexes honed to feline quickness by his years on the street, he dodged the blow and seized the other man's forearm before he could recover. Tony growled and tried to pull free, but Zander dug his fingers into the muscle and held fast. "I don't want to fight you," he pleaded, "but I will if I have to."

"Yesu's balls, cut it out, both of you." Zander felt Sonia squeeze between him and Tony. She planted a hand against his chest and shoved, breaking his hold on the other man. Zander staggered back a step. "We don't have time for this!" Sonia said. "We've got to get away from here before the polis come sniffing." She turned to face Tony. "Can you make it back to my uncle's place?"

Tony sucked in a pained breath. "Have to."

Sonia reached out to take Zander's hand, but he refused her touch. The hurt her deception had created was too sharp, too immediate. It rendered even that small intimacy unbearable. She shook her head and started down the alley, picking her way around sodden heaps of garbage.

Tony flicked a cold glance at Zander. "You coming?"

After a heartbeat's hesitation, Zander followed.

25

battle of wills

Jourdessa sat at the head of the conference table, drumming lacquer-hardened nails on the arm of her chair. From her vantage point she eyed Jon Santo as he stared out the casement window at the fearsome display of natural fury lighting up the skies over the city. A late spring storm—blown up from the south—hurled violet electrical discharges toward the ground from the bottoms of fat purple clouds. No rain fell to rinse the coal soot from the air. This was a rare, dry storm, but its powerful winds would scour the worst of the pollution from the Nue Bayona basin.

The Alcalde had deliberately chosen the smallest and least ornate of the palace's three conference rooms for their parleys, but not because she wished to demean Stefan's envoys. Though they'd tried to hide it, she'd seen the envy and resentment in Santo and Higar's faces as they'd taken in the opulence of the palace's public spaces since their arrival several days ago. Discontent, she'd realized, would make them far less willing to accept concessions. She hoped a sparser, more intimate chamber would serve to blunt some of their acrimony.

A simple rectangular roble-wood table, large enough to seat sixteen, took up most of the room. The matching chairs, though plain, had cushioned seats. An arrangement of dried leaves and flowers in a blue ceramic vase stood at the center of the table. At a sideboard, a young palace attendant poured iced limón water from a glass pitcher into tumblers and placed them on a metal tray. She circulated about the room, setting a tumbler at each place before returning to her own chair by the door.

Mari sat behind and slightly to Lourdessa's left, pen and notebook at the ready, a telephone on a small table next to her elbow. Alehan had taken the seat to his mother's right, directly across the table from Dominic Higar. His languid hazel gaze roamed the other man's face, a tiny smile curving his lips. From their first meeting, Alehan's attitude toward Higar had been one of admiration, bordering on an obsequiousness that irritated Lourdessa.

"The storm's worsening," Santo remarked. "I'm worried for our jelly."

"Your jelly is safe, Señor. It's being well provided for in a covered stall," Lourdessa assured.

Santo left the window and returned to his seat beside Higar. "Thank you, Dama," he said. Removing a pair of spectacles from his breast pocket, he put them on and began to scan a sheet of notations handed to him by Higar.

Lourdessa retrieved her own notes from their previous day's discussions and made a show of studying them, though she had no real need. Her position had been set long before the Castilians' arrival and would not change.

Outside the storm raged. The windows rattled in their frames. Mari stifled a cough and Higar discreetly squirmed beneath Alehan's frank perusal, his eyes fixed on his own notebook.

At last Santo laid his paper aside and spoke. "Dama Alcalde, we've been negotiating for several days now. Our demands are not unreasonable. We supply much of the unskilled and all of the skilled labor. Why should we not share equally in the profits?"

"Señor Santo," Alehan switched his attention away from Higar to his superior. "My great, great grandfather and his brothers discovered the gas and coal deposits in the hills above Nue Castila when your city was little more than a squatter's camp."

Santo's bushy salt-and-pepper eyebrows met over the bridge of his nose as deep furrows cut across his forehead. Alehan's mild insult had not gone unnoticed by either of the Castilians. Higar frowned as well.

Lourdessa continued. "My family supplied the technological expertise and the money needed to get the coal and gas out of the ground."

"Your family grew rich exploiting those whom you call squatters," Santo replied. "Those men were our great, great grandfathers. Many of them got hurt or killed in those early days. Without their willing labor, the coal and gas would've stayed in the ground."

"May I also point out that there were Sedanos who died as well," Lourdessa countered.

Alehan's languid smile grew smug. He said, "The Sedanos raised the living standards of every man, woman, and child on this continent."

For the first time, Dominic Higar spoke. "The Sedanos didn't raise our living standards." He met Alehan's eyes with unconcealed scorn. "We did that ourselves by using our own ingenuity."

Lourdessa studied Santo's golden-haired aide for a few moments, wondering why she hadn't noticed his beauty before now. Slowly she said, "Our blood earned us the right to control those resources."

Higar shifted his gaze to Lourdessa. "That may have been true a hundred years ago," he replied, "but it's our blood on the line now. The mines are just as dangerous as they were back then. Perhaps more so. Your managers care only about keeping production high, but nothing about our workers."

Such outrage in one so young and handsome amused the Alcalde. Finally she understood her son's fascination with Higar. The flush in the aide's cheeks, the flare of elegant nostrils, the flash of green fire in his eyes—all conspired to produce in her an unexpected ache of desire. Lourdessa entertained a brief fantasy involving Higar's unclothed backside and a whip. *But business first, my dear. Frivolity later,* she thought.

Santo cleared his throat. Higar's jaw clenched. Glancing at his boss, he tapped his pen against his notebook, but kept his mouth firmly shut.

"I must once again raise the question of the Tiqui." As Santo spoke, Higar began to write. "We want slave labor abolished," Santo continued. "Not only is the practice deplorable, it allows your company to reduce Castilian employment and undercut wages."

"We've been over this, Señor. The Tiqui have always been slaves," Lourdessa said. "They arrived on Nuetierra in bondage to our ancestors. It's their natural state. The system benefits both races."

"We refuse to accept that. The system is corrupt and immoral," Higar interjected. His pen now hung motionless over his notebook. "The Tiqui fled the cities after the Great War for good reason. Your family had no right to re-enslave them. You raid their villages, steal their young people..."

"A young Tiqui male is as strong as a full-sized man," Lourdessa said. "His small stature allows him to go where a Castilian miner can't." Lourdessa's gaze touched on each man's face in turn. Speaking with deliberate slowness, she added, "Consider how Stefan will deal with your people's anger when they can no longer afford to heat their homes or cook their food."

"Those are all just excuses, Dama," Santo replied in a voice as chill as winter fog.

Lourdessa counted to twenty, determined to keep a leash on her temper. Santo sat as still as a trance-held mystic and regarded her with diamond-hard eyes. Higar bristled like a riled guard perro. Mari continued to write on her notepad.

"Enough about the Tiqui," Lourdessa said, breaking the tense silence. "We are here to negotiate gas and mining contracts, not debate morality."

"I agree," Santo said. "However, the plight of the Tiqui is an integral part of all this. Morality aside, their presence directly affects the economic health of our city. In this, Alcalde Stefan is adamant. He wants a gradual phase-out of Tiqui labor and Castilian citizens hired at fair wages to replace them."

"What do we get in return?" Alehan asked.

"Stefan will agree to a sixty-forty split of profits."

Lourdessa made a show of studying her fingernails. "And if I refuse?"

"Alcalde Stefan will seize control of the mines and the gas pipeline. He will not hesitate to cut Nue Bayona off."

"That would be a mistake," Lourdessa replied in a low voice. Her eyes met Santo's. "I would have no choice but to force him to relinquish control of what is not within his rights to seize."

"That sounds like a threat, Dama." The furrows in the chief envoy's forehead deepened into crevasses. A stain of color crept above the rim of his starched white collar to suffuse his heavy jowls. Higar's eyes darted between his notebook, his superior, and Lourdessa as he scribbled furiously.

Deciding she had goaded the pair about as far as she could—Santo looked ready to rupture a blood vessel at any moment—Lourdessa changed tack.

"Gentlemen, please. Let us not allow acrimony to derail our purpose." She rose from her chair, beaming. "Tea, anyone?"

Santo's scowl dissolved. "Tea would be nice, thank you." He sank into his chair like a deflated balloon, running chubby fingers through his thick, gunmetal hair. Higar blinked like a spiny *mola* plucked from its burrow.

Lourdessa snapped her fingers at the palace attendant, who promptly rose from her chair. "Full tea service," she ordered.

"Yes, Dama." With a crisp curtsy, the young woman opened the door and scurried out of the room.

"Now, then," Lourdessa began. Her next sentence died on her lips as the conference room door swung open to admit Arturo Deltoro. He looked pale against the black of his pinstriped suit. "What are you doing here?" she demanded, frowning in surprise.

Ignoring the others, the Chief of Police crossed the room and placed his mouth close to Lourdessa's ear. "There's been an attack on the Red Hill police station." His low voice was grim.

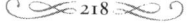

"What?" Lourdessa recoiled in shock.

"What's going on, Mother?" Alehan rose from his seat.

Mari and the Castilians sat motionless, staring.

"How?" Lourdessa whispered.

"A bomb," Deltoro answered.

Lourdessa felt a cold knot form in her gut. She glared at the Chief. "Mierda…are your men stupid, or just lazy?"

Deltoro's nostrils flared. "That's not fair, Dessa, and you know it."

"Arturo, by the Blessed Madre, if you weren't married to my little sister…"

Deltoro did not respond. They both knew her implied threat carried no weight. The Chief owed his current position and allegiance to her brother Gregorio, not her. "I've got to get to Red Hill. I'll call you as soon as I know more," he said.

"Then go," Lourdessa snapped. As the door closed on Deltoro's retreating figure, she turned to the expectant Castilians. She forced a tight smile to her lips. "It seems there's been a small incident."

26
impasse

Like an auburn-haired ghost, the girl glided down the dim corridor. The soft leather soles of her shoes whispered on the clay tiles. She ignored the distant voice of her nanny, calling out her name from somewhere behind her.

She arrived at the apartment she shared with her older sister, certain that no one had seen her. From a niche above the doorframe she retrieved a hidden key and unlocked the door. She paused at the threshold to listen, but heard only the ticking of the porcelain mantle clock. She closed the door and made her way across the sunny dayroom to her bedchamber.

A quartet of dolls sat at a small table in the center of the room, a hand-painted china tea service laid out before them. The girl selected a chair between the doll with long black hair and the one with blond ringlets and sat. She inspected her hands, her dress, and her shoes until satisfied that nothing was amiss. Hands clasped in her lap, her eyes rolled up in their sockets. She slumped forward, head lolling.

"Miss Ceilia! Where have you been?"

Ceilia jerked upright, drawing in a deep, convulsive breath. Fragments of memory—a man crumpled beneath a car, a screaming girl, a noise like a giant door slamming, the smell of smoke—flashed across her mind's eye.

None of the memories belonged to her.

She looked at Freeda, her nanny, who glowered at her from the bedroom doorway.

"I...I've b...been here...with my dolls. We're having our tea."

"Maria and Yesu...give me patience!" Freeda's meaty hands fluttered above her head like agitated birds. "I came to tell you not to spoil your dinner, but you weren't here. I've been running around for the last half hour looking for you. The whole place is in an uproar. There's been another bombing."

"My friend said something bad was going to happen, but he told me not to worry." Ceilia spoke in a voice meant only for the dolls, but Freeda's ears had always been sharp.

"What friend? Who are you talking about?"

Ceilia shook her head. "No one." She lowered her gaze to the table. "I'm sorry if I scared you."

Freeda muttered something about "fey child." Ceilia didn't understand what "fey" meant, so she paid no heed. "The dolls and I will finish our tea now." She picked up the teapot and filled each cup with imaginary brew.

"I've told you time and again not to go out alone without telling me, child. Yesu knows I'm not your jailer...but if anything should happen to you, I'll catch all the blame."

Ceilia wanted to reassure the old woman, but she dared not. When the pale, green-eyed boy had first come to her shortly after Papa had gone away, he'd made her promise to keep his presence a secret. It was the only way he could protect her, he'd said. Other than the drawings of him she sometimes made, she'd kept her end of the bargain, but as they'd grown older, he'd become more careless. That worried her.

"I'm sorry," she repeated. She heard Freeda sigh. In an agitated rustle of skirts her nanny departed, leaving Ceilia alone once more.

"I wish he wouldn't keep sneaking out like that," she told her porcelain companions with a frown.

If the dolls had anything to say, however, they kept their opinions to themselves.

Between Deltoro's departure and the palace attendant arriving with the tea service, Lourdessa related to the Castilians what little she knew about the Red Hill bombing.

"It appears your resistance movement is growing bolder, Dama." Santo glowered like a dyspeptic bull vaca. "The common citizens of Nue Bayona won't tolerate oligarchy forever."

Lourdessa fought the urge to fling her teacup at the chief envoy's sanctimonious head. "I mean no offense when I say this, Señor…but you speak from a position of ignorance. The commoners want a firm hand and decisive leadership. They desire, above all else, order and safety. My government provides both."

"The resistance is made up of malcontents and criminals," Alehan added with a dismissive flick of his hand. "Human trash, pure and simple. The people reject their tactics."

"We've heard their leader—a man called Faustin—is actually an elite who has joined in solidarity with the commoners," Higar said. "Such a man would stand as a powerful symbol for democracy."

"Faustin is a traitor and a terrorist," Lourdessa replied, tight-lipped. "When he is finally captured—and he will be captured very soon—he will stand trial for his many crimes, including murder."

Santo and Higar exchanged subtle, sarcastic glances over the tops of their teacups. Lourdessa felt her simmering temper begin to boil over. She ate two sweet biscuits in rapid succession, drained her cup and sighed. Pastry and strong tea always had the power to soothe her nerves. She glanced at her wristwatch. Deltoro had left for Red Hill over twenty minutes ago.

He should have some news by now.

As if conjured by her thoughts, Lourdessa heard the soft chime of the phone in the background, followed by Mari's quiet answer. Before the secretary could announce the caller, Lourdessa snatched the receiver from her hand. "Well?"

She didn't need to see her brother-in-law's face to comprehend the horror left in the wake of the bomb's destruction. His voice conveyed its full measure. "A few minutes before the bomb exploded, there was an auto accident in front of the station," Deltoro said. "I've spoken to the desk sergeant, who suspects now that the whole thing was staged as a diversion. Shortly afterward, the bomb detonated." He paused, then said, "It's bad, Dessa."

Exquisitely aware of the Castilians' eyes upon her, Lourdessa rose from her chair. Telephone in hand, she stepped away from the table and retreated to a corner. "Is anyone in custody yet?" she asked, keeping her voice low.

"We're on it. But the three that staged the diversion almost certainly wore disguises. They won't be easy to find. That is, if we can find them at all."

"I don't want to hear any excuses, Arturo. You have to find these criminals and bring them in for questioning." From the corner of her eye, she saw the Castilians had begun gathering their papers. "Call me back in ten," she ordered. She hung up on Deltoro's response.

"Dama Alcalde, it's clear our talks are over," Santo said as Lourdessa returned to her chair. "Higar and I wish to go back to our suite now."

"Please, let's not allow this bit of minor trouble to interfere with the important work we're doing here, Señor." Lourdessa placed the telephone into Mari's waiting hands.

Santo shoved the last of his notes into his black satchel and secured the flap. "Dama," he huffed, jowls aquiver, "in the four days we've been at this, you've made it abundantly clear that you intend to give up nothing substantive. We are at an impasse." He pushed the satchel toward Higar, who tucked it under his arm. "I see no reason for us to stay. We're leaving tomorrow morning."

Lourdessa affected as contrite a look as she could manage. "I am sorry to hear that, Señor. I had such high hopes for these talks."

Santo's mouth twitched. Higar snorted and shook his head.

Ignoring the implied challenge to her sincerity, with unwavering politeness, Lourdessa said, "I'll summon a guard to escort you." She watched the Castilians depart and then resumed her seat at the conference table. "Insufferable, self-righteous prigs," she muttered.

"Oh, but such a delicious prig, that Higar. Eh, Mother?" Alehan leaned back in his chair, folded his arms behind his head and grinned. "I saw how you were looking at him. Naughty, naughty."

Feeling a mix of chagrin and grudging amusement, Lourdessa glared at her son. "I could say the same for you, cheeky mono."

Before Alehan could reply, the conference room door swung open to admit a rumpled Saviero Nunyez. "Dama, I apologize for my tardiness," he said. "I rushed over here as soon as I heard, but bicycling through all that wind and lightening, well…"

Alehan glanced at the Minister of Intelligence with narrowed eyes, looking as if he smelled something unpleasant.

Lourdessa waved at the chair beside her. "You should have called. I would've sent a car for you. Have a seat." As Nunyez settled in, the phone rang again. This time Mari picked up the receiver and handed it straight to Lourdessa.

In the infinitesimal slice of time between thought and speech, Lourdessa made a decision. "Arturo, I'm turning over the investigation of this latest attack to the Ministry of Intelligence."

Silence, punctuated by soft bursts of static and faint background voices met her declaration. In her mind's eye, Lourdessa could see Deltoro's face, scarlet with indignation. After several seconds, he said,

"Dessa, I must protest. My City Police were the ones targeted. I, myself, should lead the investigation."

"You have your hands full with all the usual crime that goes on in this city."

"Nunyez and his Specials can't, or won't, stop Faustin's gang. It's time to give the job to me."

Can't or won't... Deltoro's oblique aspersion gave Lourdessa pause. She couldn't deny the truth, but then, the Specials owed allegiance to her, alone. Deltoro was her brother's creature. She thumped the table with her fist. "Damn it, Arturo, this isn't a pissing match! My decision is final. Have all the evidence your men have collected at the site delivered to the M.O.I. by this evening." She slammed down the receiver.

Nunyez, quiet throughout the entirety of the tense exchange, said, "I'll have my best operatives on this immediately."

"The resistance is growing bolder, Nunyez," Alehan said. Fresh sweat slicked his brow, despite the coolness of the room. His hands, steady for the last two hours, had begun to twitch. "Today they struck a police station. Tomorrow...it might be the palace."

Noticing her son's condition, Lourdessa allowed herself a brief moment of maternal concern, but she pushed it aside. She had no time to deal with his bad habits now.

"The resistance hasn't the resources to penetrate palace security," Nunyez said. "You are perfectly safe within these walls, Señor Estes."

Alehan frowned dubiously.

Lourdessa poured herself another cup of tea. "We have to cut off this serpent's head—make an example of him. Only by utterly and publicly destroying Faustin will we crush the resistance once and for all."

"What of the Castilian problem?" Nunyez snagged a biscuit and nibbled off a corner with surprising delicacy.

"I gave them nothing, of course. Santo will return to Nue Castila and report his failure. No doubt Stefan will make good on his threat."

"Does that not worry you, Dama?"

"On the contrary," Lourdessa replied. "It's exactly what I want him to do. It gives me the reason I need to justify a military attack against him." She looked at Nunyez and Alehan in turn. "Nue Castila's days as an independent city are numbered. I intend to return it and its satellite towns to their rightful places as our vassals. Only then can we assure absolute and uninterrupted control of the resources we need."

The disparate elements of her plan were falling into place. Lourdessa found it hard not to become intoxicated with excitement. "The entire continent will soon be ours."

27
disillusionment

Zander stared at the front page of the *Nue Bayona Observer*, his breakfast forgotten on the bar in front of him. Sonia rode the stool beside him, tucking into her own plate of eggs, *jamón*, and toast. Though the common room was near full capacity, they had the bar to themselves.

**ALCALDE VOWS TERRORISTS RESPONSIBLE
FOR LATEST BOMBINGS WILL BE PUNISHED**

The screaming headlines crowned grainy photographs of the demolished Red Hill precinct and Hall of Records. Guilt made a wreck of Zander's appetite as the image of broken bodies flashed across his mind's eye. His close relationship with Sonia teetered, irrevocably damaged. Her unwillingness to tell him the truth had done more than wound him emotionally. It had deprived him of his right to make a critical decision about his role in the resistance. As a result, the blood of every innocent bystander spilled on that terrible day would forever stain his conscience.

The sounds of morning on Escarpado Street drifted in through the inn's open front door. The tinkling bell of the milk seller's cart, the shouts of the vegetable vendors and fishmongers, a woman haranguing a wailing child, the rough laughter of a work crew laying bricks in the empty lot next door—Zander heard it all without conscious thought, so preoccupied was he with his own remorse.

"Zander." Sonia's exasperated voice at his elbow interrupted his melancholy reverie.

He lowered the newspaper and looked at her. "What?"

"Are you listening to me?"

"I am now."

Sonia sighed and shook her head. "I *said*…I'm getting really worried." She took a bite of toast and washed it down with a gulp of café. "I haven't heard from Alberto yet."

"He's probably laying low, like the rest of us." Zander shuddered at the unpleasant memory of the chubby bomb maker's lascivious eyes and soft, moist handshake.

"But he's never stayed out of contact this long," Sonia replied. "Besides, he loves my uncle's cooking."

"That's obvious," Zander quipped, then in response to Sonia's frown, added, "You're afraid something happened to him at the Hall of Records."

"Maybe. But the explosion wasn't nearly as big as at Red Hill, and Alberto is always so careful. I can't imagine he'd get caught in his own blast."

Zander folded his newspaper and gazed around the common room at the faces of the breakfast crowd filling the comfortably worn chairs and benches. These were the working people of the city—carpenters, gardeners, delivery drivers, laborers, shop clerks—whose liberation Faustin supposedly fought for. Yet, with each strike, Zander realized that the rebel leader succeeded only in tightening the noose around the collective necks of them all.

The Hall of Records attack, following so close on the rump of Red Hill, had given the Alcalde the excuse she'd needed to impose martial law on the city. Daylight hours saw squads of blue-uniformed City polis patrolling working-class Red Hill and Quarry with belligerence once reserved only for The Maze. A sullen glance now earned a beating as quickly as a snarky remark. Many a young man staggered or had to be carried home, dazed from a truncheon-cracked skull.

Night belonged to the Special Police of the Ministry of Intelligence. Their armor-plated black cars rolled like desolation through the darkened streets. Any soul unlucky enough to be caught outside would earn a trip to the detention cells. Guilt or innocence played no part in deciding who got seized.

"People are starting to grumble," Zander commented. "I even heard your uncle questioning Faustin's tactics. And he's been a staunch supporter since the beginning."

"Uncle Guermoe should know better," Sonia said.

"Maybe..." Zander paused, ever mindful of her explosive temper these days.

"Maybe what?" Sonia's lips tightened and her eyebrows drew into a shallow V.

"Maybe things could be done differently...without violence."

"What do you mean?"

"No more bombings," Zander replied. "No more attacks of any kind. The people want a leader who claims the moral high ground, someone they can rally behind and march for in the streets. Someone they can love."

"Eduard Hernaan is in jail. There is no one else."

"Yes there is."

Sonia's eyes grew bright with unshed tears. "You're talking about Deanna, aren't you?"

Though he knew how much it would hurt her, he nevertheless refused to pull the punch. "Yeah, I am."

Sonia lowered her head. Her hair fell across her face like a dark, silken curtain. A short week ago, Zander would've desired nothing more than to kiss her tears away, but her lie had curdled his affection, leaving only melancholy regret in its place.

"No one knows where she is." Sonia spoke to her clenched fists as they lay on the table in front of her.

"Roberto Gomaz might. Or if he doesn't know, he can find out," Zander replied.

Sonia's head snapped up. "He's a Special. What makes you think he'd tell you anything?"

"Something he said that night at the Marian House. I think he's not entirely what he seems."

"He's a Special," Sonia repeated.

"He said if I ever needed his help, I could contact him through Mother Elizabette. Why would he offer if he didn't mean it?"

"To get you to incriminate yourself. Or to lead him to the rest of us." Sonia's eyes had gone cold and her face had lost all softness.

Zander refused to turn away from her black-ice stare, though it chilled him to his core. When she looked at him that way, Zander almost believed her capable of killing him if she felt it necessary. "I don't know why," he said slowly, "but I trust him. I need to find Deanna, wherever she is. And he's the only one I know who can help me."

"I won't let you." Her voice, though steely, was barely audible above the background tangle of conversation and clattering crockery.

"You can't stop me." Zander seized his fork, stabbed a lump of egg and lifted it to his mouth. It had gone cold and rubbery. He pushed the plate away. "I'm not hungry anymore."

As he rose from his seat, Sonia caught his hand in hers. Though her lower lip trembled, he saw no sign of surrender in her eyes. He pulled his fingers from her grasp and walked out of the Rosa Blanca, into the noise and bustle of Escarpado Street. With no clear destination in mind, he allowed his feet to carry him wherever they willed.

Most of the structures along Escarpado were at least two centuries old. Built primarily of bricks made from the heavy red clay dug out of ancient, dry riverbeds, the old buildings housed a hodgepodge of businesses. Private dwellings occupied the upper floors. A butcher, a dry goods store, a locksmith, and a pawn shop all shared the block where the Rosa Blanca stood, the only sizable wooden structure in the neighborhood.

Zander kept to the curb, avoiding the main flow of pedestrian traffic filling the uneven sidewalk. In the street, bicycles whizzed past and a delivery truck rolled by, rattling and squeaking as it bounced over the potholed pavement. The breeze of its passage ruffled his hair. A snarling mass of fur rolled out of an alley in front of him, gradually resolving into a pair of stray perros battling over a half-eaten *gayoh* carcass. A man wearing a smudged apron rushed from a storefront and swung at the animals with a broom handle. Yelping, they scurried back into the alley, tails tucked between their legs.

Zander rounded the corner onto Caya Uno and wandered past Alma's Bakery, its windows crammed with golden-brown rolls, heavy dark loaves, trays of iced pastries, and decorated cakes. On any other day he might have stopped to savor the yeasty aroma and gaze with childlike longing at the display. But today his thoughts, like storm clouds, drifted in dark and shadowy masses through his mind, leaving no room for daydreams.

The precinct bombing had done a lot more than damage a building. It had stripped away much of the romantic veneer sheathing the resistance, leaving Zander to battle his growing disillusionment. It didn't help that Faustin had released several communiqués in the days since, full of bluster and grandiose promises. Zander wanted to believe in the cause, but the thought of more bloodshed sickened him. His own role in creating that bloodshed sickened him even more.

It came as no surprise when he looked up to find himself outside the Marian convent. He reached out to pull the bell rope, but the memory of Sonia's words—*I won't let you*—stopped him. Though she'd spoken in a whisper, she might as well have shouted. He reluctantly lowered his hand. He'd always known where Sonia's primary loyalties lay. She loved him…was in love with him, but she also counted herself among Faustin's top lieutenants. And what if she was right? Could he live with the consequences?

Gomaz is a poli. I have no proof, other than a hunch, he's anything other than what he seems. He could be out to trick me. I can't take the risk...can I?

Glancing up at the pale sky, Zander wiped his perspiring brow on his bare forearm. The day had already warmed well past comfortable, though it was not yet noon. With one final look at the weathered wooden gate of his childhood home, he turned his back on the convent and started the long, lonely walk back to the Rosa Blanca.

28

a night of celebration

Reed Valley drowsed in the heat of late afternoon. During the sleepy hours between midday and dusk, many Tiqui adults worked indoors on small home repairs or personal projects. Others napped on hammocks strung in the shade of their verandas. Babies dozed nestled in the arms of their parents, while cliques of older children, too restless to nap, congregated at the lake to swim and hunt ranas, or to play games on the patch of grass fronting the village meeting house.

"Deanna…Deanna! Come play with us," the young girl called, waving. Deanna smiled at the trio of children spinning wooden hoops—a game called *vuelta*—around their arms and legs.

"Not now, Dawn. Your mother wants to talk to me. And since she's the ithani, I have to obey." A chorus of mournful cries arose from the small group. "I promise I'll come back as soon as I can," she said, laughing.

Four weeks had come and gone since Strong Hand's hunting band had returned home with their unexpected guest. Unexpected to everyone, it seemed, except Yellow Bird, Ithani of Reed Valley and Principal Shaman of the Wolf Clan. As Deanna made her way back to the spacious lodge where the ithani and her family dwelled, her thoughts drifted back to that earlier day.

THE HUNTING BAND rode through a lush meadow alive with flitting, buzzing insects and into the village proper. Deanna gazed around her with fresh wonder at the small, neat houses, each set on sturdy wood pylons and adorned with sculpted wooden lintels and doorposts. A running eelat, a pair of pinya trees, a swirling cloud bank—love of the natural world was apparent in each beautifully rendered carving.

Boxes filled with fragrant herbs and flowers hung beneath many of the windows. From within open doorways, or standing at the railings of verandas, Deanna glimpsed women in white blouses and colorful, striped skirts, some holding babies, still others clutching the hands of small giggling children. Their bright garb stood in sharp contrast with the neutral tones worn by the hunters. She felt like she'd ridden straight out of the bush and into a rainbow of joy.

A group of men with worried faces fell in to escort them, peppering Strong Hand and Shadow with questions.

"Who is this alta?"

"Where did you find her?"

"Why is she here? Are there others?"

"Is the valley in danger?"

Deanna wanted to offer assurances, but silence seemed the wiser course for now. She sensed no overt hostility; rather, the men exuded a collective aura of wariness, as if faced with a potential menace that had yet to be fully evaluated.

Strong Hand raised his free hand, keeping the other firmly on the reins of his mount. "This girl is no threat," he said. "We're taking her to see Yellow Bird. Come if you wish to learn more."

The ithani's lodge stood near the center of the village, no different from any other except for its size. A woman dressed all in white watched from the veranda as the hunting band, still surrounded by its escort, drew rein and dismounted.

Deanna did not need to be told that this was Yellow Bird.

Before her senior husband could explain the presence of an alta woman in their midst, the ithani had descended the steps to stand before Deanna. She raised a slender hand and reached toward Deanna's face, stopping just shy of contact.

Yellow Bird's eyes met hers. For an instant, Deanna felt like she could fall without fear into their sparkling amber depths.

The ithani lowered her hand. "I know you," she said. "You are most welcome."

THE MEMORY OF that first meeting still filled Deanna with warmth and wonder. At the time she'd accepted Yellow Bird's statement without question. But days had turned to weeks, and the ithani had yet to dispel the mystery of how she could know someone she'd never met.

Perhaps now, Yellow Bird would finally explain herself.

Deanna mounted the shallow steps of the ithani's home and limped across the veranda, rubbing her thigh as she walked. Her leg still ached from the jelly sting, though the wound itself had healed, leaving behind a puckered red scar.

A pair of bloodwood statues—carved in the semblance of the wolf totem, symbol of Yellow Bird's clan—stood sentinel on either side of the doorway. Their stylized, toothy snarls; wide-eyed stares; and lolling tongues signified their role as guardians of the family within. Deanna paused before the idols and removed her shoes.

With a bow of her head, she recited, "Revered Protectors, I greet thee and ask leave to enter." Ghost Dog had taught her the ritual greeting on the day she'd first arrived. She waited for a few heartbeats and entered, ducking lest she crack her skull on the carved lintel. While her eyes adjusted to the dim interior she lingered on the threshold, the crown of her head grazing the rafters. "Yellow Bird, I'm here," she called out.

The ithani's warm contralto voice beckoned, "Come in, child."

Deanna dropped her Tiqui-made leather slippers among the collection of footwear beside the door, then made her way to where Yellow Bird sat on a carved bloodwood chair draped with the plush black pelt of a mountain pantera. "It's easy to forget how quiet the lodge can get when the family's not around," she said, grinning.

Yellow Bird returned Deanna's smile. "Yes, that's so," she agreed. "We should take advantage of this time for a private talk." She pointed to the floor.

Deanna sat cross-legged at Yellow Bird's bare feet on a thick mat of woven reeds. She gazed up at the ithani, marveling yet again, as she had so often since coming to Reed Valley, at Yellow Bird's beauty.

Lustrous black hair fell in a thick braid across the small woman's left shoulder. A white kirtle, embellished at neckline and hem with sprays of colorful, embroidered flowers, graced her trim figure. A bone pendant, carved in the shape of a dolora bird on the wing, hung from her neck on a leather cord. Her golden eyes, punctuated by a spray of fine lines at their outer corners, glimmered with shrewdness and intelligence.

In the short time she'd lived in Reed Valley, Deanna had come to realize that Yellow Bird's authority, which draped her like a rich mantle, did not feel at all like the brutal version wielded by Lourdessa.

Yellow Bird doesn't rule her people. She guides them with wisdom and love, she thought.

The ithani gestured to a red clay teapot on a stool by her knee. "Would you like some tea?" Deanna noted that the warm red tones of the Tiqui woman's skin mirrored the color of the clay to perfection.

"Yes, dama, thank you." Yellow Bird poured the steaming amber liquid into two small, hand-thrown clay cups. The pungent fragrance of corella flowers filled the air. She handed a cup to Deanna and took a single sip from her own before setting it aside on the stool.

"It's been only a few weeks since you came to us," Yellow Bird began, "but you've already done so much for the village. Volunteering at the school, helping in the vegetable garden...the improvements to our irrigation system alone..."

"All I did was make a few suggestions." Deanna had shown the village farmers how to build a pedal-driven pumping system to raise water from the lake to the fields, replacing their inefficient hand-crank system.

"You are too modest, child." Yellow Bird patted Deanna's knee. "None of us have your mechanical knowledge. Because of what you've shown us, we'll have the ability to increase our yields. That means more trade and a more comfortable life for everyone."

Deanna allowed herself a moment of pride. That her skills had bettered the lives of her new friends gave her more sense of accomplishment than anything else she'd ever done.

She blew on her still-steaming tea and took a cautious sip. "Little Horn and Meadow are turning out to be excellent apprentices," she said. "They're both such fast learners." The teen boy and girl had come to her soon after she'd arrived. They'd begged her to teach them all she knew of her skills, and—eager to give back to the community—she'd agreed.

"With your training, we'll soon have two engineers of our own," Yellow Bird said. "They, in turn, will train others in the future. This means so much to us. To me. I am truly grateful."

"You gave me a place when I had nowhere else to go, Ithani," Deanna replied. "I could do no less."

"My son tells me you've discovered a way to fix our old generator?"

Deanna nodded. "I just need to get my hands on the right part. Ghost Dog says we might find it at Dry Creek Station." A few days after her arrival, Ghost Dog had told her of a trading post located a half-day's ride east of the valley. There, Wilds-dwelling alta and Tiqui met to barter or sell everything from pelts and tanned hides to groceries, coal oil, and manufactured goods. High-tech salvage and the occasional luxury item could also be had, for a price.

"Strong Hand found that generator several seasons back, abandoned at an old mining camp," Yellow Bird said. "We were able to coddle it for awhile. The entire village had electricity, at least for part of the day. Last winter it developed a cough like an old man with lung fever, then it died." The ithani sighed.

"In Nue Bayona, only the district around the palace has electricity," Deanna said. "The middle class use gas to light their homes. Or fuel cells, if they can afford them. Which are better, because they last a long time and they can't explode and cause fires, like gas. The poor make due with coal oil lamps or candles."

"The comforts the city dwellers take for granted come at a very high price for the Tiqui." A hint of steel underpinned Yellow Bird's soft tone. "So many young people have fallen victim to the slavers over the years. Thank the Ancestors, Reed Valley has been more fortunate than some other villages. Our best defense is our seclusion. We've been raided only once in my lifetime."

"Ghost Dog told me of that raid. Shadow lost his brother Rain." The memory of the *nexa's* bitter anger retained its sting. Deanna gazed into the amber depths of her tea. "I wish I could atone, at least in part, for the terrible things my people have done to yours," she said. "But I don't know how. I'm just one person."

"No one here expects you to personally answer for the injustices perpetrated by the alta upon the Tiqui. That would be an injustice itself." Yellow Bird leaned forward and touched Deanna's cheek. "There is a reason, though, for why my family found you."

"I don't understand."

"You were meant to come here, Deanna," the ithani murmured.

"When I arrived in the village, you said you knew me. How is that possible?" Deanna searched Yellow Bird's face for any clues, but the ithani gave nothing away.

"Come with me now, Deanna. There's a special place I want to show you," the ithani said, rising from her chair. Intrigued, Deanna obeyed. After donning her shoes, she fell in beside the older woman. Together they made their way down the front steps.

The path the ithani chose led away from the main cluster of houses to join with another that skirted the southwestern edge of the village proper. Yellow Bird set a purposeful pace, humming a soft tune in lieu of speech. Though bursting with curiosity, Deanna remained silent.

After several minutes of walking they reached the lakeshore. The sounds of splashing and children's laughter rose from among the reeds.

Yellow Bird turned aside onto yet another path that led toward a grove of trees near the southernmost end of the lake. After another minute of silent trudging, Deanna finally asked, "Ithani, where are we going?"

"Be patient. We're almost there," Yellow Bird replied with a tiny smile.

Deanna huffed and bit her lip, then took a deep breath. *I suppose it's part of a shaman's job to be mysterious*, she thought.

By the time she and Yellow Bird entered the grove of tall pinya and hoary roble, Deanna's forehead and armpits prickled with sweat. The deep shade beneath the trees felt like a refreshing drink of water after a long run. She paused for a heartbeat to savor the coolness before setting off after Yellow Bird's retreating figure.

The ithani led the way along a narrow trail strewn with a thick layer of dried pinya needles. Her small, sandaled feet made almost no sound as she walked. Ahead, Deanna could see the trail's end at the edge of a clearing. Yellow Bird paused, waiting for Deanna to catch up.

"Welcome to my sanctuary," the ithani said.

Within the circle of trees dominated by an ancient, lightning-split pinya, corella and rosa bushes in full bloom stood in neat rows. They were interspersed with low-growing, woody shrubs that Deanna didn't recognize. Abehas and other insects flitted from flower to flower. A heady mix of fragrances filled the air. "It's beautiful," she exclaimed, delighted.

"Every shaman keeps a sacred garden in which to cultivate *mezcala*. This is mine." Yellow Bird removed her sandals. "I love the feel of the soil between my toes," she said. "It helps me connect to the energy that flows from the heart of this world."

Without hesitation, Deanna shed her own shoes and followed Yellow Bird into the garden. "Is this where you come to scry?" she asked.

"Sometimes," the ithani replied. "But mostly, I come here to meditate. It's the one place that's always quiet. No children." Deanna smiled.

Yellow Bird wove a path through the rows, stopping near the garden's center. There, she settled among the plants. Deanna sat beside her. "This is mezcala, the sacred herb of the Tiqui shamans," the ithani said. "Your people know it as sueño." She plucked a slender, spiky, mottled green-and-red leaf and placed it into Deanna's hand. "The tea brewed from the dried leaves unlocks the shamanic gift of foresight. The flowers," she crushed a six-petaled white blossom between her fingers, releasing a burst of spicy scent, "are used in healing, as a sedative and pain reliever."

"No wonder I'm a little light-headed," Deanna said.

"I brought you here, child, because I wanted to show you my sacred place. But more importantly, I want to give you some answers. You asked me how it was possible that I knew you, even though we'd never met. For many months before you came to Reed Valley, my scryings showed me that a girl of the alta people would come to dwell among us, and that her fate and ours were inextricably linked."

Deanna felt a flutter in the pit of her stomach. "What does that mean? Please, tell me."

"I can't. At least not yet."

"Ithani, with respect, you said you'd give me answers." Deanna crossed her arms, frowning. "Instead, all you've done is create more questions."

"I can see your frustration, child. And I'm sorry," Yellow Bird said, "but know this. The future is not set. It changes with each choice made or not made. Your feet were placed on a road that led to this valley by a series of choices. The best possible future for both our peoples can only come to pass if you continue to choose a particular path from among many."

"What I've been through doesn't feel like I had a choice at all. Quite the opposite, in fact," Deanna said.

"I know it seems that way now. So much is still hidden, even from me." Yellow Bird sighed. For an instant her gaze lost focus; it then snapped back to full intensity. "But in this I am certain," she continued. "My people have a role to play in insuring you choose correctly."

The ithani's expression told Deanna it was pointless to press her further. All she could do now was wait, and trust that Yellow Bird would tell her what she needed to know when she need to know it.

"Now that I've mystified you completely, let's talk about the feast tonight," Yellow Bird said with a smile. A celebration to honor the ithani's birthday was to take place on the village commons, starting at sundown. "New Moon and River have a big announcement planned," she continued. "I already know what it is, but the rest of the village doesn't, at least not formally."

Deanna's mood brightened. "I've heard some of the other women talking. It's hard to hide the truth from them."

Yellow Bird nodded. "Especially since my poor daughter is having such a difficult time with her morning sickness. None of my usual remedies are working. I hope Ghost Dog can trade for some jenjibre root at Dry Creek."

"Back home, jenjibre flowers are used to make perfume," Deanna said. "I didn't know the plant had a medicinal use."

"A potent nausea remedy can be extracted from the root, but out here in the Wilds it's extremely scarce and expensive," the ithani explained. "Fortunately, I have something I think will meet any reasonable asking price." She stood up and brushed bits of debris and soil from her skirt. "Time to go. We have a party to prepare for."

"It's been ages since I've been to a good party," Deanna said, smiling.

"Then we shall take special care to make sure you have fun."

Deanna climbed to her feet. Together she and Yellow Bird headed back to the village.

The celebration began as dusk cloaked the valley in purple shadow. Coal oil lamps hung from wooden poles that ringed the village commons. A large bonfire crackled in a pit at the center. The tantalizing aroma of roasting meat, mingled with wood smoke, hung heavy in the air.

The entire area had been cleared of all capras, which the Tiqui raised for their meat, milk, and hair. The herdboys had carefully combed the grass to remove every dung ball they could find.

Dressed in a new, alta-sized green-and-red-striped skirt paired with a blouse of white algodon—both made for her as a gift by Little Horn's mother Gazela—Deanna paused at the commons edge to take in every detail of the festive scene.

Trestle tables and benches—enough to seat the entire village—had been set up around the fire. The happy crowd swirled in constant motion as people traveled from table to table, stopping to sit and talk with one group before moving on to the next. A quartet of musicians on pipes, drum, and a stringed instrument Deanna couldn't name serenaded the crowd from a low wooden stage, in front of which a gaggle of children hopped and capered. Their youthful abandon made her smile.

Deanna spotted Yellow Bird and Strong Hand seated at the table nearest the outdoor kitchen, their arms about each other, faces touching like young lovers. As she watched them, Shadow arrived and sat beside the ithani, who then drew him into her embrace along with Strong Hand. Together, the trio, arms linked, laughed and talked with everyone who stopped at their family table.

At that moment, Deanna saw them for what they truly were—the unassailable heart and soul of the community.

As she pondered the depths of love and commitment shared by the ithani and her husbands, a small hand slipped into hers. She looked down to see Dawn, Yellow Bird's eight-year-old daughter, gazing up at her with wide, liquid brown eyes. Her baby brother, White Fox, clung to her skirt like a pilot fish on a *tiberon*. "Come sit with us, Deanna," the girl pleaded.

Smiling, Deanna allowed the children to lead her over to Yellow Bird's table.

Strong Hand spotted her first. "Ah, there you are," he said. "Join us." He waved to a pair of reed-stuffed cushions stacked against the table edge. As Deanna settled on the comfortable pile, Dawn released her hand; then she and White Fox scampered to their parents. Shadow welcomed the little boy onto his lap.

"You look beautiful tonight, Deanna," Yellow Bird said.

Deanna smoothed the folds of her new skirt around her knees. "Gazela is a wonderful seamstress. Everything fits perfectly."

Strong Hand picked up an earthenware jug, poured foaming brown liquid into a mug, and pushed it, sloshing, toward her. "Have some of this."

Deanna took a swallow. What tasted like fresh bread mixed with nuts and fruit warmed her empty stomach and filled her head with a light fog. She grinned.

"Best celebration beer brewed among the clans," Strong Hand said. "Shadow's recipe," he added with a smile for his brother spouse.

Deanna risked a glance toward the nexa, afraid of his usual lacerating stare, but tonight, she saw only contentment in his black eyes. "It's delicious." She tipped her mug back for a long, deep drink.

"Careful. You'll land flat on your back before dinner is served," Strong Hand warned in a teasing voice.

Deanna laughed, raising her mug in salute to the quality of the drink and the sheer joy of the moment. "It's a party," she said.

For a time she basked in the warmth of community. Friends came to greet her and offer compliments on her new clothes. Kids ran by, shrieking. Village perros circulated from table to table, whining and sniffing. Deanna felt sympathy for them, her own belly rumbling in response to the delicious aromas filling the air.

"Where have you been?" Yellow Bird asked, eyebrows raised, as Raven, her middle son, appeared by her side out of breath. Though the boy called both Strong Hand and Shadow "father," his prominent nose and high forehead marked him as Shadow's blood son.

He gasped, "Me an' Two Rabbits an' Coyote Moon were racing around the lake. I won!" Deanna knew that Raven and his two best friends had just counted their fourteenth summers. The three were already dreaming of their manhood ceremonies, which would take place next spring. The boy hopped from foot to foot, his excitement irrepressible. "We came to see if it's time to eat yet."

"Two Rabbits and Coyote Moon are welcome to sit with us, if they'd like," Shadow said. His son whooped and darted off, returning a few moments later accompanied by a pair of lanky youths. Deanna recognized both from their many visits to the ithani's lodge. After respectful greetings to their elders, the boys joined Raven at the far end of the table, where all three sat in a huddle, whispering.

"I remember when I was that age," Shadow mused. "My friends and I, we thought we were so grown-up then. We wanted to stand apart from the adults. And yet we still needed them, still wanted to be close in some ways."

Yellow Bird sighed. "I sometimes wish all the children could remain babies forever."

"But that would mean changing dirty diapers forever as well, suna-iya," Strong Hand replied, wrinkling his nose. His comment elicited a burst of good-natured laughter from his spouses.

Near the kitchen a bell clanged. With a final flourish the music stopped. People moved to take their places at the trestles in anticipation of the coming feast.

"Where are the others?" Deanna asked, looking around and suddenly realizing she'd not yet seen Ghost Dog, New Moon, or their respective mates.

Strong Hand tsked. "Young lovers...they don't wish to sit around with the elders and the children when they can make merry with each other."

"I saw them all sitting with Black Wolf and Paloma," Raven spoke up from the end of the table.

Yellow Bird patted Deanna's hand. "If you'd rather go join them, we old folks won't mind."

"I'll stay, Ithani," Deanna replied. As much as she enjoyed the company of the younger couples, she didn't wish to intrude in the special, pair-bonded space Ghost Dog and the others had created for themselves.

The bell clanged a second time, heralding the imminent arrival of dinner. When the last stragglers had found their seats, the feast began.

Servers brought out platters heaped with steaming, roasted white and yellow patoks; bowls of fresh raw greens sprinkled with wine vinegar and *ani* seed oil; tureens of boiled red beans; crocks of roasted, spiced *griyos*; great bunches of bloodbark fruit; and baskets of fresh-baked crusty flatbread. The centerpiece consisted of an entire capra, roasted all day in a ground oven until the meat was fall-off-the-bone tender. Deanna counted seven similar roasts leaving the kitchen, destined for the other tables.

Conversation dwindled to sporadic words of praise and pleasure as everyone concentrated on the meal. Deanna took a portion from each dish as it made its rounds of the table, except for the griyos. When Strong Hand offered to serve her a generous scoop of the insects, she politely declined.

The initial flurry of eating subsided. The *natome* laid down his fork, took a swig from his mug, and loosed a hearty belch. Shadow echoed with one of his own, as did Yellow Bird, though hers was softer.

Even though Deanna had grown used to this peculiar Tiqui custom, it still made her giggle. She hid her smile behind her hand. For a Tiqui not to belch after an especially savory meal was considered the height of bad manners. With the help of a large gulp from her own near-empty mug, she conjured a passable compliment of her own.

Yellow Bird dabbed her mouth with a cloth. "It's time for the announcement," she said. Strong Hand and Shadow nodded. She rose from her seat and waited for the crowd to notice. Within moments, the happy chatter died away to expectant silence as all eyes looked toward the ithani.

"My friends and family," she began. "Today is my birthday...but that is not the only reason we are celebrating tonight." Her gaze swept the gathering and came to rest on the table where New Moon and River sat, arm in arm. "I have joyous news to share," Yellow Bird continued. "My firstborn daughter and her husband will welcome their firstborn at the start of the cold season."

The crowd erupted in a chorus of cheers. Deanna added her voice to the ecstatic outpouring of love and congratulations.

When the people quieted again, Strong Hand and Shadow both stood beside Yellow Bird. "Every new, free-born Tiqui life is a blessing," Strong Hand said. He raised his mug. "To our first grandchild!"

Shadow then raised his mug. "Our Ancestors gave us the greatest gift possible. As a people, we honor their blood sacrifice by remaining free. To the Ancestors."

The crowd cried the toasts in unison and drank.

As Deanna drained her mug, she thought about the deeper meaning behind the two men's words. *Nothing is more important to these people than their freedom. They live with the possibility that it could be snatched away from them at any time. Yet they don't allow fear rule their lives. Love and community are their strength.*

Bayonans used to have that, before...

Deanna quickly shoved away her creeping melancholy. Tonight she would allow no sad thoughts of home to spoil her mood.

The toasts finished, the ithani and her mates resumed their seats. Calls for more refreshment rose from multiple tables. As if on cue, the volunteer servers sprang from their places and scurried to the kitchen. They returned laden with plates of sweetmeats, more beer, fruit juice, and milk for the children. Empty platters and dishes were whisked away as folk grew too sated from eating, but not yet too full for more drink. The musicians returned to their little stage, took up their instruments, and launched into a lively tune. People abandoned their seats for the dance space until most of the tables were empty.

Raven and his friends had left after the toasts and before the sweets, *no doubt on some secret "boys only" business,* Deanna thought. Nursing a fresh mug of beer, she gazed at the bobbing crowd, her head filled with a pleasant fog.

Yellow Bird stood, holding a hand out to each of her spouses. "Come, husbands. Let's dance." Her face shone with a young girl's giddy delight.

"Join us, Deanna," Strong Hand added.

Deanna rose and followed the ithani and her husbands, but as she drew closer to the dance space, a strange reluctance overcame her. She stopped just beyond range of the flickering firelight.

Yellow Bird, Strong Hand, and Shadow joined the rapturous throng of dancers. Babies in their mother's arms, scampering children, young lovers clinging to each other like climbing vines, silver-haired elders—all swayed, stamped, and twirled to the music, an entity of many bodies with a shared soul.

Deanna watched with the envy-tempered joy of an honored guest who, despite the welcoming embrace of her hosts, still suffered the loneliness of the outsider. Homesickness bit deep, and wrung a spate of tears from her eyes.

Damn it. I swore I wouldn't let myself feel this way.

She tugged on the chain around her neck and pulled her own locket and Zander's ring from their hiding place beneath her blouse. The feel of them in her hand offered a measure of much-needed consolation.

I hope you're safe, dulzor. I miss you so much.

Ghost Dog materialized beside her. "Why are you standing here alone, Deanna?" He looked up into her eyes with an expression that seemed to convey understanding of her inner turmoil.

Deanna gazed over the top of his head at River and New Moon as they moved in rhythm with each other, laughing. She let the jewelry drop back between her breasts and dabbed her wet cheeks on her wrist.

"I love it here, Dog…I do. The village welcomed me, though I had no right to expect it. I've tried to contribute, to make myself useful."

"You have, Deanna." Ghost Dog took her hand and squeezed. "Has someone made you feel otherwise?"

Deanna thought of Shadow, but knew nothing could be gained by speaking against Ghost Dog's adoptive father. "No," she replied. "I can't quite explain why…but right now Reed Valley doesn't feel like my home."

Ghost Dog pulled gently on her wrist until she sank to his height. Taking her in his arms, he whispered, "It's your home if you want it to be."

"Thank you, dear friend."

Ghost Dog released her and she stood. "Come dance with me," he said.

Smiling, Deanna allowed him to lead her into the circle.

29

dry creek station

The sun had not yet reached zenith when Deanna and Ghost Dog approached Dry Creek Trading Station. They'd started out from Reed Valley before sunrise, Ghost Dog leading the way, a pack eelat tethered to his saddle. After riding for hours along bush trails and dirt roads with only one brief rest stop, Deanna's full bladder and sore backside had her aching for the journey's end.

The station's collection of weathered clapboard structures sprawled amid a sheltering grove of sawtooth trees at the end of a rutted track. In a clearing on one side of the two-story main building, several hard-used autos and a small truck were parked in the shade of a rusty water tower. Four drowsy eelats stood tethered to a long hitching post near the base of the raised porch.

Ghost Dog and Deanna rode beneath an entrance arch of unshaven logs and across a plank bridge spanning the dry watercourse that gave the station its name. The thick litter of fallen, serrated leaves formed a crunchy gold carpet beneath their mounts' three-toed feet.

At the far side of the bridge a quintet of rough-coated perros, lean as saplings, greeted them with a chorus of shrill barks. Grim threw up his head in challenge, his lip rippling in time to the growl emanating deep in his throat. The pack eelat jerked hard on the leather lead tying it to Ghost Dog's saddle, wringing a curse from the young Tiqui hunter.

From an alleyway between the main building and a smaller windowless shed, a woman came running. She shouted a barrage of threats that sent the perros slinking to the far side of the porch, where they flopped in the dirt, tongues lolling. The woman strode toward the new arrivals, a bridle slung over one broad shoulder. "Ghost Dog, you young reprobate. It's been awhile."

Ghost Dog flung his leg over Grim's rump and slid to the ground. "Hausi, Maya. It has indeed. Almost six months."

The middle-aged alta woman standing before them had the look of one who'd been tempered in the fires of hard experience. She wore a loose unbleached algodon work shirt and a long leather skirt that hid all her womanly curves beneath a cover of strict utility. The ebon lagrima pendant hanging around her neck served as her sole adornment.

She eyed Deanna from head to toe. "Who's your friend?"

Deanna eased off her own mount, acutely aware of the discerning shrewdness in the woman's gaze.

"This is Deanna," Ghost Dog replied. "She's living in the valley with us for now."

The woman's eyebrows disappeared beneath the fringe of silver-streaked black hair ornamenting her broad forehead. "Oh?"

Deanna limped forward. "Hola," she said with a half-smile.

"Maya runs this station," Ghost Dog explained.

Though clearly curious, Maya asked no further questions. Instead she said, "I've known this one since he was nuthin' but an itty-bitty pup coming in with his daddy Strong Hand." She gave them both a gap-toothed smile. "Garcea is here with some of his boys. If you've got any medium-sized fuel cells, he's looking to trade."

Ghost Dog slapped the bulging load secured to the pack eelat. "We had excellent luck on our last salvage trip. I've got three medium and a dozen small. I've also brought some nice hides—gazela mostly, and a few pantera pelts."

"I promised to try to fix Reed Valley's generator," Deanna said. "Do you know if anyone has any machine parts for trade?"

Maya shrugged. "Most days there's someone here with a few stray parts. Don't know if you'll find what you need today, though." She passed a professional appraiser's gaze over Deanna's face and body. "Y'know, girl, you're pretty. If you've a mind to make yourself a little extra scratch, you'd find plenty of opportunity here. I'd only take ten percent."

Deanna felt her cheeks ignite. "Not interested."

Maya sighed, a look of mild disappointment on her weathered face. "Well, if you change your mind…"

"Got any jenjibre today?" Ghost Dog asked.

"I might," Maya replied. "I'll have to look. Is it for someone in particular?"

"My sister," Ghost Dog said. "Nothing in my mother's medicine bag has helped her morning sickness. I can pay well for the good stuff." The ithani had sent along with Ghost Dog one of her most prized possessions, a large amethyst crystal, specifically to purchase the drug.

Maya pursed her thin lips and tsked. "Poor girl. My first one was like that. Swore I'd never let another man near me. Went on to have five more. Hah!" She grinned and slapped her thigh, then said, "You two can stable your eelats in the big box stall at the end of the back row." With a brusque nod she turned and stumped off toward the main building, the jingle of the harness across her shoulder punctuating each step.

"I can't believe that woman thought I might want to…to…"

Ghost Dog patted her arm. "Life is hard out here for your kind. Most come to the Wilds because they have no other choice."

"And the women do what they have to in order to survive." Deanna knew in her heart that under different circumstances she too might consider the previously unthinkable. "Why should Maya believe I'm any different?"

"That's a good thing, Dee. If Maya doesn't know who you are, then most likely no one else will either." Ghost Dog tugged on Grim's bridle. "Come on. Let's see to the eelats, then we'll get something to eat."

"Before we do anything, I really need to pee."

Ghost Dog frowned in sympathy. "Why didn't you say something sooner? The outhouse is on the way to the barn."

AFTER TENDING TO their animals, Ghost Dog and Deanna made their way from the barn to the main building. "General store and tavern on the first floor, rooms for rent on the second," Ghost Dog explained as they walked. They rounded the corner and he stopped Deanna with a hand on her forearm. "Everyone's supposed to be equal here," he said. "Maya doesn't tolerate any trouble. So nobody'll say anything, at least not out loud. But still...expect some stares."

"From your people or mine?"

"Both. Folk come together out here for trade, but there's not much socializing between the races. You being with me...that's going to cause a stir."

Deanna squared her shoulders. "You and I are friends. I don't care what anyone here might think."

Ghost Dog smiled and released her arm. Together they mounted the steps. Deanna pushed the tavern door inward and held it while she and Ghost Dog stepped through together.

"Oh, mierda," Deanna murmured. "This is...interesting."

At first glance, the station's common room looked as if a taxidermist had set up shop inside a junk-filled warehouse. Multiple snarling felion and pantera heads glared down in frozen anger from every wall, interspersed with gazela and striped *cebre* hides. Racks of cervena antlers had been fashioned into light fixtures. A diverse mix of objects hung on wires from the darkened ceiling beams. Deanna saw everything from old animal skulls and stuffed birds to broken machine parts; worn-out boots; and an enormous, preserved sky jelly beak. It seemed not a single nook or cranny had been left unfilled.

Warped shutters hung open to admit stray breezes and natural light. Drifts of sawdust covered the rippled plank floor, lending a pleasant woodsy note to the blended aromas of smoke, burning coal oil, candle wax, and roasted meat.

"It can be a little overwhelming at first," Ghost Dog said, his eyes twinkling with suppressed laughter.

"Just a little," Deanna replied.

Midday had brought a sizable crowd to the tavern eager to break bread and escape the heat with cool mugs of beer and wine. Most of the mismatched tables and chairs—some sized for altas and others scaled for the Tiqui—were occupied by pairs or small groups. A trio of alta barmaids worked the room, along with four other alta women whose cheap finery proclaimed their profession. Deanna saw no Tiqui women there.

As the door swung closed, the group of alta men sitting closest to the door looked up from their card game to peruse the newcomers. For a split second, Deanna froze. *What if someone recognizes me?*

The men returned to their game. Deanna exhaled in relief and wiped damp palms on her pant legs. *Don't be silly. No one out here knows who I am.*

"There're some empty tables at the back," Ghost Dog said. Deanna followed him past a cold, soot-blackened fieldstone fireplace to the last pair of free tables, one Tiqui-sized and the other alta. Before he asked, Deanna volunteered. "I'll manage." She inspected the floor, saw no egregious debris in the shavings, crossed her legs, and sat.

As she settled, Deanna noticed a Tiqui man dressed in worn brown leathers, sitting alone at a table in the back corner. *That's odd*, she thought. *Tiqui held the bonds of community as sacred. Why is he on his own?*

The man slouched over a bowl of stew, slurping with single-minded intensity. His long hair, a tangle of bead-strung braids and oily hanks, fell about his sparsely bearded face. An irregular, polished blue stone, strung from a twisted strand of bronze wire, dangled from one earlobe. A sheathed knife the length of his forearm hung at his hip. The other Tiqui in the room did not acknowledge him, nor he them. His isolation seemed as much his own choice as a state imposed upon him.

Deanna nudged Ghost Dog, lifting her chin in the direction of the lone Tiqui. "You know him?" she asked.

Ghost Dog scowled. "Yes. He's from the valley. His name's Broken Knife. He's been a bully and a troublemaker since we were boys."

Broken Knife picked up his bowl, sucked down the last of the stew, and belched. Deanna kept her eyes on Ghost Dog's face. "I don't remember seeing him in the village," she said.

Contempt stiffened Ghost Dog's posture and roughened his voice. "Two summers ago, he and a couple of his friends played a stupid prank on another man named Little Bear. Little Bear lost the use of his hand because of it. As punishment the three were offered a choice. Work for one year as bond servants to Little Bear and his family, or suffer banishment from Reed Valley for the same time period. Broken Knife's friends chose service, but he chose banishment and has yet to return. He'd rather live as a solo hunter and salvager than live in community with his people."

Deanna perused the room as Ghost Dog spoke, careful to not let her gaze linger overlong on any one person. The alta denizens of Dry Creek Station seemed of a kind—men and women alike—rough-hewn and weathered from hard living. Most wore patched leathers and unbleached homespun. Ghost Dog had told her firearms were prohibited in the common room, but Deanna noticed knives hanging from many belts. Two men riding adjacent barstools, dressed in shabby frock coats and trousers, looked like a pair of city clerks on the run from the law.

Deanna found the neat dress of the Tiqui a notable contrast. She wondered if it was a conscious effort on their part, a form of psychological protection against real or perceived alta bigotry. *Like when a girl from Red Hill puts on her best dress to go have a cup of tea at a Valencea café,* she thought.

Only Broken Knife shared the same hardscrabble appearance as the tall folk.

"It can't be easy for him," Deanna said, glancing once more at the lone Tiqui man. "Living as an outcast, ignored by his own people."

"He's not an outcast," Ghost Dog insisted. "He can return any time he wishes. He doesn't want to."

"Still, it has to be a very lonely life."

Ghost Dog snorted. "Don't waste any sympathy on him. He doesn't deserve it."

Before Deanna could reply, a blonde wearing a tight-laced red corset and white pantaloons strolled up to their table. With one hand on her hip and the other hanging loose, her languid gaze lingered on Deanna for a moment and then slid to Ghost Dog. "You looking for a good time, dulzor?"

The woman's heavy black eyeliner, powdered cheeks, and crimson-painted mouth could not disguise the telltale signs of aging. Deanna guessed this woman neither wanted nor needed her pity, but she felt sorrow nonetheless. *Mierda, she's old enough to be my mother.*

Ghost Dog's voice was gentle, but firm. "No, we aren't."

The woman cocked her head. "You sure? I'll do both of you for time and a half."

"We're sure."

Raucous shouts rising from the card game near the front of the room grabbed the woman's attention. "Looks like someone's won big," she said. With no further acknowledgement she turned and walked away, heading for more promising prospects.

Deanna forced herself to relax, surprised at how tense she'd grown. "I've never been propositioned by a puta before. I'm not sure how I feel about it."

"Don't worry. They'll leave us alone now," Ghost Dog said. He gave her arm an affectionate squeeze.

She shook her head. "You know, Dog...I was the Alcalde of New Bayona's daughter...and I knew nothing about any of this." That an entire society could exist out here in the Wilds, and thrive, independent of any city control, amazed her.

"Does it bother you that you didn't know?" Ghost Dog asked.

Deanna had a hard time admitting to herself, let alone to another, that her father might not be the paragon of forthright honesty she had always imagined. That he could keep such a big, important truth hidden from her aroused a fierce ache in her heart.

"Yes, it does," she said, "even though my father didn't exactly lie to me. I know he must've had his reasons, but still…"

"Maybe he was trying to protect you."

"From what?"

Ghost Dog shrugged. "I don't know. But as you said, he must have had his reasons."

Father, I'm certain you never dreamed I'd end up out here, and yet... here I am. If we ever see each other again, we'll have a lot to talk about.

Without warning, from a hidden well of memory, an image of Zander raising a beer mug to his lips floated through Deanna's mind. Loss pierced her heart like a stiletto as tears blinded her eyes.

"Dee, what's wrong?" Ghost Dog laid gentle fingers on her cheek. "You're crying."

"I'm all right," she murmured, wiping her eyes on the back of her wrist. "I was just remembering someone…that's all."

Ghost Dog's mouth twitched, but the question in his golden eyes remained unasked.

With a deliberate smile, Deanna said, "I'm starving. What do we do to get served around here?"

"Order at the bar." Ghost Dog slid from his chair, but Deanna climbed to her feet and stopped him with a raised palm.

"I'll go. What do you want?"

"Steak and a beer, please."

Deanna threaded her way between the tables, trying not to make eye contact with anyone. As the only alta woman in the room not at work, she felt conspicuous. But aside from a few desultory glances tossed her way, she was ignored.

The bar itself, fashioned from a single shaved sawtooth log, anchored the north end of the room. With a soft apology, Deanna pushed between a buckskin-clad Tiqui man perched on a stool and a shaven-headed alta whose face bore a terrifying burden of scars. She shivered as the disfigured man cast a one-eyed glance at her before returning his attention to his alta companion.

A slate board hung from a peg on the wall behind the bar. The menu selections, scribbled in chalk, read *cervena steak, gazela steak, puerco stew*. As Deanna considered the limited choices, she found herself listening to the scarred man and his companion.

"...happened about a month ago," the scarred man said, his voice little more than a harsh croak. "Red Hill Precinct and the Hall of Records. Whole city was in an uproar."

Unsettled by what she'd heard, Deanna couldn't help but glance at the scarred man. He met her gaze and she quickly looked away.

"The resistance is gettin' bolder, Calderone. That's Yesu's honest truth," his hook-nosed companion replied.

The scarred man clicked his tongue. "Killed a bunch of polis. Alcalde slapped a curfew on the city the next day, and the Specials came down like the Madre's own wrath. Lots of blood and busted heads all over The Maze. In Red Hill, too. Lots of folk rounded up and hauled to detention."

The hook-nosed man stirred his drink with a forefinger. "You can beat a perro only so much before it turns and bites. Seems to me like it's time folks started biting. Maybe next time, the rebels'll bomb the palace."

The scarred man took a swig from his beer mug. "That'd take some mighty big *cojones*."

Madre, things back home are getting worse, Deanna thought. *The more Faustin's organization strikes at her, the more Lourdessa will punish the people. And what if they do target the palace?*

An image of Ceilia lying like a broken toy in a mound of rubble flashed before her inner eye. She leaned past the bulk of the scarred man's shoulder to catch the attention of his companion. "Excuse me. I didn't mean to eavesdrop, but…"

The scarred man looked at her from the corner of his one, slate-hard eye. "You did anyway." The hook-nosed man tsked.

Deanna resisted the urge to retreat. "I'm sorry. I've been gone awhile. I haven't heard much news."

The scarred man swiveled on his stool to face her. She couldn't tell if the twist of his lip was deformity or contempt. "Do you know if any people were hurt? By the bombs, I mean," she asked.

"Some civvies got caught in the Red Hill blast. A few died."

"You were there when it happened?"

He sniffed. "Yeah."

Deanna pressed. "Are the people protesting against the crackdown?"

The scarred man's demeanor morphed from impersonal to cool menace. "You sure are a curious one, girlie. You're out here, living with the *camarons*," he tilted his head toward Ghost Dog, "far away from city troubles. What do you care?"

His challenge, flung in her face with cold disdain, chilled her like a dousing of ice water. Chastened, she turned away, imagining she could still feel his single eye boring into the side of her head.

"What'll you have?" a barman asked.

"Uh, two cervena steaks and two mugs of your best beer, please."

The barman snorted. "We only serve one kinda beer here, girlie. The waitress'll bring your food."

As Deanna headed back to their table, from across the room, she saw the puzzled look on Ghost Dog's face.

He waited to ask until she sat down. "What's wrong?"

"Something terrible happened in Nue Bayona," she whispered. "The street resistance bombed a police station and a government office. I overheard the big man sitting at the bar telling his friend. It happened about a month ago. People died."

"No wonder you look upset."

"I'm afraid for my sister, Dog. They'll try to attack the palace, I'm sure of it. Ceilia will be in harm's way." *And what about Zander? And my father?*

"Do you want to return to the city?"

The question gave her momentary pause. *If I suddenly show up alive in Nue Bayona, Lourdessa will know that Roberto Gomaz didn't carry out his orders. She'll have him arrested and tortured. Then, it's only a matter of time before she learns who's really running the resistance. Can I risk that?*

Deanna took a deep breath and let Ghost Dog's calming presence ease her conflicted mind. "I have to. As soon as possible. I only wish I had some kind of plan."

"You must have allies who'll help you," Ghost Dog said.

Yes, but I foolishly let my fears get the best of me and didn't trust them when I should've. Aloud, she said, "I do, but I can't reach out to them. It's too dangerous. I'll have to do things on my own, in secret…though at the moment I have no idea how."

"You are much stronger and more clever than you think, Dee." Ghost Dog's golden eyes brimmed with compassion. "I have faith in you."

At that moment, those five simple words—*I have faith in you*—felt to Deanna like a warm, comforting embrace. Although worry still fluttered at the edges of her mind, now that she'd made her decision, her clarity and focus had returned.

The waitress arrived with two platters balanced on her forearms and a beer mug in each fist. The savory aroma of grilled cervena and fried patoks reawakened Deanna's appetite. Though simple rough fare, the food tasted delicious.

"We'll finish our business here as quickly as possible," Ghost Dog said between mouthfuls. "Once we return to the valley, you can decide on a plan. I'll help in any way I can, of course. You don't have to go back alone."

"Thanks, Dog. I know I can count on you, but this isn't your fight." Deanna pushed her plate aside. "I have to do this on my own. Somehow."

Ghost Dog put his knife and fork down and laid his fingers over Deanna's closed fists. "When the time comes, you'll know what to do."

The earnestness of his tone crushed her self-control. She found herself in his arms, wetting his bare shoulder with her tears.

ACROSS THE ROOM, Calderone sat at the bar, pondering his next move. He glanced over his muscular shoulder at the alta girl and her Tiqui companion.

The boss'll have to be told Hernaan's daughter's still alive, he thought.

He drained the remains of his beer in a single gulp, fished a Bayonan two-reále coin from his pocket and dropped it on the bar. The hook-nosed man looked up from the depths of his mug. "Hey, where ya goin', friend?"

"Away from here. And I'm not your friend." His erstwhile companion muttered an obscenity and returned to drinking. By the time he'd finished his second beer, Calderone had saddled his eelat and departed the station, riding hard for Nue Bayona.

30
trial by fire

Throughout the entire journey back to Reed Valley, Deanna fretted. Returning to Nue Bayona would have been foolhardy, even if Faustin wasn't escalating his campaign. And yet, how could she not go back? Ceilia had no one to protect her, and then there was Zander, her dearest friend. Had he survived detention? And if so, did he now risk his life as a member of Faustin's resistance? She had to find out.

By the time she and Ghost Dog emerged from the gap in the sheltering hills overlooking her adopted home, Deanna had made up her mind to set out for Nue Bayona the very next morning.

Below, the valley sweltered beneath the midday sun. Heat mirages rippled the air. The two young Tiqui warriors standing guard duty had returned to their posts high in the cliff walls, after first hailing Ghost Dog and welcoming him and Deanna back home.

The eelats raised their heads and sniffed, rolling and chomping their bits. "They smell the herd," Ghost Dog commented. He slapped Grim's lathered neck. "C'mon. Let's get them to their rest."

Word of their return spread quickly on the feet of the village children. When they arrived at the paddocks, Strong Hand and River were waiting.

"Hausi, my children," the natome called. He held Ghost Dog's eelat's head while his son dismounted. "How did the trading go?"

"Very well, Father," Ghost Dog replied. "I've got several bolts of algodon cloth, some coal oil, the new saw blade you wanted…"

"And, I found the part I need to fix the village generator," Deanna said.

"Marvelous," Strong Hand replied.

River steadied Deanna's mount as she swung to the ground. "What about the jenjibre root for Moon?" he asked. Deanna heard the worry in his voice.

"The Ancestors granted us the best of luck, Brother," Ghost Dog said. He rummaged in his saddlebag for a few moments, then withdrew a small cloth pouch and tossed it to River.

"Praise Them," the young redhead exclaimed, then pressed the pouch to his lips. "Moon will finally get some relief."

"It's good to have you back home," Strong Hand said, smiling first at Ghost Dog, then Deanna.

River gave Deanna's shoulder a gentle squeeze. "Both of you," he added.

"It is good to be back," Deanna replied, fighting to keep all trace of sadness from her voice. The realization that Reed Valley had indeed become her home only made her resolve to leave all the more difficult.

She sighed. "Natome, I have something very important to tell Yellow Bird."

"She's at the house." Deanna saw the question in Strong Hands' eyes. "You go on," he said. "We'll finish here."

Grateful she didn't have to explain, Deanna nodded and left her three friends to unsaddle the eelats.

She found Yellow Bird and Shadow lying together in a hammock on the veranda, little White Fox curled up between them. At first glance they appeared to be napping. Deanna paused at the bottom step, loathe to disturb them, but Yellow Bird raised her head and beckoned Deanna with a crooked finger.

"I heard that you and my son had returned," the ithani said, her voice soft and blurred from sleep. "How did the trading go?"

Deanna mounted the stairs with a delicate tread. "Very well," she whispered. "The village women will have algodon cloth to make new clothes." She paused; then added, "And, I found the part needed to fix the generator."

"Oh, that's wonderful."

Deanna glanced at Shadow's sleeping form, then said, "Ithani, I need to talk to you, but...it can wait until later."

Yellow Bird sat up and carefully swung her feet to the floor. Shadow stirred, mumbling. Yellow Bird murmured in his ear and he settled. She then rose and padded on small, bare feet to take Deanna by the arm. "You are anxious, child," she said, steering Deanna over to a bench against the wall, away from her husband and son. "Speak to me."

Deanna gazed into the ithani's liquid gold eyes, so full of a mother's affection and wisdom. "Ithani, I've made a decision. I have to leave Reed Valley and return to Nue Bayona."

Sadness replaced the look of gentle concern on the ithani's face. "Why this change of heart?"

"My sister needs me. She's alone and in danger."

"How do you know this?" Yellow Bird asked gently.

Deanna felt her cheeks ignite as she remembered the scarred man's contempt. "At Dry Creek, I overheard two alta talking. The rebels have escalated their attacks. They're striking police stations and government offices, now. I'm afraid they'll soon attack the palace."

Yellow Bird caressed the backs of Deanna's hands as she spoke. "Deanna, I understand the instinct to protect a loved one, but...I fear for your life."

"I know it's dangerous," Deanna said. "I don't care. And it's not just my sister who's in danger." She paused, gazing intently into the ithani's face. "There's my father, and my best friend Zander. No...he's so much more than a friend. I know that now," she continued. "He's my sunaiya. I need to find him and tell him how I feel before it's too late."

Yellow Bird took Deanna's face between her hands. Her gaze had turned fierce and penetrating. "Child, you must listen. You cannot return to the city. Not now."

"But...I have to go back," Deanna insisted.

"Heed my words, Deanna." Yellow Bird's voice, though still soft, now thrummed with an undeniable authority. "My visions have shown me what will happen if you take this path. Only death awaits you and those you love at its end."

No...I don't want to hear this. A single tear spilled from her eye. "Ithani, please," Deanna whispered.

Yellow Bird sighed and tenderly clasped Deanna's rigid fingers. "I'm so sorry, child. I know this is hard to swallow, but if you trust me, you won't do this thing," she murmured." You are too precious to me. I can't let you die."

Deanna yielded, sinking into the ithani's arms. "I do trust you, as I would my own mother. But...I'm so scared for my father and Ceilia and Zander. If anything happens to them..."

Yellow Bird kissed her forehead. "We're here, all of us, to give you the love and strength you'll need to get through."

IN THE LOFT she shared with the family's stores of food and winter clothing, Deanna sat on the edge of her cot, fully clothed; waiting.

When all had gone quiet and still below, she donned a pack filled with supplies she'd assembled in secret over the last two days. She secured her pistol in her belt and crept on stockinged feet down the ladder to the main room. The Tiqui custom of leaving shoes and boots beside the front door made it easy for her to retrieve her own boots without undue noise.

I'm sorry Yellow Bird, she thought, as she tiptoed across the veranda and down the stairs. *I trust you, but you've said many times that your visions only show you what may happen, not what will. I have to believe I can avoid whatever death you've foreseen for me.*

With a heavy heart, Deanna made her way through the sleeping village. Past the school, the carpentry shop, and the smokehouse she walked. Each place evoked its own special memories—the voices of children reciting their letters, the smells of sawdust and wood polish, and the taste of smoked cervena sausage. By the time she reached the communal vegetable garden her cheeks were wet with tears.

Overhead, Luna—in three-quarter phase—had just cleared the blunted teeth of the surrounding hills. Nayna was in her dark phase, so tonight Deanna cast but a single shadow. The air felt deliciously cool after the day's fierce heat.

At the eelat paddock she paused to dry her eyes and weigh the options of taking a mount against traveling on foot. After a few moments she moved on. Though she suspected her friends would hold her blameless, with no means to return the animal, it felt too much like theft.

I only have to get as far as Dry Creek, she thought. Once there, she'd find a ride back to the city. Though with no money or goods to barter, paying for that ride would be problematic.

One thing at a time, Dee.

At the edge of the north meadow, Deanna paused once more to look back at the place she'd grown to love so quickly. Though she might never return, still it would always feel like home.

Hitching the pack up more comfortably on her shoulders, she set out on the dirt path that led toward the defile in the hills. The dry grass rustled with the furtive movements of the meadow's myriad inhabitants, some tiny, others not so. Deanna felt no threat; in truth the nighttime sounds of the valley filled her heart with peace.

Deanna smelled the smoke before she caught sight of a dancing yellow light on the path ahead. As she drew closer, the light resolved itself into a small fire burning near the mouth of the defile. A figure crouched beside it, no more than a shadow against the glow.

Damn...must be one of the guards. Chagrinned that her plans for a quick and secret departure were not to be realized, Deanna approached. "Hausi, and good evening to you," she called.

"Hausi, and good evening to you, Deanna," a familiar contralto voice replied.

Shocked, Deanna sank to her knees beside Yellow Bird. After several moments of silence, she corralled her whirling thoughts and spoke. "What are you doing here, Ithani?"

"Waiting for you, child," Yellow Bird answered softly.

Deanna sighed. "You knew I planned to leave."

The ithani's eyes flashed like new-minted coins in the firelight. "I had a suspicion."

A small teapot rested atop a metal grate over the coals. Yellow Bird herself sat cross-legged on a reed mat, a light wool shawl draped about her slim shoulders. She picked up a stick and stirred the embers. "I tried with all my power to persuade you to heed my warning. You chose to ignore me."

Deanna felt a chill blow through her, despite the warmth of the fire. "Please, Ithani," she whispered. "Don't be angry with me."

Yellow Bird's smile was gentle. "Oh, no, sweet child. I'm not angry with you. Disappointed perhaps. But angry? Never."

"I trust you, Ithani, I really do. But you've said your visions aren't always accurate. Maybe this is one of those times."

"It's true. My visions don't always show me what will be. But in this, I *know* what I've seen is the only possible outcome, should you choose this path. I've scried it many times. And every time, despite small variations in events, the end is always the same."

From a leather satchel, Yellow Bird produced two tiny clay cups. She set them down by the fire. "You are a courageous young woman, Deanna, whose heart will not allow her to forsake those she loves.

Which is why I've decided to attempt something that's never been done before."

Deanna glanced at the teapot. "Ithani, is that…" Her voice trailed off as Yellow Bird fixed her with a compassionate gaze tinged with resolve.

"Yes, and there's enough for both of us," the ithani replied. "No shaman has ever shared the mezcala link with a non-initiate, much less an alta. I'm not at all certain it can be done. However, I'm willing to try so that you may see what I see, and be convinced to your very marrow of the truth."

Yellow Bird wrapped her hands in a thick cloth and lifted the pot off the fire, laying it aside on a flat rock. Rising to her feet, she shook out a second, larger mat. "This will be unlike anything you've ever experienced, Deanna," she said. "I'll be there to guide you, but still there's a real risk that you could become lost in the dream realm. I might not be able to call you back to the waking world."

"I'd go insane," Deanna murmured. "Like an end-stage sueño addict." She thought of Alehan, lost in the seductive embrace of an especially potent high. How much longer before her stepbrother fell into the abyss of insanity?

Once more, Yellow Bird knelt and took Deanna's hands in hers. The fire, collapsed to glowing coals, gave off a feeble light. "If you're ready, we can begin," the ithani said.

For one terrifying moment, Deanna felt the darkness closing in. *Am I strong enough to witness my own death?* she wondered. In answer to her own doubt she shrugged the pack from her shoulders and removed the .45 from her belt. She set both aside. "I'm ready," she said.

Yellow Bird nodded and filled the two cups with mezcala tea. Her small, graceful movements were infused with both honor and reverence. Head bowed, she murmured, "Ancestors, grant me strength to bear my gift with courage, and help me guide this seeker to the truth."

She held out a cup. "Drink quickly."

Deanna took the tiny vessel and raised it to her lips. Her nose filled with the essences of smoke and earth. She took a deep breath and drained the cup to the dregs.

"Lie down," Yellow Bird instructed, gesturing to the larger mat. "Remove your boots if you like." Deanna did as she was bid. Already her body felt strangely weightless, as if the slightest breeze could bear her aloft with no effort. Yellow Bird slipped a small cushion beneath her head. "Take slow, deep breaths," she said. "Become as a leaf upon the swift-flowing stream. Let the medicine do its work."

An ocean of stars wheeled overhead, filling Deanna's sight with its unending vastness. She felt her body falling up into the panoply of lights, and was afraid. But then the voice of Yellow Bird whispered in her mind, calm and steady.

Let go, child. I am with you.

Courage renewed, Deanna shed the last tethers holding her mind earthbound, and floated free. At first she drifted, surrounded by an infinity of glittering jewels, which elongated into streaks of light as she picked up speed and hurtled toward a vortex of colors so bright she could barely look upon it. Like a diver, she plunged headlong into the kaleidoscope.

Darkness. The feeling that large shapes hem her in on all sides is overwhelming. She tries to move, but her body is held fast by unseen hands gripping her arms and shoulders.

"Yellow Bird," she cries. "Help me!"

"Easy. I am here. Remember, none of this is real. Step out of your dream-self and become the watcher."

Deanna struggles to break free, but the grip on her shoulders grows tighter. "I don't know how."

"Yes, you do. Let go of your fear. Concentrate!"

Deanna relaxes, and the panic threatening to overthrow her sanity flows through her like water through a sieve, leaving calm in its wake. Her unseen bonds loosen. She steps away...and sees herself, standing before her stepmother in Lourdessa's mayoral office, flanked by two huge shadows that ripple in the half-light, as if made of black water. They are pinning her arms at her sides. Lourdessa sits at her desk, tapping nails like crimson daggers on the shiny wood. She regards her stepdaughter with hatred so profound, Deanna wonders how it could exist within one person.

"What did I ever do to you?" Deanna asks.

"You made me feel naked." Lourdessa flicks her hand. Sparks shoot from her fingertips and drift around the room like electric snowflakes. Take her away.

Deanna watches the shadow-Specials drag her dream-self, unprotesting, from the room. She turns and sees...Ceilia, crouching in the corner, a strange half-smile on her lips. Something in her eyes isn't right.

The scene dissolves like smoke on a stiff breeze, to reveal a dim, trash-strewn alley. Deanna senses Yellow Bird's steady presence, anchoring her to the unseen reality beyond this realm of drug-induced visions. She draws strength from it, and waits.

Soon, she hears rapid footsteps. Two figures plunge into the alley at a dead run. They hurtle toward Deanna and skid to a stop several paces from where she stands. She cannot see them yet in the shadow. Their breaths rattle and wheeze in their throats. She hears stark fear when one of them catches enough breath to speak.

"They're right behind us, Zander."

Horrified, Deanna realizes that, somehow, Zander has been caught up in this deadly scene.

"Mierda...this alley's a dead end," he cries.

A black cloud congeals at the alley's entrance. In eerie silence, it floats toward the shivering fugitives.

Deanna can only watch, helpless to intervene. "I wanted to see this," she reminds herself.

Zander takes Deanna's dream-self into his arms and kisses her with the passion of a man savoring the last beautiful thing he will feel before death.

The cloud becomes a pack of Specials. They halt and raise their ee-pistols. The barrels crackle with blue static.

Zander pushes dream-Deanna behind him, offering his body as a shield, paltry though it be, in a vain attempt to save her life.

"This is your last chance to come with us, Deanna," one of the Specials shouts.

"No," she whispers, then lays her head on Zander's shoulders and closes her eyes.

The ee-pistols discharge in a unified flash of blue-white energy.

Two bodies lie at Deanna's feet, their limbs entwined in a death state as intimate as any lover's embrace. An upwelling of sorrow and rage so intense it could burn all of existence engulfs her. She feels control of her sanity slipping.

"Deanna, listen. Look up and let the light take you. Follow the light."

It takes all her strength to tear her eyes away from the bodies on the ground. She looks up and sees the kaleidoscope. She raises her arms and lets the energy of the vortex suck her in.

DEANNA OPENED HER eyes. Instead of stars, Yellow Bird's face, serene as a valley sunrise, filled her vision. "Ithani…" she began, but then, the full import of what she'd seen seized and shook her. She flung herself into Yellow Bird's waiting arms, clinging as if to a rock in turbulent waters. Yellow Bird whispered soothing words and stroked her hair until she could speak once more.

Deanna's head felt as if it had grown too heavy for her neck. "I can't go back. I see that now," she said, her cheek pressed to Yellow Bird's shoulder. The ithani smelled of rosa, a scent that triggered Deanna's memories of her own dead mother. She wanted to remain wrapped in Yellow Bird's arms forever.

"You were magnificent, Deanna," the ithani murmured. "I've trained initiates with less raw talent." As Deanna drew back, Yellow Bird took her face between her small hands. "I thank the Ancestors you had the courage to do what you did. Now lie back. The aftereffects of the medicine can be unpleasant. I'll bring you the antidote."

Deanna curled on her side. Already, she felt dizzy, and the beginnings of a fierce headache tapped the back of her skull. "If it were only me," she said, watching the ithani sprinkle a pinch of powder into a cup, "I might not have changed my mind, but seeing Zander, my suna-iya, die trying to protect me…I can't let that happen."

Yellow Bird added a small amount of water to the cup and brought it to Deanna. "This will ease most of the withdrawal."

Deanna took the cup, lifted her head, and swallowed the bitter liquid in one gulp. As she lay back down, the pain began to ease.

Yellow Bird looked up at the sky. Luna rode directly overhead. "We'll start back as soon as you can walk," she said. "You can still get a few hours sleep before sunrise." She poured the dregs of the mezcala tea into the fire.

Deanna closed her eyes, and allowed the images she'd seen to replay themselves in her mind. Lourdessa's hatred came as no surprise, but Deanna didn't understand why their stepmother would allow Ceilia to witness her condemnation. And what of the eerie smile on her sister's face? What did it mean? Could Lourdessa have somehow turned Ceilia against her?

No, that's not possible…is it?

And then, there was Zander. Watching him die had proved more painful than witnessing her own death. How and why he'd come to be in that alley, facing a firing squad beside her, had not been revealed. The exact circumstances didn't matter. By remaining in Reed Valley she would stop them from being set in motion.

"How are you feeling?" Yellow Bird asked.

Deanna sat up and reached for her boots. "Well enough to go back now…Ithani, you said you'd trained initiates with less raw talent than I. Does that mean I could learn the ways of the shaman?"

In the dark Deanna couldn't see Yellow Bird's face, but she heard the thoughtful note in the ithani's voice. "Before tonight, if anyone had asked me if an alta could be trained in our traditions, I'd have said no. But, now, I think…yes, Deanna. Anything is possible."

"It seems the longer I live among you, the more Tiqui I become." Deanna paused. Then, wary that she might offend, she asked, "Perhaps one day you'll agree to train me?"

"Perhaps, child. Perhaps," Yellow Bird replied with a smile.

31
a terrible thing of beauty

At the north end of the cavernous hangar that served as the workshop for the AX238 project, Eduard stood with his assistant, Suela Ayenda, a new-minted graduate from the university engineering program, hovering beside him, a black binder stuffed with spec sheets clutched to her breast.

The workshop, normally filled with the dissonant sounds of construction, lay quiet. The workers had halted for the midday break. The two of them had the expansive space to themselves.

Scion of one of Nue Bayona's finest families, Suela's chestnut hair framed a face drawn in delicate lines, made lovelier by eyes the color of new leaves. She had arrived at the workshop six weeks ago to present her credentials and show him her order—affixed with the official seal of the Alcalde's office—to take up the post as his personal assistant. Eduard had accepted without argument, despite nagging worries that the pretty young woman might be his wife's agent, sent to spy on him.

Suela had proven herself to be intelligent and capable. Eduard found her advice invaluable. Maintaining his suspicions had grown more difficult with each passing day, until now, he couldn't imagine a better assistant.

"Such a thing of beauty, and yet, such a horror." Eduard sighed and allowed the schematic in his hands to curl closed. He studied the construct before him.

In the center of the concrete floor, surrounded by a cage of scaffolding, a four-meter high skeleton sketched in steel lofted toward the open ceiling. Natural light from multiple windows placed high in the corrugated walls bathed the metal bones of the machine in a soft, silvery shimmer.

"Still, you must feel some pride in what you're accomplishing," Suela said. "Nothing like this has been built in hundreds of years. It's... exciting."

"Pride?" Eduard smacked the rolled-up schematic against his open palm. "Hardly. Instead of focusing on rediscovering useful tech, here we are...working to resurrect the machine that destroyed the colonial civilization."

Suela's gaze dropped to her scuffed work boots.

Instantly regretting his sharp tone, Eduard said, "Don't mind me. I'm just a grumpy old man who needs to vent now and then. This is a great opportunity for a young engineer like you. Perhaps, while working on this project, you'll rediscover something that will make a positive difference for our city."

"We'll discover it together." She lifted her face to meet his eyes, her own imbued with a strange intensity. Eduard felt a familiar warmth, but quashed it. To do otherwise presented perils too great to risk.

"Any word from the fabricators yet?" Eduard held out his hand and Suela relinquished the binder. He flipped it open and scanned the first few pages.

"They've gotten about half the hull plating done," Suela replied. "After the mishap with the blast furnaces, I'm surprised at how fast they got back on track. The first load should arrive tomorrow."

"Working under threat is a great motivator." *A fact I know only too well.* "Those cracked plates have cost us a week's delay," he continued. "I suspect my wife has promised unpleasant consequences for the families of both the factory workers and the owners if anything else should go wrong."

Suela remained silent, but the tension in her lips spoke of her discomfort. Eduard vowed to refrain from such comments in the future. The last thing he wanted was for her to feel ill at ease in his presence.

He moved closer to the machine, Suela trailing in his wake. Though he despised it for its intended purpose, Eduard could not stop the twinge of awe and admiration evoked by its terrible beauty.

Two-centimeter-thick steel plates would armor the frame. Its weapons complement included a forward-mounted ee-cannon, a 40-mm gun, grenade launchers, machine guns, and an aft-mounted flamethrower. The cockpit windows were composed of bulletproof glass. The yet-to-be-installed power plant, a massive, semi-flash monotube boiler, would sit in a rear compartment behind a heat shield. The entire ten-meter length rested atop six multi-jointed legs, each capable of independent movement.

His earlier denial to Suela had been a lie. As an engineer, Eduard took great pride in his work. As a human being, he felt disgust and anger.

"I want you to double-check the pressure calculations for the boiler," he said.

"You've gone over them a half-dozen times, Doctor…we both have," Suela pointed out. "They're correct—forty-six kps."

"Don't you think it's time you started calling me Eduard?" He looked back at her and smiled. She bit her lip. For an instant Eduard feared he had made her uncomfortable again, but she returned his smile and nodded.

"You know those numbers are correct…Eduard."

They reached the base of the scaffolding and gazed up through the maze of struts, cables, and wires.

"I want to go up and inspect the cannon mounts." Eduard held out the binder for Suela to reclaim. He placed a foot on the bottom rung of the service ladder attached to the scaffolding.

The ratcheting sound of the hangar doors sliding back on their runners halted Eduard's climb mid-step. Two men approached them—his stepson and Raul Olivas, the Chief Engineer of Nue Bayona. Suela, clutching the binder against her breasts like a shield, edged a step closer to him.

"Where are all the workers?" Alehan's handsome face wore its usual sneer.

"The men are entitled to meal breaks." Eduard stepped away from the scaffold, his voice as mild as water. "They're scheduled to return at two."

Alehan's fair cheeks flushed scarlet and his eyes narrowed to slits. A muscle in his jaw twitched, worm-like. "Yesu's balls, are you trying to piss me off? You're already a week behind. I want those lazy perros working around the clock if need be."

Before Eduard could respond, Olivas stepped in. "Calm yourself, Estes. A week's delay isn't insurmountable. If you deny the workers their breaks, you'll only foster resentment and they won't perform at their optimum levels."

Alehan continued to glower. "My mother charged me with making sure this project is completed on time. She wants the machine ready for testing by the end of the month."

Eduard shook his head. "Impossible. We'll need at least one additional month."

"You can't have another month." Alehan's tone rippled with an undertow of menace. "Need I remind you what you stand to lose if you don't deliver?"

Madre, give me strength. "Yes, I'm well aware of your mother's promises," Eduard replied, "but that still doesn't mean we'll be ready to test in two weeks." He chose his next words with care. "Last week, a mishap at the metal fabricators resulted in an entire run of cracked hull plates. The furnaces weren't primed properly, so the metal was poured too cold. We're getting a shipment tomorrow, but only half of what we need. You didn't think to factor normal setbacks into your schedule, Alehan. If you rush us, you're risking the ruin of the entire project."

Alehan took a step toward Eduard, coming within striking distance, radiating thuggish belligerence. Eduard stood firm, refusing to back away.

"I don't care about any of your stupid excuses. Just get it done."

Eduard had known Alehan since boyhood. He'd recognized the monster hidden within the beautiful child even then. It had stared out at him through the windows of Alehan's youthful eyes, boldly challenging the man who would be his father to a death match for the soul of its host.

The monster had won.

"Eduard is right. This project can't be rushed," Olivas interjected. A sheen of sweat slicked his bald pate. He flapped a chubby hand at the scaffold-caged construct. "There's still too much to do. We need more time."

Alehan raked the Chief Engineer with a glance like barbed wire. "Mother won't like this at all."

"Your mother must resign herself to the fact that she can't have everything her way," Eduard replied. "She'll get her machine. Just not by the end of this month."

"I want to see the cockpit," Alehan said.

"It's not finished," Olivas warned, his nostrils flaring in alarm.

"I don't care. Take me up, now."

"It's all right, Raul," Eduard said. He offered Suela a reassuring smile and gestured toward the service ladder. "After you."

He waited until Alehan had scrambled to the top and lowered himself through a gap in the roof frame before following. "You're in the pilot's seat," Eduard informed him as he dropped into the second of the two sturdy padded chairs already bolted into place.

"That's fitting, since I intend to drive it when it's finished," Alehan replied. His eyes darted like hungry fish over the toggles and gauges set in the glossy, ebon-wood control console, installed earlier that morning.

Madre preserve, Eduard thought, shaken to his core. He wondered if Lourdessa knew of her son's intentions.

"How many men are needed to operate this beauty?" Alehan asked.

"Six," Eduard explained. "A pilot, copilot, two boilermen, and two gunners — one per turret. All compartments are linked via hatches both forward and rear. Communications between compartments is via telephony and we can speak to security on the ground with a wireless set. All of that has yet to be installed."

Alehan continued to stare, enraptured, at the console. Eduard continued. "The current for the electrical systems is generated by the turbine in the boiler compartment. The pilot can monitor steam pressure in all systems with these gauges." He pointed to a row of glass-fronted dials. "There are also gauges in the boiler compartment itself."

Like a man asking a friend about a potential lover, Alehan said, "Tell me about the weapons systems."

"An ee-cannon will be housed in the forward turret." Eduard pointed directly overhead. "It's powered by a bank of seven, S-grade fuel cells connected in sequence. It can be fired only three times before all the cells are exhausted, but the 40-mm gun can be brought to bear at any time."

"I thought I saw a flamethrower on the stern," Alehan said.

Eduard nodded. "You did. It's connected to the same coal-oil reservoir that flash-fires the boiler. It can fire in bursts of up to six seconds or continuously for fifteen minutes before it needs refueling. Two machine guns and eight steam-propelled grenade launchers will complete the armaments."

A slow smile curved Alehan's handsome mouth. "You really are an effing genius, Eduard," he said, his voice ripe with admiration.

Eduard took no pride in the compliment. "That's all there is to see, at this point," he said, then, without waiting for Alehan to react, he climbed out of the cockpit and started down the ladder. He reached the bottom and stood aside, watching, while his stepson scrambled down and dropped to the floor.

"I'll be back tomorrow," Alehan said. His gaze lingered for a few heartbeats on the machine before he turned and headed toward the warehouse entrance.

Suela exhaled. Slowly the color began seeping back into her cheeks.

Wringing his hands like an anxious matron, Olivas said, "Eduard... how soon can you finish? Realistically?"

"The frame is done," Eduard replied. "But we still have the outer hull plates and the weapons to install. The electrical wiring is only partially complete. And of course there's the boiler. It'll be difficult, but I think I can get it finished in another six weeks."

"I'm anxious to see how the new heat-tempered glass for the windshield performs," Suela said.

Salvagers had found pieces of toughened glass among the debris of the continent's ruins for centuries. Since his days as a university professor, Olivas had worked to rediscover the process. The added incentive of the Annihilator project provided the momentum to drive him to a final breakthrough.

Hands folded at the small of his back, Nue Bayona's Chief Engineer rocked on his heels like a happy child. "I'm quite proud of it," he said. "The commercial applications are what're most important. Think of how much safer auto windshields eventually will be. I only need to conduct a few more minor tests. I've got my two best assistants on it."

One good thing will come from all this, Eduard thought. "Let me know when that's done so we can send the specs to the fabricators." He grabbed the service ladder once again.

"Don't worry too much about Estes," Olivas said. "He may think he's in charge, but I'm Chief Engineer. I have the Alcalde's absolute confidence."

Eduard started up the ladder. "If you believe that, my friend, then you are fooling yourself."

32
the secret hostage

Four weeks had passed since the Red Hill precinct bombing. A heavy police presence in the streets kept the resistance cells in hiding, but the citizens had grown weary and restive beneath the burden of curfew. Only a direct appeal to the Alcalde by Archbishop De La Roha seemed to have had any effect; during the last few days, the cruel pressure had eased.

At the Rosa Blanca, tonight's dinner rush was winding down. Zander rode a stool at the end of the bar, polishing glassware at Beatrichia's request. Sonia sat beside him, folding dust rags. She didn't speak, and Zander didn't intrude on her silence.

The emotional aftermath of the Red Hill bombing had taken its toll on their relationship. Though they still shared a bed, to Zander, Sonia's embraces felt cooler. When they weren't coupling she treated him less like a lover and more like a casual acquaintance. Her coolness rankled, even though he knew he had no right to that emotion. After all, he'd been the one to withdraw first…not her.

Now, mistrust and the pain of unrequited love stood between them like an impenetrable wall of thorns. He didn't know if either of them had the will or desire to scale it.

Guermoe had just sent the last plate of blood sausage and fried patoks from the kitchen for the night when a ragged child scurried in. He pattered on bare feet to the bar, dropped a folded bit of paper at Sonia's elbow, and scurried out.

She opened the paper and scanned its contents. "We've been summoned." She slid off her stool, crumpling the paper in her fist.

Zander laid aside his polishing rag and trailed her out into the warm night. He didn't need to ask where they were going. Despite everything, Sonia still counted him as a member of her cell.

A twenty-minute walk beneath clear skies brought them to a warehouse in Quarry, near the city's coal-oil distillery. Winking like dim stars in Nayna's silver light, broken glass from shattered windows littered the gravel forecourt where spiky weeds struggled for survival. Rival gangs had marked over each other's symbols on the soot-stained brick walls. Faded lettering over a steel door large enough to admit a delivery van proclaimed that the building had once housed Choa and Sons Furniture.

Sonia led the way to a small side door and knocked. It cracked open and then swung just wide enough to allow them to squeeze through into the hallway beyond. Light flared, revealing a gaunt-faced young man wearing a dark, hooded jacket. He pointed his torch beam into the gloom. "Go down to the end, turn right. Mind your step."

Zander followed Sonia through alternating pools of moonlight and darkness to the main room of the derelict warehouse. In one corner the light of a bullseye lantern banished the shadows, revealing a small assembly standing around a broken shipping crate. Zander recognized Tony's wiry form next to Alberto's corpulent shape. As he and Sonia approached, Zander heard snatches of soft, tense conversation. Tony detached from the group and drew Sonia in, leaving Zander standing outside the circle. Uncertain, he hung back, watching and listening.

"It's getting harder and harder to avoid the puercos' dragnet," a short, redheaded girl was saying. Her eyes looked big and frightened in the dim light. "Eventually one of us is gonna get caught. And we all know what that means."

"Everyone, relax," Tony said. "As long as we're careful, no one's going to get caught."

You're so sure, are you? Zander thought. Hands thrust deep in his pockets, he waited, feeling apprehensive and invisible, until Sonia glanced up and waved him over. Tony looked at him but said nothing. Alberto smiled and stroked his arm. Zander edged away, putting Sonia between himself and the pudgy bomb maker.

Someone produced a bottle to pass around. When it got to Zander he took a sip, delighting in the pleasurable burn of *cirulo* brandy on his tongue. The rush helped to soothe his jittery nerves.

Off in the distance Zander heard the faint sound of a door opening and closing, followed by footsteps approaching in the dark. "Here they come," Alberto said.

Flanked by Ernesto and the hooded door guard, Faustin strode into the circle of light, trailing streamers of cigarette smoke. "Good evening, comrades," he said cheerfully.

Tonight, he wore the simple algodon work shirt, trousers, and scuffed boots of a common laborer. He had replaced the leather pantera mask with one of heavy molded paper, painted to look like a calico gahto. It covered his forehead and nose, leaving his mouth and chin exposed. A scarf of heavy black silk hid his hair beneath its tight-wound length.

As on the night a month ago when he'd met Faustin for the first time in the basement of Lucie's Tavern, Zander felt like he already knew the man behind the mask. The suspicion nagged like the ache from an old injury.

The group formed a close ring around their leader. Faustin took a final drag and flicked the smoldering cigarette butt to the cracked concrete floor.

"First off…congratulations to Sonia, Ernesto, and their crews on the success of the Red Hill and Hall of Records jobs," Faustin said. "Well done." Creases at the corners of his eyes told of the smile hidden beneath his mask. He made a point to look at Sonia, who nodded, as did Tony and Alberto. All three pulled themselves up straighter.

The memory of bloodied corpses denied Zander any feelings of pride. He crossed his arms and refused to meet Faustin's gaze, staring instead at a spot on the pitted wall above the rebel leader's head.

Faustin returned his attention to the gathering. "All our actions have gone off flawlessly. Your courage and fortitude have never waned. I should be pleased." He paused for effect. "But in fact, I'm furious. Not with you, comrades. But with the ruthless system that keeps its boot on the necks of the people."

The pull of Faustin's charisma kept all eyes riveted on him. He clenched his fists and began to pace, the group melting back to give him sufficient room.

"We have a big problem, comrades," he said. "Though we've struck blow after blow against this illegitimate regime, the Alcalde still refuses to take us and our demands seriously. Even when we proved we could strike at the instruments of her power — the police — she didn't bend. We will not be ignored. I won't be ignored!"

"What more can we do?" Ernesto stood with arms folded, scowling. "If blowing up the biggest police station in the city won't move her, then..."

Sonia spoke up. "Each time we strike, it's the people who suffer the punishment. We're losing their support. Even my uncle is beginning to question your motives, Faustin."

Zander looked at Sonia, eyebrows raised. That she would challenge Faustin in front of the whole group shocked him. The rebel leader stopped pacing. He fixed his gaze on Sonia. His eyes looked ready to defy natural law and burn her to ash. He took two steps toward her, fingers clenched. Sonia's face drained of color, but she remained rooted in place.

Zander found himself standing between them with no memory of having moved.

Faustin spun away. Zander felt like he had deflected something dangerous.

"My motives are being questioned now?" Faustin returned to pacing. His voice rose an octave. "I have more to lose than any of you!"

Since when did this become about you? Zander thought. He studied the faces around him, seeing anxiety, consternation, and puzzlement.

"I've only ever wanted one goal, worked toward one glorious achievement, and that is to bring down this criminal regime by whatever means necessary." He swept the crowd with a raised index finger. "How dare anyone question my motives?"

"No one here is questioning you, Faustin," Ernesto said in a low voice.

The rebel leader fell silent and still. His arms dropped down by his sides and his eyelids closed. As the seconds ticked by, he neither moved nor spoke. Zander sensed the growing confusion of the group. *What the hell? Has he fallen asleep?* He glanced at Sonia, who looked back at him and shrugged, clearly as mystified as everyone else.

Finally, Ernesto spoke. "Faustin?" he murmured.

Faustin's eyes snapped open. He shuddered and drew in a deep breath. "I understand the people are tired," he said. "They suffer, despite all our efforts. We need to increase the pressure so Lourdessa Hernaan can no longer refuse our demands."

Weird. It's like he doesn't even realize he's been gone, Zander sensed the built-up tension in the gathering begin to ease.

"Tell us how," Ernesto said, sounding relieved.

"We start targeting the elites, and the things they most cherish," Faustin replied. "We will sow such terror among them that *they* will force the Alcalde to capitulate." Below the edge of the painted mask, his sensuous mouth curved into a smile. "Hernaan can't ignore a strike on the Blessed Maria Girls Academy."

Yesu, he can't be serious. Zander wanted to scream his objection but the rapt faces of Faustin's followers paralyzed his tongue. *Those are children. What happened to us not hurting innocents?*

Graceful as a dancer Faustin glided past Zander, so close he could smell the tabac on the rebel leader's breath when he spoke. "We can't let the Sandstone raid go unanswered."

Two weeks ago the Special Police had raided Sandstone Primary School, claiming some of the teachers belonged to the resistance. Sandstone served as the only primary school for the entire Maze. Six children suffered severe injuries and one boy died of his wounds. The Specials had hauled five of the staff to detention. None of them belonged to the resistance.

"I heard no cries of outrage from the elites over the spilled blood of Maze children. Why should we feel any compassion for theirs?" Faustin fixed his gaze on Zander. Though at least ten kilos heavier and eighteen centimeters taller than the other man, Zander still shivered. Something cold and ruthless shimmered in the depths of the rebel leader's peridot eyes.

If we do the same things to them that they do to us, we lose any right to claim we're better than they are. Like a man confronting a poisonous serpent, Zander was desperate to step back, but the unyielding barrier of Tony's and Alberto's bodies imprisoned him. His lungs felt starved for air.

Ernesto coughed, and Faustin's gaze snapped onto his second-in-command. "You have something to say, Nez?" He stepped away and Zander felt he could breathe again.

In the dim light Ernesto's hair looked as dark as old blood. "We'll speak later." He and Faustin regarded each other in silence. Something passed between the two men, a message that needed no words.

The rebel leader clapped his hands. "Right." He spun back to the center of the group. "The elites believe we are nothing but a ragtag pack of street perros bent on anarchy. Unless we force them to fear and respect us, they will never negotiate. Let's show them we won't be denied."

Attacking their children won't gain their respect. Madre, this is insane.

Zander realized he'd reached the limits of his endurance. He glanced toward the exit, his desire to escape growing with each breath. Part of him longed for the comfort of certainty that drove so many in this room. The bigger part that needed to look at itself and not turn away in disgust, shouted at him to flee.

"I'm leaving," he whispered in Sonia's ear.

"What? Why?" She gripped his forearm, her eyes uncomprehending. Gently, he pried himself free.

"I'll see you outside," he said. As he pushed his way past them and headed for the door, Zander felt the heat of Tony and Alberto's disapproval ushering him out.

Outside, the night air felt cool on his flushed face. He leaned against the wall, staring into the dark. The rough concrete irritated the skin of his back through his thin shirt, but not enough to make him move.

I really thought he was a hero. Turns out he's just a bloody-minded pendayho.

Disillusionment tasted so very bitter.

The door swung open. "Zander," Sonia whispered. He refused to look at her

"Is the meeting finished?" he asked.

"Almost." She searched his face, her beautiful mouth twisted into a frown. "Why did you leave?"

Without a word he took her hand and led her away from the door, several dozen paces toward what had been a loading bay. Once inside he stopped to face her. "I was afraid I'd say something that'd get us both in trouble," he said in a low voice.

Sonia gently freed herself from his grasp. "What do you mean?"

"I'm only part of this group because you vouched for me. If I continue to cross Faustin, he'll hold it against you."

"What are you talking about?" Sonia's tone was almost plaintive.

Zander moved in closer. For the first time in many days, he felt like they'd regained their lost connection. "This plan to bomb the girls' school," he said. "Sonnie, it's wrong, and you know it. This isn't a principled resistance any more. It's a terrorist campaign. And none of you seems to see Faustin for what he truly is. I couldn't stay silent one second longer, so I had to leave."

"Zander...Faustin is committed to the people." Sonia insisted. "He doesn't want to hurt innocent children..."

Zander threw up his hands. "Madre, how can you say that? Weren't you listening?"

Sonia looked away. A year spent as her lover had taught Zander to read the essence of her thoughts and moods upon her face. He watched as her certainty gave way to doubt, but it lasted only a few moments. When she looked back at him, it was with the hard face of Faustin's valued lieutenant. "We have to trust him," she said. "I have to trust him. Otherwise..."

Sonia fell silent. Heartsick, Zander wondered if there was anything he could say to convince her. He could feel their brief, tenuous reconnection already beginning to dissolve, like clouds before a strong wind.

"I'm going back inside," she said. Zander remained in the shadows of the loading bay, listening to the crunch of her receding footsteps, his mind a blank. He heard the warehouse door open and close.

A faint scraping sound snapped him out of his reverie and drew him to the edge of the loading bay. Hoping it might be Sonia returning, he peered around the wall and saw a figure exit the warehouse. Its tall, slender form left no doubt in his mind as to the person's identity.

Faustin paused to light a cigarette. Then he strode off into the humid night amid a cloud of tabac smoke.

Before the dark could swallow him, Zander followed. He had no clear idea why; the impulse had taken him by surprise.

The murky streets of Quarry lay deserted and silent beneath a low ceiling of thin clouds. From somewhere close by, the high-frequency squeal of a night-hunting *buho* bird echoed. A warm breeze moaned and sighed, ruffling Zander's raven locks. The moons looked like fuzzy-edged coins, their lights attenuated by the haze of water vapor.

Faustin moved like a man late for an appointment. Zander matched him stride for stride, keeping far enough behind to remain unnoticed. He knew the rebel leader needed to go to ground before sunrise.

At first Faustin made no effort at stealth. Even without the Alcalde's curfew, the chance of encountering another soul abroad in this district, and at this hour, was remote. Once he reached Quarry Road, the main thoroughfare that separated the warehouse district from Red Hill, he dashed across it, plunging into the shadows cast by the shuttered shops and dark houses fronting the road.

The narrow streets of Red Hill fed into the wider thoroughfares of Valencea, which in turn broadened into the tree-lined avenues of Palace Hill. Instead of multistory tenements, high walls now rose on either side of the walkway. Behind them the manor houses of the elites crouched in hidden splendor. Here, electric streetlights banished the night, making it more difficult for Zander to remain undiscovered. As he darted from one pool of shadow to the next, he thanked Fortune for his cheap, near-silent rubber-soled shoes. Expensive hard-soled boots would have made too much noise.

Faustin paused to light another cigarette. Zander tried to merge with the cool sandstone of a retaining wall, his mind spinning with plans of action should the other man spot him. When the rebel leader flicked a dead match from his hand then continued walking, Zander breathed a sigh of relief. He counted to ten and hurried after his quarry.

At the outer wall surrounding the palace grounds, Faustin stepped down into a weed-choked ditch at its base, then headed north. When he paused before a section of wall overgrown with flowering *arboria* vines, a seed of suspicion sprouted in Zander's mind.

Faustin lifted aside the living curtain of vegetation and disappeared behind it. Zander waited several seconds before darting across the road. He too slipped behind the vines, as he had done countless times in the past, and stood immersed in cloying sweetness before a heavy wrought iron gate all but invisible from the street. Until now he believed only he and Deanna knew of this gate's existence. The fact that Faustin also knew disturbed him.

Deanna had shown him the gate years ago, when they first became lovers. It opened onto a remote expanse of garden at the back of the palace complex, near Deanna's isolated workshop. It had served as a convenient way for Zander to come and go unseen.

If Faustin knew about the gate, might he have an ally on the inside, a guardsman perhaps? Another possibility—Faustin himself worked in the palace and somehow had discovered the gate on his own. Might he even have a direct connection to the Alcalde herself? As a member of her staff, he'd have access to at least some of her secrets. He could hide in plain sight—a risky, but clever strategy.

Zander pushed through the gate, praying Faustin would not hear it squeak. Once inside he peered into the dark, searching for movement. It took him a moment to spot the rebel leader striding through the overgrown grass like a king on progress.

He resumed the chase.

Faustin angled across beds of rosa bushes gone seedy from neglect, heading toward the central palace. Instead of keeping to the path as Zander expected, Faustin stopped at a small shed standing in the lee of a tall hedge. After a moment's hesitation, he entered the little wood structure and carefully closed the door behind him.

Zander crouched on his haunches in the long grass, perplexed, wondering why Faustin would stop here. Perhaps he awaited the arrival of an insider accomplice?

A light breeze stirred Zander's hair. He breathed in the scents of rosa and grass, stretching to release the nervous tension in his limbs. After several minutes the door swung open again. Faustin emerged. Zander waited until the shadowy form had moved on a dozen paces before following.

Faustin's steps quickened as he neared the palace. When he reached a columned walkway illuminated along its entire length by electric lamps, he paused to adjust the hood of the long black coat concealing his face. Glancing around him, he resumed walking quickly down the path.

Zander's heart skipped a beat. He recognized this part of the sprawling complex and knew what lay at the walkway's end—a corridor that led to the private apartments Deanna shared with her sister Ceilia.

Confused, Zander lingered for a few moments in the shadows beside the lighted path. *No...I don't believe it*, he thought. *He can't be going there.*

No explanation made any sense. Ceilia lived a life as cloistered as a Marian novice. Her path and Faustin's could never cross, unless....

Zander entered the corridor in time to see the familiar door at the end swing shut. Cold dread ate at the impulse that had driven him this far. *Has Ceilia been playing games all these years? Are she and Faustin friends, or...Yesu, lovers? No...that's crazy. But I have to find out why he came here.*

He walked to the door and knocked. After several moments of silence, he tried again. When he got no response he grasped the knob, only to have it pulled from his grasp as the door swung open to a release of warm air.

Ceilia stood on the threshold, slump-shouldered and wearing a blue dressing gown she held closed at her breast. "Oh...hola, Zander. Deanna's not at home."

Zander looked past her into the empty sitting room beyond. He searched it, but saw no sign of Faustin. A single dim lamp did little to chase away the shadows filling the corners. "May I come in?" he asked quietly.

Ceilia twirled a strand of auburn hair around her forefinger. "Deanna's not here and neither is Freeda. You're a boy and it's very late."

Zander detected nothing amiss in Ceilia's demeanor. Her lack of guile astounded him.

"I'm not just any boy, Cece. We're friends."

Ceilia cocked her head and rested her chin on her fist. "Hmmmm. It's very late and I really should go back to bed."

Zander tried to ease across the threshold, but Ceilia blocked him with a deft sidestep. Dropping all pretense, he said, "Cece, I know he's here."

She regarded him with a puzzled expression. "I don't know what you mean."

"Yes you do." Zander caressed her shoulder. "I only want to talk to him. Please let me in."

Ceilia bit her lower lip. An expression too quick for Zander to read flickered across her face. "Well...all right, but only for a little while. Freeda will be back soon." She melted aside to allow him to enter and closed the door behind him.

Zander stepped into the middle of the room, flushed with uneasiness. "I know you're here, Faustin," he called out. "I followed you from the meeting."

"I...I don't understand. No one's here except me." Ceilia pulled her dressing gown closer about her body, fingers pale against the dark blue algodon.

"Cece, please." Zander stepped closer. The faint aroma of tabac smoke touched his nose. "This isn't a game." He glanced at the hallway leading to her bedroom. "He's not your friend, dulzor. He's dangerous."

"I'm not playing any games. You're starting to scare me."

Her soft voice and unwavering air of childlike innocence sparked Zander's anger. That the rebel leader would involve an ingénue like Ceilia in his ruthless plans only fanned the flame. He took a step toward the rear hallway. "Faustin, I know you're in there, pendayho."

Ceilia's fingers clamped onto his wrist with strength enough to bruise. "Stop yelling. There's no one here."

Zander spun, and grasping her shoulders, he growled, "Don't lie, Cece."

Her face crumpled into a mask of terror as tears spilled down her cheeks. "You're hurting me," she sobbed.

Street instinct drove Zander to pull Ceilia into a protective embrace and draw the shiv he kept hidden in his waistband. "Last chance, Faustin...get out here now."

Ceilia sighed and twisted in his arms. The eyes that looked into his had lost all trace of innocence. "You had to follow me, you stupid raton. That was a mistake." Her voice had dropped a full octave.

"Diosa mia," Zander whispered.

"Get off me," she snarled.

He pushed her away, heart galloping. Ceilia's bent shoulders straightened. Regarding Zander with cold appraisal, she said, "You know our secret now."

Zander shuddered. "Our secret?"

Ceilia edged closer. "You want to talk to me. Here I am."

"I want to talk to Faustin."

Ceilia jabbed a finger at her face. "I'm right here, idiot."

Zander shook his head, feeling like all of reality had just been knocked off-kilter. "Are you telling me you're Faustin?"

Ceilia threw up her hands. "At last. The blind man sees."

"This is insane. If you're Faustin, then where's Ceilia?"

The girl tapped her forehead. "She's in here. With me. When she feels threatened or there's important work to do, I take over. She needs me. I protect her."

Zander stared at the familiar face, searching in vain for any sign that the sweet girl he knew still existed. "But...how is this possible?"

"Don't know. Doesn't matter." Ceilia cocked her head, her lips in a pout. "You don't believe me."

"I don't know what to believe."

She tapped his breastbone with a forefinger. "Maybe this will convince you. You spent a week in detention getting the mierda beaten out of you every day. Dear, sweet Aunt Bea nursed you through the worst of the aftermath. Sonia told me everything, of course."

Zander felt as if a fist had squeezed all the air out of his lungs. There was no way Ceilia could have known about that.

"Now, do you believe me?"

The truth stared Zander in the face with peridot eyes, the same that had looked out from the holes of a painted mask earlier that night.

"You have to admit this is the last place Lourdessa would look for me." Faustin grinned. "Who would ever suspect poor, crazy Ceilia of anything? Certainly not of leading the resistance."

Sweat prickled Zander's brow and armpits. *Of course. She...he...can come and go as he pleases.* "Ceilia's just a kid."

Faustin seized Zander's hand and pressed it against Ceilia's breast. "Oh, no she's not."

Zander recoiled.

Faustin smiled and slowly ran the tip of Ceilia's tongue over her lips. "Did you know our sweet Cece has always had a huge crush on you?" he said. "She's a bit, well, let's be honest…she's a lot jealous of her sister because you chose Deanna over her. I have to admit I find you very attractive as well." Abruptly, his smile vanished. "Your loss."

"You'd better not be using Ceilia's body for…for…that." Zander swiped a hand through his hair, sick with fury and fear.

Faustin twisted Ceilia's mouth into a sneer. "Relax, idiot. Our little dulzor is still pure as the day she was born."

Every instinct screamed at Zander to run, but that meant abandoning Ceilia to something so alien that nothing in his experience lent it any context. "I don't know what exactly you are, and right now I don't care. You're putting Ceilia in danger. I can't stand by and do nothing." He paused to take a deep, steadying breath and said, "I don't know what else to do. So I'm going to the Church."

"What will you say? That Ceilia Hernaan is possessed?" Faustin chuckled. "Even those sanctimonious fools don't believe in demons anymore." He reached into the pocket of Ceilia's robe and pulled out a straight razor. With deliberate slowness he drew the gleaming blade across the white skin of her forearm. Blood trickled from the cut and dripped off Ceilia's fingertips to spatter the carpet. "You tell anyone about me, Zan, and the next time I cut her it'll be her wrists."

Horror threatened to upend all Zander's senses. "No."

Ignoring the dripping wound, Faustin flopped into an upholstered chair and tucked Ceilia's legs demurely beneath her, the bloodied razor still in her hand. He pointed to the sofa opposite. "Sit," he ordered, "and I'll tell you what happens next."

Trembling, Zander obeyed, his eyes never leaving Ceilia's face.

Faustin stared at Ceilia's blood for a long, agonizing moment, then said, "You keep your delicious mouth shut and we go on as if nothing's changed. Our little Cece won't remember any of this, so feel free to breeze in and out of her life like always. Though, if I were you, I'd take advantage of her crush and give her what she wants."

"Eff you," Zander whispered.

Faustin guffawed. Zander couldn't recall ever hearing Ceilia make such a sound. "You can remain a part of my resistance and, as long as you choose to stay, you'll follow my orders. Sonia seems to think you're useful. I can guess what for."

The smell of his own fear thick in his nostrils, Zander stared at Faustin, his mind still grappling with the dissonant evidence of his eyes and ears. The body slouched before him like a lounging gahto might look like Ceilia, but the entity gazing from the windows of her eyes was something made of pure malice.

"I want to talk to her," Zander demanded.

"Well, she doesn't want to talk to you."

"I think it's you who won't let her talk."

Faustin shrugged. "Believe what you like."

"Ceilia may be more child than woman," Zander replied, "but she knows right from wrong. Killing innocent schoolgirls is wrong. She'd fight you if she knew."

"Cece doesn't ask any questions. She's content to leave the grown-up stuff to me."

Like murder, Zander thought. Aloud, he said, "How can you talk about freeing the people from oppression while planning to slaughter children?"

Faustin remained silent, his peridot gaze unwavering.

"You son of a bitch," Zander whispered.

"Sometimes it's necessary to shed blood for a righteous cause."

Bitter helplessness fueled Zander's laughing reply. "The only cause you believe in is yourself!"

"It doesn't matter, as long as the results are the same." Faustin closed the razor and laid it on Ceilia's lap. He glanced at the cut on her arm, now clotted, and frowned. "Gotta bandage that."

Close to emotional collapse, Zander closed his eyes. "You're going to pay for all this," he said.

"We'll see."

Zander stood, and praying she could hear him, spoke to his lost friend. "I'll find a way to help you, Ceilia. I promise."

Faustin pointed at the door. "Get out."

Zander fled.

33

a problem resurfaces

If she had been a queen from ancient Earth times, Lourdessa would have strangled the messenger standing before her with her own hands—Sedano Black Corps agent or no. How dare he come to her office with this news? She surged out from behind her desk, hands clenched. "What do you mean…my…stepdaughter…lives?"

Though his scarred face remained passive, the set of Calderone's shoulders suggested he was unfazed by Lourdessa's fury. "I saw her at a Wilds trading post about a week ago. She's living with the camarons in a place called Reed Valley. It's one of the bigger villages in the Amariyo watershed."

The man reeked of sweat-marinated leather and eelat. Lourdessa fished a perfumed silk handkerchief from the pocket of her skirt and covered her nose.

His lips curved upward. "I came straight to the palace as soon as I arrived. Figured you'd want to know right away." The amusement in his voice grated, but Lourdessa had to admit to herself that he was correct.

Steady, Dessa. Calm yourself. "You're certain it was her?"

"I heard the Tiqui buck she was with call her by name."

Lourdessa closed her eyes. *How could this happen? Nunyez will make this right. Or suffer the consequences.*

"You called, Dama?"

Lourdessa opened her eyes. The Minister of Intelligence stood in the doorway, regarding Calderone with hooded eyes. Glaring at his pinched visage, the Alcalde said, "Nunyez, you've failed me."

His thin brows arched upward. "Dama?"

Lourdessa waved a hand toward the scarred man. "Calderone's just returned from a sojourn among the malcontents and criminals in the Wilds."

Nunyez frowned.

"He's discovered something very interesting. Deanna is still alive."

"Dama, that is impossible. My man Gomaz is completely reliable." A tiny muscle in Nunyez's jaw jumped beneath his parchment-thin skin.

Lourdessa slammed her fist down on her desktop. "Then he lied to both of us."

"The heart..."

"Someone or something else's, obviously." Lourdessa returned to her chair and sat. Waves of heat rolled through her body, dizzying her. Perspiration soaked the underarms of her lavender silk blouse and trickled down her face. She reached into a drawer and withdrew a fan. Opening it with a snap, she sighed as the self-made breeze cooled her skin. "Calderone, tell Señor Nunyez what you saw."

As the Sedano agent related his story, Lourdessa studied the Minister's face. Nunyez had never given her cause to doubt his loyalty, but how was she to accept this news? He had personally selected Gomaz and vouched for his reliability. Such a critical lapse in judgment seemed unbelievable in a man as wily as Saviero Nunyez.

And yet...

Nunyez remained motionless as Calderone fell silent.

"Well?" Lourdessa prompted.

"Dama, it is clear Gomaz has betrayed us," he said at last. His face revealed nothing of his emotions. "I shall deal with him personally. As for your stepdaughter…"

"I want the traitor Gomaz arrested along with his family," Lourdessa said. "Order an armed airship to be made ready to sail at once. Calderone," she addressed the Sedano agent. "This Reed Valley. Can you find it?"

He nodded. "It's well hidden, but I know where to look."

"Good." Lourdessa turned her gaze back to Nunyez. "I want Deanna found and dealt with. I don't care how many of the vermin sheltering her must die. The ones left standing can be brought back to work the mines."

"I will instruct my men to obtain more definitive proof this time. Her head, perhaps?" Nunyez said.

Lourdessa pretended to recoil. "That is truly disgusting, even for you." She paused. "But it would be easier than hauling back the entire body."

Calderone cleared his throat.

Lourdessa returned her kerchief to her nose. "What is it?"

"The Tiqui are tougher than you think, Dama. They'll fight like demons if put to the test."

"They're no match for a fully armed Bayonan airship," the Alcalde countered.

"I'll see to the arrangements now, Dama," Nunyez said.

Lourdessa watched him go, doubt once again scraping at her trust. After a moment she pushed it aside.

No. Nunyez is loyal. We were both duped. This man Gomaz will live to regret his treachery.

She turned her attention back to Calderone. "You're the one who pinched the Bayona District One crystals from beneath Gabril Ledesme's nose, aren't you?"

"Yeah."

A man of few words, Lourdessa thought. "Well done. You have some time before the airship leaves. You may use the showers in the kitchen staff bathroom."

"Thanks."

As he headed for the door, Lourdessa added, "Ask for a meal as well." His thick scars turned his smile into a grimace. Lourdessa wondered at the catastrophe that had left such ruin in its wake. She picked up the telephone handset. When Mari answered, she said, "Tell my son I want him. Now."

THE TELEPHONE ON the watch sergeant's desk jangled to life. Caught dozing—it had been a slow night—he awakened with a snort and snatched up the handset, pressing the black cone to his ear. "Palace Hill Station. Sergeant Mendoza speaking."

He listened. "Uh, yes, he's here. I'll transfer you. Hold on."

The sergeant pressed a button on the base of the phone and a second voice answered. Mendoza spoke again. "Uh…yeah. Gomaz. Call for you."

Sounded none too happy, Mendoza thought. He replaced the handset then leaned back in his chair to resume his nap.

BLACK COATTAILS FLAPPING in the wind, the Minister of Intelligence steered his battered bicycle past the guardhouse and through the north palace gate. Old gears squeaked as he pedaled, hunched over handlebars gripped in bony fingers.

The stately ranks of roble trees lining the broad avenue that circled the palace splintered the sunlight within their tangled canopies, casting shards of light and dark upon the asphalt.

The shaded streets of Palace Hill were always quiet, even in the middle of the workday. A grocer's van glided past, venting steam in wispy trails, headed in the opposite direction. A woman in an emerald-green dress, her hair a mass of brassy curls spilling from beneath the confines of a broad-brimmed hat, strolled the sidewalk. A small perro, like an animated bundle of white yarn, capered at her hem. The Minister saw no other living thing.

Gliding to a stop before a wrought-iron gate set within a fieldstone wall, he dismounted, gave the gate a shove with his foot, and wheeled his cycle through. He made his way up the flagged path, through a garden gone feral from lack of tending, toward a small half-timber-and-fieldstone manor house. Leaning the bicycle against the trunk of an old manzaniya tree near the porch, he climbed the stairs to the door. He fit a plain brass key into the lock and let himself into the relative coolness of the entryway. He pushed the door closed behind him.

The minister hung his coat on a garment tree and headed down a narrow hallway, floorboards creaking beneath a threadbare blue-wool runner, to the back of the house. As he pushed open the door to his study, his thin lips crimped with displeasure.

Anna has been cleaning in here again. Infernal woman. I told her to stay out.

Crossing the room to his desk—an antique ebon-wood roll-top that had belonged to his wife, dead ten years this Fevrero—he glanced at the pile of the day's unopened reports that Anna had stacked with great precision at the exact center of the now dust-free surface. The reports would have to wait. He had much more important business to attend to.

He moved past the desk to a small table beneath the room's only window and pulled the canvas dust cover off a telegraph machine. A brass clock perched on the fireplace mantel kept a steady rhythm while he waited.

Three minutes later, the clock chimed a run of soft, sweet notes, paused, then sounded the hour—one o'clock.

Nunyez tapped out a two-sentence message:

The hunters have returned empty-handed.
Time to move forward.

34
vulnerabilities of a lonely heart

Eduard removed his spectacles and rubbed his tired eyes. He shoved aside the diagrams he had been studying. The small brass clock on his office desk informed him midnight had come and gone. Out on the shop floor, shrouded in shadows, the AX238 Annihilator waited like a sleeping behemoth for the spark that would awaken it to life.

The former Alcalde rose from his chair, went to the office doorway, and stepped out into the darkness of the workshop. It took a few seconds for his eyes to adjust to the dimness. The machine gradually emerged like an apparition from the deeper blackness. The light spilling from his office door created a dim sheen across the cockpit windshield. He moved toward the machine with an unconscious reverence, like a worshipper approaching an altar of the Madre.

Nearly two months of study, design, and intensive labor had culminated in this—the greatest technical achievement of the current age. As Eduard gazed at what he'd wrought, the sheer magnitude of the feat filled his engineer's soul with pride.

Holy Madre Maria, he thought, as shame replaced pride in quick succession. *What kind of man am I, to take satisfaction in such handiwork?*

He circumnavigated the machine, feeling only despair.

He knew that whatever plans Lourdessa had for this monster, they did not end with the defense of Nue Bayona. His prototype would serve as the template for a fleet of re-created AX238s. With such an arsenal, the entire continent would fall before the might of the Sedanos.

Nue Castila will fight back, but even with a flotilla of airships, it stands little chance. When it falls, the smaller towns will be next, then the wilderness outposts, and finally...

The Sedanos would round up the Tiqui and return the diminutive race to bondage. The ones that dared to resist would be slaughtered.

I have to stop this, but how?

Eduard slumped against the machine's heavily armored forward leg, weary and dejected.

"I thought I might find you here."

The sound of Suela's voice, unexpected at this late hour, startled him. He straightened to his full height. "Madre, I thought you'd gone home hours ago."

She materialized from the darkness and settled in beside him. The faint scent of jazmin flowers filled his nostrils. "I did, but I couldn't sleep," she replied, "so, rather than stay home, tossing and turning in bed, I decided to return and get some work done."

Appreciative of her dedication, Eduard said, "Truth be told, I'm not the least bit sleepy either, so I'm glad of your company." He felt her shoulder brush his. The sensation sent a little shock coursing down his arm to his belly. Heeding the prick of warning at the back of his mind, he edged away.

"You're worried about something," Suela said.

He sensed her face turn toward his, imagined her eyes seeking his in the dark.

"No. I'm just preoccupied with all the last-minute details. You know the Alcalde wants a test run in less than a week."

"Eduard, you don't have to pretend," Suela chided gently. "We're friends now. You can talk to me."

Despite his best efforts, Eduard's resolve to maintain emotional distance from his young assistant had steadily eroded over the weeks they had worked together. Her kindness had drawn him out from behind the high walls he had erected, exposing his crushing loneliness. That same kindness had acted as a balm, transforming their relationship.

"Yes, we are friends," he agreed. "The truth…I'm worried about how my wife," the word tasted bitter in his mouth, "will use what you and I have made together. This machine should never have been resurrected. It's too powerful. I can't help but feel it's somehow animated with a…a kind of malevolent awareness. Foolish, I know."

"No, not foolish," Suela replied.

"Yet, at the same time," Eduard continued, "I look at it and think… how magnificent, see what you've done, Eduard. You are the greatest engineer of your generation." He shook his head. "Madre, what hubris."

"Please don't punish yourself like this," Suela murmured. "You don't deserve it." She laid her hand atop his. "You're a man of great integrity. The idea that something you made will be used for evil distresses you. I know because I feel the same way."

Eduard turned to face her, and though the darkness concealed her full expression from him, he heard the sincerity in her voice. "I believe you do," he said.

He felt her breath, warm against his cheek, and then her mouth, soft and gentle, on his.

He pulled away. "Suela…"

"Oh, Yesu…I'm sorry, Eduard," she gasped. "I…I shouldn't have done that."

But I'm not sorry you did, he wanted to reply. Instead, he entwined his fingers in hers and said, "Please, don't apologize."

For a time they sat in silence, holding hands, Eduard exquisitely aware of Suela's shoulder pressed against his. He knew he walked a dangerous line that, once crossed, there could be no returning.

Suela spoke first. "I lied, Eduard. I'm not sorry at all."

He released her hand and stepped away from both her and the machine. "We can't do this," he insisted, even as he wanted to sweep her into his arms.

"Why not?" she said. "I respect you and I think you feel the same about me."

"I'm old enough..."

"To be my father?" She laughed. "Since when did that ever make a difference?" She stood and moved close enough for Eduard to smell the scent in her hair. "All that matters is that I'm old enough to make my own choices."

"I'm a prisoner twice over, sweet girl. Of both a loveless marriage and a usurper who happens to be my wife." He paused to breathe through a swell of pain, and continued, "If those reasons aren't serious enough to scare you away, then you have no sense of self-preservation."

She didn't speak. Instead she lifted his hand and slipped it beneath her clothes. Soft warm flesh met his fingers. With a start he realized he touched her breast. Instinct took over. He pinched her nipple to hardness between his thumb and forefinger and felt his own flesh respond as she gasped.

Warning cries echoed at the back of his mind, but his aching need for the touch of another human being drowned them out in a rush of heat.

Once again she pressed her sweet, soft lips to his. Eduard felt himself falling into the vortex. Seizing her hand, he led her on trembling legs to the tiny room off the main workshop floor that served as his private chamber.

He pulled her through the door and locked it behind them, then leaned with trepidation against the jamb.

"Are...are you absolutely sure you want to do this?" he whispered, wanting desperately to tear her clothes off, but steeling himself to crush his swelling passion.

Suela undid the buttons of her coveralls and shrugged free, letting them slip to the floor.

Stepping into Eduard's embrace, she yielded to his hungry kisses. Before he could catch his breath, she had his shirt off. As she stroked his chest and belly, he gripped her silken hair in his fists, his breath ragged. Ripples of pleasure so intense as to approach agony flowed throughout his body, wracking him with shudders.

He could feel the pressure approaching detonation.

He pushed her away. But before she could misconstrue, he lifted her into his arms and carried her to his cot, where he laid her atop the coverlet. She sighed and stretched her arms toward him, languid as a drowsy gahto.

Eduard slipped free of his pants and stood at the foot of the bed, drinking in the sight of Suela's beauty. Her small, firm breasts, flat stomach and slim thighs framing a triangle of dark pubic hair reminded him of a painting he had once seen. She was that masterpiece of art, come to glorious life. He wanted to savor the moment, stretch it to the breaking point, but his need was too great.

He fell into her eager arms. The loneliness and despair crippling his spirit burned away in a joyful bonfire of passion.

As the last ripples of climax died, they lay cradled in each other's arms. Eduard breathed in the mingled aromas of sex and sweat, and for the first time in six long, desolate years, he felt at peace.

"What are you thinking?" Suela asked after a long silence.

Eduard caressed her face. "About how happy you've made me tonight."

"I'm glad. You deserve to be happy."

"I've been alone for so long. I'd almost forgotten how good it feels to be this close to a woman."

"You never have to feel lonely again, Eduard." She pulled him into a deep, lingering kiss, leaving him breathless when they finally parted. He sank into his pillow and closed his eyes.

"Eduard," Suela murmured. Her forefinger traced a lazy circle on his breastbone.

"What is it, dulzor?"

"I want to ask you something, but I'm afraid you'll be angry with me."

Eduard propped himself on an elbow to gaze into her eyes. "I could never be angry with you, dear girl," he replied.

A fleeting smile played about Suela's lush mouth, then was disappeared. "It's about the Annihilator. What if..." She paused.

"Go on. I'm listening. What if...what?"

"What if we built in a weakness somewhere? A faulty valve, or a flaw in the boiler?"

For an instant, Eduard couldn't breathe. He shivered and said, "You're speaking of sabotage." The words felt heavy and cold as they fell from his lips.

"Would that be so wrong?"

Eduard wanted to say no. In fact his mind had already harbored such thoughts. Instead he laid a tender hand on Suela's cheek. "Don't ever say anything like that to me again, dulzor. You're so young and you have your whole life ahead of you. You shouldn't trust anyone right now, least of all me."

"Eduard, we just made love. How can I not trust you now?" A single tear spilled down her cheek to splash on his hand.

"I'm a prisoner of the state, that's why." His peace shattered, Eduard lay back and squeezed his eyes shut against the fresh pain clawing at his gut.

Suela massaged his shoulders with gentle pressure. "I'm sorry, Eduard," she whispered. "I didn't mean to upset you. I promise to respect your wishes." As her hands worked their way down to his chest and belly, he felt the pain dissolving in the fresh fires of rekindled desire. By the time her hand reached his hip, he stood ready.

LATER THAT NIGHT, Eduard woke to a cooling indentation beside him in the narrow bed. No feelings of abandonment rankled him; he knew Suela couldn't risk anyone seeing her emerge from his room at daybreak. In truth he felt relieved she'd gone, for his thoughts were dark and dangerous. He dared not jeopardize her safety by sharing them.

Arms crossed behind his head, he lay staring at the ceiling, examining the seed of a plan germinating in his mind. Suela's talk of sabotage had merely watered what had already been planted weeks ago.

Eduard had determined that he would not allow his consummate engineering skills to serve his wife's mad thirst for more power. The machine he'd resurrected, along with all the schematics, must be destroyed. Even at the cost of his own life.

A series of explosive charges wired to a single detonator would accomplish the goal. Obtaining the necessary parts would be difficult. But in all matters pertaining to the project, Lourdessa had given him free rein. With careful planning he could have everything he needed delivered to the warehouse, hidden among the routine supplies.

He would assemble the charges during the small hours, after Suela had fallen asleep. Only after the work crew had gone home and the warehouse watchman who doubled as his jailer had locked him in for the night, could he work unobserved. He understood the implications should Suela awaken and discover his covert project. The last thing he wanted was to put her at even greater risk. By allowing her into his bed he'd already endangered her enough.

There was still the fact that Lourdessa had sworn to do harm to his daughters if he crossed her. But, he knew, those threats would be rendered pointless if he died in the blast. And after he'd turned his wife's megalomaniacal dream into a smoking ruin, no other engineer in the city, not even Raul Olivas, would be able to give it back to her.

It's a good plan. Eduard pulled his blanket up to his chin, sighed, and closed his eyes. The steady ticking of the bedside clock soon lulled him back to sleep.

Suela paused before the side-door exit and tapped lightly to alert the guard waiting outside to her presence. The door swung open, and a hand seized her arm, dragging her forth into the cool night air.

"Did he say anything?" Alehan demanded, his face a mere shadow in the dim light of the warehouse yard.

Suela shook her head, grateful that the darkness hid her tear-filled eyes. "I suggested that we sabotage the project," she said in a hoarse whisper, "but he shut me down. He warned me not to mention it again."

Alehan grabbed her shoulders with bruising force and yanked her close. "My mother is soft and blind when it comes to Eduard," he sneered. "That's love for you. Now me, I think with my head, not my *verga*. It's only a matter of time before he tries to betray us. Your job is to find out when and how."

"I understand what's required of me, Alehan," Suela replied, trembling.

"I hope you do. Think about your mother, Suela. What do you suppose your father would do if he learned the truth about her?" His voice was smooth, friendly almost, which only heightened her fear. "Or even worse perhaps, what would happen to your family's precious name—and your mother herself—should her bad habits and indiscretions come to light?"

He slipped one arm around her waist and leaned in, sniffing, delicately, like a gahto nosing a dainty treat. "Maria's tits, you smell…like sex." He nibbled on her neck, his breath hot and sour against her skin. Suela shuddered and tried to pull away but his grip was too strong. "I should eff you right here and now. But then why bother with my stepfather's leftovers?"

"You're disgusting," she whispered.

Alehan laughed and pushed her away, aiming a playful slap at her buttocks. "Just remember who owns you, dulzor."

Suela watched the Alcalde's son climb behind the wheel of his sleek, low-slung roadster and speed away. When the taillights had disappeared around the first turn in the road, she buried her face in her hands and wept.

35

race for their lives

"They're coming for you." The line clicked and went dead.

For an instant Gomaz couldn't breathe as raw terror kicked him in the gut. The next moment, all his years of training took over. With a steady hand he dialed his home number.

His wife Izabela answered. "Hola."

"Izzy, dulzor, the time has come. I'll see you soon."

"Sweet Yesu...Please be careful, Beto."

Gomaz replaced the handset and paused to listen. He heard only the sounds of routine activity in the squad room beyond the closed door of his office. Aware that his window for escape was closing fast, he decided against flight on the bicycle he'd ridden to work that morning. He needed to get home as quickly as possible, which meant he'd have to take a patrol car.

The small, bare office held nothing of value to him other than the little gilt-framed photograph of his family resting on the desk. He removed the photo from the frame and tucked it into his shirt breast pocket. Retrieving his black cloak and cap from the coat tree in the corner, he secured his ee-pistol and neural baton to his belt, then stepped out into the squad room.

The evening had been unusually quiet for Palace Hill Station. Most of the blue-uniformed City polis were out on patrol. A pair of civilian clerks moved about on various tasks. The watch sergeant sat dozing at his desk. In the drunk tank, a lone man lay curled on the floor, his coat folded beneath his head, snoring.

Through a door at the end of a back hallway lay the precinct garage. Several squad cars were usually kept fired up and ready to answer calls. Gomaz prayed that one remained as he strode across the bright-lit room.

"On your way home, sir?"

"Yes, finally," Gomaz said, acknowledging the friendly inquiry of the clerk, a woman named Bettina.

"You have a good night, Señor Gomaz," she replied with a smile, then returned to her filing.

Gomaz reached the back hallway without speaking to anyone else. He paused at the door to shrug into his cloak, pull on a pair of black leather gloves, and settle his cap into place.

In the garage the smell of engine oil, heated metal, and rubber filled his nostrils. The air hung moist and warm, despite the large doors standing open to the night-shrouded street. All the bays stood empty save for the one closest to him. Gomaz breathed a sigh of relief at the sight of steam venting from the coupe's boiler.

The garage attendant sat hunched over a workbench, his back toward the door. With bold strides, Gomaz approached. "I need a car tonight, Rey," he called out.

The man jumped from his stool and faced Gomaz. "Evenin', boss," he said, wiping his hands on the legs of his dark-blue coveralls. "Didn't hear you come in." Sounding apologetic, he pointed at the coupe. "This one's all I got right now."

"It'll do fine," Gomaz said as he climbed behind the wheel.

"I'll go get the sign-out sheet."

As Rey moved toward the workbench, Gomaz released the hand brake and eased the car through the open doors into the street.

Ignoring the attendant's surprised shout, he stepped on the accelerator and sped into the night.

The warm breeze caressed his face through the partly opened window. Nayna had newly risen in the western sky, but her light was dimmed by the glare of Palace Hill's electric streetlights. Gomaz schooled his breathing to a slow cadence and focused on the tasks before him—rescuing his family, getting them to the Marian convent, fleeing the city. All according to plan.

For a split second he succumbed to uncertainty. *Holy mierda. What have I gotten myself into?*

With the last of Palace Hill's gated estates behind him, Gomaz allowed himself to relax. *Everything's prepared. Izzy knows what to do. There's time. Stay calm.*

A low-slung roadster whisked by, heading in the opposite direction. A few moments later, Gomaz overtook and passed a chauffeured limo. Several minutes ticked by before another set of headlights appeared ahead. As the car—a sleek black sedan—flashed past, Gomaz paid it little attention. His thoughts remained focused on one thing: reaching his family before the Specials did. Though never a religious man, he found himself praying to the Blessed Madre that the head start he'd been given would be long enough.

Another sedan blew by, rocking Gomaz's coupe in its wake.

He glanced in the rearview mirror and felt his confidence dissolve. Both cars had slammed on their brakes, swung around, and were now speeding after him.

With grim determination, Gomaz trained his eyes on the road. Broad and tree-lined near the top of the hill, at the bottom, Palace Hill Road funneled into Caya Palaceo, a narrow avenue lined with high masonry walls, intersected by even narrower alleyways. Forced to slow down, Gomaz checked his rearview mirror again. To his dismay, he saw that the sedans were gaining on him.

The glowing blue discharge of an ee-rifle flashed past his window. Ahead, a section of wall exploded, showering the car with chunks of red-hot brick as it rocketed past. A second flare lit the night. Cursing, Gomaz bent low over the steering wheel, smelling the acrid tang of scorched metal. At the first intersection he turned right off Palace Hill Road onto Caya Valencea. An instant later, a third energy blast cut across his windshield. A droplet of molten glass hit his cheek. Hissing in pain, he clawed at the wound with one hand while keeping the other clamped tight on the wheel.

Realizing the sedans would soon overtake him, Gomaz stomped on the brakes and wrenched the steering wheel hard to the left. Tires squealing in distress, the car careened into a skid. Gomaz's shoulder muscles popped with the strain as he struggled to regain control. The car at last screeched to a stop, the stench of burning rubber wafting around it.

His car now faced the black sedans as they barreled straight at him. Gomaz floored the accelerator, sending the two-seater hurtling toward the two Specials.

Their oncoming headlights blinded him as they converged. He heard the pop-pop-pop of slug pistol fire. He hunched over the wheel, a yell of defiance bursting from his lips.

At the last moment the two sedans parted as Gomaz's coupe shot between them. The driver to his left lost control and crashed into a shuttered storefront. The second driver pulled a swift U-turn and resumed the chase.

Undaunted, Gomaz pushed the coupe's engine to its limits.

The flash of ee-rifle fire again lit up the rearview mirror. The coupe lurched and swerved out of control. The steering wheel bucked in his hands and, with sick certainty, he knew one of his tires had been shot out. A wooden railing flashed into view through his windshield.

A split-second later, amid an explosion of shards, the coupe plunged headlong down a steep overgrown embankment.

Gomaz clung with desperate strength to the wheel. The car bucked and rattled before slamming with bone-jarring force into a water-filled slough. His forehead cracked against the steering wheel and erupted in a flash of pain. For a few seconds he drifted in blackness.

A siren's wail galvanized him out of his stupor. He fumbled for the door latch and tumbled out of the car into muddy, ankle-deep water. His foot slipped in the muck and he fell to his hands and knees.

A voice from high above shouted his name.

Behind him he heard two heavy splashes. A pair of roving torch beams pierced the darkness. *Gotta move*, he thought.

Scrambling to his feet, woozy and nauseous, Gomaz abandoned the wrecked coupe and staggered ahead in the darkness, fleeing his pursuers. Several meters later the slough dead-ended at the mouth of a brick culvert set into the base of a bramble-covered slope. Chunks of shattered concrete lay strewn at the water's edge.

Gomaz grasped a handful of spiky vegetation and began pulling himself up the hill.

A voice from behind shouted for him to stop. Ignoring the order, he reached for another handhold with stinging palms.

"Stop now…or by Yesu, I'll shoot!"

Gomaz froze, still clinging to the slope. For a second, he sagged into the weeds, then released his grip and slid back down into the slough.

The Specials approached him with pistols raised and their torch beams fixed on his face. Gomaz raised one hand to shield his eyes, then looked down at the water swirling around his ankles.

The two officers splashed to a stop a stone's throw away. "Drop your weapons," one of them ordered.

Gomaz gripped the butt of his neural baton and stepped clear of the muck onto a chunk of concrete. "My baton first," he said, then in one smooth motion, pulled it free, plunged the tip into the water and pressed the trigger.

The electrical charge crackled and the water glowed blue. The smaller of the two Specials screamed and fell backward into the slough. The larger man shuddered yet remained on his feet, retching. Heart racing, Gomaz triggered a second burst from his baton. The Special dropped into the muck like a stone.

Wedging the baton between his teeth, Gomaz pulled himself up the embankment. When he reached the top he cautiously lifted his head above the weeds and scanned the road.

In the darkness he saw nothing but empty asphalt in both directions. Still, he waited, unmoving, certain that the two Specials lying unconscious in the slough had at least one other partner. His ears strained to catch any sound—a whisper, the scuff of a boot heel—that would warn him of imminent danger. All he heard was the sighing of wind through the branches of the roble trees lining the road.

I can't stay here any longer. I've got to risk it, he thought, then scrambled onto the gravel verge. For a few heartbeats, he crouched, hand pressed to his temple, as the pounding in his head blurred his thoughts.

"Don't move, Gomaz. It's over. Time to give up."

Gomaz looked up to see a figure materialize from the darkness, resolving as it approached into a man he recognized as part of the Alcalde's personal squad. The Special halted a few meters away, holding his neural baton in one hand and his ee-pistol, pointed at Gomaz's chest, in the other.

Gomaz remained in a crouch, careful to keep his own hands in front of him. "I'll give up when I'm dead, Hermez," he growled.

"No one wants you dead," Hermez replied. "The Alcalde has some questions for you, that's all." He waved the pistol. "Now. On your feet."

Gomaz scooped up a fistful of gravel as he stood and faced the other man.

"Drop the baton," Hermez ordered.

Gomaz complied, making note of where it fell.

"Now your gun."

Gomaz removed his ee-pistol and laid it next to the baton. "I only want to get my family to safety," he said. "They're innocent. For their sake, let me walk away."

"I can't. You know what'll happen to me if I fail to bring you in." Gomaz thought he heard an undertone of regret in Hermez's voice.

"I understand, Max," he said, letting his shoulders droop. "You have a family, too."

Hermez stepped within reach, the muzzle of his pistol dropping a fraction. "Is it true, Roberto? Are you part of Faustin's terrorist gang?"

"Is that what the Alcalde is saying?"

"That's what we've heard."

Gomaz edged closer. "Do you believe it?"

"I don't know what to believe. You've always been a straight arrow, Roberto. A poli's poli."

"The Alcalde is wrong," Gomaz said. "I've never been a part of Faustin's gang." He captured and held Hermez's gaze with his own. "You know me, Max. I'm not lying. Let me go."

Hermez's pistol wavered. "I'm sorry, Roberto," he said, his eyes pleading. "I can't."

"I'm sorry, too," Gomaz whispered as he hurled the gravel into the other man's face.

Hermez yelped and jerked back, his free hand clapped over his eyes. Gomaz drove a swift foot into the man's groin. Hermez doubled over, the ee-pistol dropping from his fingers.

Gomaz scrambled backward and bent to grab his baton. He straightened and turned as Hermez lunged, swinging, the live tip of his own weapon ripping a glowing blue arc through the darkness.

Gomaz blocked Hermez's baton on the shaft of his own, then twisted beneath the other man's arm and spun away.

Hermez had a professional boxer's build, and a longer reach, but Gomaz was the better fighter. As the Special whirled to face him, Gomaz swung his baton low, catching his opponent on the thigh.

Hermez howled and fell to his knees, reeling. Gomaz closed, and touched his baton to side of the other man's neck. The Special toppled onto his face and lay still.

Gomaz snatched up his gun, and then took off running, back toward where his car had gone over the embankment. He slowed as the Specials' black sedan came into view, doors flung open, deserted. With a thanks to the Madre on his lips, he tumbled behind the wheel, pulled the doors closed, and shot away amid a rattling flurry of gravel.

Buildings and trees, the occasional passenger vehicle or pedestrian out for an after-dinner stroll—all swept by in a blur as Gomaz fled the Valencea business district, racing toward a tidy, two-story adobe brick townhouse. Blood and sweat mingled on his face. He could taste their metallic, salty flavors when he moistened his lips.

A sudden, painful realization lanced through him. He was about to bring down calamity on his family, and he loathed himself for it. For a few bitter moments, Roberto Gomaz, ex–Special Police officer and agent of the true resistance, wept. And yet he dared not indulge in self-pity for long. The hounds had his scent. He'd gained himself but a temporary reprieve. They'd corner him soon enough if he didn't hurry.

Gomaz abandoned the sedan in an alleyway two blocks from his own home. At the alley's mouth, he paused to watch and listen. Satisfied that the street beyond was deserted, he hastened along the walkway, avoiding pools of light cast by the street lamps. His destination lay another three blocks away—a small public park, little used and overgrown with neglect.

The ferocious pain in both his head and face hammered at his concentration. He fished a handkerchief from his pocket and pressed it to the wound in his cheek. All his senses felt stretched to their limits, straining to catch the slightest hint of danger.

A block from the park Gomaz slowed his pace and—with the stealth of one experienced in tracking and surveillance—he approached the back fence. He spotted his own car parked in the shadows beneath a large tree. He could barely make out a figure sitting behind the steering wheel.

Still cautious, he glided closer, stopping near the rear bumper. "Izzy, it's me," he whispered.

Izabela bolted from the car and flung herself into his arms. For the second time that night, Gomaz wept.

"Thank the Madre you're safe, Beto," she murmured against his shoulder.

"As are you, my darlings," he replied. Their three children had clambered from the back seat to huddle around them like frightened gazelas.

Izabela eagerly tasted his lips, but then pulled away, gasping. "There's blood on your face. What happened?"

As she reached out to caress his injured cheek, he grabbed her fingers and kissed them before they touched the wound. "No time for that now, dulzor. Did you get everything out of the shed?"

Several months ago, Gomaz had filled a rucksack with survival supplies and five thousand reáles in cash. He'd hidden it—along with his spare Poltro .45, three boxes of bullets, and six fuel cells for his police-issue ee-pistol—in a secret space beneath the floor of his wife's potting shed.

"It's all in the boot." Izabela had always been levelheaded and strong. Gomaz heard no trace of anxiety in her voice, though he knew she must feel terrified inside. He also knew she would maintain her outer calm for the sake of their children.

Gomaz looked into the faces of his three offspring: oldest daughter Julia, nut-brown and raven-haired like her mother; middle child Madelina, with tresses like honey; and baby Lalo, his son and the only child to inherit his sandy hair and ruddy complexion.

"My darlings," he said, "your papa is so very sorry we have to leave home like this, but I promise you, everything will be all right." He bent down to kiss each small face, sensing their confusion and fear, but also, their confidence in him.

Knowing that his family trusted him kept the fear circling through his own mind from closing in and crushing his reason.

"Everyone, get back in the car," he said. Once the children settled themselves in the rear, Gomaz slid behind the wheel and glanced at Izabela sitting beside him, her hair confined by a dark scarf. She caught and held his gaze.

A sudden sound, carried on the night breeze, set Gomaz's heart racing.

Sirens.

The Specials had arrived. Even now they were surrounding his house.

Izabela smiled and touched his knee. No words passed between them; none were needed.

Gomaz released the hand brake and stepped on the accelerator.

Perhaps the unseen hand of Madre Maria guided him. Perhaps he'd developed a sixth sense during his years as a poli. Whatever the reason, Gomaz safely brought the car to a stop in an alleyway several blocks northeast of the convent. He turned to regard his family.

The children had remained silent throughout the journey. Their faces looked like pale dolls' heads in the light of the twin moons.

"I'm going to walk ahead to make sure it's safe. Then I'll come back for you," he said. "If I don't return in ten minutes," he looked at Izabela, "drive to this address. This man is a friend." He pulled a card from his pocket and pressed it into his wife's hand. She held it close to her face and gasped.

"But this is..."

Gomaz nodded. "Nunyez is one of us. He'll help you. Trust me."

Izabela's eyes gleamed like dark stones in the faint light. "I do trust you, Beto. With my life." She caressed his uninjured cheek. "Be careful, my love."

He stepped from the car and moved down the alley toward the street. His shoes made little sound on the pavement as he walked. Stopping at the entrance to the alley, he looked both ways before heading south.

This section of Red Hill housed skilled laborers and artisans. The tenements on either side of the street were well kept, the gutters free of trash. Savory aromas wafted from open windows, along with fragments of melody and muted conversation.

The rear wall of the Marian convent rose like a cliff of deeper black against the night sky. Ee-pistol in hand, Gomaz approached, all senses engaged. Hearing voices, he paused for several seconds before daring to peek around the corner. A knot of black-cloaked Specials stood at the front gate. A half-dozen squad cars formed a haphazard road blockade.

"Mierda." He melted back into the shadows, heart racing, and leaned against the gritty sandstone, his mind in a furious whirl.

He cursed himself for a fool. His attempt to throw the hounds off his trail had been in vain. They had known all along where he would go to ground. The Marian convent was the only place in the city where the police—the Specials included—could not enter without permission.

Gomaz took off at a trot back toward where his family waited.

"Is it safe, Beto?" Izabela asked. She'd taken little Lalo onto her lap and now rocked the child in her arms.

"The Specials have beaten us here," he replied quietly. "We can't get in through the front gate."

Izabela covered her mouth with her hand, her hazel eyes wide. "Then, what'll we do?"

Gomaz motioned for them all to exit the car. "There's another way in," he said, his voice grim, "but it won't be pleasant."

36
sanctuary

Gomaz smelled the rank aroma of sewage long before he and his family reached the convent's main outflow drain at the base of the rear wall. He signaled for the others to stop and ran ahead to where the pipe emptied into a ditch. Crouching in front of the iron grate, he grabbed the slimy metal in both hands and heaved. The grate didn't budge. His whole body ached from the pummeling it had taken earlier, but failure was unthinkable. Gritting his teeth against the pain, he heaved again.

The metal groaned and abruptly gave way, sending Gomaz down on his rump into the sludge. Tossing the grate aside, he scrambled to his feet, then ran back to fetch his family.

When the children saw where their father proposed to lead them, they balked. Lalo burst into tears. "Papa, it smells bad," he wailed from the protective circle of Izabela's arms.

"I know, dulzor, but you need to be brave," Gomaz said, stroking the boy's silken cap of hair. "This is the only way inside."

"We'll be right here with you," Izabela murmured. "You can do this."

Sniffling, the child nodded and said, "Put me down, Mama."

Izabela set him on his feet. "It's all right, Lalito," his big sister Julia said, taking the child's hand. "Hold on to me. It's not far, right, Papa?"

"Not far at all," Gomaz replied. He adjusted the pack on his shoulders to a more comfortable position and activated the hand torch secured to the top flap. He dropped to his hands and knees, the torch beam shining over his head to illuminate the drain's slippery brick walls. "Come on, everyone. Follow me," he called over his shoulder as he splashed forward into the malodorous stream.

The pipe closed around them, barely wide enough for Gomaz to remain on all fours without having to shed the pack. The stink seemed like a living, palpable thing, clogging his nose and throat. He'd never before suffered from a fear of enclosed spaces, but he felt his chest tighten and his mouth drying up. "Is everyone all right?" he called out. As he received his family's assurances, Gomaz felt some of his anxiety dissipate.

Forcing his mind to think past what he was crawling through, Gomaz concentrated on the tunnel ahead. As promised, they didn't have far to go. The torch beam met a solid, slime-coated brick wall. An iron ladder led up into darkness.

"Everyone, wait here 'til I call you," he whispered, and mounted the ladder. The rungs ended at a round iron hatch. With one hand clutching the ladder for balance, Gomaz shoved upward with the other. Metal ground against stone as the hatch slid aside. Sweet, clean air wafted across his sweating face.

He gripped the edges of the hole and pulled himself up into darkness nearly as deep as that in the sewer. High overhead, he spied a square of night sky pricked with stars. Gomaz drew in a deep breath and sneezed. The sound bounced off close, stone walls. He wiped his face on his sleeve, realizing he'd emerged into a small courtyard.

He shed the pack and bent over the open hatch, pointing his torch beam downward. "All right, darlings," he called. "I'm coming down for you."

Bright light flooded the courtyard. Gomaz sprang to his feet, his hand on his pistol butt. An instant later, he relaxed. Three women, their long black robes and veils swirling as they walked, approached him. One held a lantern.

"Good evening, Señor Gomaz," the oldest said. A brief smile flashed like white tile against her ebon complexion. "We were expecting you a little sooner."

"Good evening, Mother Elizabette," Gomaz replied. "It's been a very long night."

CLAD IN LOOSE gray robes, still damp from the showers, Gomaz and his family perched on wooden chairs within the whitewashed walls of the convent's office. Mother Elizabette sat behind her heavy roble-wood desk, thumbing through the wallet of cash Gomaz had laid before her. Tonight the old woman wore the simple white wimple and black veil of a common sister rather than the elaborate, winged headdress that proclaimed her rank as Mother Superior.

For a time only the hiss of the gas lamps and the chirp of griyos in the shrubbery outside the half-open window broke the silence. Mother Elizabette finished counting the bills, then swept the wallet into a drawer.

"I trust the amount is adequate?" Gomaz asked.

The Mother Superior nodded. "More than adequate, Señor. You've been a good friend to this house. Your family will be safe with us."

The money helps, of course, Gomaz thought, *as does the fact I've turned a blind eye to your dealings in the underground market all these years.*

"While you were cleaning up, I received a phone call, Señor," Mother Elizabette said, her voice bland. "From the M.O.I. himself. Most unusual. He had a message for you." She slid a folded piece of paper across her desk. "Now. I must go deal with the Specials." She pushed her chair back, grasped a rope dangling from a hole in the wall behind her, and gave it a brisk tug. "A Lieutenant Alonzo has been cooling his heels in my reception room for the past hour. A novice will be here shortly to show you and your family to your accommodations. There will be fresh clothes for you there."

Gomaz snagged the note and read the words penned in neat, block letters—GUNSHIP LEAVING AT DAWN FOR REED VALLEY. "I won't be staying, Mother," he said, crumpling the paper in his fist. Beside him, he felt Izabela's body tense. He laid a reassuring hand on her arm.

"At least stay long enough for our infirmarian to dress the cut on your cheek," Mother Elizabette urged.

Gomaz had forgotten about the wound. Quiescent until now, it flared perversely to life with a ferocious sting. He resisted the urge to rub it. "Thanks, but I don't have time."

"Very well, Señor." As the Mother Superior stood, Gomaz rose, gathering his family around him.

"I'll leave the same way I came in," he said.

With a wave of a brown hand, Mother Elizabette replied, "That won't be necessary. There's a secret passage beneath the north wall that leads to an abandoned pump house nearby. When you're ready, one of the novices will take you there." She paused before the office door. "May the Madre be with you, Señor Gomaz." In a swirl of black robes she was gone.

"I wish she'd told me that before now," Gomaz muttered, a wry smile on his lips.

"It doesn't matter," Izabela sighed. "We're all safe now…and yet, you're leaving us."

Gomaz sat down again, took his wife's elbow and pulled her onto the chair beside him. "I have to, my darling. I was hoping to delay this for a few more weeks, but things are moving much faster than we'd anticipated."

Lalo whimpered. Izabela took the boy onto her lap and cradled him against her breast. "Hush, baby," she whispered, and kissed his hair.

"Everything will be all right." She looked at her husband with eyes that pleaded for candor. "Can you tell me any more, Beto?"

Until now he'd kept from Izabela all but the most basic details of his secret work, in order to protect her and the children. None of that mattered anymore. Gomaz knew the time had come to tell his wife enough of the truth so that she could understand why he must leave her and their children behind.

"You've known all along that I work for the resistance—the true resistance, not Faustin's terrorist network," he began.

"Yes, darling," Izabela answered. "And I've supported you from the beginning."

"And that's meant everything to me. Tonight, I told you that Saviero Nunyez is one of us. In fact, he's our leader. It was he who called the station to warn me that the Specials were coming."

"Señor Nunyez has saved the life of my children's father." Izabela clasped his fingers with hers. "For that he has my undying gratitude. Sweet Yesu, the agonies of conscience he must suffer. However does he bear it?"

"I don't know," Gomaz said. "He never talks about himself. He's committed, body and soul, to thwarting Lourdessa Hernaan's imperial ambitions, and to the restoration of democratic rule. To that end he's devised a plan. I wish I could say I have one hundred percent faith that it'll work, but I'd be lying if I did. There are so many variables. Still, I knew the risks when I joined, and I still believe in the cause. My job now is to see things through to the end."

"What is this plan?" Izabela asked.

"It sounds unbelievable, but Nunyez and Raul Olivas—yes, he's one of us, too—think it's possible. They've discovered a map showing the approximate location of a Great War–era Annihilator. It's buried somewhere out in the Siyera Desert. The plan involves recovering and reactivating it, then using it to force the Alcalde from power."

"How will the resistance ever get a centuries-old machine working again?"

"That's for Eduard Hernaan to figure out."

"But, he's in prison...oh…" Izabela's hand flew to her mouth. "Diosa mia. You're planning on freeing him."

"Doctor Hernaan is a brilliant engineer. We need his expertise."

"And what better way to rally the hopes of the people than to know their legitimate leader has escaped captivity?" Izabela said. "Of course, the Alcalde will only deny that he's escaped."

Gomaz felt a surge of pride. *Izzy, my love, you've always been so quick to see everything.* "She'll try at first," he replied, "but eventually, she won't be able to contain the truth."

"What's your role in all this, Beto? I know you say you must leave the city without us…" Izabela fell silent, and for the first time that night, she looked close to panic. "No, darling. Can't someone else go?" she pleaded. "The Siyera Desert…it's too dangerous."

Gomaz hated to see such fear in his wife's eyes. "I won't be alone, Izzy," he said, wishing he could offer more soothing words. "Besides, I can't stay in the city. My cover has been compromised. I'm in worse danger than if I go."

Izabela wiped the tears beading her lashes on the rough sleeve of her borrowed robe. "You are a man of honor, and I love you. I know you must do this, but I'm still afraid. I don't want to lose you."

Gomaz took his wife in his arms. The ache in his throat made speech difficult. "You won't lose me, I promise." He knew he had no right to promise anything, but he could not leave her otherwise. "I'm not going to the Siyera just yet," he added. "First, I have to find and retrieve Deanna Hernaan."

Izabela pulled away and stared at him, frowning. "What do you mean? Isn't she here with the Marians? The Alcalde's announcement said she'd taken holy orders."

"That was a lie," Gomaz said, "concocted by Lourdessa Hernaan to cover up the fact that she tried to have the girl murdered. We saved her life and tried to get her to Nue Castila, but things didn't quite go as planned. She's been living in the Wilds, but the fact that the Specials came for me tonight means the Alcalde now knows Deanna's still alive. She'll almost certainly send one of her agents to find and kill the girl. I can't let that happen."

"Do you even know where to look?" Izabela asked.

"I know someone who does. With any luck, I'll be back in a few days to take you and the children to a safe-house outside the city."

The convent bell tolled, sounding the hour with nine, brassy notes.

Time is running out, Gomaz thought. *The longer I stay, the greater the likelihood that I won't get to Deanna before the Alcalde's assassin does. Yesu's balls, but I wish I had a cigarette.*

Until now, the children had been silent save for baby Lalo's occasional sniffle. Eight-year old Madelina seized Gomaz's hand in her small fingers. Her blue eyes sparkled with tears. "Please Papa. Why can't you stay?" she begged.

Before he could answer, Julia spoke up. "Papa has something very important to do, Maddie. He needs us to be safe so he can do it."

Gomaz stared at his oldest child. The look of serene comprehension in her eyes filled him with a mix of incredulity and admiration. "Yes, dulzor, you are right." He stroked the ten-year-old's dark curls. "When I'm done, I promise I'll come back for all of you. Now, give your papa a hug." He embraced both girls. As their arms encircled him, he felt as if his heart would shatter.

A soft knock sounded on the door and a droopy-eyed girl clad in a smoke-gray habit entered the office. She sketched a quick curtsy. "I'm to show you to your rooms."

"Thank you, Sister," Gomaz said. "Please, lead on."

The girl bent her knee a second time, then smiled shyly at Gomaz and his family from beneath the overhang of her veil. "Follow me, please."

Luna had neared zenith by the time Gomaz's car bounced into the pothole-strewn front yard of a small, darkened farmhouse. He set the brake, killed the ignition and slid from the driver's seat. Snatching his pack from the boot, he approached the house.

Several moments of pounding raised a muffled shout from behind the front door. "Maria damn you, I'm coming!" A dim wedge of light sliced across Gomaz's boots. "It's effing two in the morning. Who is it?"

"Diego, it's me," Gomaz replied to the peeling wood. "Let me in."

The door swung open to reveal a dour-faced old man holding a bullseye lantern. A twist of thin lips passed for a smile. Stepping aside, he said, "If you're here, things can't be good."

Gomaz shut the door behind him. "My cover's blown."

Six years ago, Migeyl Diego had held the rank of captain in the Nue Bayona City Police. He'd chosen exile on this isolated farm rather than submit to the new regime. Nothing much could surprise him, yet, Gomaz watched as the implications of his news turned the other man's face into a mask of consternation.

"Damn. That means…" Diego sniffed and shrugged a bony shoulder. "Come on back then. I'll put on the kettle." He turned to stump down a cobweb-strung hallway toward the rear of the house, his shadow huge against the flaking walls. Gomaz followed, mindful of his footing. Loose floor planks warped by age and piles of unidentifiable junk along the baseboards presented a myriad of hazards.

Diego led the way to a small kitchen, which stood in contrast to the hallway by virtue of its tidiness. A round table filled the center of the room and a wood-burning stove, still radiating heat, squatted against the far wall. Another door, pierced by a curtained window, opened to the back yard. Gomaz unslung the pack from his shoulder, pulled out a chair, and sat. "Got anything stronger than tea?"

"Nope." Diego set the lantern on the table, grabbed a battered kettle from a shelf, and moved to the sink to turn the tap. The antique pipes produced clanks and groans before a thin stream of water gurgled into the kettle's open top.

"That's best, really. I need to wake up." Exhaustion dragged at Gomaz's eyelids. He craved nothing more than a few uninterrupted moments of sleep, but the urgency of his mission precluded such bliss.

"That cut on your face looks nasty," Diego commented. "I can give you something for it." He placed the kettle on the stove to boil.

Gomaz fingered the injury with care, lest he restart the bleeding. "I would appreciate that." He listened to Diego's footsteps recede to the opposite end of the house. After several moments, the old man returned to place a small, circular metal tin on the table.

Gomaz flicked off the lid to release a sharp, medicinal scent. "I have to find a place called Reed Valley. Ever heard of it?" He scooped yellow ointment onto a fingertip, then dabbed gingerly at his wound. When the sharp sting of burnt flesh subsided, he gave silent thanks for small mercies.

"So that's where those Tiqui were from." Diego sat at the table opposite his guest. "It's somewhere in the hills above the Amariyo River, but I couldn't tell you how to find it. How in the Blessed Madre's Name did the Alcalde figure that out?"

"I'm not sure. A Sedano agent must have seen the girl there."

"Not likely. The Tiqui don't usually let altas too near their villages. More like he spotted her at Dry Creek Trading Station. It's the only place in the area where altas and Tiqui mingle. Someone there might give you directions to Reed Valley, though I guarantee the residents will know you're coming long before you ever reach it."

"The Alcalde is sending a gunship. I have to get there before it does."

"Tall order," Diego said. "Country's too rough for your car, and I don't have a trike. You'll have to go by eelat. Can you ride?"

Gomaz shrugged. "It's been a few years." He recapped the ointment tin and set it aside. "How far to this trading station?"

"'Bout five day's hard ride from here. Six if you spare my beast."

Gomaz muttered a tart expletive. "Five days is too long. That gunship will have been and gone by then."

"The Tiqui are tough and smart," Diego said. "They haven't survived this long because they're easy prey. I wouldn't bet against them. Hernaan's girl could do a lot worse for defenders."

"They might be tough, but a heavy gunship packs flamethrowers and at least one ee-cannon. Can the people of Reed Valley defend against that kind of firepower?"

"Don't know. Maybe. All you can do is see for yourself. Like I said, Hernaan's daughter could do a lot worse. And she's no weakling. She survived that damned sky jelly attack, after all."

"I'm still amazed by that. I wonder how she..."

The cheery warble of the kettle whistle stilled Gomaz's tongue. Diego fetched mugs, spoons and a pair of tins. "I've got *sweetbush* and *corella* flower," he said as he poured steaming water into the chipped, mismatched cups. "There's also milk if you want."

For a time, the two men let silence reign, each made pensive by the comfort of strong, hot tea. After he had drained half his cup, Gomaz spoke. "I've never put much stock in religion," he said, "but I've found myself praying a lot tonight." He lifted his eyes to the smudged ceiling and looked into Diego's storm-colored eyes. "If there is a Blessed Madre, then I hope She's watching over Deanna Hernaan right now, because I don't know if this scheme of ours will work without her."

"Did you tell her everything?" Diego asked.

"Enough to get her to trust me, or so I thought. I was wrong. Damn it!" Gomaz hammered his fist on the tabletop. "If only she hadn't bolted. I wonder what spooked her?"

Diego shrugged. "You can ask her when you find her."

Gomaz reached for his pack and stood, leaving the cooling remains of his tea untouched.

With a sharp nod, Diego hooked the lantern handle in a two-fingered hold. He pointed to the back door. "Stable's this way."

Together they crossed the rear yard to the shed that sheltered Diego's transport. A fat-tired bicycle, scattered flecks of red paint still clinging to its otherwise naked steel frame, leaned against the slats of a single box stall. Hay, manure, and musk blended their separate fragrances into an aroma that was not unpleasant to Gomaz's city-bred nose.

"Heya, old girl. My sweet old girl," Diego crooned as he secured the lantern to a hook protruding from a support post. A soft whuff of exhalation and the pop of shifting joints answered his greeting from the dimness beyond the stall gate. The hairless piebald head of an eelat mare thrust out of the dark into her master's waiting hands. Diego scratched the sensitive area behind her ear holes, eliciting a contented groan from deep within her barrel chest.

"Don't let this sweet act fool you," Diego said, chuckling. "Meriah here can be a handful when she's feeling contrary, but she's sturdy and long-winded."

The last time Gomaz had owned a pet—a little white gahto—he had been a boy of twelve. He recognized the look on the other man's face, for he too had felt that same kind of love. "I'll take good care of her."

"Saddle, blanket, and bridle are over in that corner." Diego pointed and Gomaz retrieved the tack. The old man led the eelat from the stall and secured her halter rope to a post outside the shed. He then ducked back inside the stall to retrieve the lantern.

"Take the road out to where it ends," Diego instructed as he tossed the blanket and saddle onto Meriah's broad back. "You'll see a dirt track angling south. Keep to it. There'll be other tracks branching off and intersecting. You have a compass, I assume. As long as you keep heading south by southwest, in two days time you'll come to the Amariyo."

He tightened the girth. "The path continues south along the bank. The nearest crossing is about two hours downstream. It's been a dry spring, so the river should be pretty low. Once you're across, it can get confusing, but there's one track that's marked with a post. That's the one you want. It'll lead you straight to Dry Creek."

"I guess I should expect a cool welcome," Gomaz said as he passed Diego the bridle.

"No great mystery why folks out there are wary of strangers," Diego adjusted the straps on the headstall. "But money always smooths the way, as you well know."

Meriah tossed her head and mouthed the bit. A froth of pale foam flew from her lips, splattering the front of Gomaz's coat. Though she stood no higher than a meter and a half at her withers, to a weary Gomaz it seemed as if the beast's back scraped the stars. He rested his cheek against the saddle skirt for a few moments before grabbing the horn and swinging into the seat.

Diego secured his pack to the cantle while Gomaz adjusted stirrup leathers fitted for a shorter man. Meriah seemed resigned to the loss of her rest. She no longer fidgeted, but stood quiet while her rider made ready to leave.

Diego rested a hand on the eelat's smooth shoulder. Gomaz sensed a change in the older man's mood. "This is probably a fool's errand, my friend," he said. "You can't outrun that gunship."

"After all the things I've survived this night, I have to believe there's a chance," Gomaz replied quietly.

Diego scratched his grizzled head and nodded.

Gomaz gathered the reins and tapped his heels against Meriah's sides. The eelat responded with a snort and a smart step. Diego walked beside her, his hand touching her shoulder as if he feared to lose their connection. The old man would not speak the words, so Gomaz spoke for him. "I know this mare means a lot to you. I promise I'll return her safe."

"She's my only real friend." Diego quickened his pace to trot past the side of the house toward a gate, which he unlatched and pushed open. Gomaz guided Meriah through and pulled her to a stop beside his temporarily useless car.

"I've got a place to hide your machine," Diego said. He peered up at Luna, ensconced amidst a fleecy nest of clouds. "You'd best be on your way. It'll be sunrise soon."

Gomaz kept one hand on the reins as he reached out to offer the other to his fellow ex-poli. Diego had the grip of a working man—strong and callused. "Good luck and Maria protect you, Roberto," he said.

"And you, Migeyl."

With a final caress for Meriah's nose, Diego turned to head back toward his house. The eelat crabbed sideways, intending to follow her master, but Gomaz pulled hard on the reins to set her straight.

"You answer to me now," he said, and dealt her a sharp kick to the ribs. Stubby tail lashing, the mare bolted out of the yard into the road, trailing farts like pistol shots. Together, man and mount sped southwest toward the coming dawn.

37
fire and blood

Beneath the old pinya tree near the center of her shamanic garden, Yellow Bird sat cross-legged, weaving tufts of sweetgrass into a rough human figure. She swayed as she wove, her voice rising in the minor chords of a funeral dirge. Ashes of mourning smeared her forehead, and her long black hair hung disheveled about her shoulders. Tears streamed down her coppery cheeks, spattering the soft white algodon of her blouse with salty drops.

That morning she'd awakened from a disjointed dream of fire and blood that had left her shivering with dread. "Ancestors, I beg of you... spare us," she murmured, despite suspecting that her plea would be futile.

When she'd finished the poppet, she laid it atop a flat rock next to a sprig of corella, a polished moonstone, and a scrap of serpent skin; all symbols of peace and rebirth. Her ritual cairn complete, the ithani closed her eyes and whispered a prayer to center her mind.

Ancestors, if some of us must die soon in order to spare those yet to be born a worse fate, then grant your children the strength to accept this sacrifice.

The shamanic gift of foreknowledge could be both a blessing and a curse.

The ithani brought her other senses into sharper focus. The spicy scent of mezcala in full bloom overpowered the more delicate aromas of corella and rosa. A ray of sunshine slanted through the spreading branches of the old tree, warming the right side of her body, while her left side remained rinsed in cool shadow. Overhead she heard a pair of striped *ardiyas* scolding her with squeaks and puffed tails from their nest hollow midway up the fungus-studded trunk.

Yellow Bird breathed in the heady aromas and, with them, the peace of her sacred place. In the distance she could hear the faint sounds of the village going about the daily business of life. Gradually she felt the tightness squeezing her heart begin to ease.

After a long interval of stillness, the ithani opened her eyes. Though sorrow still coiled, heavy and gray, within the center of her being, she felt in control of it, rather than it having control of her.

Gazing at her surroundings and delighting in the beauty of the well-tended beds, Yellow Bird suddenly found her attention snagged by an inexplicable wrongness near the rear of the garden. Troubled, she rose from her knees to investigate.

At the edge of the outermost bed, where thriving mezcala plants once grew, she saw only hacked stumps and a scattering of broken roots amid the disturbed soil. Disbelief and confusion swelled within her like knives cutting her flesh. To dishonor sacred tradition by stealing from a shamanic garden—who would have done such a terrible thing?

Sorrow mixed with anger, heaped upon still more sorrow. Yellow Bird wept fresh tears, but only for a few moments. Wanting only to rage against the unrelenting cruelty of her burdens, instead she brushed the ashes from her forehead and blotted her eyes on the hem of her blouse. Gathering her hair into a thick twist, she secured it with a pair of carved vaca bone combs.

I must be strong, she thought, *for the sake of the community and my family.*

After brushing away the crumbs of soil clinging to her skirts, Yellow Bird picked a mindful path through the rows of her garden, heading back toward the village. By the time she reached the veranda of her longhouse she felt serene once more, and ready to face the trials yet to come.

Deanna walks on an empty savannah, alone under a night sky strangely devoid of stars. Her body casts a double shadow in the light of the twin moons. Tough grass rasps the skin of her bare feet. Coming from everywhere and nowhere at once, she hears the sound of bells. She stops to listen, for the mournful peal carries an urgent message she knows she must heed…yet she can't quite remember how.

Without warning, a multi-forked lightning bolt splits the sky and…

A noise like thunder tore Deanna from sleep. Her narrow bed trembled. She bolted upright with a startled cry and glanced around the storage loft that had served as her sleeping quarters since she'd arrived in the valley. Drifting in from the little window beneath the eaves, she heard the steady clangor of alarm bells.

The village is in danger. Dressed in only a thin algodon shift, she rolled from her bed. Crouching to avoid the low ceiling, she scurried down the ladder that led into the main room.

Shirtless and rumple-haired, Strong Hand sat on the floor by the front door, already pulling on his boots. Raven stood wide-eyed at his father's back, fists clenched at his sides. Yellow Bird crouched beside them with her two youngest children in her arms, her unbound waist-length hair covering her shoulders like a cloak of black silk.

A second and third explosion rolled through the village, shivering the walls of the house like a slap from a giant's hand.

Deanna jumped from the ladder and rushed to Yellow Bird's side. "What's happening?"

"We're under attack," the ithani said, sounding strangely calm.

Deanna gasped. "By whom?"

"An alta gunship," Strong Hand replied. The natome and his wife exchanged a look of such harrowing intensity it lacerated Deanna's heart.

"No," she whispered. "Why?"

"Slaving raid," Strong Hand said.

"Natome...I want to help," Deanna declared. "I'm a good shot."

Strong Hand nodded. With a brace of savage tugs, he finished lacing his boots and scrambled to his feet. "Get dressed and follow me to the armory."

He kissed his wife. With Raven at his heels, he bolted out the front door.

Deanna scrambled back up to the loft and with shaking hands pulled on her shirt and pants. Another explosion sent a shockwave through the house. Debris showered the thatched roof in a staccato burst. The acrid sting of smoke and burning coal oil infused the close air. She stifled a cough and scrubbed at her watering eyes. Below she could hear Yellow Bird trying to calm her wailing babies with quiet reassurances.

"Hurry, child!" the ithani shouted.

"I'm coming!" Deanna laced her boots over threadbare socks and reached under her bed to retrieve Gomaz's Poltro. Checking to make sure the safety was engaged, she shoved the slug pistol into her waistband and slid down the ladder, hitting the floor at a run.

Yellow Bird caught her arm as she passed. "Deanna, wait."

Deanna paused, flushed and trembling.

"The alta gunship carries one who comes hunting you," the ithani murmured. Her eyes burned with a peculiar intensity. "I've seen his face in a vision. It is horribly scarred."

"I've seen him myself," Deanna replied. "At Dry Creek Station." The implications added to the fear already savaging her gut.

"This man will find you tonight, child," Yellow bird continued. "If you die, then all is lost; for the Tiqui and for the loved ones you've left behind in your world. If you live, the disaster can be averted. I've seen glimpses of both futures."

"Then I'll have to live."

Yellow Bird reached up to pull Deanna's face down to hers. She kissed Deanna's forehead, stepped back and gathered her children to herself. "Go," she whispered.

Deanna turned and rushed into the night. She ran through the village, dodging grim-faced women carrying sloshing water buckets, barking perros hurling themselves to the limits of their tethers, and young people gripping whatever they could seize to use as weapons: axes, staffs, hoes, slug guns. Thick smoke roiled in gray, stinging clouds between the houses. Somewhere to her left, a man screamed for help to douse his flaming roof.

She found Ghost Dog, New Moon, and River at the armory, helping Shadow and Strong Hand distribute the firearms the village held in common to those who did not have them. She did not see Raven.

After the last of the slug rifles had been assigned and the defenders dispatched to the battlefront, Strong Hand, Ghost Dog, and Shadow moved to the back of the shed where a long rectangular wooden chest rested against the wall. A thick, forged steel padlock secured the lid. Strong Hand produced a key and released the hasp. His arm muscles cording with strain, he and Shadow lifted the heavy lid and maneuvered it to a corner. Ghost Dog reached into the chest and retrieved something that looked almost as long as he was tall. The glow cast by burning thatch rippled like orange water along the gleaming barrel of an ee-rifle.

"I hope you have more of those," Deanna said.

"Only two," Ghost Dog replied, "but we had none the last time the altas came."

"Natome, Nexa." Three Stars emerged from the smoke, eyes streaming. "The raiders are at the north pasture."

Strong Hand and Shadow exchanged grim looks.

Ghost Dog passed the rifle to his brother-in-law and reached back into the chest for its twin. "River and I can try to get close enough to kill the jelly or hit the boilers, if it's a steamer."

"No!" New Moon seized her husband's shoulder and turned fierce eyes on her brother. "It's too dangerous. Do you want my child to lose its father and uncle both on the same night?" Her free hand pressed the swell of her quickening belly.

"Your brother is right, Daughter," Shadow said, gently touching New Moon's arm. "It's the best chance we have to destroy their ship."

New Moon looked at the tense faces of her menfolk and bit her lip.

The crack of gunfire heightened Deanna's sense of urgency. "I need a rifle," she said, holding out her hands. "My pistol won't be enough."

Shadow regarded her with a mixture of incredulity and contempt. "You would take up arms against your own kind, alta? Why?"

"You are my friends." She refused to shy away from the fury and heartache in his stare. After a moment of silence, the nexa tossed her a weapon. A box of bullets followed.

"Go now," Strong Hand ordered. "Don't let any of them get into the village."

Ghost Dog and River took off, the bulky ee-rifles slung from thick straps over their shoulders. New Moon started to follow, then stopped.

"Daughter, I know you want to fight…" Shadow began.

New Moon's raised hand silenced him. "I'll gather a few of the women and go stand guard over Mother's garden." She grabbed a rifle and darted away into the murk.

Deanna looked at Strong Hand, who nodded and said, "Ancestors protect you." Shadow's mouth remained compressed and silent.

"And you, Natome." Deanna shifted her gaze to Shadow. "You as well, Nexa." Gripping her rifle, she took off toward the north edge of the village.

Shouts, screams, and the constant barrage of gunfire greeted her as she rounded the corner of the northernmost house and saw for the first time what the Tiqui were up against. Illuminated by the garish light of flaming grass and wood, a midsize steam-powered gunship hovered at the far end of the north pasture. Empty rope ladders dangled over the sides, but muzzle flashes from the gunwales betrayed the presence of armed men still aboard.

A bullet hummed past her ear, knocking a chunk of wood from the wall beside her. A lash of pain scored her cheek. She ducked behind the cover of a low fence, risked a glance and saw scattered, furtive shadows gliding toward the village from across the meadow.

With a shudder of fear, Deanna realized she was about to be overrun. *I can't face a squad of armed men alone.* Heart in her throat, she sprang up and ran back the way she had come.

A flurry of loud pops sounded just ahead. Deanna skidded to a halt between two houses, the rifle raised and her finger on the trigger. The memory of her father's patient coaching at the palace shooting range steadied her hands. Thick smoke and darkness confounded her vision and burned her throat raw. She swallowed hard to suppress the coughing spasm that threatened her aim.

Multiple footsteps pounded down the path toward her. She heard a sharp report; the blue flash of an ee-rifle discharge illuminated three fleeing Tiqui. One screamed and fell, the rifle in his hand spinning away. Deanna held her fire, waiting. A much taller dark shape loped past the fallen Tiqui. She stepped into the path and squeezed the trigger. The invader fell without a sound.

A feeling of unreality sluiced through her. *I just killed someone.* An actinic flare crackled overhead.

Can't think about that now…

She sprinted after the two retreating Tiqui. The echo of gunfire bounced off the walls around her. *Madre, they're in the village. I have to get back to Yellow Bird and the children.*

A clutch of women and youngsters rushed out from a side alley. Their eyes were wide and wild in their small faces. "Go to the woods behind the ithani's garden!" Deanna yelled as a volley of bullets peppered the dirt. "Run!"

To draw the gunmen away from the fleeing Tiqui, she plunged into the alley, shouting, "I'm over here, you effing pendayhos!" She stopped and pressed her back to the plastered wall, chest heaving.

Several moments passed with no sign of pursuit. Deanna sidled to the alley mouth and peered out. The path was deserted.

Afraid and relieved at once, she paused to listen. Damn it…where had they gone?

A trio of flashes lit the sky to the north, followed by the bass roar of flamethrowers. Dog and River were firing at the gunship. Torn between the desire to stand with her friends on the frontline and the obligation to offer whatever protection she could to Yellow Bird, Deanna chose the latter.

Abandoning caution for speed, she took the most direct route toward the ithani's longhouse, swerving only to avoid dwellings engulfed in flames. She prayed that all the children and elders had escaped to the woods. Rounding a corner, she snagged her foot on an exposed tree root. It sent her down hard on one knee, cursing. Pain shot up her leg and the rifle flew from her hands. It landed beside a small body sprawled in the dirt of the pathway.

"No, no, no," she moaned. "Raven!" With frantic fingers she searched at neck and wrist for a pulse, but found none. Her hands came away sticky with blood. The boy's small hand, resting limp at his side, still curled loosely around the grip of a pistol.

Sobbing, Deanna gathered Raven into her lap and cradled him to her breast as if he were her own son. Too sunk in grief to hear approaching footfalls, she recognized her own peril only when it spoke her name.

"Deanna Hernaan."

She looked up into a familiar, ruined face. Its single eye sighted along the barrel of a rifle trained on the center of her forehead.

I'm so sorry Yellow Bird, she thought. Aloud, she said, "If I'd known you were my stepmother's thug, I would've stuck a knife in your ribs that day back at Dry Creek. Tell that bitch I said to go eff herself."

The scarred man laughed. "You've got guts, girl. If it makes you feel any better, this is nothing personal."

Deanna eased Raven's body to the dirt and stood to face her assassin.

The knowledge that the news of her demise might never reach those she cared about most in the world felt more tragic than death itself. She took three slow steps forward and—wishing to hasten the inevitable by goading him—said, "Do it then, you mother-effing piece of mierda!"

The crack of rifle fire made Deanna jump. The top of her would-be executioner's shaven skull shattered like a ripe melon dropped on pavement, sending a spray of blood across her face and clothes. Like a felled vaca he crashed to his knees, and then toppled facedown at her feet.

38
tears for the dead

Deanna backed away from the corpse as Strong Hand emerged from the shadows, his rifle poised to fire another round. "Are you hurt?"

Shock pared Deanna's voice to a whisper. "No, I'm…I'm fine."

Strong Hand prodded the dead man with a booted toe, rifle still at the ready. "Thank the Ancestors I got here when I did."

"Natome…" Deanna glanced back to where Raven's body lay, still hidden from his father's sight by the dark. The agony of what she must now tell Strong Hand filled her with such despair that she thought she might die herself. She tried to speak the words that would break her friend's heart, but they emerged as little more than a formless exhalation.

Bursts of crimson light flooded the sky to the north. Fresh explosions shivered the ground underfoot. "I'm needed at the meadow," Strong Hand shouted. He turned and disappeared into the darkness, leaving Deanna alone and immersed in the metallic smell of death.

Heartsick, she returned to Raven and crouched beside him, too weary to move, but then the thought of Yellow Bird waiting and praying for the safety of her loved ones infused her with a fresh rush of energy. Gathering the body into her arms, she struggled to her feet.

"Let's get you back to your family, Raven," she whispered, rocking the dead boy as if he were asleep.

Stepping over the lifeless body of her own would-be assassin, she began making her way toward Yellow Bird's longhouse.

The path she walked twisted between houses that had sustained heavy damage. The dark and her heightened awareness turned familiar shapes alien, and every doorway teemed with menacing shadows. The bitter haze from burning coal oil, wood, and dry grass enveloped her, filling her mouth with the taste of ash.

Deanna spotted the glow of lamplight spilling from the open doorway of Yellow Bird's home, and paused to gather her resolve. Though he weighed no more than an alta toddler, Raven's cooling body had grown heavy in her arms. She gazed at the boy's pale, still face, surprised that she'd never before noticed his beauty. Pulling him closer to her breast, she started toward the longhouse.

She reached the bottom of the porch before realizing that the continuous rattle of gunfire from the meadow had subsided. Deanna strained to hear any sound, but an eerie silence had fallen over the village. For several heartbeats it reigned unbroken; then, one by one, ululating cries rose toward the starry sky to combine into a full-throated chorus of victory.

"It's over," she whispered, feeling a brief moment of gratitude. But then she glanced down at Raven, and once again remembered what her friends had yet to face. *No, it's not. It's only just begun.* She started climbing.

Yellow Bird met her on the top step, a thin wail rising from her throat. Deanna passed Raven into the arms of his mother and followed the ithani as she carried the boy inside and laid him on the woven reed mats before the hearth. Yellow Bird collapsed beside her son, making a cradle of her warm flesh to hold him.

Desperate to offer any comfort, Deanna sank cross-legged beside her friend and clasped Yellow Bird's sweat-dampened hand, holding tight as if to a lifeline. Dawn, until now huddled by the hearth with baby White Fox in her arms, scuttled over to sit by their mother. The toddler, as if sensing his mother's distress, began to bawl.

"I prayed to the Ancestors, begged them to spare me this sacrifice, but they took what they would from me anyway," Yellow Bird murmured through her tears.

Deanna drew in a sharp breath. Only now did she realize the ithani had seemed unsettled and melancholy for most of the day. *Sweet Yesu, did Yellow Bird foresee what would happen tonight?* she wondered.

The clatter of boots on the longhouse steps interrupted her thoughts. Deanna looked up to see Shadow bounding through the door, his slug rifle raised in jubilation. "Wife, the altas have turned tail and run."

Yellow Bird's gaze never left Raven's face. "Sunaiya, our son is dead."

As if touched by some dark force, Shadow froze. His fierce, joyful grin melted into a grimace of horror. His arms dropped to his sides and his rifle slipped from his fingers. He crossed the room on unsteady legs and fell to his knees beside his wife. Shock and disbelief contorted his angular features as he stared at Raven's body.

"I found him near the school," Deanna said, reaching a tentative hand toward the nexa's shoulder, then letting it drop. "He was still holding his pistol. I...I'm so sorry, Nexa."

Shadow groaned. Snagging his fingers through soot-dusted hair, he yanked as if he would tear out every strand. Yellow Bird raised herself from the floor to slip her arms around him. In utter desolation they clung to each other, weeping. Dawn leaned against her mother, her small face crumpled, sobbing almost as loudly as her baby brother.

Sensing the children's need, and wanting to offer the comfort their parents were too mired in grief to provide, Deanna opened her arms. "Dawn, dulzor," she beckoned softly, "come here." As both children snuggled, whimpering, against her bloodstained shirt, Deanna pressed her face against the tops of their rumpled heads and closed her eyes.

For a time her mind drifted in a blank haze of exhaustion, until Ghost Dog's voice crying out for help roused her from her torpor. He swept through the door with Three Stars lolling like a broken doll in his arms, her eyes blank and staring. Blood droplets like scarlet beads welled from an ugly wound in the Tiqui girl's head.

Deanna tensed in shock. Only the children in her lap prevented her from leaping to her feet. *Diosa mia*, she thought. *How much more could this family endure?*

"Mother, Star's been shot!" Ghost Dog staggered to a halt, his eyes darting between the faces of his parents and dead brother. In the horror of the moment, he did not seem to know where to look.

"Ancestors, no..." Shadow exclaimed.

"Mother..." In a voice like rusted metal, Ghost Dog pleaded.

Yellow Bird rested her cheek against Raven's forehead for a moment and kissed the pale skin. "Ghost Dog, my son...your little brother has gone to join the Ancestors."

Shadow tenderly gathered the boy's body into his arms. "The living need you now, Wife," he said. "Our son can rest awhile by the hearth."

Yellow Bird nodded, wiping the tears from her eyes. She stood and went to her firstborn. "I can do nothing more for Raven," she said, gazing at Three Stars' waxen face. "But, perhaps it's not too late for your Star." She pulled the pantera pelt from her favorite chair, and spread it on the floor.

Ghost Dog knelt and gently laid his betrothed on the soft, black fur. "Mother will make you well, sunaiya," he whispered. Raising her slack fingers to his lips, he kissed them.

"I'll need my medicine bag," the ithani said as she settled on the floor at Three Stars' side.

From beside the fireplace, Shadow answered, "I'll get it." He left the room and returned a moment later carrying a leather satchel that he passed into his wife's waiting hands. He said, "I'll get water and bandages from the kitchen."

Yellow Bird nodded and bent close to examine the girl's wounded forehead, her brow furrowed. She did not touch the damaged tissue.

After a few moments she sighed and turned to Ghost Dog, sitting in tense expectation beside her. "Son, it doesn't look good. See here," she pointed to Three Stars' temple, "the bone is broken and there's a piece pressing into her brain."

"Please, Mother. You have to try," Ghost Dog begged in an agonized whisper.

The ithani brushed a snarled lock of hair from her son's tear-streaked face. "I'll try."

Hesitancy had kept Deanna silent until now. "I'd like to help, if I can, Ithani," she offered.

"We don't need anything from you." Shadow had returned from the kitchen, bearing a basin of water in each hand and several strips of cloth draped over his forearms. He set his burdens down and knelt beside Three Stars' head. "This is your fault, alta," he added.

"I didn't want…" Deanna began, but Yellow Bird interrupted.

"Peace, Husband. Now is not the time."

Shadow yielded, but the look he gave Deanna could melt iron. Unable to meet his searing gaze, she instead focused on Yellow Bird's quick, sure moves. The ithani reached into her satchel, withdrew a small lump of soap and washed her hands. "Hold her steady, Husband," she said, dipping a cloth into the second basin. While Shadow braced Three Stars' head between his hands, Yellow Bird sponged blood from the wound, revealing the gleam of bone amidst torn flesh. Deanna saw the distraught look that passed between the ithani and her husband, and she knew in her heart what neither could bear to say aloud within earshot of their son.

From a series of small packets, Yellow Bird made an herbal poultice that she soaked in water and applied to the wound. She then swathed the unconscious girl's head in a clean bandage. Tying off the ends, she turned to Ghost Dog and said, "I've done what I can for her, Son."

Ghost Dog pressed Three Stars' limp hand against his cheek. "Is there nothing else?" He sounded as if he would shatter at any moment.

"I can keep her comfortable. The rest is up to the Ancestors."

Pointing a rigid finger at Deanna's face, Shadow warned, "If Star dies, her passing will be yet another death on this alta's head."

"Husband…" Yellow Bird murmured, clasping Shadow's forearm.

"No, you can't blame…" Deanna's protest froze on her lips as she remembered the cold, one-eyed gaze of her would-be assassin.

The nexa glared at his wife. "Strong Hand believes the altas came for more slaves. But I think they came for her," he retorted. "We never should have brought her here."

Deanna had no words to offer in her own defense. She knew Shadow was right.

Into the fraught silence, Yellow Bird spoke. "No, sunaiya. Deanna is not to blame."

"How can you defend her, Wife?" Shadow asked.

"Because it's true," Yellow Bird replied. "Deanna already knows I foresaw her arrival in our valley," she continued in a quiet voice. "At first I didn't understand, but each succeeding vision brought increased clarity. I believe the Ancestors guided her here for a reason."

"What reason? Why would our Ancestors concern Themselves with an alta girl?"

"You think because she isn't Tiqui, the Ancestors don't care about her?" Yellow Bird replied, shaking her head. "You're wrong, Husband. The Ancestors care about all living things in this world. They showed me that our people's destiny and Deanna's are entwined."

"No. I refuse to accept that," Shadow growled.

"In my visions I've seen many possible futures," the ithani continued, "but only one in which both the alta and Tiqui live in harmony and mutual respect. Deanna is the key to that future, but only if she makes the correct choices."

Tears once again coursed down Yellow Bird's cheeks. "The Ancestors also warned me there would be great sacrifices, for her and for us. Tonight brought the first of those sacrifices."

"If this is what The Ancestors have decreed for us, then curse Them," Shadow exclaimed.

Yellow Bird's face paled. "You don't mean that, sunaiya."

"Yes, I do," Shadow replied. "They took our son from us, in exchange for her." He pushed to his feet, his face a mask of pain. "Get out, alta! Leave this house now, before I lose all control."

Trembling, Deanna shrank from the anger in the nexa's hoarse shout. The two children in her arms began wailing once more. Ghost Dog continued to stare at Three Stars, seemingly oblivious to his adopted father's outburst.

"Sunaiya." Yellow Bird stood and embraced her husband. Caressing Shadow's tangled hair, she murmured, "We need love to get us through this, not hate. Husband, you must let go of your rage. For all our sakes."

Overcome by the raw anguish of Yellow Bird's family, Deanna felt her own emotions begin to spiral out of control. "Ithani," she said, "Your husband is right. I should leave." As tears for the dead and dying stung her eyes, Deanna released Dawn and White Fox and slowly climbed to her feet.

Ignoring Yellow Bird's pleas for her to stay, she fled the house into the night.

As she ran through the village, Deanna passed knots of folk mopping up the last of the fires. Someone called out to her for news of the ithani's son, but she didn't answer. Guilt and grief fueled her speed as she followed the dirt path past the southern perimeter of the village toward the lake.

She stopped running when she reached the fog-shrouded water. Among the tall shoreline grasses she collapsed, hugging knees to chest, her body shaking so hard her teeth rattled.

Raven is dead, Three Stars is dying, and...Madre, I killed a man tonight.

Until this moment, she'd kept that sickening truth walled up behind a protective barrier of distraction. With devastating swiftness, the barrier crumbled and the memory punched through to savage her. *Yesu, I'm a murderer!*

She screamed until her voice failed, then she curled on her side in the grass like a wounded puppy. The last remnants of Deanna the child—the idealist, the sheltered elite—had been torn loose by tonight's tragedies, slain with the same bullet that had felled her would-be killer. She had no idea who the new person inhabiting this shell of her old self would become. The realization frightened her.

If I'd gone back to Nue Bayona, none of this would've happened, she thought. But then she and Zander would both be dead, and the terrible future Yellow Bird foresaw would come to pass, dooming all the Tiqui, not just her friends in Reed Valley.

Sucking in deep breaths of the humid air, Deanna allowed the sounds and scents of the night to calm her feverish thoughts. The oscillating whir of griyos hidden in the grass, along with the deep croaks of amphibious ranas in their watery lairs among the reeds and the spicy-sweet fragrance of night-blooming *loto* flowers—they all acted in concert to lull her with near narcotic potency, until she eventually fell into an exhausted sleep.

THE GURGLING CALLS of *ganso* birds paddling among the reeds roused Deanna from a tangle of disturbing dreams. Images of fire and blood faded from her waking mind, leaving her queasy. She rose from her bed of crushed grass, dew-dampened and stiff from hours spent lying on the hard ground. The thin pall of mist hanging over the lake's mirrored surface shimmered in the early morning sunshine. Shivering, she raised her hand to shade her eyes and watched the gansos diving beneath the water, emerging seconds later with tiny fish or crustaceans wiggling in their spoon-shaped beaks.

As long as she stayed here watching the birds she could pretend that last night never happened.

But it did happen. And I have to face the consequences.

Turning her back on the lake, Deanna started walking along the path leading toward the village. As exertion restored some warmth to her chilled body, she felt a burning pain in her cheek. Amidst the night's greater traumas, she'd completely forgotten about the wound. She explored the area with careful fingers and found a laceration—swollen and tender, but thankfully shallow, and already crusted over with a fresh scab.

If only the wounds inflicted on Reed Valley could heal so easily, she thought.

When she reached the community vegetable garden, Deanna paused, conflicted. She wanted to learn how Three Stars fared, but that required her to return to Yellow Bird's house and risk facing Shadow. She wasn't sure she had the courage.

In the end, concern for Ghost Dog overcame her fear. With fresh determination in her step she continued on, keeping to the village outskirts while heading for the ithani's home via the back pathway.

At the bottom of the longhouse stairs, Deanna once again paused. She gazed up at the open doorway, feeling an indefinable sense of dread sink its chill talons into her psyche. Her straining ears caught the faint sound of voices chanting, barely audible above the whisper of her own anxious breath.

As she stepped on the first riser, a heartrending cry from inside the house shattered the silence and sent her racing up the steps and through the door.

What she saw stopped her cold and smote her heart like a hammer blow.

Atop the long table at which she'd shared many a meal with Yellow Bird and her family, the bodies of Raven and Three Stars lay side by side, covered to their chins with thin multicolored blankets. Surrounding them stood the ithani, her family, and a few others, hands linked, chanting softly and swaying in unison. Deanna recognized several of the village council among the mourners. At the head of the table, held up by his father Strong Hand's arms as if he'd lost all strength to stand, Ghost Dog tore at his hair, weeping.

"Oh, no, no," Deanna whispered.

She started toward the gathering, hoping to remain unnoticed, but then Shadow turned and looked straight at her, as if he'd somehow sensed her presence. With a scowl he left his wife's side and came to block Deanna's way. "Three Stars is dead," he said.

"I'm so sorry," Deanna murmured.

For several heartbeats Shadow stared at her, stony-eyed and silent. Then he spit in her face.

Deanna reeled backwards, her leg muscles turning to wet dough. She fell on her knees, too stunned to think. For a brief moment, the room spun in a lazy arc around her as she struggled to regain her shattered equilibrium. Then a soft voice spoke in her ear.

"My father had no right to treat you so cruelly, but please…forgive him. His grief is nearly unbearable."

Deanna looked over and saw New Moon kneeling beside her. The Tiqui girl's cheeks were flushed and glistening with tears. "I…I'm fine, Moon," she whispered. "I understand that your father is in a lot of pain. He needs to blame someone for what's happened."

New Moon pulled a cloth from her belt and tenderly blotted the spittle from Deanna's face. "He can't blame you. I won't allow it."

Deanna gave her friend a wan smile. "If only it were that simple," she said.

The group chant ended. The mourners stood in silence for a heartbeat. Then Strong Hand began anew, his voice raised in a solo dirge. Deanna climbed to her feet. "I think it's best for everyone if I find somewhere else to sleep."

New Moon caressed her shoulder. "The hayloft is comfortable. You can sleep there until you're ready to come back."

I don't know if that will be possible, Deanna thought. With Shadow's animosity curdled to outright hatred, her presence would only have a poisonous effect on Yellow Bird's marriage and family life.

"I have to rejoin the circle," New Moon said, her voice apologetic. "Please, don't go yet. Mother wants to speak to you after the *cheiya* ceremony is done. It won't be much longer."

"I'll wait by the door," Deanna said.

New Moon nodded and slipped back into the circle. Deanna lingered a few moments longer, watching the people she'd come to know as family. Though she longed to show them in some small way the depth of her own sorrow, she instead retreated to the doorway, feeling more like an intruder than kin. Closing her eyes, she leaned against the wall, listening to Strong Hand's lament. The words, sung in a language she did not understand, carried the full measure of his fatherly grief. Ghost Dog's hoarse sobs filled the pauses between stanzas.

Dog and Three Stars were supposed to be married in only a few weeks. Now though, instead of a bridegroom's bright colors, her friend would wear ashes and rags for as long as his shattered heart remained un-mended.

Deanna sighed. She opened her eyes in time to see Ghost Dog reach over and pluck Strong Hand's bone-handled hunting knife from his belt. She watched in horror as she realized his intent.

"Dog, no!" she screamed as he raised the blade to his throat.

Shadow and Strong Hand lunged together, bearing Ghost Dog to the floor beneath them. The room erupted in a babble of voices, all crying out in alarm. Ghost Dog struggled against the combined weight of his fathers' bodies, pinning him. "Let me go," he howled. "I want to be with her." Twisting his hand free, he once again pressed the knife to his neck.

Rushing over to the three heaving bodies, Deanna pounced upon the knife and, with grim determination, pried it from Ghost Dog's fingers. As she backed away, a hand touched her wrist. She spun to see River, standing behind her. "Take it," she gasped, relinquishing the weapon to him. She then went to hunker by the hearth, feeling powerless to do anything more.

Dog and I are iyahuya. If he dies, a part of me goes with him, she thought.

Though she questioned the existence of deities in general, she honored the Tiqui belief in their sacred Ancestors.

Perhaps there was something she could do after all. She clasped her hands beneath her chin. "Please, Tiqui Ancestors…Help Dog to see how much he is loved and needed…now, more than ever. Don't let him die."

Yellow Bird had fallen to the floor beside Ghost Dog and had begun to stroke his sweating face. "My son," she crooned, "this isn't what your sunaiya would want." Her quiet voice and gentle touch seemed to have an effect, for the suicidal fury slowly drained from him. His two fathers relaxed their hold upon his limbs, allowing Yellow Bird to gather him into her arms, where she rocked him, humming.

The shared moment of pain between mother and son proved too intimate for Deanna to bear. She looked away.

The village elders had departed, leaving the ithani's family to mourn in private. Deanna decided she would depart as well, to wait in heavy-hearted solitude until Yellow Bird felt ready to speak to her.

As she crept past them out the front door, none of her friends seemed to notice.

The shady porch offered a pleasant refuge from the morning sun's heat. Deanna wiped her brow on a grimy forearm, frowning. Glancing around, she spied a large dented cooking pot sitting a few paces from the doorway, filled to the brim with water. Recalling her blood-spattered state, she commandeered the pot and abandoned the porch for a patch of grass beneath the longhouse eaves.

She stripped off her filthy shirt and, clad in only a camisole and pants, doused her head and shoulders. With fingers made stiff by disgust and sorrow, she scrubbed the worst of the gore and grime from her face and neck, mindful of the throbbing cut on her cheek. When she'd done what she could, she returned to the porch. Settled on a stool too small for comfort, she leaned against the shaved pinya logs of the longhouse wall and tried to ignore her aches while she waited.

Reed Valley's inhabitants had risen early to begin the strenuous work of rebuilding their devastated community. The rasp of saws made a rough counterpoint to the clangs and thumps of hammers. A pile of still-smoldering cinders that had once been the thatch roof of the house next door infused the air with an acrid tang. Folk shouted to each other across fire-blackened railings and traded surprisingly cheerful banter over mounds of debris. Perros barked, children shrieked, and capras bleated. To Deanna's ears, the village sounded much like it did on most mornings, a testament to the Tiqui's strength and resiliency.

The soft strains of a cheiya, sung this time by Yellow Bird, drifted from the interior of the longhouse. Deanna reflected on her own mother's funeral, held in Nue Bayona Cathedral nine years ago. Her memories of the opulent ceremony had lost none of their clarity. She could still smell the incense and hear the choir singing the Rites for the Dead in ethereal tones. The Tiqui's simple mourning rituals stood in sharp contrast, yet were no less moving.

She bowed her head and tried to empty her mind of all thoughts. As all else but the sound of Yellow Bird's voice began to fade, shouts of alarm rose from the northern edge of the village, shattering Deanna's tenuous peace. She surged to her feet, tipping the stool on its side, and stared toward the sound of the commotion.

A few moments later she spotted a young man pelting up the path toward Yellow Bird's house, his long black braid slapping his back as he ran. She recognized him as one of River's friends. He reached the stairs, and without slowing bounded up and through the door, ignoring Deanna while shouting, "Ithani! Natome! Nexa!"

Madre, what now?

Reluctant to follow him inside, instead Deanna stood at the threshold, listening. The young man spoke with quiet urgency. Though she couldn't make out every word, she caught "scouts" and "alta" and "gap." The message propelled Strong Hand, Shadow, and River to their feet. They rushed to the door and snatched up their weapons. Deanna jumped aside as they ran past her down the stairs. She followed them to the bottom and cried, "What's happening?"

Without breaking stride, River shouted, "More raiders!"

39

lives in the balance

Gomaz reined his mount to a halt and surveyed the terrain ahead.

The trail dipped to cross a sluggish stream. It then wound up a shallow slope and disappeared into a narrow defile between high cliffs. Perfect place for an ambush, he thought.

A silver ten-reále coin had purchased directions to Reed Valley from a bushy-bearded trapper with no front teeth, met in the common room of Dry Creek Station. With no time to spare he'd pushed Meriah hard to reach this place, stopping only to feed and water the eelat and catch a couple hours' rest.

Gomaz removed the bandanna from his head and mopped the sweat off his face. No doubt Reed Valley's Tiqui defenders already had him in their sights and were waiting for him to enter the bottleneck before making their move.

Meriah snorted and scraped at the hard-packed dirt with a three-toed foot.

Gomaz retied the damp bandanna over his sweat-plastered hair. Can't put this off any longer, he thought.

Reaching into his saddlebag, he fished out a scrap of white cloth tied to a stick, a precaution he'd prepared before leaving Dry Creek. With the flag held high, he picked up Meriah's reins and urged her into the creek. Submerged weeds, like shreds of bright green cloth, fluttered around her fetlocks. Midstream, she stopped to drink. Gomaz pulled up hard on the bit, forcing the eelat out of the water and into the deep shade of the cliff face.

He stopped before the opening to the defile and peered into the gloom. They hadn't shot him yet. Good sign. The trail threaded between two massive boulders sheared from the granite walls, and disappeared.

They'll let me get past those rocks, first.

Gomaz cupped his free hand to his mouth. Waving the parley flag, he shouted, "I'm alone. I don't want any trouble." He waited, listening to the echoes rebound and die away to silence.

The rattling slide of dislodged pebbles coming from somewhere within the defile might be random or the result of a Tiqui defender's incautious change of position. Deciding that going in on foot was a better option, Gomaz dismounted and flipped the reins over Meriah's head. He tugged, and she followed him into the cool shadows.

The rock walls closed in around him. The eelat's padded feet made little noise on the sandy trail. When she hesitated, tossing her head, Gomaz stopped and shook the parley flag. "I don't want any trouble," he repeated. "I've come to speak to Deanna Hernaan...if she's still alive."

Meriah grunted and jerked at her reins, her rubbery lip lifted to expose yellowed teeth. Gomaz scanned the clefts and crevices above his head, wondering how badly he was outnumbered. Lawman's instinct screamed at him to take cover.

Fresh runnels of sweat trickled down his back and sides. A near unbearable itch had sprung up between his shoulder blades. He took a deep breath to steady his nerves. "I'll drop my weapons," he called out. Only echoes of his own voice answered him.

With deliberate slowness, Gomaz freed his ee-pistol from its holster and laid it on the ground, then reached to the concealed holster at the small of his back and removed his Poltro. It joined the ee-pistol at his feet. He raised his hands and waited.

As the seconds ticked by in silence and stillness, Gomaz felt his anxiety morphing into irritation. "Are you ever planning on showing yourselves," he said, "or are you just going to leave me to stand here for the rest of the day?"

As the echoes died away, one by one a group of diminutive, pistol- and rifle-wielding men began emerging from concealment among the clefts. They slid down to the trail and soon had him and Meriah surrounded.

For one awful moment, time stood still. Gomaz stared down the muzzles of a score of guns trained at his chest and head. *Relax, Beto*, he thought. If they'd intended on summary execution, they'd have done it already. He ran his tongue over dry lips.

Gomaz had seen his first living Tiqui only two days past, at Dry Creek. Like those he'd encountered at the trading station, these small men wore well-made clothes of algodon cloth and leather. They had skin tones of copper brown, and their hair color ranged from mahogany to black, with one notable exception—the tallest among them, a young man striking for his red hair and fairer complexion.

One man with threads of silver shot through his hair and a close-cropped beard stepped forward. His eyes raked Gomaz from crown to boot tops. "Drop all your weapons, alta," he said. Though no taller than an adolescent boy, kilo for kilo the small man's chiseled physique easily matched his own. *If I had to fight this hombre hand to hand, I might lose*, Gomaz thought. A half smile curving his lip, he nodded in salute to the other man's canniness. From a leather sheath in the top of his boot, he withdrew a slim knife and dropped it to the dirt. "That's all, I swear."

The Tiqui regarded him with the warmth of a midwinter dawn, but lowered his rifle. The others followed suit.

Another Tiqui, clean-shaven and younger but with the same air of authority as the older bearded man, stepped forward to claim Gomaz's arsenal. He ran an appreciative hand over the ee-pistol's chromed barrel before tucking it into his belt. The .45 and the knife he handed to his older comrade, then the two bent their heads together. Gomaz strained to listen, unable to make sense of their rapid, oddly accented speech; but their disagreement was plain. The younger man glanced repeatedly at him with dark, angry stares.

The older man finally spoke. "Last night, an alta raiding party attacked our village. People were killed. Perhaps you are one of them, come back to trick us," he pointed to Gomaz's white flag, "into letting our guard down, so as to gain entrance to our valley."

"I'm completely at your mercy," Gomaz replied. Fifteen years experience as a poli helped him keep his voice calm and his gaze steady. "You could've shot me anytime, but you haven't yet, which tells me you understand and respect what this flag means."

The Tiqui man's face remained impassive. "What business do you have with Deanna Hernaan?" he asked.

"I have information about her father." The itch between Gomaz's shoulder blades had resurged with hellish intensity, but he dared not move a muscle. He sensed his fate teetered at the edge of a slippery precipice. One false move could get him punctured by a volley of bullets.

Finally, the older Tiqui said, "Come with us."

Gomaz lowered his arms, hopeful now, but still wary. "Thank you."

The semicircle closed around him and Meriah, forming an escort. Gomaz tugged on the eelat's reins, urging her forward. The Tiqui walked in silence, the echoes of their footfalls bouncing off the quartz-veined granite. The walls of the ravine soared to end in a sliver of violet sky overhead. At this hour no sunlight reached the bottom to warm the chilly air, but light from both entrance and exit provided adequate illumination. When they reached the far side of the defile, Gomaz got his first look at Reed Valley.

At the far end of a lush meadow, alive with flitting, buzzing insects, he saw a collection of thatched wooden structures interspersed with small patches of green. A tiny lake sparkled in the distance.

No wonder they fight so hard to defend this place. It's beautiful....

His escort led him down a gentle incline and across the meadow into the village. As they walked down a lane past the charred ruins of what had once been a row of small houses, Gomaz studied the details of his surroundings with police-trained precision: a doorpost carved into the sensuous curves of a rampant felion, its beauty unmarred despite scorched forepaws; the tailored fit and embroidery of vines on the Tiqui leader's blue algodon shirt; a split-rail enclosure within which a clutch of black-and-gray-spotted capras milled about in bleating complaint; the ease and familiarity with which these small warriors handled their guns.

Men bent to repairs with hammer and saw paused in their labors to stare at him with blank faces. Women gathered fawn-eyed children into the folds of their multicolored skirts, whispering or else hurling bold imprecations like pistol shots. From a partially ruined doorway, an old man pitched a stone that smacked Gomaz in middle of his back and erupted in rusty laughter as his target whirled in surprise. Gomaz grimaced, stretching his arm in a futile attempt to massage the stinging welt.

The group emerged onto a grassy patch fronting the biggest house Gomaz had yet seen in the village. Though its neighbors had sustained damage in the attack, this home had come through unscathed. On the bottom step stood a woman too tall to be Tiqui.

Gomaz breathed a sigh of relief. *She's alive.*

Deanna left the porch and approached, slowly at first, staring at him with uncertainty. She paused, her hands flying to her mouth. "Roberto!" she cried and ran toward him, the Tiqui parting ranks to let her through. She stopped at arm's length, then reached out to clasp his outstretched hands. "I'm so glad to see you."

For a few moments all Gomaz could do was drink in the sight of her.

Sunlight kindled bronze highlights in hair that fell in dark waves across her bare, tanned shoulders. A damp algodon camisole clung to her small breasts. Canvas breeches, patched at both knees with swatches of soft leather, ended in frayed hems. A thin smear of soot painted a false bruise on her forehead, while an inflamed laceration stood in angry contrast across her cheek.

Finally he rediscovered his voice. "Yesu, it's good to see you too, Deanna."

"Clearly you know this man," the older Tiqui said, a hint of suspicion coloring his voice.

Deanna looked down at him, smiling with a daughter's affection. "Natome, Roberto is a friend. You can trust him."

"That remains to be seen," the Tiqui replied, but Gomaz thought he saw a slight thaw in the small man's dark eyes.

"I know about the raid." Gomaz clasped Deanna's shoulders and squeezed. "I'm sorry for the losses your friends suffered. I'm just thankful you survived."

"I almost didn't," Deanna replied. "How did you find me?"

Gomaz glanced around the half circle of Tiqui, still watchful as a pride of hunting felions. "With some tracking skills and a great deal of luck. This place is well hidden."

"Roberto, I know now I should've trusted you. I'm sorry," Deanna said, her gaze fixed on her shoes.

"Don't worry about that now," he replied softly. "Is there somewhere we can speak privately?"

"Before you may speak to Deanna, you first must go before the ithani," the man called Natome said. He looked pointedly at Gomaz. "Wait here." He signaled to his second-in-command and the young redhead. Together, all three men climbed the stairs and entered the house.

"Who, or what, is the ithani?" Gomaz asked.

"Ithani means 'chief'," Deanna explained. "Reed Valley's ithani is called Yellow Bird. She's a very wise and compassionate lady." The look she gave Gomaz laid bare her heart. "I've come to love her like a mother. She has shown me nothing but kindness since I arrived, and I've repaid her by bringing death and destruction to this beautiful place."

The deep sorrow infusing her voice touched a chord of sympathy and regret in Gomaz's heart. "Deanna," he said, "whatever happened here, none of it is your fault."

She shrugged. "I wish I could believe that."

The young redhead appeared at the door. Looking at Gomaz, he said, "The ithani will see you now."

As Deanna started up the stairs, Gomaz stopped her with a hand on her forearm. "I'll gladly meet with the chieftess," he said, "but then you and I must speak in private. Nothing I have to say involves your Tiqui friends."

Deanna's lips paled. "You're wrong, she replied. "They're very much involved, more than you know."

Gomaz didn't see how, but he kept his doubts to himself and followed Deanna up to the doorway.

"Watch your head," Deanna warned as she stooped to pass beneath the wooden lintel, carved in the graceful whorls of a bank of storm clouds. Gomaz bent near double as he followed. The coolness of the longhouse interior felt marvelous to his heat-stressed body. He shuddered with relief. A few steps over the threshold, he paused in a crouch while his eyes adjusted to dimness. Wary of standing too fast lest he crack his skull, he straightened by slow increments until he felt the tickle of thatch on the top of his head.

Awning-shaded windows softened the glare of natural light illuminating the large, open room. Densely woven reed mats cushioned his footsteps. Gomaz trailed Deanna toward a group of people clustered near the center of the room.

Though he had never met Yellow Bird, Gomaz surmised that the small woman seated on a fur-draped chair could be no one else. An air of strength, mingled with a profound sadness emanating from her, struck him like a velvet-sheathed slap.

The posse leader and his second stood in grim-faced watchfulness to either side of her. A girl wearing a younger version of the ithani's face sat cross-legged at her feet. Gomaz didn't see the young redhead.

"You've already met Strong Hand and Shadow, the ithani's husbands," Deanna said in a low voice. "Strong Hand is the senior. The girl is New Moon, her eldest daughter...Ithani." Deanna addressed the chieftess in soft tones of respect. Glancing next at each man she said, "Natome, Nexa, this is Roberto Gomaz."

Acutely aware of how he towered over the Tiqui and in a gesture meant to show his own respect, Gomaz dropped to one knee. "Ithani Yellow Bird, mere words can't convey how sorry I am about what happened here."

"No, they cannot, Señor Gomaz," she replied. "But the right ones can hint at what is truly in your heart."

Though the ithani regarded him with equanimity, Gomaz recognized the telltale marks of grief on her face. He marveled at her composure. "Then know my heart is aching," he said. "It's been a long, hot ride from Dry Creek. May I have some water?"

"I'll get it," New Moon said. As she rose to her feet, Gomaz, a father three times over, recognized her condition. Izabela had moved with the same awkward beauty.

"Deanna assures me you are a friend, Señor Gomaz," Yellow Bird said. "She says we should trust you. That is not easy for us, and I'm sure you know why." Her husbands nodded in response. She leaned forward, fixing him with a golden gaze that seemed to bore straight into his thoughts. "Tell us why you've come to Reed Valley."

Gomaz felt his belly tighten. "It's complicated, Ithani," he replied. "I suspect Deanna's already told you something about me and the cause I serve."

"She has, but I want to hear it from you."

Before Gomaz could begin, New Moon returned, a ceramic pitcher in one hand and a cup in the other. With a grateful nod he accepted the cup, holding it steady beneath the lip of the pitcher as she poured. He drained the cool, clean water in three strong swallows, and then wiped his lips on a dusty sleeve redolent of eelat.

"Thank you," he said. Then, to Yellow Bird, "I'll keep kneeling if that's your wish, Ithani. But I'd rather sit, if I may."

"One of the benches out on the porch should hold him," Strong Hand said.

"I'll help you," Deanna volunteered. She and the natome left the room to return a few moments later carrying the bench slung between them. They positioned it before the ithani's chair; after eyeing it for a few seconds' hesitation, Gomaz rose from his knee and sat. The wood groaned with the strain, but held.

"This is better, Ithani. Thank you."

He paused to collect his thoughts, acutely aware of the semicircle of small, intense faces before him. No matter that Deanna had vouched for his character. Gomaz suspected his life still hung in the balance. He found himself reaching into his shirt pocket for cigarettes that weren't there.

"Ithani," he began, "I came to your valley hoping to find Deanna alive. Thank the Madre, I did. For your courage and willingness to defend her, my colleagues and I owe you and your people a debt of gratitude."

Yellow Bird touched elegant fingers to a carved-bone dolora bird pendant hanging from her neck. "I am not only ithani of this community, Señor," she said. "I am also its shaman, entrusted by our Ancestors with the sacred gift of foresight. Deanna's destiny and the fate of my people are inextricably entwined. If your cause is hers, then it's ours as well."

Once again Gomaz felt the power of the ithani's penetrating amber gaze. Again a cold twinge roiled his gut. "Dama, you speak of Deanna's destiny entwined with that of the Tiqui. What do you mean?"

"I can't say with certainty. The journey is too new. I only know that her path and ours must converge."

"Then Ithani, truly our fight for liberation is yours as well." Excitement began to crowd out the anxiety in Gomaz's mind as he explained. "The true resistance — those of us who are working to restore democracy — has remained hidden for too long. We've allowed a dangerous demagogue, one who pretends to be a champion of the people, wreak havoc in our city without challenge. It served a useful purpose in the beginning, but now it has to stop."

He reached out to where Deanna sat on the floor by his bench and touched her shoulder. "We need a symbol. Someone who has the unconditional love of the common citizen, and who can become the public face of our cause. That someone is you, Deanna."

He felt her muscles tense beneath his hand. "What about my father?" Deanna asked. "He's the rightful Alcalde. He should be your symbol, not me."

After all you've survived, you still doubt yourself, Gomaz thought. "It's true that your father is loved and respected by the people," he said. "But after so many years, they've begun to doubt he'll ever win his freedom. Deanna, we need your youth and vitality to convince the common people that there's hope. The Alcalde is right to be afraid of you. She knows the people would rally if only you'd step forward to challenge her."

"Roberto, the day we first met you said the resistance needed me. Do you remember my answer?"

"I remember."

"That hasn't changed."

"I understand, but hear me out. Afterward it may." He refocused on Yellow Bird. "Ithani, the Alcalde of Nue Bayona is a usurper. She rules the city by fear."

"Deanna has already told us of her stepmother's ruthlessness," Yellow Bird replied.

"What neither you nor Deanna knows is that Lourdessa Hernaan isn't content with maintaining the Sedano stranglehold on Nue Bayona. Her ambitions are much greater. She aims to bring the entire continent under her control. The biggest obstacle standing in her way is…"

"Nue Castila," Deanna interjected.

"You have a better grasp of things than you realize, Deanna," Gomaz replied, smiling. "Nue Castila's Alcalde has demanded a more equitable share of the continent's coal and gas resources. He's also demanding the abolition of Tiqui slave labor and the hiring of Castilians at fair wages. If Lourdessa refuses to meet his demands, he's promised to seize control of the pipelines and mines and cut off Nue Bayona's energy supply."

"Perhaps your Alcalde welcomes such a move," Strong Hand spoke up for the first time. "It gives her the perfect excuse to launch an attack, does it not?"

Gomaz regarded the small man with fresh admiration. "It does, Señor," he said.

"Nue Bayona has its own defense force, but it's nowhere near big enough to take on Nue Castila's," Deanna pointed out. "Lourdessa will have to mandate a draft. But even so, Stefan can match her man for man."

"That's true," Gomaz agreed, "but she's counting on attaining an advantage so overwhelming that no army Nue Castila fields can stand against it."

Deanna frowned. "What could give her such an edge?"

"A weapon unlike any this world has seen in over four hundred years. Deanna, your stepmother wants to resurrect an Annihilator."

"But...that's insane," Deanna whispered. "How...?"

"Lourdessa got her hands on the schematics and an operations manual."

"Our oral traditions tell of great machines that brought about the destruction of alta civilization," Yellow Bird said. "'War walkers,' they were called."

"War walker...Annihilator...AX238. All one and the same," Gomaz replied. "The Alcalde ordered a prototype and put Deanna's father in charge of the project."

Deanna's face went pale. "She's coercing him, isn't she?"

"Your stepmother holds your sister's life in her hands, Deanna. And she's threatened your life as well. Your father would've never agreed to her scheme otherwise."

"If he succeeds in producing a working prototype, then..."

"The next step will be to construct an entire fleet. If that happens, Lourdessa will be unstoppable."

Gomaz watched the implications of his words furrow Deanna's brow and darken her gaze.

"I'm sorry, Roberto," she said, "but nothing you've said has given me any reason to be hopeful. You keep saying the resistance has a plan. Whatever it is, I hope it doesn't rely on divine intervention."

"A religious man might pray for that," Gomaz replied, "but we're counting on something far more concrete. Thanks to a stroke of blind luck, we have something the Alcalde doesn't…a map showing the approximate location of a Great War–era Annihilator. Intact and, we pray, operational. Its weapons are so far beyond today's technology, one machine could stand against a dozen modern reproductions."

Yellow Bird's grip tightened on the arms of her chair. "You and your comrades are determined to find this ancient machine," she said. "And when you do…" She fell silent, and for a heartbeat, her eyes seemed to focus inward. "You intend to reawaken it," she finished, softly.

Does she know everything? Gomaz thought, astounded. "Yes, Dama, we do."

For a few moments no one spoke. Gomaz remained hypervigilant, but he'd begun to sense a change in the atmosphere. It felt much less like a trial and more like an inquiry.

Finally, Yellow Bird said, "How will you do this thing?"

Gomaz allowed himself to relax. "Deanna's father is the best engineering mind in Nue Bayona," he replied. "If the machine can be reactivated, he's the one with the skills to do it."

"But my father is in prison," Deanna said.

"He won't be for much longer."

"How is that even possible?" The hope on her face stood in stark contrast to the incredulity in her voice.

"Nunyez controls security at Central Holding," Gomaz explained. "He's arranged everything."

"Have you or your comrades considered what you'll do if the machine can't be reawakened?" Yellow Bird asked.

Gomaz sighed and rubbed his eyes. Days of unrelenting stress had begun to creep in and sap both his physical and mental strength. He had to struggle now to stay alert. "We have complete confidence in Doctor Hernaan's abilities," he said. "But…yes, we've discussed the possibility. If he can't reactivate the Annihilator, then we'll have to mount an old-fashioned insurgency. It will mean more blood in the streets, a prospect none of us relishes."

"No," he heard Deanna whisper fiercely. "My father may be the best engineering mind in Nue Bayona, but I'm his daughter," she added. "There isn't a problem we can't solve if we work together."

"You've changed your mind."

She smiled. "Yes, but not because I think I'm a symbol the resistance can rally the people behind. I'm doing it for my father. I can't let him take on this crazy, dangerous task alone. I'm also doing it for my sister and for Zander, because they'll never be safe as long as Lourdessa is in power."

Gomaz felt all of his fatigue vanish. "I never doubted you for a moment, Deanna."

The sun still blazed high and bright in the sky when Gomaz emerged, no longer a captive, from the relative cool of the ithani's longhouse onto the porch, Deanna by his side. With her gracious permission, he and Deanna had withdrawn from Yellow Bird's presence so that they might speak of more private matters.

Deanna pulled a stool away from the wall and sat, while Gomaz chose a sturdier bench. "That couldn't have been easy for you in there, Roberto," she said. "You seemed so calm…"

Gomaz chuckled. "Believe me, I was anything but. It was all training. A good poli knows how to keep his emotions hidden." *Even when he thinks he might die.*

"I never believed for a moment that Yellow Bird would've allowed any harm to come to you."

That makes one of us. Aloud, Gomaz said, "The ithani is indeed a wise and compassionate lady."

For a few moments, Deanna stared past him, unfocused, as if her mind roamed beyond the present. Then, she sighed and looked him in the eye. "Roberto...I owe you an explanation. When you left me at that farmhouse, I thought I'd come to grips with everything you'd told me... but night fell and the man you'd said would come...he never did. I waited all night, and by morning I'd convinced myself you'd told me nothing but lies. I got scared, so I ran."

"Darkness and silence does strange things to the mind, Deanna. I'm sorry you had to endure that." Gomaz raked a hand through his hair. "When I drove away, I expected Diego to retrieve you. I never would have left you alone, had I known."

Deanna frowned. "Known what?"

"Diego had fallen ill with *cerebra* fever. He lives in the countryside, with no easy way to get word to us in the city. By the time he'd recovered enough to come for you, you'd already bolted. He's an excellent tracker though, the best I've ever known. He picked up your trail easily enough, but you'd gotten a good day's head start on him. He caught up in time to watch you get eaten by a sky jelly."

"Oh, mierda," Deanna whispered.

Gomaz nodded. "He thought you were dead. He tried to retrieve your body, but the Tiqui found you first. When he saw you'd in fact survived, he decided to let them take you instead. He knew he hadn't the skill to save you from the jelly poison, but he suspected the Tiqui might."

"How did he know they wouldn't kill me?" Gomaz thought he heard a note of anger in Deanna's voice.

"Diego has lived in the Wilds before. He's had dealings with the Tiqui. He trusted that they'd recognize you were no threat to them."

"I only survived the poison because of Yellow Bird's eldest son, Ghost Dog," Deanna said. He's a *curaro*, a special kind of healer," she explained. The look in her eyes told Gomaz that this Tiqui held a special place in Deanna's heart. "Once a curaro saves the life of someone, he and that person become iyahuya, or bonded. That bond is unbreakable."

"It sounds a lot like true love," Gomaz said.

"In some ways it is the same, but the Tiqui word for a person's soul mate, their true love, is sunaiya."

"Zander Montoiya...is he your sunaiya?" Gomaz asked.

Deanna's lips curved in a wistful smile. "Yes, he is." Her smile faded and her entire body grew tense. She reached out and touched the poli's arm. "Please tell me you were able to find him."

"You can rest easy," Gomaz said. "He was at a tavern in Red Hill, a little ragged around the edges, but considering he'd just spent a week in detention, he looked pretty good."

"Oh, thank the Madre," she murmured. "I've been so worried..." Her voice caught and for a moment Gomaz expected tears, but then she sighed and all the tension seemed to leave her body. "Did you give him my message?"

"Word for word."

"How did he react?"

Gomaz recalled with sympathy Montoiya's soul-baring confession—*Deanna means everything to me...* "Like a man in love," he replied gently. "It all made sense then. You love him as much as he loves you."

"I'm sorry it took me so long to realize that," Deanna said. She hid her face in her hands.

With a father's tender understanding, Gomaz leaned forward and clasped her trembling shoulders. "Your Zander's tough, Deanna. And so are you. The two of you will find your way back to each other, I'm sure of it."

Wiping away her tears on the backs of her wrists, she whispered, "Thank you."

"When I'm back in the city, I'll let him know you're safe," Gomaz said.

Deanna nodded. She sat for a time, her chin in hand and her gaze focused inward. Gomaz remained quiet, granting her the mental space he sensed she needed.

The burden she'd agreed to shoulder was heavy and perhaps unfair for someone so young and inexperienced. But Gomaz had witnessed Deanna's courage. He had faith in her strength.

At last, Deanna emerged from her reverie. "What about your family, Roberto?" she asked. "Are they safe?"

With everything she has to deal with, she can still think of others. "For the moment," Gomaz replied. "The Marian Sisters are looking after them. Thank you for asking."

"Tell me something. How did Lourdessa explain my disappearance to my father? She couldn't very well admit she had me murdered."

"A few days after you left the city, the Alcalde claimed that you'd taken holy orders and had renounced public life to live as a cloistered nun."

"Why would she make up such a ridiculous story?" Deanna shook her head, incredulous. "I haven't a pious bone in my body. My father knows that."

Gomaz shrugged. "Perhaps she was aiming to convince the people rather than your father. She knows how much the common folk respect you."

"And she also knows slandering me would only rouse suspicion," Deanna replied. "Well, I'm certain Father didn't believe her." She stood and walked to the edge of the porch, and then turned to face him, a hand on her hip. All trace of her previous emotional fragility had evaporated. "So. What do we do next?"

"I must return to Nue Bayona," Gomaz said. "My colleagues are waiting for news. You need to stay here. This is the one place I can feel reasonably sure you'll be safe. Nunyez can forestall any further attacks on the valley, at least until after I've escorted your father out of the city."

"What about my sister? Father won't leave unless he knows Ceilia's safe."

"We'll get her to the Marians. Not even Lourdessa would dare cross that line," Gomaz said.

Deanna started to pace, twirling a lock of dark hair around a forefinger. "Roberto," she said, "my father believes Nunyez is Lourdessa's creature. He won't trust anything the Minister says. He certainly won't leave his cell without proof that he's not walking into a trap."

She makes a good point. "What do you suggest?" Gomaz asked.

Deanna pulled a necklace from beneath her shirt, upon which hung a gold ring and locket. Touching the locket, she said, "Have Nunyez give this to my father. He must say 'The perro barks, the gahto purrs. My sister's hair is full of burrs.'"

Gomaz began to chuckle at the silliness of the message, but seeing Deanna's cheeks flush, he stifled his mirth. "Forgive me," he pleaded, chagrinned.

"It's from a poem I wrote when I was eleven." Her mouth relaxed into a slow grin. "At the time it sounded unbelievably clever. Father will remember." She slipped the chain from her neck, removed the locket, and dropped it onto Gomaz's palm.

"I'll take this to your father myself," he promised. An enormous, jaw-stretching yawn caught him completely by surprise. *I really need to sleep soon*, he thought. He sniffed at his armpits and with a grimace, said, "I could use a bath."

The delicate crimp of Deanna's lips spoke volumes.

Gomaz's entire body shook with laughter. "Don't think I didn't notice how our hosts kept wrinkling their noses."

"There's a bath house around back," Deanna said between giggles. "You'll have to stand up in the tub, though."

Gomaz pushed himself to his feet. "Lead the way."

In the dark, still hour after Luna-set, Yellow Bird dreamed.

She stands alone on a featureless plain. In all directions, only gray, empty horizon. Overhead, a pearlescent mist obscures the sky. She hears a faint sound, like the mewl of a puppy. Looking down, she sees an infant in her arms. Her son, Ghost Dog, newborn again.

The silence is ominous, oppressive. Filled with dread, she holds the baby to her breast. She senses the approach of something massive and dangerous.

The tumult begins as a low hum, rising steadily until she and the baby are immersed in a rhythmic, metallic roar. The ground beneath her feet shakes. Ghost Dog is curiously calm, even as she fights looming panic. She spins around, searching for the source of the cacophony, and sees....

A towering black whirlwind, approaching amid roiling clouds of dust. She can only watch, transfixed. Its shadow races ahead of it, and soon she and the baby are engulfed in profound darkness. Desperately, she clings to her son as the shrieking winds batter her to her knees, and then...

All sound ceases. She is blind. Trembling, she waits.

A white beam of light flares to life, lancing downward to catch her in a pool of brilliance as blinding in its own way as the darkness. She shades her eyes with a hand. Ghost Dog burbles. Beside her, a voice whispers her name. She turns and sees....

Deanna, her hand outstretched. Glancing down, she finds that her arms are empty. Ghost Dog stands before her, a grown man once more. He smiles and touches her cheek. He and Deanna join hands. Together, they turn...

And are swallowed by a boiling mass of fire and lightning.

She screams...

Yellow Bird awakened in darkness, shattered and breathless. She sat upright, a cry on her lips. Strong Hand sat up beside her, caressing her shoulders and arms. "Easy, Wife...easy," he murmured.

Shadow, also awake now, slipped from the large bed. Yellow Bird heard him strike a match, then a heartbeat later the little bedside lamp flared to life, filling the sleeping chamber with soothing golden light.

From their shared pallet at the foot of the bed, she heard Dawn and White Fox whimpering.

"Ghost Dog, my son...my son," Yellow Bird moaned, then crumpled back into the pillows, weeping in soul-searing desolation.

Strong Hand cradled her from behind, his face pressed against the silky hairs at the nape of her neck. "It was only a bad dream, sunaiya," he murmured.

"No. It was a vision," Yellow Bird whispered. She squeezed her eyes shut but couldn't expunge the bizarre and frightening images from her mind's eye. *Ancestors, why do you ask me to give up so much? Isn't one child enough?*

Shadow returned to bed, a sniffling child tucked beneath each arm. He passed Dawn into Strong Hand's waiting embrace and lay down facing Yellow Bird, White Fox cradled between them. "What did you see, sunaiya?" Shadow asked as he gently brushed a lock of ebon hair away from her face.

Yellow Bird shook her head, too drained to speak. Shadow clasped her fingers and kissed them.

Outside, a neighbor's *perro* whined and yipped before it was hushed with a sharp rebuke. The gentle breeze sighing through the eaves earlier that evening had swelled to a whistling bluster. The old *naranha* tree anchoring the south corner of the longhouse slapped the plank walls with windblown, leafy limbs.

Beside her, Yellow Bird's little ones settled back into sleep, their small bodies smelling of herbal soap and *uva* berry jam. Her two husbands lay on either side of the bed, forming a sheltering enclosure of muscle and bone. Their quiet, steady presence soothed her enough to allow sleep to return, but true rest eluded her.

The morning sun woke her with bars of light through shutter slats, touching her closed eyelids with golden dazzle. Exhausted and heartsick, yet practical to her core, the ithani rose to face the new day and all that must be done.

IN THE LOFT of Reed Valley's community barn, Deanna lay within her nest of hay and blankets, watching the sky through a lattice of blackened roof beams. The sweet fragrance of dried fodder, mingled with eelat musk and the bitter scent of burnt wood, filled her nostrils. She could hear Gomaz, snoring softly from where he'd bedded down in the opposite corner.

Though the roof had caught fire during the gunship attack, only a section near the double-paneled entrance had sustained any serious damage. As the sky paled from indigo to violet with the rising sun, Deanna—too restless to remain abed—threw back her covers and sat up. She pulled on her shoes, crawled to the ladder, and descended to the hard-packed clay floor. By the doors she paused to listen for any sign that Gomaz might be stirring, but the ex-poli's snores rattled on, unabated. Relieved, she pushed open one panel and slipped out into the fresh dawn air.

The barn stood at the northeast edge of the village, separated from the nearest houses by a large grassy paddock. Much of the wood railing, as well as a small storage shed close by, had suffered heavy fire damage. The sight of the nearly demolished shed tore at Deanna's heart. Less than a week ago she'd seen a pair of nesting *palomas* flying in and out of the eaves, carrying wriggling insects in their beaks to feed a clutch of voracious, newly hatched chicks.

With no aim beyond taking advantage of the early morning solitude in order to think, Deanna walked to a hay bale resting against the barn wall and sat.

The true resistance...this plan of theirs...it seems so insane, and yet... could Father and I actually reactivate an Annihilator? And if we do succeed, what will that mean?

Deanna felt a sudden chill within her belly. She wondered if bringing back something so terrible, even for a just cause, was a moral act. That machine had been hidden for a reason. Perhaps some things should remain buried, no matter how much of a moral imperative existed for digging them up.

Then again...Lourdessa is a tyrant, and Faustin is an effing madman! She knew they'd happily rip Nue Bayona apart between them, no matter the cost in innocent blood.

The chill deepened as she thought of Zander. His idealism had made him vulnerable to Faustin's seductive, but ultimately false rhetoric. *Oh, my sunaiya. Every day you run with that terrorist might be your last.*

The true resistance believed that by resurrecting the Annihilator and bringing it back to the city, they could force an end to the terror. Deanna suspected they might be right. If that were so, then didn't she have a moral duty to help in any way she could?

Roberto had said the machine was hidden somewhere in the Siyera Desert. That meant a long journey across an unfamiliar wasteland, full of unknown dangers. *What if Father's not up to this? What if I'm not?*

If this plan fails, if Father and I fail....

I wish I could know for sure if I'm making the right decision.

A flutter of bright green drew Deanna's focus out of the turbulent realm of her head and onto the flame-damaged storage shed. From a hole below the scorched eaves she saw the male paloma emerge and take flight. A few seconds later the drab brown female popped out. She soared after her mate.

Deanna gasped in shock, amazed that any creature could have survived.

She waited, watching, her heart beating wildly. A few minutes later the palomas returned, a fluttering insect in each tiny beak. One at a time they squeezed into the hole and disappeared.

Deanna leapt to her feet and ran to the shed. From within she heard the robust cheeps of a hungry brood. *How is this possible? The entire shed looks like it was engulfed in flames, and yet....*

Somehow the nest with its precious cargo of new life had survived the fire.

As she stood peering up at the sooty eaves, the male paloma burst from the hole again and streaked away, shedding a single emerald feather that floated down to alight on Deanna's shoulder.

Like a ray of sunshine punching through heavy clouds, hope poured into Deanna's soul. She felt her doubts begin to evaporate within its brilliant light. She removed the feather and pressed it to her lips. *The universe has given me a sign.*

She would carry this feather with her on the perilous road ahead. It and Zander's ring would be her talismans. She'd hold them against her heart whenever she felt her courage flagging.

Still cautious, yet resolute, she turned and headed back toward the barn.

40
tying loose ends

Within the confines of her private garden, amidst lush beds of purple lavanda, crimson rosa, and yellow butter-bells, Lourdessa held court, lounging on a cushioned bench beside a splashing fountain. A commodious, fringed green canopy provided protection from the sun's heat and glare.

Raul Olivas and Saviero Nunyez occupied ornate, wrought-iron garden chairs in the shade beside her, while Alehan prowled an aimless course among the bushes. Sweat dampened the armpits of his white linen shirt.

Stationed at a discreet distance, yet close enough to leap to Lourdessa's defense, two members of the palace guard stood watch. The chromed barrels of their ee-rifles glinted in the late morning sun. A blue-coated palace attendant with a towel draped over his arm hovered at her elbow, exuding bland attentiveness.

The Alcalde stared at the printed schematic of her war machine, laid out before her on a marble-topped table strewn with empty iced café glasses and cake crumbs. She was angry, and not even the sweet perfume of her prized blooms could soothe her. "No more excuses," she snapped. "My husband's had plenty of time. I want the Annihilator ready for testing by this Lunes."

Olivas shifted in his chair as if the cushion beneath him had suddenly sprouted thorns to prick his ample backside. He hooked a finger beneath the high collar of his shirt and gave the starched white fabric a tug. "Dama Alcalde, I'll let Doctor Hernaan know of your request, but…"

"It's not an effing request." The Chief Engineer flinched at Lourdessa's epithet like a vaca from a drover's goad. "It's an order. Tell him that."

Alehan wandered over into the shade. "I'll go to the workshop today, Mother." He flopped onto the bench, forcing Lourdessa to gather up the hem of her skirt and tuck the slithery gray silk beneath her knees. "Why are you getting so stirred up? You've got Eduard's cojones in your fist."

Ignoring Alehan's comment, Lourdessa turned to Olivas. "Tell me how you and my husband plan to test my machine."

The Chief pulled a handkerchief from the pocket of his rumpled linen jacket and dabbed his flushed face. "We haven't decided on anything specific…"

"We need something big, showy…Let the people know what kind of power the Alcalde now wields." Alehan's voice oozed smugness.

"By 'people,' you mean the resistance," Nunyez commented in a quiet voice.

Lourdessa glanced at him as if she'd forgotten his presence. "I need this machine to protect the interests of this city. That includes the welfare of the citizenry."

Alehan snorted, his beautiful mouth in a curl. "Really, Mother? Is that why?"

Brat, Lourdessa thought.

The wisp that masqueraded as Nunyez's left eyebrow shot upward. "It would certainly be a bonus, if during the testing some resistance members were captured or better yet, killed. As an example, perhaps?"

"It would be…helpful," Lourdessa agreed with a tiny smile.

"Uh, Dama…" Olivas glanced toward a rosa-draped gazebo nearby. "Perhaps we shouldn't speak of these things in front of your stepdaughter."

Lourdessa followed his gaze and spied Ceilia, sitting cross-legged amid a crimson scatter of fallen petals, bouncing a doll topped with blond ringlets on the lap of her lavender silk frock. A pink ribbon restrained the luxuriant fall of her hair in a loose ponytail. A white gauze bandage covered her forearm.

The Alcalde sniffed and flicked her hand. "Never mind her. She comes here often to play. She has no idea what we're talking about." In a bright tone, she called out, "Ceilia, dulzor, would you like to visit your papa?"

Ceilia smiled, her eyes never leaving the doll's face. "Oh, yes, Step-mama, very much so."

"Doctor Vega fixed your arm, I see. Does it hurt?"

"No, Step-mama."

"Clumsy twit," Alehan muttered.

Though Lourdessa agreed, her son's insensitivity annoyed her. "Take Ceilia with you to the workshop, Allie."

Alehan sprang from his seat, puffed with indignation. "Maria's tits, Mother, must I?"

"Watch your language," Lourdessa snapped. "That *also* wasn't a request. She'll remind Eduard of how much he has to lose if he crosses me. Go now, before it gets dark."

With an exaggerated sigh, Alehan strode over to Ceilia, grabbed her uninjured wrist and hauled her to her feet. "C'mon." Meek as a baby, she followed him. Lourdessa waited until they had passed through the garden's trellised exit, then clamped ring-bedecked fingers to her face and growled like a thwarted pantera. "Why is *nothing* going right?"

"Dama?" Olivas asked.

Lourdessa dropped her hands. The Chief Engineer cringed like a schoolboy caught scribbling graffiti on his desk. "Don't you have an important project to oversee?" she said in tones of ice-slicked steel.

"Of course, Dama." He glanced at Nunyez and received a faint nod in return. "I'll report back tomorrow by telephone, if that's acceptable."

"Yes, yes." Lourdessa replied.

Olivas rose, donned a wide-brimmed straw hat, and with a quick bow, departed.

"Now that he's gone, you and I can speak freely," Lourdessa said.

"Regarding what?" Nunyez asked.

"Don't play coy with me, Señor. You know very well what." Lourdessa met Nunyez's cool gaze with smoldering ire. "Calderone was one of our best agents! I can't believe he failed." She clicked her tongue in disgust. "How can one skinny girl elude a trained assassin?"

"I've suggested this to you before, Dama. You should consider letting the matter go," Nunyez said. "After all, what harm can your stepdaughter do? She's exiled among Tiqui vermin and far from civilization, with no easy way back."

Lourdessa wanted to shake the wretched man until his mottled melon of a head flew from his wizened neck. "She's an effing loose end."

"That may be. But is it really worth the effort, not to mention expense, of tying this particular loose end up?"

Dislike him though she might, still Lourdessa could not deny the wisdom of Nunyez's advice. She took a deep breath. "Maybe you're right," she said. "Exiled, dead…in either case, she's out of the picture, and this way I have no blood on my hands. It'll make it easier when I finally have to tell Eduard she's gone."

She rose from her bench. "I'm going back to my office now."

"I will accompany you," Nunyez said.

With the Minister by her side, Lourdessa made the short walk down a raked gravel path, up a sun-warmed sandstone staircase, and along a blissfully cool marble-floored hallway, to the double doors of her office antechamber. She waited for Nunyez to open the door before marching through.

"I won't have to lie, at least not very much," she said as she whisked past him. "Alehan will be angry, though. He still believes Deanna's taken vows with the Marian Sisters."

"Your son will get over it, no doubt."

Something about his tone raised Lourdessa's ire once again, but the sight of Mari bolting from behind her desk, radiating alarm, forestalled her withering response.

The secretary scurried forward, face the color of suet, blue eyes shimmering with tears. "Dama, it's horrible. Just horrible."

"Mari, what in Yesu's Name is going on?"

Quivering, the small woman pressed her knuckles to her mouth, gulping like a landed fish, as if the news she bore was too painful to spin into words.

Lourdessa seized Mari's shoulders, lacquered nails spiked into the crisp, white cotton of her blouse like *aguila* talons. "Damn it, woman. Speak or I'll slap it out of you."

Between sniffles, the secretary said, "Dama...the Palace Hill police station called... A bomb exploded just now at the Blessed Maria Girls Academy. Many of the children are dead."

Nunyez hissed like an angry serpent.

Eyes squeezed shut, Lourdessa screamed, "No, no, no!"

ALEHAN TURNED THE key in the ignition and slumped back against the leather seat of his roadster to watch the boiler pressure-gauge needle creep upward. The faint aroma of coal oil suffused the warm air; clustered beneath the eaves of the small garage dedicated for mayoral family use, a flock of green palomas rustled and cooed.

Ceilia sat beside him, pale and lovely, hands primly folded on her lap. She hadn't spoken since leaving the Alcalde's garden. He cast a sideways glance at her, a flush of desire heating his body. The dress she wore, though suited more for a child, couldn't hide the ripe swell of her woman's breasts. He imagined slipping his hand beneath her skirt, past the barrier of delicate lace pantaloons to find that warm, silken place heretofore untouched by any man. He wondered how she would react. Would she cry out in alarm? Or would she giggle and allow him to continue?

"The car's ready," Ceilia said in a clipped monotone.

Alehan fixed his full gaze upon her, startled. Peridot eyes met hazel in steady regard, rinsed clear of any vestige of childishness. Even the timbre of her voice had changed. Momentary confusion upended his equilibrium. He checked the pressure gauge and turned back to Ceilia, who still watched him with uncanny clarity. "You're right. I didn't know you knew anything about cars." Unease and the first tingling ache of withdrawal turned his fingers into clumsy sticks as he fumbled in his shirt pocket for the little pouch of sueño leaf he was never without.

"Deanna knows a lot about cars. She shows me things. I miss her. You know what happened to her, don't you?"

Alehan loosened the drawstring, retrieved a pinch of the drug, and pushed it beneath his tongue. It wasn't his favored way of getting a fix, but he'd left his pipe on the nightstand by his bed. He closed his eyes to await the slow crawl of bliss that would calm his jangled nerves. "She joined the Marian Sisters."

"No, that's not what happened at all."

Alehan frowned, confused anew by her certainty. "What do you know, Ceilia?"

She caught a lock of hair and twirled it around a forefinger. The girlish gesture seemed at odds with the finely honed edge of her voice. "Deanna went away, but I don't know where. I thought Zander might know, but he doesn't either."

Alehan bristled at the sound of his rival's name. "You've spoken to Zander Montoiya? When?"

"I don't remember exactly." Ceilia touched her bandaged forearm. "He came to my apartment. I asked him if he knew where Deanna had gone. He didn't…though he talked about some strange things."

"What do you mean by strange?"

"I didn't understand, really." Ceilia sighed and lowered her head. "Something about helping a man blow up a machine."

Alehan stared, riveted. "What else did he say?"

"He needed to find Deanna. He seemed very angry that I didn't know where she was. I made him go home."

"Home?"

"Yes, back to the Rosa Blanca. It's where he lives now, with his friends."

Alehan basked in a warm swell of euphoria, part drug rush, part excitement engendered by the revelation he'd just heard.

From the mouths of simpletons….

He shifted the car into gear, released the brake and stepped on the accelerator. The roadster rolled out across the sun-washed courtyard to the driveway. Wild laughter burst from his lips. The wind combed his fair hair into snarls around his face. He glanced at Ceilia, who smiled sweetly, once again the child-woman he'd known since adolescence. The odd notion that he'd seen a change in her dissipated in the whirl of fierce exhilaration.

Perhaps I won't have to get my hands dirty after all. Faustin smiled at Alehan with all of Ceilia's alluring innocence. *This effing junk-head will take care of my problem for me.*

41
ultimatum

"Diosa mia...Alehan! Why is Ceilia here?"

Eduard set aside the spec sheets he'd been studying, his instinct to protect his daughter prodding him to act, though he knew he could not. He stood rigid with anger, watching Alehan cross the expanse of hangar floor, towing a pliant Ceilia by the hand.

When he had closed the distance between them, Alehan mumbled a petulant reply. "Mother made me bring her."

"Papa!" Ceilia broke Alehan's grip and flung herself into Eduard's arms. "I've missed you so much," she murmured against his neck.

Well-versed in Lourdessa's manipulative ways, Eduard understood his wife's implied message. "I've missed you, too, dulzor." He stroked the tousled mass of her auburn ringlets. Spotting the gauze bandage encircling her forearm, he whispered, "What happened to your arm, dulzor?"

Ceilia's lower lip quivered. "I...I don't remember." Her eyes seemed to harden for an instant. Eduard felt as if he had stepped into unexpectedly deep, cold water. He had always believed his daughter incapable of deception, but he couldn't shake the impression that she wasn't telling him the truth.

"Step-mama says you're building something very grand and important," Ceilia said with the guilelessness of a small child. She pointed over her father's shoulder toward the nearly finished machine, crouched at the center of the work floor like a massive, steel-clad insect on six jointed legs, each ending in a four-pronged footpad. "Is that it?"

Eduard kissed her forehead. "Yes, that's it, and your stepmother thinks it's very important."

Turning to face Alehan, she said, "Thank you for bringing me, Allie."

Alehan looked like a singed gahto. "Don't effing call me that."

"You don't speak to my daughter in that manner," Eduard warned. "You know she means no harm." Ceilia placed her hand in the crook of his elbow. A tiny smile curved her lips, and then vanished. Eduard felt another chill race through him.

Alehan dismissed his anger with a flip of a hand. "Mother wants the Annihilator tested this Lunes."

"It's not ready yet."

"Then get it ready." His handsome face made ugly by rage, Alehan advanced to a threatening closeness. "Work around the clock if necessary. You have my machine ready for testing by Lunes or I swear to Maria, you'll be sorry."

So it's your machine now, Eduard thought. He remained steady, even as a fleck of spittle flew from Alehan's lips to splatter his cheek. Ceilia leaned into him. He stepped forward to place his body like a shield between her and his stepson. Staring into hazel eyes dilated and simmering with drug-fueled violence, Eduard forced his voice into a soothing cadence. "The boiler hasn't arrived yet. The fabricators promised they'd deliver on Lunes. It will take at least a day to install."

Alehan's clenched fist drifted upward, then fell back to his side. He blinked as if waking from sleep. "Martes, then, but that's it. Not a day longer. You've had more than enough time to finish. Don't think Mother and I haven't noticed how you've dragged your feet." His eyes scanned the machine where a half-score of coverall-clad men watched in wary silence from perches on the superstructure.

Alehan pointed to a gaping hole at the stern. "What's missing, and why?"

"That's where the boiler's to be installed," a female voice answered.

Eduard turned to see that Suela had materialized at his side. Though clad in loose-fitting coveralls, a kerchief binding her chestnut hair, she still held the unconscious power to stir his flesh to aching desire. He saw that same emotion mirrored in Alehan's face, but sullied with a measure of contempt. He quashed the urge to step between his stepson and his lover. "Alehan. We're wasting time standing here talking," he said. "You've set me a tough deadline. Let me and my crew get back to work."

Alehan closed his eyes and massaged his temples. "My head's effing killing me," he muttered, then snapped, "I'll be back Martes morning… and by the way, I've decided on the perfect test."

Eduard's throat tightened in trepidation. "Have you now? And what might that be?"

"Let's just say it's going to be spectacular," Alehan said, glancing at Ceilia. His playful grin only sharpened Eduard's unease. "Come on, Cece." He thrust his hand out. "Time to go home."

Ceilia edged away. "Must we? We've only just arrived. It's been weeks since Papa and I have spoken."

"Come with me now or walk back," Alehan replied, his voice flat. "Your choice."

Eduard took his daughter by the shoulders and gently turned her to face him. "Go on, dulzor," he said, smiling. "It's too far for you to walk on your own. Besides, Father's Day is only a couple of weeks away. I'll see both you and your sister then."

"Oh, yes. You'll see me for certain, Papa." Ceilia stood on tiptoe and gave Eduard a peck on his cheek, then brushed past Alehan, heading toward the open hangar doors. Without turning around she called, "What are you waiting for, Allie? Let's go."

Scowling, Alehan muttered, "Don't call me Allie." With one last venomous glance at Eduard, he stalked after Ceilia's retreating figure.

Eduard watched his daughter and stepson's silhouettes dissolve like watered ink in the glare of afternoon sunlight, trying to shake off a gnawing apprehension. Something about Ceilia's demeanor had seemed different, but the change was too subtle to define. *Maybe I'm imagining things,* he thought.

Alehan's cryptic statement about testing the machine presented an even greater cause for concern. Anything that so obviously pleased his stepson made Eduard nervous.

Suela, still standing by his side, must have sensed his apprehension. "Don't worry, Eduard. Alehan won't hurt her."

"I'm not worried, not about that," Eduard replied. "It's Alehan's test that worries me. I wish I knew what he's planning."

Suela reached out as if to touch his forearm, then let her hand drop. "You shouldn't fret about something over which you have no control."

Eduard sighed. He wanted to take her in his arms, but remained ever mindful of their secret. Instead he contented himself with a soft smile. "You're right, of course."

Though Alehan pushed the roadster to a reckless speed up the long, curving grade of Palace Hill Road, Faustin felt no fear. In fact he was giddy with delight. *Oh, Allie, Allie. Your plan is perfect. I couldn't have thought up a better one myself.*

"What are you grinning at?" Alehan shouted over the roar of the wind through the open top. "You look like an effing kymera!"

"I'm having a lovely time, is all," Faustin replied, glancing sideways through the whipping strands of Ceilia's auburn hair.

Alehan frowned and shook his head. "You're completely insane."

Faustin burst out laughing.

Upon Alehan and Ceilia's departure, the workmen had resumed their tasks. The shop echoed with the pounding of steam hammers and the metallic screeches of power saws. A shower of sparks cascaded like falling stars from the forward gun turret where one man applied finishing touches with a welding torch. From the interior of the machine, Eduard heard raucous laughter, mingled with the pop of rivet guns.

It amazed him how the crew could still manage to find some enjoyment in their work, no matter that they labored under the threat that their families would suffer if they faltered. He knew from the many furtive expressions of support he'd received that most, if not all, the men still considered him to be their rightful leader. Because of that, they trusted him to keep them safe.

"Doctor." The worker waved to catch Eduard's attention. "I'm finished with the turret." He pushed his welding goggles onto his flushed forehead. "You can come up to connect the ee-cannon now."

Eduard had insisted the sympathetic crew call him Doctor rather than Alcalde. Lourdessa may have stripped him of his office, but she couldn't rob him of his academic title. "Yes, I'm coming," he replied. As he mounted the ladder leading to the gun turret platform, he heard Suela calling his name. He paused in mid-step, apprehension pricking his gut, watching her hurrying across the workshop toward him. She stopped at the base of the ladder and looked up, her face pinched and leached of color. Eduard felt apprehension flare into full-blown alarm.

"What is it?"

"There's been an attack at the Blessed Maria Academy," she cried, then turned and ran back toward the office. Eduard swung with reckless haste off the ladder, cold dread spinning visions of horror in his mind.

When he reached the office, Suela turned the volume up on the little radio nested among the clutter of his desk. Through bursts of static, snippets of sentences painted a scene of mayhem and death. "Damn this thing," Eduard growled, spinning the antenna first one way then another, attempting to catch the full signal. After a handful of frustrating seconds, the voice of the reporter again crackled forth in urgent cadences.

"...is pouring from the pile of rubble. The school day was not yet over, so the classrooms were full...the City Police are already onsite. They won't confirm, but the rumor going around is that this was an attack by Faustin's rebels. The reporter paused and said, "What's that? How many? Damas and señors, the Headmistress has just told us that there were at least a hundred girls and over a dozen staff in class today. Wait...wait... Maria in Heaven. The firemen are bringing out more bodies."

Suela sucked in a breath and then let it out in a long, soft moan. In slow motion her legs buckled, landing her in a chair beside the desk. "Those poor girls."

"Damn him," Eduard whispered. In furious sorrow, he slammed his fist on the paper-strewn wood and switched off the radio. *The ultimate blame for this atrocity can be laid at your feet, Dessa. There'd be no Faustin, if not for you*, he thought. "The rebels have just crossed a line. It's one thing to attack a police station, but to target *children*..."

"Why would they do such a terrible thing? It's...it's barbaric," Suela said.

Eduard remembered a small article he'd read in the *Observer* a few weeks past. "The Specials raided a primary school in The Maze two months ago, on the excuse that several of the teachers were rebels. At least one child died. Today's attack could be in retaliation for that raid."

"Yes, you could be right," Suela said, nodding.

"If Faustin believes ratcheting up the violence will make my wife lose her nerve, he's sorely mistaken. What he's actually done is give Lourdessa the perfect excuse to lock down every district except Palace Hill." Eduard looked through the office door at the fruit of his forced labor, and shuddered. "She knows he and his cells hide among the people of Red Hill and The Maze. What better show of force than this machine to flush him out."

"Do you think that's what Alehan meant when he said he had 'the perfect test'?" Suela asked.

"I suspect that's exactly what he meant."

"Faustin and his followers are terrorists and murderers, and I want them brought to justice, but…" Suela fell silent for a moment, her face pale and drawn, then said, "How will it be possible to tell who's a terrorist and who isn't?"

Eduard traced the line of Suela's jaw with a forefinger. "Precisely," he said, "Which is why the test can't happen."

"You asked me never to speak of this, but…it sounds like you've made up your mind."

Eduard didn't need to hear her say the word. The fear in her eyes showed him that she understood, at least in part, what he meant to do. "You needn't worry about me, dear girl," he replied, hoping to soothe her fright, "and I swear you won't be implicated in any way."

Suela opened her mouth to speak, but Eduard stopped her with a thumb pressed gently to her lips. "It's time we get back to work," he said.

As Eduard strode from the office, Suela buried her face in her hands. Maria help her, despite every barrier she'd erected to keep him out, Eduard Hernaan had claimed her heart. To find the strength to betray him, she knew she must somehow divorce herself from all the tender emotions he raised within her. The sound of his voice whispering her name, the touch of his hands on her skin, the heat of his body as they made love; she had no choice but to push those memories aside.

Alehan Estes had chosen her for his spy because he'd known how easy it would be to coerce her. Her feelings for Eduard, no matter how strong and real, didn't matter. The reputation and honor of a family name as old as hers deserved to be protected, and her mother's safety must be preserved at all costs. Suela knew where her duty lay.

Please, Blessed Maria, she prayed, *show Eduard another way. Spare us both.* Suela brushed away the tears beading her lashes with the cuff of her sleeve. *Eduard will hate me,* she thought, *but I'll hate myself even more.*

42
día de sangre

One, two, three, four...done. Zander tossed patok slices into a metal pan and snagged another tuber off the seemingly endless pile Guermoe had set him to chopping for the evening's menu of roasts and stews. The knife in his hand was razor sharp and cut through the tough, starchy roots as if they were made of butter. Zander knew that Guermoe prided himself on the keenness of his kitchen blades.

Zander enjoyed working in the inn's kitchen during late afternoon. The day shift had gone home and the evening staff had yet to arrive; he had the large room to himself. The simple tasks of peeling and chopping vegetables allowed him to retreat into a serene, mental place where life's difficulties could be ignored, at least for a time.

One, two, three, four...done. Zander dropped another handful of slices into the metal pan. As he reached for a fresh tuber, from the common room he overheard cries of dismay. Laying down his knife, he went to investigate.

He found a small crowd of patrons gathered at the bar, listening intently to Oskar, the portly beer deliveryman. "I heard about it over at Nola's place," Oskar said, punctuating his words with a fist smack to his open palm. "It's bad...real bad."

Zander saw the look of stricken horror on the faces around him and felt his mouth go dry. "What's happened?" he asked. Some of the men moved aside to grant him a place at the bar.

"Another bombing. At the Blessed Maria Girls Academy," Guermoe replied grimly. He and Beatrichia were both huddled behind the bar, their round faces pale and somber. Tears glistened in Aunt Bea's eyes.

"When?" Zander croaked.

"Not more than a few minutes ago," Beatrichia sobbed, her hands pressed to her cheeks.

"The radio said an entire wing's gone," Oskar added. "A lot of kids have died."

Faustin, you effing monster. For an instant, a red mist clouded Zander's vision. He blinked, inhaled sharply and shook his head. "Guermoe, may I borrow your bicycle?" he asked.

"Of course, Son. Where're you going?"

"The girls' school."

Guermoe frowned. "I know you want to help, but is that wise? It's Valencea. There'll be polis swarming everywhere, and you know how they treat folk they think don't belong." He touched a meaty hand to Zander's forearm. "If you got thrown back in detention…" His voice trailed off in a husky whisper.

"I have to go," Zander replied, and for a moment, he knew the warmth of a father's concern. It felt good. He squeezed Guermoe's hand, then turned and dashed back through the kitchen to the inn's rear door. On the covered porch outside he retrieved Guermoe's old bicycle. An instant later he was pedaling out of the alley onto busy Escarpado Street.

Sick fury drove him to push the limits of safety as he wove in and out of the sluggish afternoon motor traffic, heading for Valencea. Even from a distance he could discern a thick plume of black smoke rising skyward like an accusatory finger. Several minutes of strenuous effort brought him, sweaty and breathless, to tree-lined Solis Road. Closer to the school's high brick walls, he could see fire trucks and police cars clogging the street.

A block from the entrance Zander dismounted and wheeled his bike past the parked trucks, avoiding thick canvas hoses lying like fat brown serpents in his path. A stinging haze of smoke hung in the air. When he reached the stately black wrought-iron gates, he spied a cordon of blue-uniformed City Police officers restraining a well-dressed crowd. "Family members only!" he heard the polis shouting above the cries of terrified parents as they jostled one another to enter the schoolyard.

Zander knew his threadbare clothes would mark him as an outsider. The polis would bar him as soon as they spotted him...*if* they spotted him. *No. Can't take that chance,* he thought. I can get in another way.

He hopped on his bike and pedaled away from the main gate, following the base of the wall. The commotion faded as he turned the corner, heading for the rear of the compound. With any luck, the service entrance would stand unguarded.

When Zander rolled up, he found a locked gate and no polis. Relieved, he steadied the bike against the wall and climbed onto the seat. Gripping the rough brick edge with white-knuckled determination, he pulled himself up and over. He dropped to the gravel below, staggering a few steps to catch his balance. He looked around.

Zander found himself in a long, narrow yard behind a seemingly undamaged two-story brick hall. Though he heard many voices shouting and crying close by, none seemed to emanate from this building. He saw no movement in any of the windows. The hall appeared deserted.

He made his way along a gravel path toward the front of the hall. As the sounds of frightened people grew louder he broke into a run, skidding to a stop only after he'd rounded the corner onto a scene of utter devastation.

Before him stretched a grassy quadrangle, at the far edge of which stood the smoking ruins of a smaller hall. Men in shirtsleeves were crawling over the wreckage alongside uniformed firemen and polis. A group of women stood nearby, weeping and calling out for the men to hurry. Zander stared, shocked, at the extent of the damage. He wondered how any child caught in that blast could have survived.

Driven by a terrible sense of urgency, he started running across the quadrangle toward the ruin. He dodged groups of girls dressed alike in blue sweaters and matching skirts, sobbing and clinging to one another. Many of them had bleeding cuts scored into their foreheads and cheeks. A man in the long black gown of a teacher shouted something to him as he darted past, but Zander ignored him.

When he reached the debris pile he scrambled in among the shattered bricks and began digging.

He found a body almost immediately. The girl lay facedown, the back of her head cracked like an egg. Blood matted her long blond tresses. *At least she died quickly*, Zander thought as he freed her from the rubble. Lifting her in his arms, he looked around and spotted a nearby fireman pulling chunks of stone away from a collapsed doorway.

The sharp edges of broken masonry cut into the thin soles of his shoes as Zander gingerly navigated the jumbled terrain toward the fireman. "Hey," he called. "Hey, over here."

The fireman turned, frowned, and strode closer. "Is she alive?"

Zander shook his head. The fireman took the little corpse from his arms, as gently as if she were merely asleep. He cast a quick glance over Zander and said, "Only family allowed, young hombre. You can't stay." His gruff voice sounded more concerned than reprimanding.

"I want...I need to help," Zander said. "Please."

The fireman shook his head. "I'm sorry."

"All right. I'll go," Zander promised.

The fireman stared at him for another moment, his blue eyes softening. With a tiny nod, he turned away and began picking a cautious path off the debris, the dead girl held against his canvas-clad chest.

When the fireman had gone, Zander resumed his search.

He found the second body a short time later. Even so, he felt as if he'd been digging for hours. Heat and thirst depleted his strength and his thin shirt clung to his sweat-soaked torso. His hands bled from a multitude of cuts and abrasions.

This child lay curled in a pocket beneath a buried desk. Groaning under the strain, Zander shoved the desk aside and lifted her out of her masonry tomb. Near his physical limit, he sat on a concrete slab and drew the girl across his lap. As he straightened her torn, bloodied uniform and smoothed her black curls, he gazed at the child's pale face. "I'm so sorry, dulzor," he whispered. No longer able to hold back his grief, he broke down and wept.

Through his veil of tears he saw the girl's lips move.

Zander's heart skipped a beat. He bent his cheek to her mouth and felt a feather-light exhalation. "Yesu, you're alive," he muttered. Galvanized, he scooped the girl into his arms and pushed to his feet. "I'll find you help, just hold on."

He saw two firemen approaching the ruins from the direction of the entrance gate. At the top of his lungs, he hollered, "Help! This girl's alive!"

They ran toward him, clumsy in their thick fire suits and heavy boots. Zander met them at the rubble's edge, breathing hard. One of them gasped, "Give her to me," and reached out with gentle urgency.

Zander passed the limp form into the fireman's embrace. The man turned and lumbered toward the waiting ambulances. The other fireman paused to sweep Zander with a discerning eye. "Hey."

Zander looked at the man, expecting a rebuke.

"I said you couldn't stay. Lucky for that little girl you didn't listen."

Zander inhaled sharply and opened his mouth to reply, but the fireman cut him off. "You've done a lot of good here, young hombre. Thanks. Now I'm dead serious. Go."

Zander could only nod, suddenly too exhausted to speak. As the fireman stumped off, Zander began making his way toward the main gate, where he hoped to find water to slake his fierce thirst. It seemed as if the distance had grown to klims, though in truth it was only a few dozen meters.

A glint in the grass caught his eye. He stopped and saw a green leather purse with a metal clasp. A child's purse. He bent and picked it up.

The little bag was finely made and embossed with a family crest. Inside, Zander found a small silver-framed mirror, a matching comb, and three one-reále coins. He plucked out the mirror, turned it over in his hand, and saw the name Marta engraved on the back. "I hope you survived, Marta," he murmured, his eyes once more brimming with tears.

"Hey! What d'you think yer doin'?" a voice shouted from close behind him.

Zander spun around to see a City poli, brandishing a leather-wrapped truncheon in his gloved fist. The man glared down at the purse in Zander's hands. "Filthy street raton. How'd you get past the gate, eh? Answer me!"

Zander went cold with fear. "I came to help…"

"Thought ya could find some easy pickings, eh?" the poli snarled, making it clear to Zander that he had no interest in the truth. He swung at Zander's hands, knocking the purse to the ground but missing his fingers. "Well, ya won't get away with it."

"I'm not here to steal anything." Zander edged backward, his pulse racing and his hands up. "Listen to me, please."

"Shut up, raton, before I thump ya." The poli raised the truncheon.

In the space between two heartbeats, Zander's fear crystallized into cold anger. "Eff you, puerco," he growled.

The poli lunged, swinging. Zander threw himself backward but his foot slipped, sending him sprawling. As he struggled to rise, the truncheon caught him squarely on the crown of his head.

Zander's vision exploded in a burst of white light. He felt the poli seize his arm, then begin dragging him like a sack of flour through the grass. Each rap against the ground sent a spike of pain through his skull, but he was too dazed to resist.

The poli hauled him to the edge of the lawn and onto a gravel walkway, where he gave Zander a sharp poke in the ribs with the tip of his truncheon. "On yer feet, raton," he spat. For a few moments Zander lay without moving. Then, summoning his strength, he pushed onto his hands and knees. His stomach lurched. As the poli stood over him, frowning, he vomited onto the gravel.

"Disgusting," the poli muttered. "On yer feet, I said, unless ya want s'more of my stick."

Zander obeyed, one hand pressed to the swelling knot on the top of his skull. The poli poked him again. "Move," he barked.

Zander thought he would choke on his rage, but he dared not make a stand. The memory of his last imprisonment still burned too raw and fresh. The school entrance lay only a few meters away. With the poli trailing close behind, he staggered along the path to the gate, where a line of blue uniforms blocked the exit.

"Coming through!"

The line opened up. The poli grabbed Zander's shoulder and shoved.

Zander stumbled forward and measured his length on the sidewalk. Fearing a parting gift of another truncheon blow, he scrambled to his feet. "I caught this raton skulkin' around inside, looking for loot!" he heard the poli shout. Cries of disgust and horror rose from the group of waiting parents.

On unsteady legs, Zander fled from the screams and epithets of the angry crowd, back toward where he'd left Guermoe's bicycle. He dared not look back, nor did he slow down until he rounded the corner, out of sight of the mob.

The bike remained where he'd left it, leaning against the rear wall. Zander stopped to catch his breath and examine his hands. Skinned knuckles and scraped palms were a small price to pay for the life of a child, he thought. Add to that the painful knot on his skull and a bruised rib, and he still considered it all a bargain.

He mounted the old bike and pedaled toward home.

Later that night, Zander sat at the bar, drinking only water, nursing his sore head and a new resolve born of anger and disillusionment.

The dinner rush was over and all the staff had gone home. Complaining of a sore back, Aunt Bea had retired early, leaving Guermoe to tidy the glassware and polish the bar. The big man had been strangely subdued all evening; no jokes or snippets of song had accompanied his commands.

"It was horrible, Guermoe," Zander said. "All that blood…I'll never get the sight of those dead girls out of my mind." He paused to breathe through a wave of vertigo and added, "If only I'd had the chance to do more." Though a draught of amapola juice and a couple hours of sleep had restored his coherence, it had not restored his full vitality.

"You saved a child's life. I'd say that's a lot." Guermoe patted Zander's forearm. "You're a brave, goodhearted young man, Son. Don't be so hard on yourself."

"Thanks," Zander replied, blinking back tears. "No one's ever said anything like that to me before."

"'Bout time someone did then." Sonia's uncle nodded. "You've had a nasty crack on the head. Maybe you should go back to bed."

"No. I'm too angry to sleep," Zander replied. "No one had to die… Faustin's gone too far this time." He saw concurrence in the older man's gray eyes.

"They were just children, for Yesu's sake," Guermoe muttered, scowling. He picked up a beer mug and began polishing it with a rag. "Innocent children. Why should they have to pay for their parents' sins?"

"Faustin is a fraud, in ways you can't imagine." Zander recalled his bizarre, terrifying confrontation with the entity controlling Ceilia's body. He grew cold, remembering the rebel leader's cruel laughter. "I still believe in the revolution, but this isn't what I signed up for," he said. "I can't be a part of it any longer."

Guermoe carefully laid down the mug and rag. "What are you going to do?" he asked.

"What I should've done when I first saw his true face," Zander said. "Expose him for who and what he really is. Once the others know the truth, he'll be finished."

"What truth are you talking about?" Sonia said as she slid onto the stool next to Zander.

He wasn't surprised he hadn't heard her approach. When she wished to move without a sound, she could. He took a sip of water, wishing it were beer. "Faustin is a liar *and* a lie, Sonnie," he replied. "He doesn't really exist, at least not in any way you could understand."

Sonia's jaw tightened. "That makes no sense." She reached out and pinched his arm. "Faustin is flesh and blood, as real as you or me."

Zander gritted his teeth, but did not flinch or draw away. "No, he's not," he insisted. "He's...mierda, I don't know *what* he is. But, if you pull off his mask...it's Ceilia Hernaan's face you'll see."

Guermoe let out a startled exclamation.

Sonia bit her lip. After a drawn-out moment of silence, she murmured, "That's insane."

"I saw it with my own eyes," Zander said. "Somehow, Ceilia Hernaan and Faustin are one and the same."

"Son...that's simply not possible." Guermoe shook his head. "Whatever it was you saw, it couldn't be *that*."

"My uncle's right." Sonia agreed, crossing her arms against her breasts like a barrier. Her voice grew chilly. "I don't know what you saw, Zander, but you'd better not go spreading that story around."

Zander pushed off his barstool, then stepped forward and gently gripped Sonia's rigid shoulders. Meeting her dark, unbending gaze, he said, "I can't keep this to myself, Sonnie. He has to be exposed. Every moment Faustin is in control, he puts Ceilia in danger. She's completely innocent. I'm doing this for her as much as for the cause. The rebellion needs a new leader, a true revolutionary. Not a sadistic lunatic who murders children."

Sonia let her arms fall to her sides. "I can't let you, Zander. You'll tear the organization apart."

"Maybe. Or, it'll become stronger. For Ceilia, I'm willing to take the chance."

"Please…" Sonia gripped the hilt of the slim knife she always wore on her hip. "Don't make me choose."

Zander curled his fingers around hers and pulled the blade halfway from its sheath. His gaze never left her face. "You're prepared to do whatever it takes to stop me, aren't you?"

He felt Sonia's hand tighten around the knife hilt. Finally she whispered, "I'm sorry, Zan."

"Blessed Madre," Guermoe groaned, shaking his head. A single, fat tear rolled from his eye to splash the bar's polished surface.

Zander released Sonia's hand. He glanced down at the knife. "You'll do what you feel you must," he said. "And so will I."

Sonia slipped off her stool and stood facing him, her lips drained of color and her eyes bleak. After several moments of silent regard, she turned and made her way to the inn's front entrance, where she paused for a heartbeat and then pushed through into the night.

"Zander," Guermoe rumbled, "my niece loves you, you know."

"I'll sleep on the back porch from now on," Zander replied.

43

Ashes of Despair

Propped up in bed, an embroidered silk coverlet draped over her lap, Lourdessa glared at her son in bleary-eyed indignation. "I agree it's the perfect target, but we can't just attack without any warning." She looked to Olivas and Nunyez, sitting in green silk-covered chairs next to the bed, for concurrence. Both men nodded. "Honestly, Alehan, you must think I'm some kind of bloodthirsty monster."

She pressed a linen handkerchief to her inflamed nose and blew. The effort proved futile. Her nasal passages remained blocked despite three days of steam treatments, hot compresses, and bitter medicinal draughts. Springtime had always been a misery for her.

"What I *think* is that you're too soft, Mother," Alehan commented from his seat on the far corner of Lourdessa's spacious bed.

The Chief Engineer, crimson-faced and moist as usual, pursed his fat lips and said, "This is supposed to be a demonstration aimed against the resistance, not the citizenry, Dama."

"If we attack with no warning, all we do is succeed in terrorizing the general populace," Nunyez added. "We'll hand Faustin the best recruiting tool he could ever hope for."

Lourdessa felt the tickle of an imminent sneeze. She buried her nose in her already sticky handkerchief, flush with regret that she'd called this meeting, instead of napping away the afternoon as she should have done. Still, such details must be handled appropriately. "I have to agree with you, Señors," she said thickly.

Alehan threw up his hands and stomped across the chamber to flop down on a sofa near the cold fireplace. With an exaggerated sigh he stretched out, arms crossed behind his head.

Lourdessa cast a discerning glance at her son and massaged her aching temples. "What is your plan, Señor Nunyez?" she asked.

"A squad of my Specials will enter the building beforehand," Nunyez began. "Any resistance members will be admonished to immediately come forward for arrest, in order to spare everyone—rebel and innocent patron alike—from being taken into custody. After two minutes we'll clear the building, either way. Then, Doctor Olivas will proceed with the test."

"What a stupid waste of time," Alehan called out, his tone dripping disdain. He propped himself up on an elbow. "Faustin's ratons will never give themselves up willingly. And *Nunyez*, while your Specials are trying to corral a bunch of panicky peasants, the rebels'll slip your noose like they always do."

If the Minister was offended by Alehan's gibe, he showed no sign. "Your proposal amounts to murder," he replied.

"My proposal announces to Faustin that we're done playing games."

"That you consider what we've been doing as little more than games displays your profound stupidity, Señor Estes."

Alehan shoved to his feet, snarling. "You effing son of a puta…I should smash your pasty face!"

Nunyez's thin nostrils flared.

Olivas cringed.

"Enough," Lourdessa cried, flinching as a wave of pain rippled behind her eyeballs. "Maria's holy tits! Alehan, calm down, it's settled.

We're following Nunyez's plan. And, Señor," she glared at Nunyez, "do not insult my son."

Nunyez lifted an eyebrow, but remained silent.

Alehan returned to the sofa and sat, arms crossed and jaw clenched.

"Well, now that that's settled," Olivas said with a gusty sigh, "there's the question of the crew." He pulled his ever-present handkerchief from his breast pocket and patted his glistening cheeks. "We'll need two boiler men, two gunners, a pilot, and a copilot."

"I shall personally select the crew from among my Specials," Nunyez said.

"I'll pilot, of course," Alehan stated.

Olivas flinched as if poked by a stick. "But...but..." he spluttered. "It isn't an oversized auto, Señor. You can't just turn the key and drive. It requires training. I've had two drivers preparing for a month."

"Then you'll train me, and in half that time." Once more Alehan bounded to his feet, excited. "Mother, think about it. This project was never simply about crushing Faustin's rebels. The ultimate goal has always been to bring Nue Castila to heel. When the time comes, who better than the Alcalde's son to lead a squadron of Annihilators against the Castilians?"

Lourdessa studied her son's face. Could she really trust him with such a critical responsibility? Was she mad to even consider it?

Perhaps, but, Yesu, he's my beautiful boy. "Doctor Olivas, you will train my son to operate our prototype."

Alehan crowed in triumph.

From the corner of her eye Lourdessa saw Nunyez and Olivas exchange glances. Both men seemed unhappy—Nunyez displeased, Olivas more dispirited—but she simply didn't care.

She lay back against the soft mound of pillows beneath her shoulders. "Get out, now. All of you. I need to rest."

Eduard glanced at the clock on his desk. *It's six. The crew will be leaving soon.*

The former Alcalde paused, his pen poised over the little ledger he'd been jotting figures in, and listened to the sounds of the workmen stowing their tools and gathering their personal belongings. Snatches of conversation drifted in through the open office door: a drink invitation and polite refusals on the grounds that wives and children waited at home, a good-natured complaint about aching joints, heartfelt wishes for a good night.

They all expect to return tomorrow morning and find everything exactly as they left it, Eduard thought. He laid his pen aside and closed the ledger just as Suela entered the office with Julio Colón, the crew foreman, at her back. Eduard's heart beat faster at the sight of his beautiful young assistant. He still found it amazing that she'd chosen to give herself to him. "Julio and Martin have finished with the last boiler couplings," she said as she sank onto the creaky wooden chair next to Eduard's desk. Colón remained standing on the threshold, twisting his grimy cap in his hands.

The crew boss was built like a tree stump: squat—only a little taller than he was wide. "She's ready to fill, Doctor. If you want I can stay."

The specially designed semi-flash boiler had arrived that morning on the bed of a coal hauler; the crew had worked until well past midday to install it. Eduard regretted that the men had to push themselves so hard to finish, but the threat of reprisals acted as a strong motivator for them all. "No, Julio," he replied. "That won't be necessary. You go home."

"We can fill the boiler first thing tomorrow," the crew boss said.

Eduard nodded. "Thank you, Julio. I truly appreciate how hard you and the crew have worked these past months. I know I haven't said it nearly enough, and I'm sorry."

Colón scratched his silver-stubbled jowls, one shaggy eyebrow raised. "Uh...sure, Doctor. You're welcome."

"Have a good evening," Eduard said.

"You too, Doctor." Colón slapped his cap on his head and touched the brim. "Señorita Ayenda," he added with a smile for Suela.

Neither he nor Suela spoke as the sound of the crew boss's heavy footsteps receded across the warehouse to the side exit. When Eduard heard the Special assigned guard duty close and lock the door behind Colón, he sighed. "Another day behind us."

Suela rose from her chair and moved around the desk to stand behind him. She bent to kiss the side of his neck and began massaging his shoulders. His eyes fluttered closed. Her touch felt exquisite. "The guard..." he whispered.

"Doesn't care what we do," Suela replied, continuing to work his knotted muscles with strong fingers. "You know that."

Since the night they'd first become lovers, Suela always arranged some pretext for the crew's benefit to allow her to stay behind after hours. That she worried about protecting their secret from the workmen and not the Special acting as Eduard's jailer seemed odd to him, but he was too hungry for her company to press her on the point.

During their precious time together they'd share a simple meal, talk, laugh, and make love until, exhausted, they'd fall asleep. Inevitably Eduard would wake to find her gone, vanished into the predawn darkness. At eight the next morning Suela would arrive with the crew, cheerful and ready to work, her greeting to him no more than what was appropriate for a respected colleague. The pain he felt when he saw her and yet could not touch her, nor speak openly of his feelings, never eased.

That pain was minor compared to what he felt now. For in order to carry out his final night's work, he must send Suela away. He reached up to lay his hands atop hers. She paused and said, "What is it, my darling?"

"I need to be alone tonight, dulzor." He could barely speak the words.

"Eduard..." she whispered. "Please, is there no other way?"

He stood and pulled her into his arms. Her entire body trembled against his. He buried his face in her silky hair, breathing deeply, imprinting its scent in his memory. "Go home, dear girl," he murmured. "And whatever you return to in the morning, remember how much I cared for you."

Suela pushed out of his embrace, staring at him, wide-eyed. She looked like a child bereft of all hope. Eduard ached to embrace her once more; kiss her full, flushed lips; take her to his bed; and make love to her. Instead he took her hand and led her to the office door. "Go now, before I lose my nerve."

She took a deep, shuddering breath and fled into the darkness. Eduard remained rooted in place until the echoes of his lover's rapid footfalls ended with the slam of the exit door. Still he waited, listening. After several more minutes had passed in silence and stillness, Eduard moved swiftly into action. He estimated he'd have no more than an hour before his jailer came to check on him.

From the bottom drawer of his desk, he retrieved a hand torch and tucked it in his back pocket. With a light tread he exited the office onto the warehouse floor. Silver moonlight streamed in through the high windows, casting bright rectangles onto the concrete below and providing enough illumination by which to see. His goal was a long-unused storage closet at the rear of the cavernous space, tucked into a small side chamber that he suspected might have once housed a machine shop.

Because of its secluded location, the closet had proved to be perfect for his needs. Over the span of a few days Eduard had filled it with an assortment of crates to provide cover in case one of the crew—or worse, a guard—should get curious and decide to glance inside.

Only after he reached the closet, slipped inside and closed the door did Eduard dare turn on his torch. Three steps took him to the back wall. He bent to open a crate marked FOR COCKPIT and pulled aside a wad of packing hay to reveal a coil of thin nichrome wire, a small fuel cell, and three magnesium fulminate blasting caps, all resting atop a folded burlap sack. He placed the items in the sack as if each were made of the finest crystal, then switched off the torch before exiting the closet.

As he made his way back to the main floor, Eduard reflected on how the beauty of his plan stemmed from its relative simplicity. He had most of what he needed already at the warehouse, and an extra fuel cell and a roll of wire would not raise any suspicions should Olivas or Lourdessa bother to review his supply orders.

The blasting caps had been the riskiest to obtain because Eduard had no valid reason for ordering them. He'd bet his entire plan on the thin ice of Lourdessa's trust, and he'd won. The caps had arrived two days after he'd ordered them, mixed in with a shipment of miscellaneous hardware.

Eduard reached his office door and once more stopped to listen. Faint strains of music drifted from a little room near the front of the warehouse where Moreno, the guard, spent his nights smoking, drinking café and listening to the radio. Eduard knew that the man wouldn't bestir himself to investigate any noises coming from the main floor, as long as they weren't too loud. Satisfied that Moreno had settled in for at least another hour, Eduard sat at his desk, took up pen and paper, and wrote a short note to his daughters. He folded the paper, placed it in a little steel lockbox and wedged the box behind the bookshelf next to his desk.

Dee, Cece, I wish I could hold you both one last time, he thought. *Please, Madre, let my letter survive, so my children will know I did this for them.*

After clearing a space among the papers, Eduard emptied the contents of the burlap sack onto the desktop. For a few moments he stared at the objects before him.

The Annihilator had to be destroyed, utterly and completely. Three charges placed fore, midship, and aft, to reduce it to slag. A blasting cap submerged in a bottle of coal oil to act as a primary incendiary. Surrounding it, four welding-torch canisters. Nichrome bridge wires to the fuel cell detonator would connect all three charges. Simple and effective.

A single spark, followed by a flash of light, heat, and a great roar, and it would all be over for Lourdessa…and for him.

He picked up a blasting cap and a pair of wire cutters.

Several minutes later all three caps trailed long tails of nichrome. He gathered them up and stuffed them, along with the fuel cell, back in the burlap bag. Standing, he headed out to the main floor.

Eduard imagined that the machine lay in wait for him in the darkness like some great beast, hungering for his blood. No matter that he had given the Beast new life and was its creator in every sense. He would strangle his monstrous child in its cradle before it could take its first steps. Though to do so meant his own death.

He grabbed a handcart, wheeled it to where the welding equipment lay, and began loading it with canisters. He struggled to focus on the task, desperate to keep his own gibbering fear from overwhelming him. A central tenet of the Marian faith held suicide to be a sin. Though not especially pious, Eduard still considered himself a believer. *Am I consigning my soul to Hell?* he wondered.

How could committing an act in which self-destruction was an integral part—but which prevented a terrible evil from happening—damn an otherwise worthy soul? Church teachings abounded with stories of men and women who sacrificed themselves willingly to thwart evil. Rather than damnation they received sanctity, and became the beloved celestial companions of the Madre and her Son.

The Madre is Love and Justice. She'd never let me burn in the pits of the Adversary for what I'm about to do.

As Eduard loaded the last canister, he felt his fear evaporate and a profound sense of peace enfold him like a warm blanket.

He worked steadily until all the charges were set and wired.

Now for the final bit.

It was not enough to destroy the Beast. Eduard knew he must also destroy the means for any future attempts at resurrection. That meant all of his original design notes and schematics must be consigned to the conflagration. Yes, Lourdessa still possessed the data crystal containing the original schematic of the ancient AX238; and yes, Raul Olivas was not without considerable engineering skills. However, at his core he was unimaginative and unwilling to push beyond the boundaries of his experience.

It might take him months to re-create Eduard's design, if he could accomplish the task at all. By that time Eduard prayed that Lourdessa's financial supporters would have lost confidence, or Gregorio Sedano would wake up to his sister's folly and quash it, or Nunyez's Specials would capture Faustin and destroy his terrorist network.

Nothing was certain, he knew. But it was the best that he could do.

Returning to his office, Eduard went to a metal filing cabinet in the corner and emptied its contents onto the handcart. He then collected every scrap of paper from his desk and added them to the pile. Nothing even remotely connected to the project must survive.

Finally, he removed from its gilt frame the little photo of his daughters and their dead mother he'd kept on the desk, and slipped it into the breast pocket of his shirt. He drew in a deep breath.

I'm ready.

Pushing the laden cart before him, Eduard left the office for the last time.

"Eduard."

At the sound of his name, Eduard halted. He spun around to see Suela emerge from the darkness. "Madre, why are you still here?" he gasped.

"I came back...to talk you out of this, dulzor," Suela replied, her voice trembling. "If you go through with it your life will be over."

She moved closer and reached for his hands, but he stepped away, unwilling to let her touch him. "What life, Suela?" he retorted. "Once this project is done I will lose you, and Lourdessa will bury me again in that underground cage. Only a couple hours of sunlight and fresh air a month...the agony of knowing the world goes on without me, my daughters must go on without me...that's no life, my darling. I have one chance to stop this evil, so I must go through with it, Suela. My conscience won't allow me to do otherwise."

"But...it's suicide," Suela whispered.

"It's sacrifice," Eduard replied, "and I'm making it willingly."

"Please forgive me, but I can't let you die…I can't." Suela stepped away from him and cried, "Come now…you have to stop him."

From several directions at once, shadowy figures rushed toward him. Confusion and alarm surged along every nerve. Eduard dropped into a defensive crouch, but the crushing weight of multiple bodies knocked him to the floor. He fought to break free, but his attackers proved too numerous and strong. He felt himself lifted to his feet and locked into place, arms pinned by his sides.

The warehouse lights flickered to life. Eduard bit back a shout of dismay.

A pair of Specials held him fast, their black-gloved fingers gripping each arm with unbreakable force. Two more formed a solid barrier behind him. Suela stood a few steps away, breathing in short bursts as if her lungs no longer had room to expand. Tears spilled down her flushed cheeks.

"Suela...what have you done?" Eduard cried.

A sharp reply echoed across the huge space. "Stopped you from ruining my plans and, incidentally, saving your life, fool of a husband."

In numb disbelief, Eduard watched Lourdessa approach from the direction of the guardroom, a swaggering Alehan by her side and two more Specials at her back. The taste of betrayal bitter on his tongue, he said, "Truly I have been a fool, that's clear now." He glanced at Suela, who stared back at him with haunted eyes. "Once again I let my heart rule my head. You'd have thought I'd learned my lesson with you, eh, Dessa?"

"I think it's another part of your body that rules you, dulzor, not your heart," Lourdessa replied. Her low-cut evening gown of midnight blue silk showed her trim, youthful form to perfection. "I trusted you when I shouldn't have. That was my fault," she added.

"Lucky for you, Mother, I never did." Alehan walked past his mother to wrap his arms around Suela's shoulders. "Good work, darling," he said. She struggled to break free, but her efforts only seemed to amuse him. "Your little lover here has been ever so cooperative, Papa." One hand dropped to squeeze Suela's breast. "When you spilled your secret tonight, she called me right away."

"He made me, Eduard," Suela whispered, her cheeks scarlet. She ceased struggling and sagged like a broken doll within Alehan's embrace. "I had to save my mother...my family..." Her words dissolved into soft weeping.

Alehan's cruel laughter tore at Eduard's heart. He thought he would choke on the anger rising up to scald him. No matter that Suela's betrayal had cost him everything, still his feelings for her ran deep and true. "Get away from her, you little pendayho," he growled, twisting against the hands of his captors, to no avail.

To his astonishment, Lourdessa snapped, "Alehan! Have some pity, for Maria's sake. Let the girl go."

Alehan continued to snigger, but opened his arms. Suela staggered a few steps and crumpled to the cool concrete floor, where she lay curled on her side, her face veiled by her thick, auburn hair.

Horrified, Eduard called out her name, but she remained still and silent.

Ignoring the collapsed girl, Lourdessa moved closer to the machine. She paused to study the construct of brass, rubber, riveted steel, and glass. "Eduard, this is magnificent," she breathed. "I knew you could do it." The frank admiration in her voice felt like salt poured into an open wound. After a few more moments of silent perusal she came to stand before Eduard, stern as a judge about to pronounce sentence.

"You knew what I could do to your daughters if you crossed me, and yet you still tried, Eduard," she said, a note of puzzlement in her voice. "Why risk such a thing?"

"If you need to ask, then you don't know me at all. And there's no point in explaining," he replied.

Lourdessa sighed. "You may not believe this, but I do still have some affection for you, Husband," she said, her expression softening. "You are a truly brilliant man. And, because you've delivered exactly what I wanted, I promise that Ceilia will always be safe...from me, at least."

Eduard's throat tightened with fresh alarm. "What about Deanna?"

"I wish I could have broken this news to you under...less difficult circumstances, dulzor," Lourdessa said.

Eduard would have believed the look of regret on his wife's face, had she been anyone else. "What, Dessa?" he pressed. "What's happened? Tell me."

"Two months ago, Deanna turned down a proposal of marriage from my son to run off with a dirty street raton," Lourdessa replied, her tone rich with disgust. "Apparently this creature has been her lover for several years now. Saviero Nunyez says that they've left the city and have disappeared into the Wilds."

"Diosa mia," Eduard murmured. He suddenly found it hard to breathe, as if all the air had been sucked from the room. Before he could respond, Alehan had rounded on his mother with incandescent fury. "What? That can't be true. She'd *never*...she couldn't..."

Lourdessa glared at her son but her voice remained cool, in sharp contrast to his shrillness. "Apparently she could."

Alehan stabbed a forefinger at his mother's face. "You said Deanna had joined the Marians...*mierda*!" Shoulders hunched like a disconsolate, defeated child, he clasped his fingers through his chestnut curls. "Damn you, Mother," he moaned. "Why did you lie to me? You know how much I love her."

"Because, my darling, I knew the truth would hurt you even more," Lourdessa replied. She laid a hand on her son's arm, but he shook it off.

"I'm going to the Wilds, and I'll find her and that son of a puta, Montoiya," he vowed, "and I'll cut off his cojones and stuff them down his throat. And then I'll bring Deanna back."

"Don't be ridiculous. You'll do no such thing," Lourdessa said.

Eduard thought he'd been prepared for anything, including death, but this….

My child is lost somewhere in the Wilds…He tugged once more against the restraining polis. They tightened their fingers in response. "All of this happened weeks ago," he said, wincing, "and yet you didn't feel it necessary to tell me…until now?"

Lourdessa turned and ambled over to Suela. "I knew you'd be angry and distracted," she said, prodding the girl's thigh with the toe of her black kidskin slipper. "I wanted you to finish the project first." Suela moaned and pushed herself upright. A tiny frown on Lourdessa's crimson lips curled into a smile.

When she looked back at Eduard, the smile had transformed into a smirk. "I'm sorry, Eduard, but it's time you faced the truth about your precious Deanna," she said. "She's always been a willful, wanton girl…a troublemaker. More so since you've been gone."

"I've been gone *because* you betrayed me, Dessa," Eduard grated.

Ignoring his accusation, Lourdessa replied, "Deanna spurned my son and chose to run off with a raton. I told the city that she'd joined the Marians, out of respect for you and the Hernaan family name, Eduard."

"Respect? Oh, that is rich." Eduard felt the bitter irony like a punch to the gut.

"Madre knows she didn't deserve my help after what she did," Lourdessa continued. "Now she'll have to suffer the consequences of her foolishness, though it may cost her her life."

Eduard saw with perfect clarity Lourdessa's sadistic plan to destroy what remained of his dignity; still he found himself helpless to resist. If not for the Specials holding him upright, he would have sunk to his knees. "Damn you to the ninth Hell, Dessa," he whispered.

Without warning Suela surged to her feet and, with an inarticulate shriek, hurled herself at Lourdessa's back. Instantly one of the Specials lunged, catching her with a brutal punch to her jaw. She reeled and went down.

Aleħan cackled with glee.

Eduard dropped his head and wept.

"Oh, for Maria's sake!" Lourdessa shouted. "Get her out of here."

Two Specials swept Suela into their custody, half-dragging, half-carrying the unconscious girl toward the warehouse entrance.

"Suela," Eduard murmured through his tears. Lourdessa moved closer until a mere handspan separated them. The scent of her perfume triggered bittersweet, unwelcome memories. His fingers curled shut as he imagined his hands wrapped around her throat.

"Really, Eduard. Get hold of yourself. This is so unseemly," she said.

Eduard raised his head and gazed into his wife's beautiful dark eyes. "I thought I hated you before this, Dessa. I was wrong," he replied.

"I'm disappointed you feel that way." The hurt on Lourdessa's face seemed genuine.

"I never want to see you again."

"As you wish…Husband." Lourdessa nodded to the Specials. "Take him back to detention."

44

Annihilation

Raul Olivas considered himself a cautious man. If pushed, he'd admit to a distinct lack of bravery. But even cowards could sometimes overcome their natural state. Joining Nunyez's clandestine resistance cell had taken reserves of courage that the Chief Engineer hadn't realized he possessed.

Within the machine's cramped cockpit, Olivas tried in vain to settle his ample girth more comfortably in the narrow copilot's chair. In his mind's eye he visualized a list of tasks needed to ready the Annihilator for departure.

Open cockpit air vents. Reaching overhead, he grasped the handle of a brass flywheel and gave it a vigorous spin. *Check.*

Initiate electrical systems. He pulled down on a polished brass lever set within the console. Light from the now illuminated gauges bathed the cockpit in a silvery glow. *Check.*

The Chief sighed. *If only Eduard had succeeded, I would have been spared this grim exercise, Madre help me.*

He considered the former Alcalde's sacrifice, which in turn reminded him of the high stakes for which he, Saviero Nunyez, and the rest of his comrades in the true resistance played. He knew the endgame—had known before he'd agreed to join—that they all must be willing to do whatever was necessary to see this plan through to its end.

The Chief pulled a pocket watch from his waistcoat and checked the time. *Estes was supposed to be here twenty minutes ago*, he thought. He wiped his brow on the cuff of his shirtsleeve. *Perhaps he won't show. What a blessing that would be.*

The Annihilator's crew, handpicked by Nunyez himself, had already arrived and had taken their places: two boilermen in buff canvas coveralls, and a pair of black-uniformed Specials to man the guns. The boiler had been fired up, and the pressure gauge needle stood at FULL.

Olivas looked at his watch once more. *It's nearly seven. We can't wait any longer for you, Estes.*

With mixed emotions—he felt relieved that he wouldn't have to deal with the Alcalde's volatile son, and yet he worried that he might not be able to drive the machine alone—Olivas lifted the telephone headset from its cradle and settled it over his thinning brown hair. He flipped a toggle switch and, adjusting the microphone, opened the line. "Boiler, are you ready?"

"Ready, Chief," came the reply.

Before Olivas could query the gunners, the roof hatch swung open to reveal Alehan's flushed, grinning face. "Not trying to leave without me, are you Doc?" he said.

Olivas felt grim disappointment like a kick to his gut. "No, of course not," he replied through stiff lips. "But you did cut things quite close."

Alehan slithered, feet first, through the hatch into the pilot's chair, reeking of sueño and jerez. He flexed his neck and shoulders, donned his headset, then said, "Boiler, give me one-quarter power."

High above the roof of the Rosa Blanca Inn, Gregorio Sedano's private airship, the *Danza*, circled. Its ultramodern, twin-cylinder, reciprocating steam engine made almost no sound. To further mask its presence the captain had extinguished all the exterior running lights. To any observer on the ground the ship would appear as a deeper patch of black against the night sky.

Ten minutes later all the interior lamps save one had been extinguished, leaving the plush, wood-paneled parlor in flickering dimness. Lourdessa stood before the panoramic windows, gazing through silver-chased binoculars at the inn's black-shake roof. Her brother Gregorio sat by her side in a simple wheeled chair crafted of manzaniya wood. His longtime valet, Delrey, stood in attentive silence nearby, hands clasped at the small of his back.

"I know you still have doubts about the Annihilator, Greg," Lourdessa said. She lowered the binoculars to regard her elder sibling with smug certainty.

"My only doubt is in your ability to cajole the rest of your financiers into coughing up the money needed to build more," Gregorio replied.

Lourdessa crossed the parlor to settle on a gold-velvet-upholstered banquet. Her brother spun his chair to face her. "They'll open their purses once they see what my Annihilator can do," she said. "I sent them all invitations to my little demonstration two weeks ago. Not a single one declined. They're far too curious...and a little afraid, I hope."

Gregorio studied his sister with eyes that could strike fear in the souls of anyone but her. "You'd better pray Eduard is as brilliant as you think. If this machine of yours fails…"

"He is and it won't."

"Señor Sedano, Dama Alcalde." The Captain's voice crackled over the cabin's loudspeaker. "Word from the ground. Señor Nunyez has given the order for the Annihilator to proceed."

Lourdessa laughed and clapped her hands. "You'll be a believer soon enough, Brother. Delrey, pour me a drink."

Olivas whispered a short prayer and held his breath. Through the barrier of steel plating, he heard a *chuff* as the first blast of exhaust vented. A second chuff followed a few seconds later, then a third in half the time as the pistons revved.

"All hands, ready for departure," Alehan barked into his headset. He eased his foot off the brake. The Annihilator lurched forward. Alehan whooped, his teeth bared in a predatory snarl.

On the warehouse floor the crew scrambled well away from the swinging strides of the machine's six insectile legs. Through the cockpit window, Olivas saw both fear and awe on the men's faces as they stared up at the mechanized behemoth. The grinding sound its clawed metal feet made on the concrete floor bounced in stark echoes off the walls and high ceilings.

Beyond the open doors of the warehouse a double rank of black, armored Special Police cars waited to serve as the machine's escort through the city. Olivas could see the gleaming barrels of ee-rifles pointed outward through the open windows of every car.

He glanced at the console, scanning the gauges. "All systems functioning at optimum," he called out. Alehan replied with a manic giggle.

The Annihilator cleared the hangar doors with scant room to spare. Olivas flipped a switch and the dual electric headlamps mounted on the machine's blunt bow flared to life, bathing the brick-paved warehouse forecourt in blueish light while throwing the shadows of the police sedans into stark relief. "Take us out to the yard and then wait for Nunyez to give the order," Olivas said.

"I know what to do, Doctor," Alehan snapped. He steered the machine to the middle of the forecourt and set the brake. Plumes of white water vapor, vented from exhaust pipes beneath the rear of the fuselage, swirled up to dissipate in the sultry night air.

The wireless set crackled to life. "Doctor Olivas, Señor Estes, are you ready?" Nunyez's voice rasped.

"Yes!" Alehan exclaimed, slamming his fist on his chair arm. "Maria's tits…let's *go*."

"Steady, Estes," Olivas murmured, afraid that a stronger rebuke might provoke a more violent outburst. Alehan regarded him with icy disdain. "Boiler, give me full power," he said in a clipped voice and released the brake.

Led by Nunyez's two-seater, the convoy rumbled from the forecourt onto Quarry Road, which would take the procession into the heart of the Red Hill district. Like a queen surrounded by attendants, the Annihilator walked the center of the road past rows of shuttered warehouses, a rhythmic burst of vented steam accompanying each step.

Alehan had settled into a cool focus that Olivas found surprising, given the other's clear state of intoxication. The incessant jiggle of his knee seemed to bleed off his excess energy. He held the steering wheel with a light touch that kept the machine to its course, moving at a steady pace. With grudging approval, the Chief privately acknowledged that his unwanted student had learned his lessons well.

Olivas refocused his attention on the machine. His trained engineer's senses attuned themselves to every vibration translated through the hull. He made a mental note to adjust the tension in the shock-absorbing spring on the portside forward leg.

On the street the glare of multiple headlamps illuminated rows of one- and two-story workshops interspersed with narrow, multiple-family tenements. The feeble gleam of oil lamps and candles flickered in many windows. The convoy had reached the outskirts of Red Hill. People stood on the side of the road, alone or in small clusters, their faces stark and fearful in the electric beams of the headlamps. By the time the convoy reached the intersection of Quarry Road and Escarpado Street, the crowd had swelled. Residents jostled for space on the pavement, held at bay by a tight cordon of City Police.

Like a parade, Olivas thought to himself.

The wireless buzzed. "We are about ten minutes out," Nunyez announced. "At the intersection of Escarpado and Caya Uno, stop and wait for my orders."

"Understood," Alehan replied. "This is going to be effing *glorious*."

Olivas stared out the windshield at the rear lights of Nunyez's auto, at a loss for words. As a younger man he'd known Ricardo Estes, Alehan's father, quite well. He'd been many things, but never cruel. Olivas wondered what Ricardo would think of the man his son had become.

When the Annihilator reached Escarpado Street, Alehan engaged the throttle and stepped on the brake. The cockpit hummed and rattled as the machine's six legs swung to a halt. Alehan pulled up on the emergency brake lever, released the steering wheel, and swiveled in his seat to stare at Olivas. The console lights bathed his face in an eerie bluish glow, transforming his features into a hollow-eyed mask.

Olivas felt the already cramped cockpit grow even closer. "What is it, Estes?"

"There's been a change in plans, Doctor." Alehan leaned forward and gripped the arm of the Chief's chair. We're going to test this beast my way."

Sweat ran in long, tickling trails down Olivas's face and neck, stinging his eyes. He blinked rapidly to clear his vision. "You can't...I mean, I won't let you," he said in a harsh whisper.

"Sorry you feel that way," Alehan said with a grin.

The last thing Raul Olivas saw was Alehan's fist.

CONCEALED IN PURPLE shadow, Zander sat cross-legged in morose seclusion on the back stoop of the Rosa Blanca Inn. The sun had dipped below the peaked roof, briefly firing the wood shakes to crimson before plunging the world into soft twilight. The beer he had nicked from the bar tap not twenty minutes earlier rested in a chipped mug, half-drained, beside him. Dejected and forlorn, Zander marveled at how quickly his life had devolved.

Three days had come and gone since his last devastating confrontation with Sonia. Though they continued to live beneath the same roof, she had yet to speak a single complete sentence to him. With their relationship shattered, Zander had stopped sharing her bed. He spent his nights alone on the back stoop, bedded down on an old mattress beneath a spare blanket. Not even Aunt Bea's pleading and offerings of a cot in the scullery could move him inside. He preferred the summer night air to the muggy heat of the kitchen, and the quiet of the semi-enclosed porch suited his need for solitary reflection.

Making good on his promise to expose Faustin had proved to be far more difficult than he'd imagined. The morning after he'd learned the truth, Zander borrowed Guermoe's bicycle and made the trek to Bayona Cathedral in Valencea. The priest on duty in the confessional listened to his story. In clipped, disapproving tones he'd then admonished him to stop making up wild tales about his betters. Zander had left the sanctuary infuriated. It seemed that not even a priest of the Blessed Madre's own Church would take the word of a street raton as worthy of belief.

Of the anonymous letters he'd sent to each of the city's three newspapers, two had been ignored. The third received a terse response: without concrete proof, such accusations had to be considered as little more than the libelous scribbling of a lunatic.

Zander had finally come to the conclusion that his best chance lay with convincing one of Faustin's inner circle. Sonia was a lost cause. And Tony and Alberto, her fellow cell members, seemed as fiercely loyal to the rebel leader as did Sonia. The only opening Zander could see to exploit lay in Alberto's unspoken, but obvious, sexual attraction to him. The pudgy man's desire might make him more inclined to listen. If he could convince Alberto, then getting the others to listen might be easier.

He'd heard Sonia mention that the bomb maker rented a room over a haberdashery in Clara Street. *I'll go tomorrow*, he thought.

Zander took another sip of beer. *Dee...I miss you so much. I wish I knew where you were.* His heart, always sore for the loss of her, suddenly ached with fresh intensity.

Yesterday he'd tried to seek out Roberto Gomaz, but had failed. Not even Mother Elizabette knew the poli's exact whereabouts, or *if* she knew, she was unwilling to say. Zander didn't press; the Mother Superior had a well-deserved reputation for discretion. With no other way to contact Gomaz, his last hope of a speedy reunion with Deanna faded. Knowing she still lived, but remained far beyond his reach, filled him with gnawing despair; but Zander also suffered from pain of a different sort.

The stripping away of the last shreds of his naïve idealism had left its own deep, raw wounds on his psyche. The fierce need to belong to anything resembling a family had driven his choices, from his first liaisons with Sonia to his insistence she bring him into her cell. To admit such a painful truth hurt worse than the beatings he'd taken in detention.

From the open rear door of the inn, the comforting sounds of an ordinary dinner service spilled into the night, raising faint echoes against the high walls of the apartment block across the alley. Zander chuckled at Guermoe's shouted complaint that someone had cut the patoks for the vaca stew into the wrong size cubes. He scratched a chin made itchy by several days' growth of stubble, then sucked down the last of the beer. *Break time's over*, he thought.

From the far end of the alley, the metallic clatter of a refuse bin lid caused Zander to start. Rising from his seat, he descended the steps and peered into the heavy gloom. A sudden chill nipped the skin of his arms to gooseflesh. "Someone out there?" he called.

Only silence met his query. He lingered another moment, listening, then turned and started back up the stairs.

From the corner of his eye he caught a flicker of swift movement. Drawing his knife, he spun to meet a shadow rushing at him from the darkness. He raised his arm to block, but his assailant proved a hairsbreadth faster. White-hot pain exploded just below his left collarbone and raced like fire down his arm. Zander cried out, even as he swung his knife in a slicing arc toward his attacker. He felt the knife hit bone and heard a howl. The shadow stumbled into the patch of light spilling out from the kitchen door. Even though both hands covered his face, Ernesto's coppery hair revealed his identity. Bright red blood leaked through his fingers.

Seizing the chance for escape, Zander flung himself up the steps towards the sanctuary of Guermoe's kitchen.

"Come now, Doctor," Nunyez commanded. He let the wireless microphone fall into his lap.

Months of clandestine planning had led to this moment. The die had been cast. Tonight would stand as the opening gambit of a very long play. So much depended on the intricate lattice of skill, fortitude, luck, and secrecy he, along with many others, had constructed and nurtured.

From his vantage point a half-block away, Nunyez watched the Annihilator approach, wondering how much more terrifying the ancient pre-war machine would have seemed. A contingent of his Specials had already charged through the front doors of the inn. A blue cordon of City Police had surrounded the building, preventing any escape.

Amid the squeal of metal gears and percussive blasts of vented steam, the monster ground to a halt a block from the Rosa Blanca. The glare from its headlamps overpowered the weaker illumination thrown off by the municipal gas streetlights, honing shadows to a knife-edged sharpness. A poli photographer had set up his equipment in front of Nunyez's car. A burst of actinic light bounced off the machine's hull as he made his first exposure. The acrid smell of burnt flash powder drifted in the air.

Nunyez plucked the microphone from his lap. "On my mark, Doctor."

Silence.

"Doctor?"

Nunyez's neck prickled with uneasiness. "Olivas, do you copy? Doctor?"

Zander staggered through the kitchen door, his left arm hanging lifeless by his side. He collided with a waitress, who screamed and dropped the serving platter in her hands to the floor. It shattered with a ringing crash. All activity came to a sudden halt as the eyes of the kitchen staff focused on him. He took several more steps and found himself surrounded by a ring of crying, shouting people. Hands reached out to steady him as he swayed. He felt someone gently take his knife from his hand. One of the fry cooks yelled for Guermoe.

"Should we pull it out?" he heard someone say.

"No. Leave it in. He could bleed to death," another voice answered.

Zander looked down and shivered. A knife hilt, brass, its glistening pommel in the shape of a clenched fist, protruded from his shoulder. Blood soaked his shirt in a red trail down to the hem.

He sucked in a deep breath, reached up and withdrew the blade.

"Madre preserve, Zander." Guermoe pushed through his horror-stricken staff in time to catch Zander as he fell. "Get me something to stop the bleeding," the big man shouted, easing Zander to the scuffed tile floor.

"I'm all right," Zander muttered, even as the rush of blood from the wound told him a different story. Yet, his mind, strangely enough, had never been clearer.

A scullery boy handed Guermoe a towel, which he pressed firmly against Zander's shoulder. "Who did this to you, son?" His voice cracked with distress.

Zander glanced at the brass-hilted dagger, still clutched in his hand. "I need to talk to Sonia," he whispered. "Help me up."

"Zan, you need to be still," Guermoe insisted. "Don't move. I'll call a doctor."

Zander shook his head. "I need to speak to Sonia. Please Guermoe, help me up." As Sonia's uncle reluctantly lifted him to his feet, Zander clenched his teeth to keep himself from screaming.

"Sonnie's at the bar," Guermoe said. "Here, take my arm."

Zander sighed, grateful for the support. The staff fell back, clearing a way just as Beatrichia swept into the kitchen. "What's happened?" she cried.

"Zander's been stabbed," Guermoe responded, terse. "Call Doctor Desilva."

Beatrichia nodded, her face white.

When Zander entered the common room, leaning heavily on Guermoe's beefy arm and pressing the towel to his wound, he spotted Sonia riding her favorite stool at the far end of the bar. Tony sat beside her, one elbow propped on the polished wood, a hand resting on her knee. She leaned away from him as if contemplating flight, but her sensuous mouth wore the hint of a smile.

Zander released Guermoe's arm and started toward her, his gaze fixed on her beautiful profile. The disparate blend of sounds filling the air faded to a whisper. His wound throbbed with each beat of his racing heart. "Sonia," he said, his voice a harsh whisper.

She turned. The smile on her lips faded.

Tony slid off his stool, scowling, but Sonia grabbed his arm in restraint.

Startled bar patrons abandoned their seats, stumbling over themselves in their haste. Zander paid them no heed. He halted a step beyond Tony's grasp, raised the brass-hilted dagger and drove it point-first into the wood. "You can give this back to Ernesto," he said.

Sonia's lips trembled but she said nothing.

"Seems I'm not so easy to kill after all." Zander glanced down at the bloody towel, then back at Sonia. "But, then, you always did underestimate me..."

Through the open front doors of the inn, a strange, rhythmic metallic screech caught Zander's attention. He paused, his head tilted, listening.

Tony frowned. "What the eff is that?"

The percussive, metallic shriek grew louder. Bar patrons cast nervous glances at each other as the scuffed floorboards underfoot began to vibrate.

A frisson of terror fired Zander's nerves. With his good hand, he reached for Ernesto's knife and pulled it free of the bar.

"Zander," Sonia whispered urgently.

He turned his back to her, his gaze riveted on the door.

The tumult in the street crescendoed and then stopped.

Guermoe rushed to the doorway and peered into the night. An instant later he cried out, backpedalling into the room ahead of a squad of Special polis. They fanned out among the crowd, neural batons at the ready.

The sergeant in charge shouted, "Everyone, stay where you are!"

"Why are you doing this?" Guermoe cried. "You have no right..."

Beatrichia screamed.

OLIVAS MOANED. ALEHAN reached over, slammed the Chief's head against the console for good measure and then shoved his limp body aside. He fell back into his chair, wiped his scarlet-smeared hand on the unconscious Chief's sleeve, and readjusted his headset. "Ee-cannon, prepare to fire on my order."

Silence.

"Ee-cannon! Did you hear me?"

"Señor Estes?" the gunner replied. "The Chief…"

"I'm in charge now. You'll fire on my orders. Is that understood?"

Several more seconds ticked past.

Alehan slammed his fist on the arm of his chair. "Do you understand?" he yelled.

"Yes, sir."

"On my mark, put the first shot through the front door."

Nunyez's voice crackled over the wireless. "*Doctor Olivas, please answer.*"

Alehan flipped a toggle switch, silencing it. He fixed his gaze on the glowing windows of the inn. Through the glass he could see dark shapes moving in the room beyond. He stifled a giggle.

"Ee-cannon, ready…Fire!"

THE NORTH WALL of the common room exploded in a dazzling flare of white light.

A silent pressure wave lifted Zander and flung him like a rag doll through the air. His body met plaster with bone-jarring force. The sharp taint of ozone filled his nostrils.

"Guermoe!" he cried, but the avalanche of roof tiles, plaster, and support beams crashing around him drowned out his cry. A cloud of dust enveloped him, filling his lungs.

A second flash, and the room shook as if from the blow of a giant's fist. Bits of debris pummeled him from above like poured gravel. He fought to breathe with lungs that felt rinsed in fire. Blinking through a haze of tears, he struggled to make sense of the scene before him.

He slumped amid a crazy jumble of shadows beneath the vault of the night sky. Feeble light bleeding in from the street revealed the horror to his shocked gaze.

Nothing remained of the common room but a jagged pile of fractured beams, shattered roof tiles, chunks of plaster, broken furniture, smashed crockery and…

Bodies, torn and broken. Some moved. Others lay deathly still. Zander saw a Special sprawled nearby, his legs little more than rags of flesh and bone. A woman stood up, swayed, and then crumpled to her knees.

"Oh, Madre and Yesu," Zander whispered.

Little sounds impinged on his awareness: the squeal and crunch of shifting debris, frantic voices shouting from the street, the cries of people trapped beneath the wreckage. He tried to stand but found his ankle pinned beneath a fallen beam.

"Guermoe, where are you," he yelled, shoving hard at the weight crushing his ankle. A hand gripped his shoulder.

"Zan, it's me."

Coated in plaster dust, Sonia crouched beside him. "Let me help you," she said, and lent her strength to his upon the beam. Together they shifted its weight, relieving some of the grinding pressure against his flesh. Hissing with pain, Zander slid his foot free. He coughed and spat out a mouthful of blood-flavored snot. "What…happened?" he rasped.

Sonia pointed to a towering shape just beyond the mound of debris, visible through the illumination cast by the street lamps. It looked like a gigantic, mechanized insect with enormous, glowing eyes, emitting short, regular bursts of sound.

"What the eff?" he whispered.

"We have to get out of here *now*." She slipped her hands beneath his arms and heaved, setting off a ripple of pain through his injured shoulder. He kicked his legs clear of the rubble and stood. Though his ankle ached, it bore his weight without buckling.

Sonia grabbed his hands and pulled him close. "Listen, Zan. I betrayed you, and I'm sorry," she whispered, her breath warm against his neck. Her voice broke. She sobbed and said, "I love you, Zander. I always will."

"Sonnie," he began, but the terrifying apparition in the street rumbled to life. Its grotesque body rotated, bringing the twin headlamps to bear, bathing the shattered interior of the inn in lurid light.

Blinded, Zander lifted his hand to shield his eyes. He heard a hollow *pop-pop-pop* at the same instant Sonia shoved him hard, sending him tumbling backward. He went down, a spray of wet warmth drenching his face, flattening himself as bullets plowed into the debris around him.

Waves of agony rolled through his arm and shoulder, dizzying his senses. He ground his teeth against the pain, determined not to lose consciousness. He looked for Sonia and spotted her, sprawled just out of reach, her face turned toward him and her eyes half lidded.

The gunfire stopped. In its wake, silence, broken only by the moans and cries of the injured and dying. From behind fallen beams, overturned benches and tables, survivors emerged, crawling, limping or scrambling in a desperate bid to escape the carnage.

Zander crawled to where Sonia lay. "Sonnie?" he whispered. Blood soaked the front of her shirt. Through a tear in the fabric he saw the ragged, pale ends of shattered ribs. He touched her neck, feeling for a pulse, but found none.

Zander's eyes filled with tears. "I'm sorry I couldn't love you the way you wanted me to, Sonnie," he murmured, and bent to kiss her lifeless lips.

"Sonia…Montoiya." a voice hissed from the darkness.

Zander glanced around to see Tony peering from behind an upended table. "Sonia's dead."

Out in the street, the machine screeched and rumbled.

Come on," Tony cried. "We've got to get out."

"I'm not leaving. Guermoe and Bea are..."

"There's nothing we can do for them." Tony growled. "Don't be a fool, Montoiya. Come *on*. Save yourself."

The metal monster waded into the debris like a giant, whirring spider, pushing the remains of the front wall before it. It spun, bringing the muzzle of a massive flamethrower to bear, then sent a geyser of fire into the inn's shattered interior. The blast of heat forced Zander into a reflexive crouch, his good arm flung over his head. He trembled at the sound of people screaming as they burned.

Tony cursed and yelled, "Come now or burn, idiot. It's coming this way!"

Zander glanced one last time at Sonia's body; then he turned and crawled after Tony. They scrambled over broken furniture and fallen ceiling beams, away from the lurid orange flames licking hungrily at the debris around them. A thunderous roar filled the air as the machine advanced, demolishing another section of the inn's roof. Zander stumbled and nearly fell as the ground shook beneath him. He ducked under a splintered beam and spotted a jagged hole in the rear wall. Panting with terror, he wriggled through.

Dizzy and nauseous from pain, he collapsed onto the dirty bricks of the alley, one hand pressed to his lacerated shoulder. He could feel blood, warm and sticky, oozing through his fingers. In the semi-darkness Tony loomed over him, a black shape backlit by the fire's glow.

"You'd better go find a raton hole somewhere, Montoiya, and stay there. Whatever that thing was, we can't fight it. We're all in the mierda now." He held out his hand.

Zander reached up and, with Tony's help, regained his feet. "What about you?" he asked.

"Someone's gotta warn Faustin. After that, I don't know. Lay low..."

The wail of sirens drifted over the bass roar of the fire. Smoke and ash filled the air, making breathing difficult. "You'd better run. There'll be polis crawling everywhere in a minute." Tony turned and jogged across the alley. Agile as a lizard, he sprang off his toes to grip the top of the retaining wall and swung himself up. He paused for a moment. "I'm sorry about Sonia," he said. He dropped over the edge and disappeared.

The sirens drew nearer. Zander made his way to the end of the alley and paused for a backward look. As the flames leapt high into the night, he felt a sudden, bitter flood of fear, rage, and grief. He had to howl in despair, lest he go mad.

When the fit had passed, he fled, his face wet with tears. When he could no longer hear the sirens he collapsed in a shadowed doorway, breathing hard, his mind filled with thoughts of Deanna. He needed her now, more than he'd ever needed anyone in his life. *But, you're not here, Dee...and somehow, I've got to get through this alone.*

The Marian House, his childhood home, stood as the only place in the city that offered unconditional sanctuary. If he could reach it, he might stand a chance.

Zander climbed to his feet and started limping toward Convento Street.

LOURDESSA STOOD IN rapt silence, watching through her binoculars as the Annihilator's flamethrowers immolated the pile of rubble that had once been the Rosa Blanca Inn. Intense satisfaction, the likes of which she'd not experienced since last she made love to Alehan's father over sixteen years ago, fired her nerves. She lowered her binoculars and turned to her brother, who continued to stare at the scene below through a telescope mounted in front of the panoramic windows.

Delrey rested a light hand on the frame, ready to adjust the instrument's position at his employer's command.

"Well, what do you think now, Greg?" Lourdessa asked.

"I think both Faustin and the Castilians will be utterly demoralized after tonight." Gregorio lifted a thin, white hand, and Delrey pulled the chair away from the window. He offered his sister a grudging smile. "Congratulations, Dessa."

45

stalemate

In the meager pool of a flickering shadow cast by the overhanging entrance to a shuttered tailor's shop, Faustin took a drag from his cigarette. Twin streamers of smoke trailed from nostrils already stinging from the fumes of the conflagration several blocks away. Though Zander Montoiya would soon be ashes, and his own secret safe, sadness tempered Faustin's satisfaction. Sonia had been a good lieutenant, and he would miss her. He wished her death might have somehow been avoided.

Another unfamiliar emotion gave him pause—uncertainty.

Now that he'd witnessed its dreadful capabilities, Faustin realized he'd no inkling of how to combat the threat of Lourdessa Hernaan's infernal machine.

Faustin rubbed his smarting eyes, then pulled his scarf over his nose and mouth, flicking his spent cigarette butt to the pavement.

He'd witnessed enough. Time to get out of here.

The police cordon had begun to collapse; that, and the inexcusable blunder by the City force in not posting watches on the rooftops would aid in his escape. Faustin wondered what the Alcalde would do if she learned of her brother-in-law Deltoro's incompetence. She might have him shot. The rebel leader smiled.

After a quick scan of the street, he abandoned his hiding place and hurried past a short row of shops, making for a narrow walkway. Once there, he paused to gaze at the glowing sky and spotted the dark shape of what could only be the Danza circling above the burning inn.

Suppressing a twinge of uneasiness, Faustin headed west, sticking to back streets and alleys while avoiding the clusters of curious fools hoping to get closer to the commotion. In the alley behind the Medala De Oro Bakery he stopped to retrieve Ceilia's bicycle from its hiding place behind a storage shed. Pedaling furiously, with a fearsome grimace, he raced the moonrise back to the palace.

CEILIA WOKE IN her bed with images of fire and smoke swirling in her mind. Panting, she bolted upright, clutching her favorite doll—the one with the blond curls—to her chest.

What's happening? Where am I?

Then she remembered.

This isn't really my room. He's locked me inside my head again.

She tossed back the blankets and padded barefoot to the window. A pearlescent mist eddied beyond the glass.

How long has it been? Time had no meaning inside the prison of her mind.

She sighed and returning to her bed, lay down to wait, drifting, neither awake nor asleep.

The door rattled and swung open. She sat up, tense and expectant.

"It's all right. I'm back now." He came and sat on the bed beside her, smelling of tabac smoke and fire.

She touched his hand. "You've kept me in here such a long time. May I come out? For just a little while?"

He smiled and kissed her cheek. "But, I have so much important work left to do."

"Please? I won't stay out long, I promise."

"Well...when you ask so nicely..."

He waited while she lay down and pulled the covers up to her chin. "Perhaps tomorrow you can come out." He stroked her hair, then stood and headed toward the door.

"May I have something nice to look at through the window?"

He paused at the threshold. "Of course, dulzor. There's a garden now."

"Thank you."

The door closed. Ceilia settled in to wait.

CONTINUED...

flora and fauna of nuetierra

abeha: Small, winged pollinating insect occupying the same ecological niche as the Terran (Old Earth) bumblebee. Wild abehas make their nests in tree hollows and abandoned burrows. Each colony contains thousands of individuals. Humans domesticated the abeha soon after arriving on Nuetierra, as a replacement for their honeybee stocks, destroyed by a native virus.

aguila: Carnivorous avian, similar in size to the Terran bald eagle. Most individuals are white with black-tipped primary feathers, but there is a rare, all-black variant.

alazan: Leafy plant, similar to sorrel. Not cultivated commercially, but both altas and Tiqui gather it from the wild and eat it raw in salads or cooked in soups, stews, or as a side dish.

algodon: Commercially cultivated fiber plant genetically descended from Terran cotton.

amapola: Woody plant with tiny purple berries. Both berries and leaves contain an effective analgesic used by the Tiqui, alta Wilds dwellers, and the working class of the cities. The elite classes use the far more potent and costly painkiller known as morfo. *See also:* morfo.

ani: Herbaceous plant cultivated specifically for the light-yellow, clean-tasting oil pressed from its seeds. The oil is used for cooking and in cosmetics.

aranya bug: One of many species of beetle-like insects. These large bugs are armored with a hard carapace that changes its color to match the creatures' surroundings. Sometimes kept as pets by both alta and Tiqui children.

ardiya: A small arboreal mammal, occupying the same ecological niche as the Terran squirrel. Ardiyas have very soft, plush pelts that can vary from pure black to russet, with spots or stripes. The Tiqui hunt them for their meat and fur, which they use to line gloves or as trim on garments.

arenbale: Huge, desert-dwelling creature that resembles a cross between a shark and a centipede. Also known as the sand whale. A large female can reach 30 meters in length. The smaller males average between 18 and 24 meters. The animal propels itself beneath the surface of the sand with its hundreds of oar-like appendages, breathing through a pair of siphons protruding from the top of its spade-shaped head.

arenbales: live in pods of up to 30 individuals. Its favorite food is the sky jelly, which it catches by lying in wait beneath the sand and extending an appendage attached to its snout through the surface into the air. This appendage has a special set of graspers surrounding a bulb that secretes a scent that jellies find irresistible. When a pod of jellies flies over a pod of arenbale, many will swoop down to grab what they think is food and fall victim to the graspers, which harpoon the jelly and drag it down and into the waiting jaws of the submerged predator.

azul: Ground-running vine that produces clumps of dark-blue berries. The Tiqui eat the fresh fruit in season, but they also pick large quantities for drying and winemaking.

bacalao: A large freshwater icthyoid, found in rivers and lakes throughout the continent. Popular with alta sport fishermen and Tiqui alike.

blackthorn: Thorny shrub with small, waxy leaves and a thick, woody stem. The Tiqui brew a restorative tea from the leaves and flowers.

bloodbark: A deciduous tree of the foothill forests, the bloodbark is striking in appearance, having deep-red bark and wood, brilliant green leaves, and bright orange fruit. The Tiqui consider the fruit a delicacy and they use the wood for fine furniture and carvings.

boca: Native terrestrial cephalopod that has evolved to resemble a tree, complete with bark-like skin and a 'leafy' crown. The creatures live in small herds in the dense hardwood forests of the central continent. They move about on a mass of tentacles at the base of their 'trunks'. They also use these rootlike appendages for water absorption.

brown cap: One of several species of fungi that grow at the bases of trees such as the choa, manzanita, and bloodbark. Looks similar to the morel. The Tiqui prize its strong, meaty flavor and most often eat them cooked, but will chop small amounts into raw salads.

buho: Night-hunting avian, occupying a similar niche as the Terran owl. Its enormous eyes take up much of the space on its round head. Its short wings are suited to gliding between the trees of its forest home. Ranges in color from slate gray to ghostly white.

café: The name of both the plant and the drink derived from it. The sturdy shrub is cultivated commercially, and wild varieties are exploited by Wilds dwellers of both races. The thick, shiny brown seed pods are collected and the seeds extracted and then roasted for varying lengths of time to produce brews of different characteristics, much like coffee beans back on Old Earth.

camaron: Small freshwater crustacean resembling a cross between a sea urchin and a crab. Used as a food source by all inhabitants of the Wilds. The word is sometimes used by alta as a pejorative when referring to Tiqui.

canteen plant: A grasslands succulent, so named because of the sour juice stored in its fleshy, purple stem that can be tapped and drunk in an emergency.

capra: Genetically descended from goats brought from Old Earth. Raised by the Tiqui for meat, milk, and leather. Capra raising has fallen out of favor with alta city dwellers at the time of Deanna's story.

cebre: Grasslands-dwelling, black-and-orange-striped, three-toed herbivore, about the size of a Terran Clydesdale horse. Males sport stiff black manes of glossy quills and a ball of quills at the end of a long, ropelike tail. Females are also armed with quill balls at the ends of their tails, but they are maneless.

cervena: Forest-dwelling ungulate that lives in small herds consisting of one bull and a harem of females and their young. This animal looks like a hairless, earless, four-toed Terran deer. The males sport tall, branching horns; the females have much smaller horns. Hunted by Tiqui and alta Wilds dwellers for food and hides. The elites of the cities hunt them for sport.

choa: Grassland tree with silvery bark and bright-red leaves; the choa grow mostly in small groves, but solitary specimens are not uncommon.

cirilo: Commercially cultivated tree with small, red oblong-shaped, edible fruits. The fruit is eaten fresh and dried by city dwellers. A popular spirit, known as jerez, is distilled from the juice.

conayho: A small mammal with elongated ears, pointed snout, stubby tail, and strong hindquarters suitable for rapid leaping and running. Occupies a similar niche as the Terran wild hare. Covered in a very fine, soft pelt, the animal is prized for its fur. A domesticated breed is kept by the Tiqui, but its wild cousins are also hunted for fur and meat by both alta Wilds dwellers and Tiqui alike.

corella: The blossoms of this flowering bush are used to brew a tea enjoyed by both city folk and Wilds dwellers alike.

coyote: Grassland-dwelling canid, similar in size to the Terran animal of the same name. These small clever animals live in packs consisting of a mated alpha pair, their juvenile offspring, and the unmated adult sisters of the alpha female. Adult, unmated males of all ages live solitary lives.

dolora: Large avian with bright-yellow feathers and slender, blade-like wings. These birds congregate in small flocks to soar the thermals.

ebon: Deciduous, broad-leafed tree prized for its dark, hard wood. Used primarily for furniture.

eelat: Used as mounts and beasts of burden, this ungulate was domesticated by the original colonists to replace virally decimated equine stocks brought from Old Earth. The creature resembles a hairless llama, with four sturdy legs, ear ridges in place of external pinnae, and a stubby tail. Its three-toed feet are armed with heavy claws, perfect for digging shallow resting burrows in the hard soil of the plains where its wild cousins still live in small herds. The eelat is omnivorous and can be ill-tempered.

felion: Similar in size to a Terran lion, and genetically related to the six-legged, forest-dwelling kymera, this creature, despite its name and superficial appearance, is not a felid. Like the lion, it lives in family-based prides on the grasslands of the continental interior. A hunting pride is capable of taking down a full-grown eelat or feral vaca. The creatures' hairless hides are mottled in tones of dun, fawn, and cream, providing them camouflage. The males are crowned with a mane of quill-like hairs, and sport small, mandibular tusks. *See also:* kymera.

gahto: Genetically descended from the Terran cat. Kept as pets by city dwellers but not by the Tiqui. Gahtos come in only one size and coat-length, which is short, but with multiple color variations. A sizable feral population exists in cities and smaller alta settlements, as well as in rural settings and Wilds outposts.

gayoh: Genetically descended from the Terran chicken. There are three distinct varieties. Two are raised as food by city dwellers and the third is found only in Tiqui villages.

gazela: Small, graceful ungulate that roams the plains in large herds. The males have a single lance-like horn growing between wide-set eyes, which they can wield to deadly effect against an attacker or a sexual rival. When the creatures flee, they often spring high in the air as they run. They are highly prized by the Tiqui for their exceptionally flavorful meat and for the horn, which is used for a vast range of utilitarian and artful purposes, including jewelry, eating utensils, and buttons.

gorrion: Small avian that lives in large flocks. Both sexes can vocalize, but only the males sing. Each individual bird trills and chirps his own unique "melody" in an effort to attract and win a mate. The female is significantly larger than the male, and both sexes range in color from dun to chocolate.

griyo: Nocturnal insect that produces a chirp much like the Terran cricket. Lives in tall grass and scrub. The Tiqui prize them as a delicacy, and eat them roasted, fried, boiled, and as an ingredient in soups and stews.

jacaran: Prized for its thick, spreading canopy and pleasant-smelling white and yellow flowers, this popular shade tree is used in the cities in both private and public spaces.

jazmin: Night-blooming shrub with highly scented flowers that shade from a delicate pink to a vivid magenta. Used as an ornamental and in perfumery.

jenjibre: Herbaceous plant with a sweetly scented, delicate white flower and a fleshy root. Native to the torrid tropical regions of the southern continent, the plant is notoriously difficult to cultivate in the more temperate zones of the north. Commercial cultivation therefore is limited to hothouses in the cities. The flowers are used in the manufacture of a very expensive perfume. The root is also prized for its medicinal value as a potent anti-vomiting drug, but owing to cost, is available only to the elite class.

kymera: Large, fierce carnivore that inhabits the deep temperate forests, where its mottled gray, black, and dull-green, hairless hide provides perfect camouflage. Both sexes are of roughly equal size and armed with razor-sharp talons on all six feet, and a double pair of tusks protruding from either side of the lower jaw. The creature is crowned with a mane of long, sharp quills. Cousin to the smaller, grasslands-dwelling felion. *See also:* felion

lavanda: Flowering shrub with abundant purple flowers. Popular as an ornamental and in perfumery.

limón: Round, pale-green fruit, cultivated for the rich oil contained in its single, large seed. The oil has many uses, including cosmetics, wood polish, and cleaning products.

loto: Aquatic plant with large, pad-like leaves and a fragrant, spiky blue flower. The bulbs are eaten as a vegetable by the Tiqui.

manzaniya: The name of the fruit and the tree from which it comes. The fruit is similar in size and taste to the Terran apple, but has a deep-purple skin and lavender-colored flesh with tiny purple seeds. Eaten fresh, cooked, dried, and juiced by city folk.

mariposo: Generic name for a group of flying-insect species characterized by the brilliant, jewellike colors of their double sets of gauzy wings. Also a mildly pejorative term for a homosexual man. The mariposo is second in importance only to the abeha as a pollinator.

mezcala: The sacred herb of the Tiqui shamans, used to unlock their powers of foresight and prophecy. A powerful hallucinogen, it is also known as sueño when used as an illicit recreational drug by the moneyed classes of the cities. Alta dealers purchase their stock from Wilds traders, who gather it wild or steal it from shamanic gardens, where the best-quality herb is cultivated. If a Tiqui should ever be caught stealing the herb, he or she would suffer the ultimate punishment—banishment from the Tiqui nation. The mottled green-and-red leaves are cured over smoky fires, then a tea is brewed for Tiqui ceremonies. Alta users chew or smoke the leaves. *See also:* sueño

mono: Generic term for several species of small, arboreal primates. Monos can be found in most of the continent's forested regions. They are highly intelligent and live in small troops of related individuals.

morfo: Powerful analgesic extracted from the juice of the morfo flower, cultivated only in the cities in special greenhouses dedicated for the purpose. This plant is difficult and expensive to grow, due to its fragile nature; therefore, access to the narcotic derived from it is limited almost exclusively to the elite class, who can purchase it in pharmacies and directly from doctors. Working-class people rarely have the cash to buy even a few pills, so they rely on the much cheaper but less effective alternative, amapola. The poor almost always must do without any relief at all, other than copious amounts of alcohol. *See also:* amapola.

mola: A small, burrowing insectivorous mammal occupying the same ecological niche as the Terran mole or gopher. Molas are nearly blind and use their large, clawed forefeet to dig extensive warrens beneath the earth. They are covered in sharp spines that discourage all but the most persistent predators. When molas invade cultivated land, they can do great damage and are therefore considered pests.

naranha: Deciduous tree commercially cultivated by city dwellers for its round orange fruit, used mostly for juicing. The Tiqui also plant them for fruit and shade.

ovehas: Genetically descended from the Terran sheep. Only one variety, with cream-colored hair, survived to the post-war era. Raised commercially in the cities for wool and meat.

pacana: The long seed pods of this commercially cultivated tree contain shiny red nuts that are prized as a foodstuff by city dwellers. Eaten roasted and salted as a snack or as an ingredient in desserts and candies.

paloma: Similar to the Terran pigeon or rock dove, this social avian comes in many color variations, ranging from bright greens, blues, and yellows, to drabber russet, chocolate, cream, and charcoal gray. They live in large flocks that tend to be made up of individuals of the same color scheme, and can become pests if not controlled. Some city dwellers keep tamed palomas as pets.

pantera: Shy, secretive felid, similar in size to the Terran cougar or leopard. A solitary creature, it favors the mixed forests of the high mountain ranges, where its dark coloring gives it camouflage. Unlike the felion, the pantera grows no mane.

patok: Root vegetable similar to the Terran sweet potato. Eaten by all classes and both races.

perro: Genetically descended from the domesticated Terran dog, perros were far more diverse in the pre-war era. Of the original six breeds brought to Nuetierra, only two have survived to flourish in the post-war age; a hound-type, used by alta and Tiqui alike for hunting and as guard animals, and a small, long-haired type kept primarily by the city elite as pets.

polilla bug: Large, round-bodied insect, similar to a Terran june bug. The thick, iridescent carapace of larger individuals are used by the Tiqui for jewelry and embellishments on clothing.

pinya: Evergreen tree, analogous to the Terran pine or fir. The wood is relatively soft, but still suitable for building. The resin is very aromatic and used as an ingredient for incense by the Church.

puerco: Genetically descended from the Terran pig. Two varieties survived to the post-war era. Raised in the cities for meat and leather.

rana: Small amphibian that lives in colonies in ponds, marshes, and streams. Looks like a cross between a Terran crab and a bullfrog. Used as a food resource by the Tiqui.

raton: Small, furry, six-legged mammal, similar in size and occupying the same ecological niche as the Terran rat. Ratons are nocturnal and so have large sensitive eyes for better night vision. Their chisel-like incisors and powerful jaws allow them to chew through most any substance, including metallic wire. They are considered vermin in the cities and treated as such. The word is used as a pejorative when referring to a certain kind of person, most often a young, impoverished street dweller.

risa bird: Small forest avian with a distinctive warbling cry and brilliant, multicolored plumage.

roble: Broad-leafed deciduous tree used extensively for commercial construction and furniture.

romara: Fragrant native herb used mainly for medicinal purposes. The tiny leaves and berries are crushed for tinctures and poultices; the leaves can also be dried for tisanes. Good for blood poisoning, wound infections, and fevers.

rosa: Cultivated flower descended from the Terran rose. All twelve varieties were developed from DNA stocks brought from Old Earth. Common ornamental in both private and public spaces. Also used in perfumery.

sajaro: A busy herb that produces abundant, heart-shaped leaves, used in both remedies and as a seasoning. Good for digestive complaints.

sand mite: Multi-legged arthropod similar in size to a Terran tarantula. Lives in loose, sandy soil, in tunnels it digs in order to lie in wait for prey. This creature secretes a substance from glands in its abdomen that acts like a glue, which it uses to stabilize the walls of its tunnel. When an insect or other arthropod comes along, the mite springs from the concealed entrance to its tunnel to seize the prey in powerful, hooked mandibles equipped with poison sacs. It then drags the paralyzed, live prey into the tunnel, where it quickly dismembers and devours its meal. For some unknown reason, gahtos find sand mites irresistible and will hunt and capture them with single-minded purpose, then often present the still-wiggling prize as a gift to their owners. *See also:* gahto.

sawtooth: So-named because of its long, thin serrated leaves, this tree species is not commonly used in commercial building, owing to its softer wood; however, Wilds dwellers and Tiqui often use it for fencing, simple furniture, and small shacks or storage units.

skeeto: A tiny, voracious, blood-sucking insect. It's bite is mildly toxic to most humans, usually inducing a mild-to-severe headache seconds after it attacks. In rare cases, a person with particular sensitivity can suffer a life-threatening allergic reaction.

sky jelly: This creature looks like the airborne equivalent of a marine jellyfish of Old Earth. Sky jellies vary in size, but all are at least as big as a Terran elephant, and a very old wild male can reach the size of a Terran blue whale. At the time of AToF, the smaller domesticated breed, used for more than one hundred years as the flotation device for airships, has been rendered obsolete by the advent of modern steam technology and stronger, more lightweight fabrics. The creature's body consists of a gas-filled bladder that allows it to float. A clump of tentacles equipped with stingers hang at the front, clustered around a beak-like mouth. Sensory organs cluster above the tentacles. The neural node sits slightly behind the sensory cluster. The creature propels itself by blowing jets of intestinal gas from ventral anal slits and steers with rows of delicate fanlike fins along either flank. The animal feeds by trolling the plains for any living thing it can snag in its tentacles and hoist to its razor-sharp beak-like mouth, where it dismembers and devours its prey. The Tiqui prize sky jelly skin for the making of waterproof garments.

The poison of the wild sky jelly is fatal if the antidote is not administered within an hour of receiving a sting. The victim's skin turns a ghostly white. Tiqui curaros are capable of making the antidote within their bodies via a chemical transformation, an ability unique to only those Tiqui males who've inherited the genetic trait of the curaro. Domesticated jellies, through selective breeding, are docile and have milder venom, though a sting will still cause serious, but rarely fatal illness.

sueño: Hallucinogenic herb smoked or chewed by city dwellers. Though not illegal, the drug is frowned upon by most of society, due to its highly addictive nature and deleterious effects on heavy, long-term users. Serious, long-term side effects include paranoia, flashbacks, volatility, depression, and irreversible dementia. *See also:* mezcala.

sugar creeper: Thick, ropy vine with yellow, trumpet-shaped flowers that produce a sweet nectar irresistible to many varieties of small pollinators.

sweetbush: Herbaceous shrub, similar to Terran mint, cultivated for tea-making by both alta and Tiqui.

sweetgrass: When burned, this grasslike plant gives off a strong, pleasant aroma. Used by the Tiqui as incense in religious ceremonies.

tabac: Non-hallucinogenic, but mildly addictive plant with a short stem and broad, reddish-brown leaves. Cultivated and smoked widely among all populations on Nuetierra.

tiberon: Large, fearsome predatory saltwater icthyoid that occupyies the same ecological niche as the biggest of Terran sharks. These creatures are top of the food chain, and a full-grown adult has no natural enemies, besides a bigger tiberon. They are solitary hunters, coming together only to mate. Their hides range in color from slate gray to near pure white. Considered one of the most desirable trophy animals on Nuetierra by elite city-dwelling hunters, owing to the high expense and extreme difficulty in capturing one.

turquia: A turkey-sized, flightless, forest-dwelling avian. Hunted for food by Wilds-dwelling alta and Tiqui.

uva: A prickly vine that produces small, red berries. Not cultivated commercially in the cities, but rural-dwelling alta and Tiqui alike prize the fruit collected from the wild.

vaca: Descended from bovine DNA stocks brought from Old Earth. Three of the four original varieties survived to the post-war era. Raised commercially for meat, milk, and leather. Large herds of feral vaca roam the plains of the primary continent. The Tiqui hunt the feral animals for meat and hides.

about the author

LESLIE ANN MOORE was born in Los Angeles, California at the tail end of the baby boom, and fell in love with the works of Ray Bradbury, Arthur C. Clarke, Andre Norton, and J.R.R. Tolkien at an early age.

A practicing veterinarian since 1988, Leslie put her dreams of writing fiction aside until she attended the Los Angeles Times Festival of Books in 2000. There, bestselling fantasy author Terry Brooks told her, "Don't ever give up. Keep writing, no matter what." Those words changed her life.

She published the first volume of her Griffin's Daughter trilogy in 2012. *A Tangle of Fates* is the first volume of The Vox Machina trilogy.

Made in the USA
San Bernardino, CA
09 October 2014